"WHAT'S THAT NOISE?"

Velanda asked, just before they pushed open the bronze door.

"That is Volk!" Tep growled, pushing past her. "Something's out there!"

"Tep! No! If there are fulfs—" But Tep was already gone. His thudding footsteps caused loose stones to rattle down to the base of the tunnel's dome-shaped earth covering. Velanda peered timidly outside, now hearing Tep's bellows mingling with Volk's yowls, and with another sound, a low, penetrating gurgling. "Fulfs!" she breathed. She silently berated herself for not rushing to help Tep—but she could not move! She was as if rooted in place.

Tep saw his first fulf. Volk was lying between the huge beast's forelegs, twitching, making little mewling noises. Tep did not see all of the fulf, because its wide-open jaws spanned from its maximum height all the way to the ground—or so it seemed from Tep's perspective. Yet that threatening vista of shiny yellow fangs—hundreds of them—did not even slow him down. "You hurt Volk!" he shrilled, and leaped to the attack—right into the fulf's maw. . . .

ARBITER TALES
L. WARREN DOUGLAS

□ STEPWATER

Old human, John Minder XXIII is the current Arbiter in a line stretching back to the early pioneers. But each Arbiter before him has held the ancient data blocks, key to all knowledge on the seven races of man . . . and vital to activate the Arbiter's hidden warrior fleet.
(454685—$4.99)

□ THE WELLS OF PHYRE

John Minder XXIII will find some unknowing assistance on the desert world of Phyre. (454707—$5.50)

□ GLAICE

As Arbiter of the Xarafeille Stream, John Minder XXIII must maintain peace. Now he must hunt far and wide for the remaining few data blocks, only to learn that some of the information he needs lies buried in the ice of a remote and forbidding planet called Glaice.
(454715—$5.50)

"Sweeping, completely original . . . modern science fiction at its best."—Allan Cole

"Well-crafted and immaculately plotted."—Chris Bunch, co-author of *The Far Kingdoms*

from RoC

*Prices slightly higher in Canada.

Buy them at your local bookstore or use this convenient coupon for ordering.

PENGUIN USA
P.O. Box 999 — Dept. #17109
Bergenfield, New Jersey 07621

Please send me the books I have checked above.
I am enclosing $________________ (please add $2.00 to cover postage and handling). Send check or money order (no cash or C.O.D.'s) or charge by Mastercard or VISA (with a $15.00 minimum). Prices and numbers are subject to change without notice.

Card #________________________ Exp. Date ________________________
Signature____
Name____
Address____
City ________________ State ______________ Zip Code ______________

For faster service when ordering by credit card call **1-800-253-6476**

Allow a minimum of 4-6 weeks for delivery. This offer is subject to change without notice.

GLAICE

An Arbiter Tale

L. WARREN DOUGLAS

A ROC BOOK

ROC
Published by the Penguin Group
Penguin Books USA Inc., 375 Hudson Street,
New York, New York 10014, U.S.A.
Penguin Books Ltd, 27 Wrights Lane,
London W8 5TZ, England
Penguin Books Australia Ltd,
Ringwood, Victoria, Australia
Penguin Books Canada Ltd, 10 Alcorn Avenue,
Toronto, Ontario, Canada M4V 3B2
Penguin Books (N.Z.) Ltd, 182–190 Wairau Road,
Auckland 10, New Zealand

Penguin Books Ltd, Registered Offices:
Harmondsworth, Middlesex, England

First published by Roc, an imprint of Dutton Signet,
a division of Penguin Books USA Inc.

First Printing, December, 1996
10 9 8 7 6 5 4 3 2 1

Printed in the United States of America

ACKNOWLEDGMENTS

The archaeologists:

Dr. Moreau Maxwell (Michigan State University) of the urine-tanned mukluks, who let me turn in my 1974 paper on arctic radiocarbon anomalies a semester late; Drs. Alan Bryan and Ruth Groen (University of Alberta, Edmonton) for the use of their Edmonton home and their wonderful library; Dr. Tim Losey, the 1974 U. of A. field crew, and Oscar the pig, for the brainstorming session where the food-chain idea first came up.

The biologists:

Dr. Susan Smith (U. of Wisconsin, Madison) for nutrition and physiology, and Dr. Fred Bevis (Grand Valley State U., Michigan) for ecosystem productivity, and for working my arse off.

The oceanographer:

The late Dr. John Lucke—the original Barnegat Bay Barnacle Bill—a mentor and dear friend to whose memory this book is dedicated.

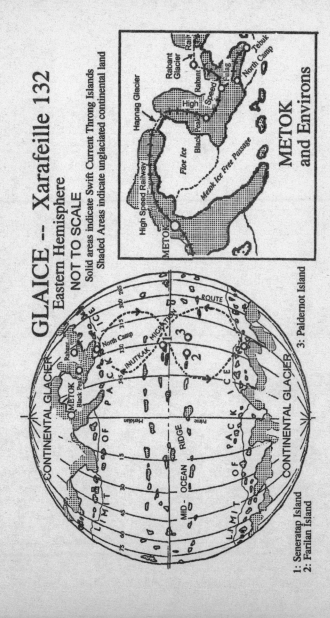

GLAICE -- Xarafeille 132

Eastern Hemisphere

NOT TO SCALE

Solid areas indicate Swift Current Throng Islands

Shaded Areas indicate unglaciated continental land

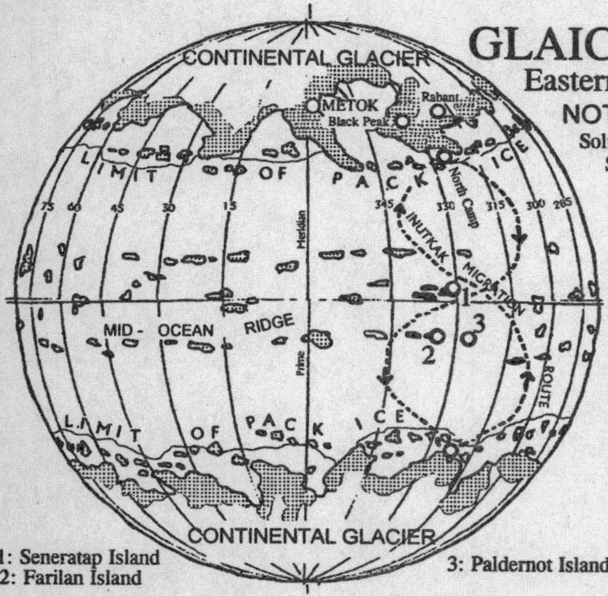

1: Seneratap Island
2: Farilan Island
3: Paldernot Island

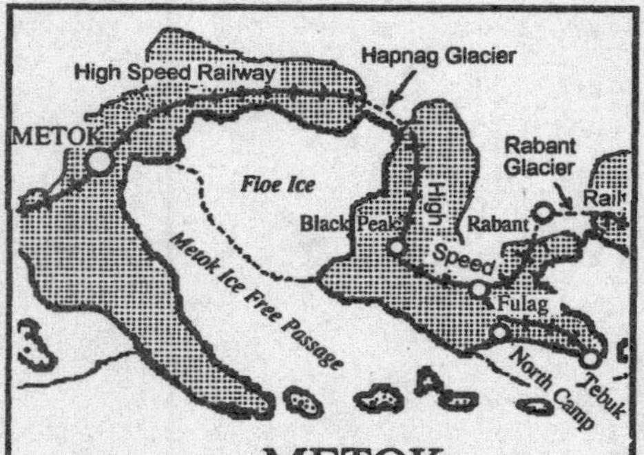

METOK
and Environs

PROLOGUE

In the first centuries of the diaspora, ikuts settled eighteen worlds, yet there are no longer ikuts on any of those. They were, it seems, too mild—too "nice"—for the shaggy white-furred men, who require arctic cold to destroy the parasites that otherwise debilitate them.

In the more than one hundred subsequent centuries, ikuts have settled only a few planets, of which Glaice is the oldest. Even those ikuts who settled there must have been desperate—their ships running low on life-support material, the colonists' vitality sapped by too many years in cold sleep—because Glaice is a nasty place even by ikut standards. Witness the elaborate migrations they must make, from pole to pole every three years. Would even ikuts have settled Glaice if they retained a shred of hope that they might find something better?

Fenwurt Maderas
First Landing
Parnoel Press,
Metok, 12202 R.L.

Volcanoes like blackened, broken teeth gnawed at the bloody sunset. The low-riding floe—flat shelf ice, hardly a respectable berg—picked up the sky's red hue and reflected it back upward, but the russet coloration of the ice was not entirely due to volcanic dust and light refraction in the air; some of it was blood.

It was a scene out of prehistory, when the races of man had fought each other with claws and bared teeth—great white-furred ikuts against lithe, brown, seal-like mantees—and as it had been then, the worst casualties were among the very young. This time they were ikut young, their soft fur no longer snowy white, but splashed with sunset and their own fluids; seventeen small bodies lay clumped and scattered about the small ice floe. Until recently it had been the site of an outing, a youthful expedition a short, supposedly safe distance from the great iceberg that was "home."

Five young bodies had already been laid reverently, with much loud wailing, in the bottoms of skin boats. The rest would follow later, when the boats returned, empty, but the ikut females would not heap their dead infants atop one another like meat.

"Meat!" snarled a big ikut male, kicking a brown and red mantee corpse off the edge of the floe to join its fellows. The cubs had given good account of themselves as they died, he reflected—there had been six dead mantees, their brown-furred skins flayed red from ankle to waist by small, sharp claws and needle-like milk-fangs. "Mantees!" he snarled. "The Ketonak are right. They aren't people at all. People would not do this. Mantees are animals. They are meat! Spoiled meat!" He *would* eat mantee as the Ketonak band had done, he growled, but only if it was fresh, rended and killed with his own huge, clawed hands.

At all times, at least one male watched to seaward, but no mantees arose through the dark waters to claim their own dead. The brown bodies remained close to the ice, bobbing sluggishly. *"Barakh!"* spat an ikut male. He thrust a spear into one floating corpse, then watched with grim satisfaction as it began to sink. He proceeded from that one to the next, until all the mantees had been punctured. They would rise again as their internal bacteria filled them with gases, but for now, he did not have to look at them.

CHAPTER 1

FYI ARBITER:
URGENTLY REQUEST ORBITAL PRESENCE OF PEACEKEEPING FLEET & RECON SATELLITE COVER ALL LATITUDES 30N-30S, AND PRIORITY ONE CALL ON ALL IN-SECTOR TROOPSHIPS. DETAILS FOLLOW. PERSONAL MSG FOLLOWS.
MARTINEZ, CONSUL, GLAICE XARAFEILLE 132

A few miles to the west of Metok City, a glacier groaned and dropped a 450-ton chunk of itself from the height of its face into the cold mud of the terminal moraine. It was summer, and glaciers often did that in summer. Not many miles farther away, but to the south, a fourteen-thousand-foot volcano vomited fire, glowing ash, and toxic gas. On Glaice, Xarafeille 132, most volcanoes did that, most of the time. The sunsets were always beautiful.

Offworlders who visited Metok considered it a suburb of hell, a glass-domed anteroom opening on the nastiest world ever colonized by men—and by women, of course, but the women mostly came because the men did, and had not volunteered, and anyway, among the worlds of the Xarafeille Stream the collective nouns "mankind" and "men" referred not only to people of both sexes, but to a variety of beings whose claim to being human sprang from their genes; most hardly resembled the root stock of ancient, forgotten Earth.

Tep Inutkak—Tep, of the Inutkak band of the ikut race of man—stood over two meters tall and was covered with white fur. His loose skin covered layers of insulating fat, which in turn hid muscles strong enough to bend or even break the bones of men of other races. Tep's bones were thus thick and heavy as well, because he was a wholly adapted man, a fine specimen of the ikut race. Actually, he was not a man, not yet. Outwardly, young ikut were neither male nor female until they reached sexual maturity, at around twenty-five years of age, but Tep knew he was going to be a man in a few years, and that colored his attitudes and his behavior. His fellow students, most of whom sprung from other kinds of parents, considered him a man mostly because he was half again the height of a lissome mantee male, weighed three times as much as a jittery fard, and was not afraid of a good rough-and-tumble with the bors males in his dormitory—whom he resembled, though bors had black fur and tended to be roly-poly where Tep looked lean.

The almost-juxtaposed crashes of calving glaciers and roar of erupting volcanoes were background music to Tep's current struggle. His paper on the food-chain paths of certain trace elements was a week late.

If he had been writing about ikut history, analyzing some aspect of the voluminous oral traditions of his folk, or about archaeological work in the ancient abandoned city of Latobak, the paper would not have been late, he told himself. But it was late, and it was not about archaeology or epics. The flow of minerals from bottom-feeding slugs that inhabited the deep ocean trenches up to the thrashing, glittering fish that ordinary ikuts caught from their ice floes was steady and inexorable, but the words that described that flow came in fits and starts, like the glowing effluvia of Mount Brastopan, looming on the southern horizon. Tep had filed his long yellow claws to blunt nubs that did not slip off his terminal's keys or obliterate the letters on them. He had adjusted his chair just so, to accommodate his stub of a tail. Those things helped, but they did not aid the flow of words and ideas from brain to fingers to keys, from the keys to the multi-terabyte data-storage crystals somewhere deep within the clammy basements of Metok U.

It would not be the end of the world if Tep did not

get the paper in by the end of the week, but he was afraid it might be the end of his academic career. He envisioned his ignominious return to the Inutkak ikut band, and his future thereafter. About now, the Inutkak were drifting north on their ice floe, probably about forty degrees north latitude, dining on *sedubik* (fish native to that clime) and on *fetuk,* a kind of seaweed that drifted north from the equatorial isles, where it grew on offshore rocks. The Inutkak *shahm,* the band's medicine man, chief, and scientist, always carefully calculated the mass and extent of the floe he selected for the northern migration, but though Glaice's water and air temperatures and the incident sunlight at a given latitude were quite consistent, there were always variables that could not be predicted. For the Inutkak ikuts, as for all the migratory ikut bands, the second half of their nine-month journey on the ice was spiced with the underlying concern that they might not make it to their northern-hemisphere camp in one piece.

Once safe in their northern winter camp, the Inutkak would feast on foods not tasted for two and a half years. Gatherers went out seeking *gitlik* shrubs—bitter seasoning for stews and pottages—and hunters sought *ritvak,* which were small deerlike creatures inhabiting the high plateau. The band's shahm sent crews to specific locations near the faces of local glaciers to find caches dug into the ice shortly before the Inutkak's last departure. If the shahm had calculated the original placement of such caches correctly, the subsequent grinding march of the ice brought the skin-wrapped, butchered carcasses of meat animals out of the ice just where the Inutkak could find them.

Then was a time of celebration: the infants conceived in the southern camp were about to be born. The Inutkak would nurse and nurture them through nine months in the north, and with the coming of warm weather they would be fat and strong, ready for the coming migration back to the south.

There was nothing wrong with the Inutkak life, Tep assured himself. Someday when he was much older, he would be ready to challenge the old shahm, to take his place as chief of the Inutkak band. But not now. He was far too young for that, and enjoyed city life far too much.

Tep struggled with the paper for another hour before he pushed his keyboard aside and waited for a printout. "Maybe somebody down at the bar can help me with the last part," he muttered. Maybe a beer or two would loosen his head just enough so he could finish it himself, too, but he had few illusions about that. Yet his decision to go to the bar was not entirely a capitulation to his inability to finish the report; in all likelihood, someone at the bar *would* be able to help, because the Last Atopak Tavern was a hangout for Metok U. grad students. People sometimes joked that every original idea for a thesis or dissertation that ended up on a graduate committeeman's desk began with a half-drunken bull session in the Last Atopak.

Before leaving his room, Tep took several small vials of pills from a drawer, emptied them one by one and counted the tiny spheres. They were dietary supplements. He—and any ikut who did not migrate—had to take them, and they were very expensive, being made offworld. Tep did not thoughtlessly indulge his considerable appetite for beer and off-campus food, because if he ran out of pill money, he would become quite ill. The Inutkak band's subsistence lifestyle did not generate large cash surpluses. Tep got almost half of the band's income from trade, and an equal share went to Fenag, his "backup," who was also a student at Metok University. They sometimes joked that their debit cards were thinner in the middle than at the edges, from having to squeeze every last credit from them. That left almost nothing for the Inutkak band—but the band did not need much from outside its self-defining existence.

The tavern's namesake, the *atopak*, was an extinct fish that had once bred in the shallows off the northern continental coasts. Now the remains of several hundred atopak decorated the walls of the tavern named for the last of them. According to campus lore it had started accidentally, and the tavern had originally been called Mopok's Midtown Bar. It had been constructed of local stone, as were most of Metok's buildings, and one block of stone near the end of the stand-up bar had contained an atopak fossil, an impressive fish almost a meter long. Only part of a jaw was exposed at first, but once sharp-clawed bors or ikut students discovered it, nothing short of a barred enclosure could have stopped them from picking at it night after night, beer after beer, until the fish in all its skeletal splendor was fully exposed in bas-relief.

Mopok, or perhaps some subsequent owner of the bar, was annoyed at the clawmarks in the walls of his booths, which made the place look shabby. No more atopak fossils had been discovered in the stone walls, but that had not stopped drunken patrons from looking for them. Mopok—or whoever—had purchased additional stones, ones that definitely had atopak fossils in them, and had them installed in and on his tavern's walls, all at a comfortable level for clawed customers. When an atopak skeleton was fully exposed, he had it moved somewhere else, and a fresh block put in its place.

No one was still around who could say for sure just when the tavern had officially been renamed or when the LAST ATOPAK sign had appeared over the door, but legend had it that not until the last atopak fossil on Glaice had been found, mounted in the tavern, and clawed from its soft stone matrix would the bar at last close down. As the atopak had been quite common, numbering in the billions, and as there were still millions of tons of atopak-bearing rocks around, owner after owner considered the name a good omen.

As luck would have it, Tep recognized a group of potentially useful fellow-students the minute he entered the bar. Also as luck would have it, they were wholly engrossed in a discussion, and did not welcome his persistent efforts to change the subject from whatever it was to food chains and trace elements.

Most of them were bors—short, heavy, black-furred people otherwise not very different from Tep. But bors were sedentary mountain folk who lived in cave towns, fine machinists and manufacturers who grew most of their food under artificial lights, in soil made from pulverized rock. To bors, a food chain was no longer than the conveyor belt from the growing cave to his kitchen, and they displayed little interest in Tep's concerns. They paid him little attention—with one exception.

"Tep Inutkak," said Velanda Torsk, a bors archaeology student, "don't you even care if the mantees kick you off your own planet?"

"Huh? Kick me off Glaice? I was born here!"

"Don't you watch the news?" Velanda and the others seemed surprised, but not excessively so. Most of them were old enough to know what it was like to be a second-year grad student. There was seldom time for anything but study. Velanda took pity on Tep, and brought him up to date.

The Ketonak band, on the other side of the planet, had purposefully disrupted their usual migration pattern so they could mate with another band that occupied the same territories, but in other seasons. Everyone knew how finely choreographed ikut migration cycles were, and how disastrous it was if a band got off schedule. If a band missed its regular voyage through the equatorial waters, they would also miss out on certain kinds of fish they needed to stay healthy, fish that dined on other fish from deeper down, who dined on crustaceans deeper still. . . . Tep understood all about the food chains that brought important trace elements from the ocean-bottom ooze up to the surface, where ikuts could consume them. He just had a hard time writing about them.

Anyway, the Ketonak missed the southern half of their migration and ended up back in their northern camp at just the time the local mantee throng arrived there to mate on the offshore rocks. Happily for the Ketonak, the mantees contained many of the trace nutrients they had missed by not completing their voyage south of the equator. Unhappily for them, the mantees, who were as human as they were, did not willingly submit to being eaten.

"Cannibals?" exclaimed Tep. "They killed and ate other people?" Members of Tep's Inutkak band—who spend nine months out of every three years in distant proximity to Metok, a worldly place with a sizeable off-world population of non-ikut humans and with its own spaceport and high-speed rail terminal—understood that mantees, whom they called "seels," were as human as they themselves. "Are they still living in the stone age?" he asked, shaking his head. They were, his fellow-students agreed.

"But that's only part of the story!" insisted Blent Dagro, another bors, a chemistry postdoc. "The Warm Stream mantee throngmother is taking them into Metok High Court. She's brought murder charges against their shahm, and there have been mantee attacks on other ikut bands, ones that didn't do anything wrong."

Tep had just drained his second mug of beer and, realizing that he would get no help with his paper from anyone present, decided to go back to his room and try again. "Well, it *is* murder, isn't it? Mantees are people too." He stood, and set down his empty mug.

"It's killing—but *murder*? The Ketonak only did it to live. In the old days before there was an Arbiter's consul or a High Court, all ikuts ate mantees, didn't they? You tell us, Tep. You're the expert on food chains."

"I wish I was," Tep said, sighing. "I never will be, unless I get this paper done, though, and since all you guys want to talk about is mantee stew . . ." He turned to leave.

"Wait, Tep!" said Velanda. "I'll go with you. Maybe I can help with your paper, and then I'll tell you the rest of the story about the Ketonak and the mantees." Tep was not sure how much help an archaeologist could offer him, but he really didn't want to walk all the way back to the dormitory alone.

"Sure," he said. "You can tell me some on the way. Especially about how what the Ketonak did affects *me*. I didn't eat any mantees."

Velanda told him. "It would have stopped right there—the court would have awarded the Warm Stream throng damages, and probably would have ordered the Ketonaks disbanded and scattered among the other bands, which is traditional, isn't it?"

"That's what people did centuries ago," Tep agreed. "But I don't think there's been a similar case in generations. I suppose now that there's a formal court and all, things are different. But you still haven't said how . . ."

"I'm getting to that. As I said, it would have stopped right there, except for Professor Rakulit, my dissertation-committee chairman. He's been putting together a book on radiocarbon dating of protohistoric sites on Glaice, and . . ."

"Rakulit? Isn't he a seel, too?"

"Tep! Don't call them that. Professor Rakulit is a *mantee.* Calling him a seel even makes him *sound* like he's something to eat."

"It's just the ikut word for mantee," Tep protested. "It doesn't mean anything bad."

"Hah! If there were an ikut encyclopedia, I wonder if 'mantee' would be cross-referenced with 'bors' and 'tarbeks' as 'other human subspecies' or with 'ritvak' and 'etolat' under 'traditional ikut meals'?"

She was joking, but Tep—even without the Ketonak incident—could have told her how close to the mark she had come. Even he, an educated person, sometimes wondered if the slim, brown, quick-moving mantees he saw about Metok would taste as good as fresh-killed, juicy specimens of the less-intelligent, non-human marine mammals ikuts also called seels.

"So did they eat your committee chairman, or what?" he asked facetiously.

"Tep! Professor Rakulit has proved that the mantees have been on Glaice longer than anyone else. Do you know how radiocarbon dating works?"

"Cosmic rays hit nitrogen in the upper atmosphere and turn it into carbon fourteen, which is heavier than ordinary carbon-twelve," he said. "It falls to earth, and enters the food chains—see? didn't you know I'd get my own subject in there?—and then it breaks down into carbon-twelve over the centuries. Right?"

"Uh-huh. And since when an animal or a plant dies, it stops metabolizing and taking in fresh carbon, something that's been dead a long time has less C-fourteen than something that died recently. When archaeologists measure the C-twelve to C-fourteen ratio of a buried house post or the ashes of a cooking fire, we can tell just how long ago the wood was alive—and how many centuries ago the people that made the fire lived."

She sighed. They were almost at the dorm. She rushed to finish the tale. In short, she said, Rakulit proved that the mantees inhabited Glaice in 650 R.L. and that the ikuts didn't arrive until around 800, and the bors a century and a half after that. That meant that the mantees were the original charter-holding colonists of the planet, and the others were there only on their sufferance. "The Warm Stream throngmother heard about Rakulit's work, and before long she had gotten all the mantee throngs on Glaice to join a class-action suit against all the ikut bands, to have them declared displaced persons who had to apply to the mantees for licenses just to remain on the planet where they were born!"

"They can't do that!" Tep exclaimed. Suddenly his own problem did not loom so large. "I belong on Glaice just as much as they do! I was born here too!"

"So was I," Velanda replied. "So far, the mantees haven't included us bors in the suit, but it's still scary. Where could we go? We'd have to appeal to the Arbiter himself, to find us a new homeworld."

"The Arbiter! Hah! I sometimes think the Arbiter is a myth, like the bogeyman who lives in holes in the ice, and . . ."

"Just for your information, Tep-with-your-head-in-the-snow, the Arbiter has opened a consulate right here in Metok. It's right down the street from the Last Atopak, as a matter of fact—and the consul himself is judging the mantees' lawsuit."

CHAPTER 2

TO: MARTINEZ, CONSUL, GLAICE, X-132
FROM: J. M. XXIII, ARBITER
REQUEST REFUSED. PERSONAL MSG FOLLOWS.
JAKE, I CAN'T DO IT. POLICY DIRECTIVES ASIDE, I WON'T DO IT. THIS ONE IS YOURS. HANDLE IT WITHOUT TROOPS OR SHIPS. AS FOR THE SATELLITES—I'LL SEE WHAT I CAN GET VIA ORDINARY COMMERCIAL CHANNELS.

The Arbiter of the Xarafeille Stream did not live in a hole in the ice, but divided his time between several grand palaces on the planet Newhome, or Xarafeille Prime. He was a young man, John Minder, the twenty-third to bear that name, and he had inherited his lofty position less than a decade earlier. His father, Rober Minder VIII, had died suddenly, leaving young Johnny quite unprepared.

Unbeknownst to John or Rober Minder, Johnny's older brother Shems (or James), who was an archaeologist, had removed seven ancient data modules from their proper place, planning to have them translated into a current, readable data format. Unfortunately for Johnny, those modules had held the operating codes for the Arbiter's fleet of white starships and the location of the secret world where he recruited his poletzai troops, warlike old-humans who were not part of the polity of the Xarafeille Stream's thousands of worlds.

The situation arising on Glaice did not call for troops or warships. It was, as yet, an internal matter. The Arbiter only intervened where hostility between the races threatened to become race war, or where governments or corporations were attempting to build interstellar warships themselves. The Arbiter was not a ruler. He was, as his title indicated, a court of last resort for disputes that proved irreconcilable, and in those cases his decisions were final.

The first Arbiter, also the first John Minder, had been a physicist living in a forgotten age long before the colonization of the Xarafeille Stream worlds. At that time there had been only seven human-colonized planets, each one chartered to an Earth-based megacorporation. A trip from Earth to even the nearest of them took years. A round trip took decades. There was little oversight from Earth—no government but corporate management, no human-rights organizations, not even a chapter of the SPCA. There should have been—as John Minder found out.

Minder worked for one of those corporations, designing and testing communications subsystems for huge, slow ramscoop cargo ships that brought the bounty of colonial mines and plantations to a depleted Earth. When he realized that the troublesome anomaly in his current project indicated that his untamed electrons not only seemed to travel faster than light, but for all intents and purposes actually did so, he destroyed his notes, faked a nervous breakdown that shed doubt upon all the work he had done for the past year, and retired to "convalesce" on a retired insystem ship converted to a small orbital habitat.

If John Minder had not come from a "good family"—one with money, connections, and an old, respectable name—the subsequent history of a good-sized chunk of the galaxy might have taken a different, and more unpleasant, turn. Having control of substantial assets, he was able to buy out the seven other residents of the small habitat and to initiate an extraordinary remodeling project—turning the hulk back into a working spaceship. If anyone seemed to question his eccentricity, he had only to give them a particularly silly smile that gently reminded them of his recent "breakdown."

There are no records of what materials John Minder

used to "remodel" his spaceship home, or how he used them. He outsourced every vital component differently, never letting one supplier know what other sources he was using, and obscured his every trail with shell corporations, bearer-bond transactions, and other devices. Later, when he was no longer just John Minder, but was the first Arbiter, he arranged for even his faintest trails to be erased. No other living person knew what he had discovered or what he had built. When he moved his habitat out of Earth orbit into a long outward-spiraling one, no one paid much attention. When he and his vessel disappeared in the asteroid belt, few but the contractors who had supplied him mourned his apparent death.

John Minder was wholly unconcerned. He was much too busy testing the very first faster-than-light starship drive ever. It did not really "drive" a spaceship faster than light. Minder was not sure just what it did do, but after a few trials, he decided that it did not matter. When he went somewhere in the ship, it took a certain consistent amount of time to reach his destination, and as nearly as he could tell, exactly as much time elapsed where he was, where he had been, and where he was going. Thus two months after his last radio check-in with Sol Traffic Control, Minder was approaching the third planet of another star. Two months had elapsed on Earth, in the asteroid belt, on the far world that was his destination, and for Minder, somewhere in between.

The place was called only TC3 in the records of the corporation that owned it, and as Minder soon discovered, it was home to several hundred thousand very miserable people. Or were they people at all? What did one call seven-foot-tall, white-furred, round-eared monsters with stubby tails? As the audio and video channels he monitored showed, the corporate types called them "teddy" if they were male, and "bitch" if female, and they only addressed them at all from the safe ends of heavy-duty cattle prods, from behind barred gates, or over an annunciator system. The managers lived in comfortable, expensive Earth-normal environments either in domes or in orbit. The teddies and their bitches lived out on the ice of TC3.

For a while, Minder himself was not convinced that teddies were human, but as TC3's surface was almost entirely ice and frigid ocean, he knew they could not have evolved there. And besides, they seemed hauntingly familiar, like short-snouted, two-legged polar bears. It took him a month to piece together what he could from the curt, businesslike radio traffic; they were humans, all right: men and women whose genes had been altered to allow them to survive on frigid, hostile, heavy-metal poisoned TC3, and they had been like that for almost a hundred years. Fish-oil-based lubricants that he had taken for granted at home, and a hundred other bulk products vital to Earth's economy and industry, came from TC3. Like everyone else, he had imagined huge factory ships combing the bleak planet's oceans with immense nets. He had not envisioned furry white slaves living on ice floes and selling their meager catches for vitamin supplements to keep their infants alive.

Minder was enraged. Was this the cost of Earth's continuing prosperity? And this was only one "colony" planet. There were five others. . . . Suppressing his rage, John Minder set a new course in his nav computers.

The next world he visited was populated by men and women of several disparate types. It took him a while, surreptitiously listening in on their corporate masters, to figure out just what they were—people with a few genes modified to make them resemble semi-aquatic mammals. The ones who lived in the north and subsisted on fish and seaweed were not really seals, but they resembled them. In the temperate zones, they were more like otters. Further south, Minder thought, they looked like dugongs. They were, he only found out much later, all genetically similar, designed in corporate labs to function in any watery environment; over a lifetime or a generation, they could adapt to all sorts of conditions. His admiration for the cleverness of the genetic engineers who had designed them was exceeded only by his loathing for what had been done by them.

At that time he suppressed those feelings and programmed in a new course for yet another world. That one was hot and dry, and the corporate slaves that labored there looked just a bit like man-sized gerbils or African desert foxes. The next planet was even hotter, with yellow, sulfurous air, and he found himself unable to compare its denizens to any earthly creature. They were orange-skinned, tall and skinny, and the males' necks were draped with great wrinkly wattles that reddened with suffused blood when they became angry or aroused.

The last corporate world but one supported bearlike men who mined its mountains, hibernating through frigid winters (thus costing nothing to maintain them), and laboring through the only-slightly-less-harsh summer months for no more reward that the few offworld supplies and tools that they bought with their world's riches. Slipshod genetic engineering, by budget-conscious low-bidder laboratories, resulted in a legacy of ills deemed unimportant by their corporate masters. One was a terrible susceptibility to the demidex mite, which caused mange. It spread rapidly in winter caves and was always debilitating, often fatal. Another was a tendency for females to miscarry, especially during a first pregnancy. Minder's anger was like a burning sore; it would have cost almost nothing to fix those things in the labs; it would have cost only a little more to supply the creatures with cheap insecticide, after the fact, but the corporations did not do even that.

The final planet—which was so entirely Earthlike that it brought tears of homesickness to his eyes—was inhabited by a race of squirrelish or ferretlike folk whose creation seemed to stem from no more than the flair and panache of their designers, for ordinary men adapted quite well to that world without any modifications at all. Yet ordinary men, he realized, could have rebelled—taken over a ship, and returned home or smuggled one of their kind on a returning ship to spread word of what was being done to them on their "colony" world. Those lithe, brown-furred, round-eared beings could not do so. They were "aliens," and they did not even speak an earthly language, but one generated in their designers' computers to be incomprehensible even to linguists who did not have the proper "key." They could not even speak with their masters without the use of elaborate hand-carved "flutes" whose notes only computers could decipher.

The tale of John Minder's labors, of the years of preparation and the final uprisings that freed the slaves and bankrupted not only the corporations but the Earth itself, was once common knowledge among the descendants of those slaves, but they were now mostly forgotten, as were the years of the diaspora, when they fled first in starships rudely converted to the task, to regions of space unseen from Earth, the far stars behind the black veil of dust that hid the sparkling jewels of the Xarafeille Stream. The laboriously developed agreement by which Minder and his descendants would arbitrate disputes between the races was not forgotten, nor was Minder's other task: to protect and control the old-humans who had rebelled with them, and who must not ever again be allowed to be more than fellowmen—never masters.

John Minder committed to one final obligation, one not without cost to him and his descendants. Under the careful eyes of a few trusted delegates from each race, the corporate gene mechanics were given one last task: to modify the genes of John Minder himself so that his children would feel no driving ambition—except in an intellectual, academic way. The men who were to become the Arbiters of all human disputes could not be allowed to *want* the power they had, and could desire no satisfaction from possessing it. Better that they be dragged to their task than that they want it at all, let alone crave it. Most of the time, down through the generations of Arbiters, that worked just fine.

For young Johnny Minder the twenty-third, it did not work so well. Shems was his father's eldest son, and by rights he should have been Arbiter, not Johnny. But the old gene modification worked quite well, and Shems, preferring the life of an obscure archaeologist to that of the most powerful man in the universe (and unable to really enjoy that), simply disappeared. If he had not taken the data modules with the code-keys to the fleet and the location of the poletzai's world with him, it would not have bothered Johnny all that much.

"Is 'teddy' a bad word, Daddy?" asked Parissa Minder, the Arbiter's youngest daughter. "I have a brown furry teddy, and . . ."

"It's only bad when you call *ikut* or *bors* that," said her brother Rober, who was quite a bit older and impatient with the five-year-old's questions.

"Why is it bad then? Purt Bleddo is a bors, and he looks like my teddy, only black."

John Minder XXIII sighed. "Once there was a man named Teddy," he said, "and someone gave him a toy made to look like an animal called a 'bear.' Everyone liked his toy, and soon children everywhere wanted bears like his. First they called them 'Teddy's bears,' then 'Teddy bears,' and finally just 'teddies.' Much later, when bad men made slaves of bors and ikut, they called them teddies because they did not consider them men like themselves. They did not value them any more than we value stuffed toys, and that was bad."

"I value *my* teddy!"

"Come on, Priss!" said Rober.

"Shall I continue the story?" their father asked. "We can wait until later, if you're tired, Parissa."

"Go on, Dad," said Sarabet, the middle child. "I want to know how Tep Inutkak became involved with your problem—finding one of the datacrystals Uncle Shems took."

"Very well then. Tep, being a member of the Inutkak band, had heard all the old Inutkak stories from his father, just as you are hearing this one from me. '*Inutkak*,' in their own speech, means 'the World's Folk.' The Inutkak legends told of an age of heroes, the founders of the tribe . . ."

CHAPTER 3

When a glacier recedes, it leaves behind more than rubble. Remember that when ice moves forward, it pushes or picks up and carries everything loose with it, but when it "moves" back, it merely melts, and everything within or upon it is dropped exactly where it was when forward movement ceased. And remember that glacial "ice" is above all dirty stuff, full of silt, sand, gravel, and boulders. It is, from the geologist's point of view, as much a "rock" as lava.

It should thus be no surprise that the creeks that run atop or within glaciers have sandy or gravelly beds much like those that run across more ordinary bedrock, that they run down to lakes or pools, and that those too have thick beds of sediment. When glaciers melt, the sedimentary topography becomes reversed: streambeds become *eskers,* winding ridges of gravel and water-worn rock; lakes, when the ice that supported their sediment-filled beds melts, become *kames*—mounds of neatly stratified sediment that are convex where once they were concave.

Fando Bumpher, Ph.D.,
Glacial Geomorphology Lecture Series,
Metok University, Glaice, Xarafeille 132, 12030 R.L.

"We Inutkak didn't always ride the ice," Tep explained to Velanda, waving her notes from Professor Rakulit's class. He had not gone home; instead, they had gone to her room, where she had shown him the notes. "The hero Apootlak was the first to discover the migration routes, when the people were starving. He led the Inutkak on their first migration, and they taught the other bands how to fish in deep waters and to steer their ice floes through the tropical islands. This stuff Rakulit told you is *keluk*!" Keluk was one of the many ikut names for ice. It meant, roughly "wormholed, soft, rotten ice about to fall apart," or "end-of-the-journey ice," worthless, treacherous stuff to be abandoned as soon as practical.

"He is a good scholar, Tep. He personally collected his carbon samples from the ikut cemeteries, and there is no question that the laboratory tests were done correctly."

"How did he get in our cemeteries? Only the shahm is allowed to go in them!"

"He had permission, and I believe your own shahm went with him."

"So much for his gratitude!" Tep snapped. "Now he wants to kick us all off Glaice!"

"He does not! He only published his findings for their historic importance. It is the Warm Stream throngmother who is twisting his work for her political ends."

"Why doesn't Rakulit talk to her, and change her mind?"

"What could he do? He only published the truth. He can't change that just because you want him too, can he?"

"But it *isn't* the truth! He says that the first ikut on Glaice, the nonmigrating ones he calls the 'Ikut One culture,' all died out by 600 R.L. and the first mantees arrived to claim Glaice about fifty years later. But they didn't die out. They were *us*, the Inutkak!"

"The first clearly Inutkak burials are in a different cemetery, Tep, and they are dated much later, around 950 R.L. If those old Ikut I culture graves were Inutkak folk also, then where are the graves of those who died between 595 and 950? That's three and a half centuries unaccounted for."

"But the sagas are quite clear! Those are our graves too. I don't know about any three-century gap, but I know Rakulit is wrong."

"Well, you do have a point," Velanda admitted. "Many oral traditions are surprisingly accurate even over thousands of years. Archaeologists often study the sagas and epic tales of modern people to help them date ancient remains, with great success. But if your Inutkak tales are right, then the carbon-fourteen dates are wrong, and that cannot be."

"Hah! Old Rakulit just won't admit his samples were bad!"

"Tep, would you like to talk with him? He has office hours tomorrow morning, I know. I can introduce you to him—if you promise to be polite, that is."

The archaeology department was in a five-story stone edifice fronted by a full-length columned porch. The spiral-fluted columns were in the style of some ancient temple or public building, and their capitals were decorated with broad carved leaves of a plant that had surely never grown on frigid Glaice, where even the "tropic" islands experienced frost at least once a year. Dr. Rakulit's office was on the fourth floor. Velanda led Tep down hallways lined with dusty showcases displaying arrays of ancient bones, pots, and other artifacts of ancient Glaice. He grabbed her arm and drew her close to one particular case.

"Look! Read that tag!" he demanded.

" 'Ikut One Culture,' " she read, " 'circa 450 R.L., from the Tepkak Bay campsite.' So what, Tep? What am I supposed to be looking for?"

"See that slate snow knife? That's just like the one my mother used to make snow shelters when we were out hunting. Wouldn't the tools be different from ours if the Ikut I people were a different culture? Now look how different the snow knives of these offworld ikut from Finnter are." He pulled her to another case displaying comparable winter-camp tools from the ikut folk who had settled Finnter, Xarafeille 1894. "See? That snow knife is shaped entirely differently."

"Come on. You can ask Professor Rakulit to explain it," she said, pulling him away from the showcases.

Professor Rakulit rose when they entered his office, but he did not come out from behind his desk. There was little room in the crowded chamber for him, all his stacks of books and papers, a bors female who was half again his size, and a belligerent-seeming ikut who was larger still. Tep eyed the mantee professor skeptically, as if anyone that small, brown, and slick-looking could not possibly be a professor at all. He had few dealings with mantees himself in recent years, and his impressions of them had been formed mostly by the other Inutkak, who thought of them as clever, hard-bargaining traders, and who did not hesitate to consider them as shifty types, at best. As a cub, he had spent a month on Seneratap, a mantee island, when contrary winds had forced the Inutkak to wait out the storm season there. He had made friends with a young mantee, Kurrolf, for a while—but even Kurrolf had, he remembered, gotten the best of him whenever they traded toys and trinkets, and his father had chastised him for that.

"How good of you to come, Sar Tep," Rakulit said, his voice sounding high and reedy to Tep, who was more accustomed to resonant ikut tones or to bellowing bors students' voices. "I, too, have a problem with just the things you have noted," he said when Tep had explained his objection to the C-14 dates. "The Ikut One and Ikut Two cultures seem remarkably similar, on the face of it. Nevertheless, the dates check out. I have rerun the tests several times.

"I have speculated that both waves of ikut immigration to Glaice were by folk from the same homeworld," he said, referring to the old snow knife Tep had remarked upon. "Considering the early settlement date, twelve millennia ago, they may have both come directly from the first ikut homeworld itself."

Tep was somewhat disconcerted by the mantee's calm, didactic manner; after all, this was more than just archaeology! Peoples lives were at stake! Still, it was better this way. He had envisioned heated argument, which probably would have led nowhere. As long as mantees and ikut could discuss these things, perhaps the violence would not escalate.

"The oral histories of your Inutkak band are less easy to explain," Rakulit was saying. "It is true that the earliest tales describe ikut living a sedentary lifestyle dependent on the now-extinct atopak fish for sustenance. It is also true that they describe the disappearance of the atopak, probably due to overfishing, and the subsequent adoption of a migratory Inutkak lifestyle. I can only speculate that those tales too were brought from some previous Inutkak homeworld where conditions similar to those on Glaice obtained. It would not surprise me if even the noun 'atopak' was an imported word that once meant only 'fish.' "

"That is all highly theoretical. The mantees—your people—are going to have us declared 'displaced persons' here! You must do something!" Tep's carefully cultivated reserve was at an end.

The professor backed up a step, even though his desk was still between him and the upset ikut. "I never intended that!" he protested. "I do not approve at all. I have suggested to the planetary council that they review the original Settlement Charter and settle this for once and for all, but I have received no response from them. I have not been able to locate the Charter, or even a copy of it."

"What charter? I have seen no charter," said Tep.

"The Glaice Planetary Charter. Every colony planet in the Xarafeille Stream has such a charter, granted by the Arbiter and defining the initial ownership of land, the type of government that will pertain, and the rights of individuals and groups of all the races that settle on it. The Charter will show who settled Glaice, and when, and will clarify the rights of your people, for better or for worse. Perhaps you, as an interested party, will have better luck with the Charter than I have had."

A charter! Of course! That would settle the matter. Tep was inclined to depart immediately, to storm the rather ineffectual fortress that was Government House. It was right across the narrow avenue from the university buildings, visible from the window behind Rakulit's desk.

All streets in Metok were narrow, compressed beneath the shelter of the huge half-kilometer glass-and-metal domes that made the town livable for the offworlders who resided there. Tep and the other ikut who lived in Metok would have been more comfortable without the domes, which trapped far too much heat and humidity for their comfort. Mantees like Rakulit were indifferent; folk of their race were adapted to a wide range of conditions, and though winter outside Metok's domes would not be their first choice of conditions, they could endure it. Bors, too, could cope with winter in Glaice's northern latitudes; though the ikuts' physical adaptation was considered to be ideal for arctic living and the bors's to more temperate ones, bors on many worlds settled high mountainous lands whose climate were actually chillier than the climates Glaice's ikut endured. Of course, bors's trogloditic lifestyle, which took full advantage of the planet's internal heat, mitigated the worst effects of Glaice's climates.

For members of other human subspecies, though, even the tempered conditions inside Metok's domes were intolerable, or barely tolerable. Few desert-adapted fards were seen on Glaice, and none had established permanent residency there. But the converse was also true; the fards on dry, desert planets like Fellenbrath (Xarafeille 271) or El Jab Al (Xarafeille 7) never saw an ikut either. There were a few wends on Glaice, because wends often congregated wherever record keepers and archivists were needed. Perhaps buried in the Arbiter's records on Newhome was an explanation for that—an Arbiter might have suggested that wends shared genetic codes with animals from forgotten Earth called "pack rats," which had exhibited similar proclivities, but the Arbiters had been quite content to leave explanations to the folk of each race themselves, who had created their own origin myths that had nothing to do with genetic manipulation, ancient corporations, or faster-than-light spaceship drives.

There were of course no tarbeks at all on Glaice. Sulfur-and-carrion-breath tarbeks could not live in close quarters with members of any of the other races, anyway, and the most hardy of them would have sickened and died in the clammy frigidity of Metok; out on Glaice's unprotected surface, a tarbek would not have had time to sicken, but would have died in hours even in high summer.

There were a few representatives of the seventh race of man on Glaice; the Arbiter's consul was one of them: an old-human. Old-humans on Glaice all occupied official positions of one sort or another; some even taught at the university. On most other worlds, a preponderance of old-humans were seminomadic or lived in slums or ghettos on the peripheries of cities. On Glaice, there was no place in the natural environment for fragile, furless nomads, so the only old-humans there had come because they needed jobs. When they retired, they usually did so offworld. An Arbiter, reviewing his ancient history files, might have likened their position to the Jews or Gypsies of lost Earth, and though few men still knew the real origins of the races, an almost-instinctive distrust of old-humans still lingered.

Tep Inutkak did not immediately leave Professor Rakulit's office to cross the narrow street to Government House. "Wait! I must show you the lab tests and the carbon-fourteen dates first." Tep did not understand why the professor thought that necessary, but he was understandably curious. Rakulit showed him not only the samples and the records of their provenance, and the test procedures themselves, but he also demonstrated how the "raw" radiocarbon dates were cross-checked against other sources.

Variations in solar output caused variations in C-14 production; those variations could be "read" indirectly in drill cores taken from the polar ice caps. Slices of trees that grew in layers year after year had been analyzed and the exact dates each tree ring represented was known. Those rings were distinguishable because each year's combination of sun, rainfall, and temperature was different, and the rings varied in distinguishable patterns. Actual carbon samples of individual growth layers had been dated in the lab, providing an accurate correlation for the field-samples' dates.

Rakulit held nothing back. Here were samples of mussel shells that had been dated to 1440 R.L., and bone collagen (not soluble in soil water, as was mussel shell) from the same location, cated at 980 R.L. "I have allowed for the solution of carbon from the shells and the redeposition of younger carbon, and treat all mussel-shell dates as 'no younger than' the recorded date."

He showed Tep painstakingly made drawings of his diggings. Each pit had been staked out and measured, then excavated two inches at a time. When a layer was removed, the surface was scraped clean and every artifact, every shift in soil coloration, was drawn on gridded paper, photographed, and carefully notated. The charts were scanned into computer programs that could reconstruct the excavation's contents and stratigraphy in two- or three-dimensional form. "This is a midden site on Paldernot Island," Rakulit said, keying his computer and bringing an illustration up onscreen. "See how the layers are defined? First the topsoil, then the midden, which is mostly mussel shells; then, beneath that, more dark topsoil, indicating that there was a break in the occupation site before the midden was made. . . ."

"What is that stuff below?" asked Tep, pointing to the next level, which the computer represented as a not-quite-natural-looking jumble.

"That is the detritus of a camp or village or an earlier time. It was burned to the ground. I think it is the oldest mantee site anywhere. I wish I knew just how old. . . ."

"You have dates on it, don't you? Isn't a lot of that dark stuff charcoal from the burning?"

"Alas! I am sorry. That material was contaminated by a spillage of fish oil in transit here. I suppose I should go back and dig another pit someday, but the times are unsettled, and . . ."

"Was there evidence of violence in the burning?" Tep asked, suddenly intense.

"Funny you should mention that," Rakulit said, eyeing Tep curiously. "There was a mantee skeleton in that level. It was not laid out neatly as for burial, but was merely sprawled under the rubble of the hut, that had burned over it. But what made you suspect it?"

"The Inutkak Cantones—our oral history—tell of a battle on Paldernot Island long ago, before there were any treaties between our peoples. It would be interesting to establish an accurate date for that—if your site is indeed where the battle took place."

"Indeed," Rakulit agreed. "Perhaps when all this other unpleasantness is over, we can go there together. . . ."

Seeming to treat Tep as he would treat another archaeologist, Rakulit showed him how every possible source of error had been accounted for. Tep had enough background in chemistry and physics to understand what he was shown, and before he left the professor's lab, he was convinced that no error of methodology had been made and that Rakulit was sincere in his belief in the dates. Still, Tep was, perhaps irrationally, unconvinced that the carbon dates were right and the sagas wrong. Perhaps the Settlement Charter would clarify things for him.

"Are you coming, Velanda? We must hurry, before the government workers take their noon break." She followed him out, giving her professor a brief nod.

"Are you convinced now?" she asked him as they waited to cross the busy street—it was crowded with pedestrians, mostly office and retail workers hurrying to get to the restaurants before the noon rush. Few vehicles were allowed beneath Metok's crowded domes.

"I am convinced that the mantee believes his own data. I am not convinced that Apootlak the Bold never lived, or that he did but on some other planet."

"Why does a long-dead hero mean so much to you, Tep?"

"He is Apootlak! He is the one who saved my people from starving when the atopak stopped coming! He is every young ikut's idol—and besides, he is my ancestor. How can I deny him his due?"

Tep's explanation did not help Velanda to believe in his cause. Quite the contrary, she became convinced that his determination was less firmly based in his convictions about oral traditions and their accuracy than in childish emotion. She did not have a chance to say so before they arrived at the door of Government House.

A wendish receptionist directed them to an elevator. "The old records vaults are all in the second basement level," she said. "Push the button marked 'two down.' " The elevator rattled and groaned. It was an open-cage type, very old, and Tep could see the bottom of the shaft through the floor's grating—a dark rectangle spotted with light patches of paper and other trash that had gathered there. Tep did not think the paper would cushion their fall much if his massive ikut body proved too heavy for the thin cables that hummed above his head.

At last the short, tense descent was finished. The cage door rattled open. "I want to see the Settlement Charter," Tep stated to the scruffy bors clerk who sat behind a too-small desk in the hallway. He noted with distaste that the bors's black fur looked oily, and bits of dust clung to it. Did bors bathe? Velanda did not seem dirty.

"You and every other ikut—and mantee—on the planet," said the bors. "I would like to see it too."

"What do you mean? Show it to me!"

"Give me a month off from my job, and money to live on, and I will go look for it. I will start my search by asking your ikut shahms what they did with it."

"It is not here?" Tep began to understand the wend's sarcasm. "It should be here!" he insisted. "It is too important to lose."

"Tell that to your shahm, then. I can show you who took it—though I do not think that will help you much."

"I do not understand. Show me. I will let him know what I think!"

The wend said, "Follow me." He led them down a corridor to a heavy metal door, which he proceeded to open.

"He is in here?"

"No one is in here. The sign-out records are in here. See? There is the book showing who took the Charter.

It is still out on the table, because the last one of you did not put it back when you left."

"The last one of me? You mean an Inutkak?"

"He was a mantee, I think. A professor from across the street."

"Rakulit? Professor Rakulit?" Tep glanced at Velanda, who shrugged. She knew what he was thinking—that the professor was indeed allied with the mantees who wanted to have the ikut disenfranchised—but she did not say anything. Rakulit never said he had not looked for the charter himself. He had only spoken of the Planetary Council's intransigence.

"There," said the clerk. "You see? It was signed out by whoever that squiggle represents. That is all I know—and that it was a long time ago."

"Is that Fedary 1, 8871 R.L.?" asked Tep, peering at the faded ink. "That is three thousand years ago! Are you saying the Planetary Charter has been missing for three thousand years?"

"I am saying nothing of the sort. I am merely showing the sign-out book to you. If I were to say anything at all, it would be that it looks more like Fedary 18 of the year 871 R.L. to me, and that was not three but eleven thousand years ago. I might say also that this is not the original book, but one of many successive copies made every five hundred years or so."

"Then how can I find the charter?"

"I do not know. I know what I would do. I told you already. If you want to hire me, now . . . I need a vacation from this place."

"You can do nothing I cannot do," Tep snarled. "Now what does that squiggle mean?"

"I can find out for you. I will start by tracing it, and showing my copy to an ikut shahm."

"I will do that! Where is paper to copy it?"

"Right here," said the bors, waving his clipboard. "I thought you might want it." He proffered a thin, beige sheet.

"It looks like a drawing of many small bugs riding a fish," Tep commented as he carefully traced the tiny icon. "I wonder what the cone and squiggle in the background is—a volcano?"

"I thought it looked like a frankowski saw myself," said the bors. "The little bumps look like saw teeth."

"What is a frankowski saw?"

"A great chain saw for cutting rock. It is a classic machine of great antiquity. We bors use them for tunneling in our mountain warrens. I thought the cone might be a heap of ore waiting to be trucked to the smelter, which is represented by the squiggle of smoke above and behind it."

"Fah!" Tep expostulated. "Why would someone draw that?"

"I have no idea. You are probably right, though. It is most likely the name-sign of an illiterate ikut. We bors have always been an educated folk, and one of us would have signed our name."

"Fah!" said Tep again, folding his completed tracing and slipping it into a pocket of his smock. On Glaice, only old-humans wore clothing for warmth; the furred races wore belts, smocks, and vests only for the convenience of belt packs and pockets. "I will ask someone who may know what this means," he said, motioning for Velanda to follow him.

"Who will you show it to?" she asked in the elevator.

"The snotty bors seemed to think it was an ikut sign," Tep replied. "I will ask my shahm."

"But how? Where will you find him?"

"It is almost the winter solstice. The Inutkak are now arriving in winter camp. I will take the train."

"Oh, can I go too?" she asked. Tep eyed her curiously. "It is a long trip and a boring one. You will pass right by Black Peak, my home. I will merely leave early for my vacation, and you can stay there one night and dine with my family."

Tep thought that was a fine idea. He would check out a portable computer from the dormitory's concierge, download his files, and he and Velanda could work on his paper en route. There was no air travel on Glaice, because atmospheric craft had proven to disrupt the breeding patterns of waterfowl vital to mantee sustenance and prized by bors and ikut as well. There were the orbital shuttles, of course, but they did not go where Tep wanted to go. So it was the train or nothing. Tep did not like sleeping on the train, which rocked and swayed, though he had done so the last two times he had visited his band when they were camped by the winter ice south of Black Peak. The first time had been six years before, when the Inutkak had arrived at the end of their migration cycle. That time, Tep had wanted to stay with them. He had been in Metok for three years, and had longed for the warmth and sociability of the Inutkak. The second time, three years ago, he had only gone because it was his duty to do so. By then he had become well adapted to city life, and he hardly remembered most of his childhood friends. Still, the band paid his board and his university tuition, in anticipation of some future day when he, Tep, would become shahm of the Inutkak band; it would not have done for him to have let them fear that he was becoming disloyal.

The robed, hooded figure stepped gingerly down the icy gangplank. Rough swells slapped the high-prowed aluminum boat and the floe ice, making the railed walkway seesaw. From beneath the hem of the person's heavy, full-length garment peeped the toes of incongruous shoes. Sandals might have looked appropriate, but not cleated, insulated boots with THERM-O-PAK® emblazoned in orange around the perimeter of the black soles.

"Ah, well," muttered the bors pilot, while struggling to keep the boat steady with a judicious balance of engine and rudder, "the real reason for the robe isn't to make him look like some ancient wizard, anyway." Indeed it was not. Such robes were equipped with an efficient filtration system because—as everyone knew, whether it was true or not—those hideous-looking, hairless old-humans reeked.

The ice was slick, its surface melted by the hot equatorial sun. The air was already above freezing, and it was not yet noon. The hem of the old-human's robe was soon wet. A huge ikut male led him to the place where the atrocity had taken place, and pointed at the white bundles of fur lined up there. "Eight of them, Consul," the Ketrap band's shahm growled with as much grief as anger. "Eight little ones."

"What killed them?" The consul saw hardly any blood, except a drop or two on a few tiny faces.

"*Poknat* ribs, tied with strips of meat," the ikut said—and then had to explain further, though it was obviously difficult for him to speak of it. The young ikuts, playing by the edge of the floe, must have been delighted when someone threw a dozen gulp-sized balls of fresh meat up onto the ice. They had swallowed the treats, and within minutes their digestive juices began working on the raw meat. The springy, sharpened and pointed strips of bone uncoiled suddenly, and slashed the little one's stomachs from the inside. They had not died quickly, but none of them lasted long enough to get help, or to tell who had given them the treats.

"There is not much I can do," said the Arbiter's consul, "unless you want me to take them to Metok for autopsies. . . ."

"We will take care of our own!" snapped the shahm. "We know who did this." The way he said it, the consul was convinced that he meant "We will *avenge* our own."

"This is how it begins," mused the consul sadly, when he was again back on board the weather station's powerboat. The population of Glaice was widely scattered, and everyone but the bors in their mountain cave cities migrated. Word traveled slowly, but it got around. The dead ikut cubs weren't the last casualties he feared he was going to see. Thank the stars the news services shunned cold Glaice, and had only a few stringers in Metok. He would have hated to see holos of those dead cubs sent out, to be plastered across holoscreens on a thousand worlds. The way his boss kept a lid on news from Glaice, the consul thought John Minder would have liked that even less.

CHAPTER 4

Two major difficulties faced the early generations of genetically altered mankind during their rapid initial spread across the Xarafeille Stream. Both stemmed from an initial decision not to divide the worlds on the basis of race, but to place colonies wherever they could thrive. There were two major obstacles to be overcome. They were (and I will have more to say on each subject later in this entry) interracial wars and interracial children. Wars, not least because they cultivated bigotry, were a barrier against interbreeding and racial dissolution, and interracial children, because bigotry was never quite universal.

John Minder IV,
Unpublished Manuscript,
Erne Museo, Newhome, 4321 R.L.

The North Continent Railroad was one of three high technology transportation systems on Glaice. The others were the South Continent Railroad—which was almost identical except for details of the terrain it traversed—and the Glaice Ballistic Shuttle, which departed Metok spaceport weekly, arriving at Amberdin, the south continental shuttleport antipodal to Metok, within slightly over an hour. Few travelers were wealthy enough to afford a shuttle ticket except on pressing business; even offworld tourists, who were an elite group composed of corporate chairpersons or princes, kings, and presidents of nations and whole worlds, seldom considered it worthwhile to see more of Glaice than could be visited within a day's rail travel from Metok—after all, what was there but more ice, rock, ocean, and volcanoes just like the ones they could see from the train's windows?

The railroad had been built by the offworld bors firm of Prang and Nudoff, on Pristine, Xarafeille 1004. P&N supported a small engineering crew in residence on Glaice to maintain it, though they hired locals as conductors, porters, chefs, and office workers. The North Continent Railroad completely encircled Glaice, weaving north and south of an average latitude of forty degrees north. About ninety percent of its rails were on the surface of the planet, and were thus usable only in local summer or in areas where snowfall was light enough to toss aside with great winged plows attached to the front of the trains. Wherever the long arms of Glaice's continental ice caps reached all the way down to its encircling ocean, the trains ran in tunnels beneath the rock—tunnels deep enough to be safe from the immense stresses of overlying, moving, grinding ice. Between Metok and Black Peak, which had a sheltered underground terminal, there was only one tunnel—where the Hapnag Glacier relieved the pressure of thousands of years' snowfall on the northern icecaps by calving enormous icebergs off into the summer sea of the Metok Ice-Free Passage, a broad bay.

Tep and Velanda tired of the unrelenting sameness of the scenery during the first leg of their train journey—there were volcanoes belching gray, noxious ash, black rocks, brown ones, scruffy slate-green trees and bushes beside the railbed, and occasional small towns that were no more than freight terminals for local bors shippers of ores and ikut traders in fish-oil products.

For a while, they found things to chat about. At school, Tep had seldom taken time for that. He reflected that Velanda was far more fun to talk with than were the uneducated ikut girls of his band—girls whom, he admitted, he had not even tried to converse with, his last visit "home." The boys—when he could tell the difference—were no better. Velanda obviously felt similarly about Tep, who was not sure just when she had decided she wanted to accompany him all the way to North Camp.

But it was a long train ride, and both of them had arisen early. They both dozed during the uneventful passage under the Hapnag ice. It had taken hours to get tickets, and they had had to get up in the middle of the night to find seats together, because it had been too late to obtain reservations. "I hope Black Peak is bigger than these little burgs we keep passing," Tep grumbled when he awakened. At some time while he had slept, the train had emerged from the Hapnag Tunnel, and it was again racing across sunlit countryside. Winter had not yet set in firmly, and there was little snow or glare, though the temperature outside seldom got above freezing; the large thermal mass of Glaice's oceans created a significant time lag between astronomical seasons and actual meteorological and climatic ones. The winter solstice, the shortest day, actually fell in what Metok residents considered early fall, and true winter did not set in firmly until the vernal equinox. The summer solstice, the longest day, marked the beginning of spring, and the autumnal equinox was high summer.

"Black Peak is not as large as Metok," Velanda replied, her pride stung by Tep's disparaging remark, "but it is a bors city, not a confabulation of offworld and local styles. It is a very beautiful place." Tep, who did not see how a warren of tunnels, a hollowed-out mountain, could be beautiful, wisely kept silent.

"There!" Velanda exclaimed. "That is Black Peak." Tep could see how it got its name. Black Peak had been formed by orogeny of the northern continent, a granitic batholith formed deep within the planet's crust then thrust to the surface and eroded by ice. Black, roughly faceted like a rude jewel by snow-filled cirques on the highest crags, it was quite unlike the red and gray volcanic cones farther south, peaks that composed Glaice's northern "ring of fire."

"Where is the town?" asked Tep. "Does it really occupy the entire inside of the mountain?"

"We are approaching from the north," she replied, "and the open adits and terraces are mostly on the other side. And no, only a small fraction of the mountain has actually been excavated, though it seems vast from the inside. We will not see the city lights, because soon the tracks will go underground to the terminal." Tep was disappointed, but said nothing. "You will see more when we leave Black Peak," Velanda said, seeing his resigned expression. "The tracks go right through to the other side. Perhaps we can find a seat in the observation car, then."

Their window darkened suddenly. "There! In a quarter-hour we will be there," said Velanda. The train had now plunged beneath the planet's surface—or at least into the side of Black Peak.

In minutes the hum and roar of steel wheels became quite loud. At full tilt across the countryside, the train rose above its track, a combination of magnetic and aerodynamic lift, but as it slowed down, wheels took over the burden. Velanda instructed Tep to swallow several times to clear his ears. "There are large tunnels overhead to exhaust the air pressure our movement creates," Velanda explained, "but some bow-pressure is saved to brake the train too. It feels no different than coming down a mountain into thicker air." Tep had never experienced that either. He had never been higher than the top of an Inutkak ice floe's crag, or at the top of a Metok building, neither of which allowed for significant pressure differentials.

Black Peak Station looked much like Metok Station at first; the train rode in a deep trench that kept the boarding platform outside at the level of the floor within, but at Metok the tracks had been covered only by the sweeping dome high overhead, giving the impression of being wholly outdoors; here the ceiling was like a night sky speckled with unnaturally large stars. It was supported upon great polished granite columns thick as houses, that were mostly black, but were shot through with veins of pink and white. Spotlights let into the pavement spread glaring light up them, while the oversized stars—floodlights—illuminated the platform and the terminal area beyond.

"Srah Velanda! Srah Velanda, over here!" someone cried out. A very fat bors wearing a ridiculously crimson sambrowne belt waved his equally ridiculous round, red pillbox hat over his head.

"Who is that?" asked Tep.

"It is Manko, my father's chauffeur," Velanda said, waving back. "Just leave the luggage. He will send someone for it." As Tep had only a small satchel containing a toothbrush, a curry comb, and several pads of unused notepaper, he shifted the bag's shoulder strap, but kept it with him; it was too small to leave lying on the pavement. Velanda had brought a bulky suitcase, which she abandoned there. "Manko," she said, running up to the fat bors and hugging him. "I missed you."

"I missed you too, bright eyes," said the chauffeur. "The palace is a dull place now. Even Vols's singing does not make up for your absence."

Velanda laughed. She glanced at Tep. "You will hear that for yourself," she said. "My brother can only growl loudly, but he fancies his voice drips like gold from heated quartz." Tep thought the simile clumsy, until he reminded himself that Velanda was at home now, among bors to whom rocks, mining, and smelting were second nature. Had she been in Metok, she might have said, "He fancies his voice is as sweet as the honeybirds that nest in the dome's high reaches," or something similar. Velanda was at home—he alone was a foreigner here. Was she going to introduce him—or did one not do that, with chauffeurs? "Oh, Manko," Velanda said, "this is Tep Inutkak, a fellow-student. He will be staying with us tonight."

"Sar Tep!" said the chauffeur, straightening to the closest approximation of military posture his bulk permitted. "Black Peak welcomes you." That seemed an odd way to put it, thought Tep, as if the chauffeur was a functionary of some kind, not a private individual.

Manko held the door of a long, silvery car open for Tep and Velanda. "This is quite fancy," Tep commented when the door had shut. "Is this a limousine? Why is there a wall between us and the driver? Can he hear us?"

Velanda giggled. "It is a state vehicle from the city

pool," she said. "I suppose it is a limousine. And no, Manko cannot hear us when that little window is shut."

Tep was not satisfied. "All those other passengers from the train got on that little trolley car. Why were there no limousines for them?" Tep realized that not only did he know nothing about bors cities, he knew less about Velanda herself, or her family. He experienced diffuse resentment that she had not prepared him for these surprises.

Velanda lowered her head slightly, and when she spoke it was as if she feared Tep's disapproval. "Perhaps it is because none of their mothers is Lady Maior of Black Peak," she said softly. "Perhaps none of them plan to sleep in the royal palace this night."

"Royal palace? Why? I do not underst . . ." He peered closely at his companion. "*Your* mother?" he murmured. "She is the ruler of this city? Does she *own* it?"

"It is something in between," Velanda said. "She rules it, having inherited her place from her mother. That is how we bors do things. She rules, but my Uncle Frant executes her rule and is more in the public eye." Among bors, Tep remembered, fathers counted for little in the scheme of things—except as mentors not for their own children, but their sisters'.

Tep was daunted by Velanda's revelation. Did that mean that she in her turn would someday be running Black Peak? Again, she seemed to read his thoughts or at least his expression. "I'm in much the same position as you are, Tep. My family sent me to Metok University to learn everything I would have to know to take my place here, someday—just as the Inutkak band sent you."

"I suppose so," Tep admitted, "but the Inutkak's ice floes and dirt-floored winter camps can hardly compare to . . . to all this." He had seen nothing of Black Peak but the railway terminal and brief glimpses of shops and business establishments—storefronts and doorways carved from the living rock of the mountain itself, though no less elegant for all that—but he was already most impressed.

"You don't have to *challenge* your mother, do you? You just walk in and take over, and . . ."

"Oh, don't talk nonsense, Tep! We both know what that 'challenge' is. The Inutkak aren't savages anymore. The only real 'challenge' you'll have to face is defending your dissertation and passing your oral exam. And speaking of that, have you made any more progress on your paper? After dinner, let's go over that last chapter again."

"After dinner" it was far too late to work on Tep's paper. First he and Velanda were let out at the palace door—a three-meter portico projecting into the well-lit underground "street." The pilasters beside the two-meter-high door were carved from brilliant black and green malachite, and the door itself was a balanced slab of polished white quartz laced with what Tep was sure were veins of native gold. The anteroom beyond towered three stories upward from a white marble floor. Two tiers of cast-bronze balconies jutted from upper-level loggias, and from within the loggias' niches emanated a clear, cold glow that Tep decided could only be indirect sunlight. Tep was thoroughly impressed—and quite intimidated by it all. Was Velanda's *house* bigger than Metok Grand Hall? This one floor of it—the part he had seen so far—surely covered more area than the entire Inutkak winter camp.

When they entered the anteroom, he was even more cowed, and a bit angry about it. They were met by palace functionaries in the same brief uniform the chauffeur wore, all standing in a line from the door well into the room. Velanda greeted each of them with varying degrees of affectionate display. Tep tried to dismiss his uneasiness as jealousy, resentment of such wealth and ostentation, but he suspected it ran deeper than that. This was just too . . . different. Ikuts did not do things this way. Ikuts were friendly when someone came to visit. Ikuts let the kids rush out and greet people. They felt welcome in an ikut camp, not threatened.

Tep, who had never had a servant—and had never even met one, to the best of his knowledge—had not realized that there would be as much interaction of personalities among masters and servants as there was among other people. Now, seeing how Velanda hugged one stubby bors female—an elderly one, to judge by her short silver-furred muzzle—and how she had merely nodded to the emaciated-looking male who stood at the head of the greeting line, he understood how it must be; each person knew his or her own role and function, but beyond that, relationships surely developed just as they did between graduate students and professors, or within genuine biological families. What a complexity of relationships! How did one keep them all straight?

By the time he had reached the middle of the line and had been introduced to half the individuals, he had forgotten the names and stations of everyone but the tall skinny bors at the head of the line. He was Trasp, the Chief Servant—clearly a formal title; Tep had heard the emphasis Velanda placed on it, and automatically supplied the capital letters in his mind. By the time he reached the end of the line, he had forgotten all but Trasp and Benat, who was Velanda's childhood nurse and later her governess—whatever that was. Trasp had greeted him coolly, with a raised eyebrow and with ears carefully held raised, neither pointed forward with ill-concealed enthusiasm nor slanting backward in thinly veiled hostility. Tep did not know what to make of him. Benat, though, flung her stumpy arms around him as if he were a huge cub and rumpled his fur affectionately. He was not sure which greeting he preferred.

"Come, Sar Tep," said Benat, tugging on his arm. "I will show you to your room." She eyed him speculatively. "Oh, dear, you are so tall! I hope the bed is long enough. Few guests here are of such a fine, manly stature as you . . ." She turned to Velanda. "And you, dear! I will help you unpack in a few minutes. I am sure you have *much* to say tell me." Again, Benat gave Tep that speculative look that he could not interpret.

"You are an old fool, Bennei," Velanda murmured, shading her eyes with half-lowered lids, her head turned to the side. Tep was not sure what the exchange meant. Bors and ikut were quite similar outwardly, though bors tended to be smaller and stouter, and their black noses did not project outward on the ends of arching muzzles like ikuts' did. Bors faces were not much different from mantee ones, actually, or old-human ones—if one were to paint the old-human's nostrils black and cover his face in short, black fur. Tep wondered if he had read Velanda's expression correctly, or if such things were as different between bors and ikut as their noses were. Had Velanda and Benat been an ikut cub and its big sister or doting aunt, he would have thought that there was a conspiracy between them, like the ones that developed between ikut females when mating time was just around the corner.

He had no time to think more on that, though. Benat was all bustle as she led him to an ornate bronze-caged elevator at the end of the anteroom. It rose silently and smoothly without cables or other observable means of support. Seeing him clutch at the perimeter handrail, Benat said, "I suppose elevators in Metok are of that terrifying cable type." She lifted her chin in pride and dismissive scorn. "This is a water lift, powered by the weight of the city reservoir, which is twelve thousand feet above us, near the top of Black Peak. There is no way this car could fall. Even if something went wrong, we would merely sink slowly back to the ground floor, where we would disembark without even mussing our fur."

From the way she had so quickly and correctly interpreted his body language, Tep was sure now that bors and ikut nonverbal expression were very much the same. He would thus have to ask Velanda, later, just what the conspiracy was all about.

His bedroom was awash with bright vermilion sunlight. There, beyond a vast window composed of tiny irregular panes held together with metal, was the setting sun. He felt a momentary disorientation, having gotten turned around as the limousine had twisted and turned through the endless tunnels below. Striding to the window, he peered outward onto a patio as large as the room itself, and over a low granite parapet onto . . . nothing at all. The patio, he realized, was no more than a niche cut into the mountainside.

Benat left him soon, as he needed little help unpacking his small kit. Everything was so elegant. Tep felt much as he had when he first arrived in Metok. He had entered his dormitory room without even having to shake sticky mud from his feet, even though it was springtime, and the Inutkak back home were slogging through thawing muck. This place was as far superior to the dormitory as the latter had been to the Inutkak winter camp. Tep found himself resenting that, and reacting to his resentment with scorn—how soft these bors were. How coddled by their warm cave city. He doubted that one of them would last a month at home—skinny Trasp, the butler or whatever he was, would not survive a trip outside to relieve himself, if the wind was up.

Tep discovered that one panel of the "window" was actually a door, and he went outside. A blast of icy air startled him as he neared the parapet. It was as cold as deep winter out there! How high up was he? He was higher, for sure, than he had ever been before. From the parapet, which he did not approach too closely for fear of being blown off, he could see the vast plateau that stretched south to the sea, and could even distinguish the shelf ice from the land itself. There, on that border between two very different but equally harsh environments, lay the Inutkak winter camp. Tep found himself, uncharacteristically, yearning for it. How far was it? He knew that the train would take several hours to get near it, tomorrow, but from where he stood, it looked like he could have walked to the sea itself in less than a day.

He heard a soft chime from within his room, and strode quickly within. His door was ajar, and he heard a childlike voice from without. "Sar Tep? Sar Tep?"

"Yes? Come in."

A small bors, a cub of indeterminate sex, stepped hesitantly in. "Dinner will be served in a half hour, Sar Tep," the cub said. "I am to see to your requirements."

Tep did not know what those might be. Did the bors

of Black Peak—the bors of the Lady Maior's palace—have special rules? What would he need besides a good currying? He asked the cub.

"I will help with your fur," the cub offered. "My name is Tabir, and I am good at that."

Tep was not accustomed to anyone helping him with matters of basic hygiene—but there were always hard-to-reach places, and those annoying mats of felted fur that formed beneath his arms could not be separated with one hand alone, and sometimes had to be clipped off. He nodded. "Thank you. I wish to make a good impression."

The cub—a female, he decided—knew her work. She had come prepared with a small leather kit bag containing several tools, some unfamiliar to him. One, he soon discovered, was a battery-powered clipper with what his helper called a "stripper" attachment that made short work of mats, removing the shed fur without harming the longer guard hairs that were still rooted. Tep grew amazed as the work progressed: the wastebasket (actually a finely cast bronze vessel with a hunting scene, bors chasing a mountain *glipter* over steep crags) was soon full of dirty-looking fur. He felt progressively lighter as the little bors's "stripper" and curry comb worked over his fur from shoulders to tail. His pelt felt softer and fluffier than it had since his mother had licked and groomed him as a cub.

Several times he stopped to shake and scratch. "Ah! That feels good. Funny, but good. I must find where to buy one of those kits like yours."

"I am sure Lady Bavant will allow me to give you this one, Sar Tep," said his groomer. "It is a small thing."

That reminded Tep of another potential omission he had not considered. "A house gift! I have nothing to give my host . . . hostess."

"Lady Velanda has taken care of that," said Tabir. "She sent my brother Fantor to the Street of Gifts for fresh flowers and sweets. It is not expected that you, a traveler, would have brought much with you on the train." Tep reminded himself to ask Velanda about paying for the gift—though his stipend from the Inutkak seldom left him with enough money for more than a few beers at the Last Atopak.

"There!" Tabir said at last. "Your lovely fur shines like fine silver. I wish my fur were so long and silky."

"Your fur is very nice," Tep said politely. "It is as black as the glassy rock from Mount Bredamog, where my folk spend winter in the south. It is as soft as a nighttime breeze off the Deep Channel islands."

"Oh," she said, turning her head shyly aside, "I am too young for such words!"

Tep, fearing that he had overstepped some cultural boundary without knowing it, said, "I am sorry! I did not mean to offend you."

"It is no offense," Tabir murmured, still not meeting his eye. "I would someday hope to hear a male speak such words to me. It is just that I have known no ikut save you, and your great size makes me forget that you are really a girl like me."

Tep was dumbfounded. Had he misunderstood? A girl? "Why do you say that?" he asked. "I am not a girl!"

She smiled—the same conspiratorial expression Tep had seen pass between Velanda and her old nurse. "I know you wish to be known as Sar Tep, not Srah Tep—if that is your true name," Tabir said. "I have heard it is often easier for women to travel unmolested when they pretend to be men—and there are even ointments that fool the nose as well. I will not reveal your secret, even though you are surely safe here."

Tep was not offended by Tabir's mistake, though members of other subspecies might have been. He now realized how it had occurred; while grooming him with her clever tools, she had obviously observed his private parts. "Tabir, I will explain. I am ikut, not bors. I am, despite what appears to you to be so, a male, but I am not yet mature. We ikut, male and female, look outwardly the same until our eighth passage—or in my case, until I reach twenty-five years of age. By this time next year, you would not have mistaken me for another female."

Tabir, unlike Tep, seemed profoundly embarrassed. "Oh!" she said softly. "Oh! Sar Tep! I am so sorry! I am only a cub, and I did not know. I . . . I must go now! I am late for . . . for something I must . . . something I had forgotten . . ." She backed out of his room, then, leaving her grooming implements strewn over the floor.

"Tabir, wait!" Tep called after her, but too late—he heard the rattle of a door latch, and by the time he reached his own doorway, he saw only a vertical bar of light at the end of the corridor, a bar that thinned and disappeared as a door swung closed. "Oh, damn!" he muttered. "I have been here an hour, and already I have stuck my foot in *pretok.*" Pretock was another ikut word for ice; it meant the thin, glassy ice that formed over a fishing hole, thin stuff that broke with sharp, knifelike edges that could slash the skin, flesh and tendons of an unwary ikut who stepped through it. What would the little bors do now? Would she relay whatever it was that had upset her to Velanda's mother? And just what was it? Tep was quite confused.

Ikut wholly lacked any meaningful sense of sexual identity until the changing patterns of days and nights had cycled fully twenty-four times—which meant eight full migration cycles for an ordinary ikut; some ikut did not even know for sure which sex they were, until that time. Tep knew only because he had been examined by the Inutkak's shahm, and had been selected as his successor. Shahms were always male. The reason for that was lost in unrecorded prehistory, and may have had something to do with some adaptation to conditions on an earlier homeworld, conditions that did not pertain on Glaice and thus seemed wholly arbitrary now. Thus Tep—who did not really care which sex he was, or would become—had not been offended by Tabir's false conclusion. Yet she had been quite distraught by her error; obviously, bors felt quite differently about such things.

Tep's only present concern was that he had not indeed stepped on pretok that would cut him—that would make him unwelcome here in Black Peak so soon after he had arrived. Thus when Velanda came for him, to escort him to dinner, he followed her with a much greater sense of anxiety than he had had before, when his only concern was with his lack of a proper house gift. The dining room was not a great hall, as he had imagined. It was not much larger than it had to be to house a table, six chairs, and a small sideboard decorated with an array of dried flowers, mostly tropical species that Tep recognized from his migrations with the Inutkak band.

Just as he and Velanda entered, others did so also. "Sar Tep," said the first of them—a bors woman, surely Velanda's mother, the Lady Maior—"thank you for the lovely flowers."

"Ah, you're welcome, Lady," Tep responded, nonplussed. He glanced briefly, gratefully, toward Velanda, who pretended not to notice.

"This is Frant, my brother," she said, introducing the second bors to enter. He was almost as tall as Tep himself, and showed scattered white fur around his muzzle. "And this is Vols."

Tep returned the nods of the males. Their demeanor seemed cold and aloof. Was that the way Black Peak males—or at least males of high station—ordinarily acted, he wondered, or had word of his offense against Tabir, whatever it was, already reached them? He wished he had paid more attention to bors, in Metok. He didn't know how to read their faces. But how could he have? Outside of classrooms and labs, bors kept to their own kind just like everyone else.

"Be seated," Frant said. "I want to know more about the crazy mantees' lawsuit—and how it may come to affect us bors."

"Frant!" exclaimed the Lady Bavant. "There will be time for politics after we eat. Now I want to hear about Metok, and the lives our young scholars lead there. Is the Last Atopak still there? When I was a student, there was a legend that . . ."

With the lady leading the conversation, things went smoothly through a first course of odd, round little leaves tossed in a thin, vinegary sauce. "These are peppery!" Tep exclaimed. "In the refectory nothing has enough spice. I wish I could bring some of this back with me."

"Is there a cold pool nearby?" asked Vols. "Watercress grows only in clear water, and only tastes good when it is almost as cold as ice itself."

Ice. They were all speaking the dialect of Standard common across Glaice, in which there were only a few words for ice. "What kind of ice?" asked Tep before he thought about it. "Some ice is much colder than water can be."

Vols smiled. *"Etok,"* he said, citing ice just forming on the verge of a still pool. "The cress prefers water as cold as it can be, without becoming ice."

"There is a pool," mused Tep, "but I am not sure the park's keepers would want . . ."

Frant guffawed. Tep cringed inwardly. These bors seemed alternately cool, then friendly and jovial. Their lack of consistent proper restraint disconcerted him—and they were so loud. He could not read their real intent or moods; all was buried beneath good cheer and laughter or uncomfortable silences. Tep, a university student, had once prided himself on his cosmopolitan poise, but he was now, and had been for some time, aware that he was still an Inutkak boy, and quite out of place.

"Vols is leading you on, boy," Frant said, obviously amused. "I told Vols about a prank I pulled when I was a student, planting cress in the Center Park pool. Before they discovered it, it had plugged the drains and filters and made a skating rink out of Government Way. I think he plans to try it himself when it is his turn to study in Metok, unoriginal as he is. Is that right, nephew?"

"Aw . . . I can find better pranks to play. But I have not yet seen Metok, or what opportunities are there."

Tep, who had not thought much about playing pranks, now considered what fun he had been missing. "There is a prank I would like to play," he mused aloud. The others, as one, urged him to tell them of it. Tep described the bors record keeper in the basement of Government House. "I would like to slip a document into one of his record books, a paper that would fall out when he moved the book. It must look as if it is quite ancient, a map perhaps, or . . ."

"A treasure map!" Velanda exclaimed. "A map of Glaice with a spot marked high on the ice cap near Mount Pesaroon, perhaps a spot labeled 'Oors.' Then she had to explain. First she told her family how the clerk had hinted several times that he wanted a vacation. She thought that a treasure map would provide him with a pretext to spend his next time off chasing shadows across the high, cold ice instead of snug at home in some bors warren. Then she told Tep about Oors. "It is one name of the legendary home of all bors everywhere," she said. "No one knows if it is a world or just a city, but considering how long ago Glaice was settled, it is not impossible that it might be here. Perhaps once the ice was less extensive, or . . ."

Thus the meal progressed. Tep told himself—once he managed to relax among them—that the bors were actually quite enjoyable company, much more fond of light talk and wit than a comparable gathering of ikut would have been. The food was excellent; the main course was a kind of fish with pale russet flesh, and several kinds of starchy tubers each with its own distinctive flavors and sauces. The servants who waited on them were so skilled that sometimes Tep did not even notice when one plate was removed from before him and another set down. His glass—cold water—was never empty.

By the time desert was served, Frant could contain himself no longer. "Now, tell me about the mantees, and just what you plan to do about it," he said.

"Us?" Tep glanced at Velanda. What had she told her family about their trip? He had not thought much beyond showing the odd little squiggle he had copied to Hapakat, the shahm of the Inutkak.

"Tep is convinced that the mantees' suit is based on a false premise," Velanda said, saving him from embarrassment. "If indeed Professor Rakulit's dates are wrong, as Tep believes, then the mantees have no case. We will first find out what the Inutkak shahm, himself a scholar of sorts, has to say about it, and then we will try to find out what has become of the Settlement Charter. The clerk seemed to think that the sigil in his sign-out book was once some sort of ikut mark, though perhaps distorted by many recopyings."

"Humph," growled Frant. "All that scholarly stuff is just fine—but I will draw up a message for Hapakat also. Being the nearest ikut band to Black Peak—at least during this part of your migration cycle—perhaps the Inutkak will consider an alliance with us, if it comes to that. Perhaps the Tehokag and Atulag will too, if he passes word to them."

"Frant? What are you considering?" asked his sister, the lady Bavant. "An alliance? To what end?"

"I would rather not say," Frant replied. "Not yet. But if the seels become too swellheaded with the success of their tricks, they might not stop with the ikuts. Without the Charter, we bors are in no better a position than your folk, are we, Tep?"

Tep agreed that it was so. He belatedly remembered that even though their territories hardly overlapped, and though bors had not been known to eat seels, there was a deep underlying distrust between bors and mantees. He would have to ask Velanda about that—but later, perhaps on the train tomorrow. Now, though, he agreed to carry whatever message Frant wanted to send to his band's shahm.

That night Tep did not sleep well. The uncommonly soft bed perhaps contributed to his restlessness, but his dreams and half-awake thoughts surely did. War? Frant had been speaking of war against the mantees, if the Arbiter's consul ruled against them.

Tep knew nothing of war except what he had read or seen on the holonews in the dormitory common. What he read was quite dry—strategies, movements of troops and weapons, logistics—but the holonews events were vivid. They seemed to dwell on the horrors of conflict—the blood, the destruction, and the weeping faces.

Tep's dreams combined both visions, books and

news, with yet another—his knowledge of Glaice, his own world. In those dreams, the wrecked city he saw was Metok, its domes shattered, blood running in its drains and gutters, clumps of brown, black, and white fur, bloodied, caught within the twisted stone and metal ruins of dormitories, classrooms, and amid the broken fossils of the Last Atopak Tavern.

He envisioned angry ikut males swarming the beaches of the equatorial island where he had played with Kurrolf, carrying heavy slug-throwers of bors manufacture at the ready. He saw brown, shadowy mantee shapes in the water, under ikut ice, and heard the dull thumps of explosions beneath the floes. Wreckage and destruction were the matrix of his dreams, and that matrix was entwined with red, the color of Glaice's bloody evening skies.

At dawn he arose, more tired than when he had gone to bed. There in the east, just within the scope of his window, the sunrise spread as a haze of rose over the ocean. Tep knew, intellectually, that the twice-daily show of color was caused by particulate matter spewed forth from Glaice's volcanoes. He knew that the volcanoes' greenhouse effect warmed the planet—just enough—for well-adapted humans to live there. Red, on Glaice, was traditionally the color of life, but now, dreaming or awake, it had an entirely different significance for Tep Inutkak.

CHAPTER 5

The genetic seat of human behaviors has not been located, though the major variations upon the genome have been known and thoroughly mapped for millennia. Phenotypic differences between the seven human races have all been traced to actions of genes located on the V chromosome—that smallest chromosome of all, with its distinctive shape*. V-chromosome genes, however, do not supply code for growth or for metabolic proteins; they merely "turn on" controller genes on other chromosomes, that in turn activate the ordinary genes of protein synthesis.

But behaviors differ between the races; no one denies the coyness of a male bors who, once mated, will remain so until he is old (or, if he loses his mate, until he goes mad). No one can ignore the disinterest of ordinary female mantees in matters reproductive—or the magnificent capacity for sexual activity exhibited by a mantee throngmother in must. . . .

Slith Wrasselty, Ph.D.,
Sex and Genes Across the Xarafeille Stream,
University Press, Thember, 12158 R.L.

"I hate war!" Parissa volunteered. "I hate holonews too!"

John Minder—not Arbiter Minder, here in his own home—raised an eyebrow. Where had Parissa seen a news show? Her viewing was carefully limited to what a young child could understand, could integrate into her fresh, naive worldview without scarring trauma.

*The "V"-chromosome's centromere is located almost at the ends of its DNA "arms," making it as immediately apparent to the eye as the equally distinctive (but specifically male) "Y"-chromosome.

"Tell me why, dear," Minder said quietly.

"There are bad things on holonews," Parissa announced. "I saw dead people and 'ploded buildings, and poletsies with guns, at Derinel's house."

"Derinel's parents should not have allowed that," her father murmured. "What else did you see? What did you understand?"

"I saw *you,* Daddy—at least he looked like you when you have your robe and hood and spooky-glow eyes on." Though he was—arguably, he thought—the most powerful man in the human-settled galaxy, the Arbiter was subject to the same prejudices as other old-humans. In public, he usually wore a full-length, concealing robe with a hood that obscured his face, with gauzy filter veils over his breathing orifices. The tales about old-human exudations and their erotic effect upon furred human folk were exaggerated, of course, but people felt strongly about them. The "spooky-glow eyes" were the sensors he wore in the courtroom, to ascertain the relative truth or falsehood of what witnesses and disputants said. All those things were part of his very mysterious public image, and no one could tell if they were in the presence of John Minder XXIII himself, or one of his many assistants.

"And what was I there for? What was I doing?"

"It was a school for grownups, sort of," Parissa replied, "and you were the teacher."

Minder nodded. "And the lesson?"

"War is very bad!" she said emphatically. "And I have to work very hard to make it not happen—and I have to come see you if Robby wants a war with me."

"I think you understand perfectly. War is very much like when you and your brother disagree, but because it involves grown-ups who are very strong, who have terrible weapons, many more people get hurt in war, and often die. Robby would never hurt you, not seriously."

That was a risky statement, he knew, because pain was very subjective, especially a five-year-old's pain, but Parissa did not rise to the bait.

"Your job is just like at home, isn't it? To make bad things not happen. That's why you showed them all the awful war things—so the grown-ups would be scared of them, and would be good."

Minder hoped his role as father amounted to more than a reign of secondhand terror, but he did not say so. "You are absolutely right, dear," he replied, lifting her up and hugging her. "And perhaps someday that will be your job—or Rob's, or Sarabet's."

"I will do a good job! I'll show scary holonewses to make everyone behave."

John Minder was not especially proud of his antiwar propaganda—mostly gleaned from the records of Arbiters over many thousands of years. There was no need to exaggerate the horrors of modern warfare. He was, however, very proud of his youngest child, who had gotten to the root of the matter so easily. Perhaps indeed she would become the first Arbiter who was not a male of his family line.

Minder signed the purchase order on his desk, for twelve commercial-grade survey satellites to be delivered to Glaice, Xarafeille 132. He did not think they would do much good. He had seen holos of the planet—vast oceans, rugged coasts, countless islands and ice floes—and all the "birds" would be good for was reporting after the fact. His consul there would only suffer the more by helplessly watching the two races slaughter each other.

Actually, he was in no better shape. He had no real idea what to do about Glaice. Did that dearth of creativity signal the beginning of the end of his still-brief career? Did it perhaps signal the end of . . . everything? No, he reflected, neither the ikuts nor the mantees had access to starships, or the skills to fiddle with them. Glaice was not an interstellar problem. It was only rough for the people who lived there—and died there.

He knew he would have to close the planet before the big news agencies discovered what was happening there. He had to consider the larger picture; if too many people began seeing how impotent he really was . . . But he still needed that datacrystal. That represented the power to "make bad things not happen," as Parissa said it. He had to gain access to the fleet codes and the poletzai. If the mantees and ikuts on Glaice wiped themselves out, he would just have to conceal it. He had no choice.

Watching Parissa playing, across the room, John Minder reflected on other men like himself, who had loved children and furry pets. He alone had access to the real history of mankind, and of ancient Earth, so he alone knew their names. Hitler. Stalin. Even Genghis Khan had probably liked children—the ones he did not slay.

Their train departed early, so Tep and Velanda did not again see members of her family after they retired to their rooms for the night. Tep had decided not to bring up the matter of Tabir, of which he had heard no more, but Velanda did so as soon as they were under way. "My little cousin has quite a crush on you," she said.

"What is a 'crush on me'?" asked Tep.

"She is of that particular age, you know. . . ." The innuendo was lost on Tep, who knew little about bors. Velanda sighed, and retreated into a cultivated, scholarly pattern of speech. "She is pubescent and soon will be sexually mature. She will then seek a mate. Among bors women, that is not a straightforward process, because bors males bond permanently with the first female they mate with, and thereafter are . . . incapable . . . with other women. So Tabir must engage in much flirtation, but must be quite careful whom she chooses, or she and her future mate will be unhappy for many years."

Tep did not understand—not really. Such things were entirely foreign to his nature and innocence. "That would not be good," he said. "But I thought she was far too young to mate. We ikuts do not do so until we are fully grown. I am sorry that something I did upset her."

"Oh, Tep, it was nothing you did. She was merely confused by her own feelings. At first she was merely impressed with you—a big ikut male. You are enough like a bors to have triggered her 'hunting instinct,' and superficially at least you would seem to be a superior mate. Then suddenly she discovered that you were—or so she thought—female, and her own earlier emotions about you confused her. Then, suddenly, you 'were' again male, and she did not have to question her own feelings for you. You see?"

"I am not mature yet. I am not ready to mate with anyone. We ikuts are not like you bors. When I mature, I will go back to the Inutkak, and will spend a whole cycle chasing females into dark places where they cannot get away. When I find one I like—and when she finds me—we will take a winter hut together just as the days begin to lengthen and she becomes fertile, and our infants will be born in the next winter camp."

"I know," Velanda sighed wistfully. "As an archaeologist, I have studied aspects of anthropology. And my avoidance of males of my own kind—necessary if I wish to remain unbonded and a student instead of a mother—must be similar to your . . . neutrality. Yet I know that you and your mate will remain together only until she gives birth to a pair of infants, or perhaps a while longer."

"That is true. But if the mating is very good, and we like each other, we will make more pairs of infants in future years, though they will not always be a boy and a girl, as with you bors. But I will not stop looking at other females, and if the shahm determines that the Inutkak needs new blood, he may command some males to wait in winter camp when the band departs, and when the Tehokag band arrives, we will mate among them and rejoin our own band later. They then will do the same, and so will the Atulag."

"The short option," said Velanda.

"Yes," Tep replied tensely, his fingers splayed to reveal his filed-down claws. "Or the long option. That is up to the males. Either way, they will suffer greatly, and no shahm should command them to take one option or the other." His vocal tone showed that deep feelings had been stirred. "It has been forty cycles since the Inutkak sought new genes that way, and it may well happen in my lifetime." Velanda, having studied ikut anthropology, knew intellectually what the long and short options were, but she was surprised that Tep, having experienced neither, would be so stirred by their mere mention.

Ikut migrations were complex enough that other folk had a hard time visualizing them, and Velanda was no exception. She knew that they had originally resulted from a dearth of vital trace elements in the ikuts' shore-bound diet, a lack that could be remedied only by eating foods not available on the continents or their shelf ice. A band member's entire life was ordinarily lived according to the three-year cycle of the ice, drifting in great figure-eight patterns from north to south to north. Ikut diet and metabolism were adapted to this great round. They were able to retain nutrients and trace elements in their body fat and specialized suborgans, doling them out as needed, replenishing them during the particular part of the drift cycle when they become available in the local, seasonal foods.

Many of those foods were, of necessity if not preference, animals and fish high on the regional food chains. As many mineral resources were almost entirely locked up in subglacial and suboceanic rock and sediment, the only available sources of them were via bottom-feeders who ingested them directly from the ocean floor. The nutrient trail was often long, but some vital substances became concentrated in top-of-the-chain carnivorous fish, sea avians, or aquatic mammaloids. That, of course, was why Tep, a potential shahm, had specialized in oceanography and marine biology.

But Velanda's thoughts then were for the mechanics of the migration cycle, and the two variations from it, the "options" long and short. After all, if the Ketonak band, halfway around the planet Glaice, had not exercised one such option, she and Tep would not be on this train right now. Three ikut bands, the Inutkak, the Tehokag, and the Atulag, all occupied a pair of weather cells centered on longitude 325, east of Metok, the prime meridian, and occupied approximately forty degrees of longitude, about 2,800 miles. Within the cells winds and currents described great circles, the framework upon which the ikut's figure-eight migrations were hung.

The Swift Current throng of mantees also occupied roughly the same longitudinal territory as the three bands, spending much of each year in permanent homes on equatorial islands scattered on both sides of the great suboceanic rift that girdled Glaice's equator.

Being a bors, of a race originally crafted to labor in mines beneath the earth, Velanda almost instinctively understood the geological processes at work. Great plumes of deep, dense, molten mantle rock rose at the planet's equator, forming the primary edges of tectonic plates. Wrinkles and folds became equatorial islands. Those islands were far below the southern horizon that the train was now racing toward, but Velanda could even now see where their rise had pushed the plates north until they met the resistance of the congealed polar plates, creating annular bands of vulcanism, the northern and southern rings of fire. From the train window, Velanda could see not one but four volcanic cones to the south, trickling ash and smoke into Glaice's atmosphere.

Glaice's symmetrical tectonics, weather, and currents influenced the life patterns of its dominant species, man, causing a millennial problem between Glaice's human variations. Mantees migrated twice annually—to the southern rocks between vernal equinox and summer solstice for mating, and to the north from the autumnal equinox to the winter solstice to give birth. Since those periods immediately followed the departure of the ikut bands, there was usually no contact between the two races, but when by accident or design they did meet there were sometimes conflicts, because mantees were, essentially, aquatic mammals whose proteins were entirely compatible with ikut digestive tracts.

At some period following the initial colonization of Glaice the colony was forgotten by the greater polity of the Xarafeille Stream worlds, and the races lapsed into semi-savagery. Latobak, Glaice's premier city—including the site where the first colony ship had set down—

was left to crumble and rust. Now, in Tep Inutkak's time, it was only a jumble of moss-covered mounds laid out in a geometric pattern, potholed here and there by treasure hunters' pits and the more regular trenches of archaeologists.

The fine distinctions and the broad generalizations that allowed such different kinds of men to live side by side in relative peace dissipated. There were few hostile incidents in any one year even during the most savage times, because the mantees established excellent defensive perimeters on their equatorial islands, and threatened the integrity of ikuts' ice-floe homes by placing explosive charges under them—a tactic against which ikuts, though good swimmers, were virtually defenseless. Besides, during their equatorial passage, the ikuts had many other sources of the trace elements they needed. Only if they stayed overlong in their winter territories did they begin to suffer—and only then did mantee-ikut hostility peak, when the mantees arrived to breed or give birth. Though mantee-ikut hostility had endured into present, relatively civilized times, it almost never escalated into actual killing. The Ketonak ikut–Warm Stream mantee conflict was a rare exception, one that now threatened not only the ikut, but the aloof bors as well.

Now she feared that the conflict was going to escalate further. Uncle Frant had given Tep a message for his shahm, proposing an alliance between not only the Black Peak bors and the Inutkak band, but with the Tehokag and the Atulag as well. That would require representatives of Inutkak, Atulag, and Tehokag to gather together in one place at one time—and the only way they could do so was for members of at least two bands to exercise the long or short options, disrupting their migrations to remain behind in camp when their bands departed, to await the arrival of the next band to occupy the camp. Those representatives would require nutritional supplements to replace what they would ordinarily have consumed during their transequatorial migrations, and Velanda had no real doubt how they would get them.

She had seen how Tep guarded his precious vials of little pills, complex products of offworld chemistry labs that—as she now understood—he took to ward off the "long camp sickness." She did not think that the band's shahm was a cheapskate, purposefully keeping his potential successor on a short leash. No, the Inutkak simply could not afford more, and she was sure that the Tehokag and Atulag bands, with no "foreign trade" or sources of cash income, fared no better. If a considerable number of ikuts had to supplement their diets while remaining overlong in winter camp, they would surely revert to the old, traditional source of supplements: the mantees who came there to birth or breed. Ironically, the mantees' legal pressure upon the ikuts, begun in order to protect themselves against being eaten, would only cause more of them to be consumed.

If there had been aircraft on Glaice, perhaps there would have been a third option, of bringing vital tropical food to the stay-behind ikuts in their camps. Even power boats would have sufficed to haul equatorial fish north or south to a long-sojourning band, but there were few of those boats, which were all small, and were all owned by the planetary police. Thus, should an Inutkak remain in the north, intending to live among the arriving Tehokag, he would, by the time the Tehokag were ready to depart for the south again, suffer from severe dietary deficiencies. He might die by the time the equatorial shallows could be reached and the lack remedied. Yet he had one option: if he could acquire a source of those missing nutrients and ration it carefully, he would survive.

Unfortunately, the only sure sources of the nutrients he would need were the mantees who came there to breed. The Inutkak would have to kill at least one mantee and freeze him in the ice, returning to his cache as his body commanded. If other carnivores found his cache and raided it, that would, incidentally, kill him unless he has another cache, yet unvisited.

"Tep? Tep?" Velanda's voice broke through her companion's doze. The train swayed and hummed, and, outside, bleak volcanic peaks reared skyward, shaped by the fall of pyroclastic ash, then sculpted by the ice that lay on their steep flanks.

Tep peered outside. "We aren't there yet, are we?" "There" meant Fulag, a minor bors town where they would change trains. They would then travel southeastward on a rattling local, a coal-powered steam train borne on great iron wheels. That leg of their journey would take as long as the first one, from Metok to Black Peak.

"No, we are not. I have been thinking, and I had a question or two for you." The soft smile on her dark face helped Tep change his mind about what he was going to say. He had been about to suggest that her questions could have waited until he awakened by himself.

"Don't your people cache food in the ice of the smaller glaciers, and collect it when they return to the camp the next time? I seem to remember reading about that."

"That is so. The shahm calculates how fast the ice is moving, and how far it will move in the next twenty-seven months. He decides where to place the caches so no one else can find them, but so they will be at the ice terminus when we we arrive."

"Why can't you catch extra fish when you're in the south, then, and freeze them in the ice floe you're traveling on? Then you could stick them in glacial ice when you arrive, and eat them when the need came upon you?"

It took Tep a moment to realize what she was talking about—trying to find a way not to have to eat mantees during a long sojourn. "That has been tried," he said. "The ice is too different, for one thing. We bury caches in *epokag,* what offworld glaciologists call firn. It is cold, crystallized snow, really. It stays cold even through several summers, so the meat does not spoil. In that way it is like the pingos where we bury our dead. Those are glacial remnants buried in the earth, from way back in time when the glaciers were bigger. They're full of tunnels."

"I know about pingos, Tep. I was asking about burying fish in ice-floe ice."

"Oh, yes. But floe ice is keluk then. It is not cold enough, and is full of little saltwater tunnels. The fish would rot, or burrowing sea creatures would get them. And besides, what if the travel-ice turns over? The cache would then be on the bottom where only mantees could get at it." Velanda had forgotten about that. If a shahm had chosen well, a travel-floe would not melt in such a way that it would roll over as its center of gravity changed, dumping his band and all their belongings into the sea. But the best floes usually contained a central mass that was actually a bulky iceberg, not just flat ice—and icebergs often turned at least once in their passage south. Turnover was not usually a total disaster, because there was usually plenty of warning, time to load valuables and children into skin boats. But Velanda knew that there would not be time to chop caches of fish out of the ice.

"I suppose it was presumptuous of me to think I had thought of something new," she said, "when your people have had thousands of years to ponder such things."

"The thought was good, though," Tep replied. "Perhaps we will not have to worry about it. My shahm is no fool. He will not accept the alliance your brother proposes unless it is vital to the band. The options are far too serious to be taken without dire need."

"That is so," Velanda agreed.

Later, they finally found time to work on Tep's paper. "If we finish it before we reach Fulag, where we change trains, you can transmit it to your professor in Metok," Velanda said. "I am sure there will be a commercial-use terminal in the station or nearby." Tep confirmed that. He had seen it on past trips—a full-capacity terminal, right next to the ticket counter.

Most of the work left to be done was purely mechanical—tables to be formatted and footnotes to be inserted. With Tep shuffling through his paper notes and dictating while Velanda typed, it went quite quickly. Long before they reached Fulag, Tep declared himself satisfied with it. Velanda then read it through, seeking out and correcting minor flaws of grammar and expression—though she admitted that much of the complex biochemistry was beyond her comprehension. "It fascinates me, though," she insisted. "Your perspective is that of an ikut who must study the food chains and the paths of trace elements from the ocean bottom upward. I wonder what applications studies like this might have for archaeology? I mean, consider that even if your hero Apootlak was a real person, he also symbolizes just what you are studying—the discovery that migration could expose the ikut clans to vital substances they could not get otherwise. Perhaps the change from sedentary life to a migratory one reflected some ecological change that denied the early ikut a resource once available to the first settlers."

Tep allowed that it might have been so—but he insisted that Apotlak had been a real person, and no mere symbol of anything. Of course he was easily satisfied just to be done with it. What he and Velanda were doing now was more interesting and much more relevant and urgent than nutrient-transfer between unimportant marine life-forms.

CHAPTER 6

The key to the easily observed differences between the sexual behaviors of bors, mantees, and the rest of us cannot, thus, be found on the V chromosome, though all other racial variations can be traced to it. Where, then? Careful observation reveals one font of human behavior that differs only in degree between us (though all behaviors found there are not always recognizable in each individual race). It is the *old-human* genome! There the entire repertoire of human behavior can be seen—the magnificent élan of a fardish chief, the ferocity of an enraged tarbek male, the diffidence of an unmated bors, and the obsessive acquisitiveness of a wend.

Lending weight to the suspicion that old-humans are the cornucopia from which all our distinctive active traits flow is the only wholly unique property of the old-human genome: old-humans alone have no V chromosome at all!

Slith Wrasselty, Ph.D.,
Sex and Genes Across the Xarafeille Stream,
University Press, Thember, 12158 R.L.

Fulag, on this trip, was no different than Fulag was at any other time. The station was enclosed, and their exposure to the town consisted of a glimpse of gray stone buildings seen at the end of the long corridor between the train they were leaving and the one they were getting on. Tep mad a quick side trip to the public computer terminal and sent his paper off to Metok, with a few final trepidations.

The new train did not groan or rattle any more as it started off than had the previous one. The difference between a main-line train and this local one was that the moaning and rattling did not stop when their conveyance reached its optimum speed; it remained firmly tied by gravity to its metal rails, which transmitted every imperfection to floors, seats, and ultimately to its passengers.

Their route now trended well south of east toward its eventual terminus at Tebuk, far out on the Farlast Peninsula, one of only five places where the northern continental landmass extended south of latitude 45 north. The terrain became both less and more forbidding as time passed; winter was still far enough off so that the land became greener as they progressed. There were a few scattered clumps of deciduous trees, still in leaf, where before there had been only conifers brought as seeds and seedlings on the long, many-stepped migration from ancient Earth. Yet the folded mountains of the long peninsular spine now gave way to thrusting volcanic peaks, many of which spewed the ash and gases that created Glaice's atmospheric blanket and kept the planet marginally habitable for Earth-derived life-forms.

They disembarked in Tebuk, where the breezes off the ocean still smelled of seaweed and salt, not ice. Tebuk was a minor port, only ice-free during summer, and the Inutkak winter camp was west of it. They had to backtrack to reach it, so they hired a ground vehicle and a driver for the five-hour, 197-mile trip along the rocky coast. Happily, he was a loquacious bors, and his running commentary kept their minds occupied; the road, such as it was, was far too rough, and their four-seat utility vehicle too stiffly sprung, for them to have relaxed or dozed. "I know a few of you Inutkak folk," he commented. "Sepulak, for one. You know him? The big fellow with the crooked nose?"

Tep had to think a moment. "Oh, yes. He trades in fish oils, doesn't he? Lubricants or something?" Tep suddenly realized how much he had distanced himself from his own people. Once, a younger Tep would not have hesitated; he had known every Inutkak's name, occupation, and face. Now even someone as distinctive as he remembered Sepulak to be was a vague impression at best. When he tried, he found he could picture only three faces clearly: his mother, his father, and Hapakat, the shahm. When he tried to picture Kelisat—Lis—once his favorite playmate, he could conjure only a generalized, though delicate, ikut face and certain sensory memories: the scent of wet fur after a swim, the prickle of milk-teeth on his arm, thigh, or neck when the rough-and-tumble play got out of hand. There should be, he thought sadly, more than that.

"What's wrong?" whispered Velanda, who noticed his withdrawn look.

Tep explained. He felt like a foreigner, not an Inutkak—a city boy. "I wish I had never thought of this," he said. "I should have sent Hapakat a letter and a copy of the squiggle, instead." What really troubled him was what Velanda would think. Ikut were practical folk who lived close to the planet—literally close—and to the progression of seasons, the slow drift of ocean currents. It was a strong, hard life, with little room for frills and decorations, and none for paved sidewalks or water-lift elevators. Ah, well, at least it was late in the season and the camp's muddy paths would surely be frozen. Had Velanda ever gotten mud on those small (by comparison with his, at least) black-furred feet?

Tep did not say that his secondary mission, imposed by her brother, was what troubled him. He had not even been thinking of that, but Velanda, assuming that it was at the root of his unease, tried to reassure him. "Very possibly nothing will come of this, Tep. We will find the Charter, and everything will be back to normal."

The Inutkak camp was a quarter-mile in from the coast, where house pits could be dug into the rocky soil. The peninsula's furthest extension southward just reached 30 degrees north latitude, where the depth of permafrost in summer was almost three feet, so there was little problem digging the pits. In full summer, exposure of the dark dirt to the sun at high noon melted a few inches of soil. Sequentially, over many days, a shelter could be scraped out.

Inutkak houses' domed roofs were built of a variety

of materials—layers of dry bunch grass laid like thatch insulated against winter cold, and animal skins stretched over the grass kept the penetrating winds out. The domes were framed of driftwood and the ribs of whales that often came near shore to die, rafters entwined with woody twigs and the long, pencil-thin roots of the straggly spruces that grew in low, wet, sheltered places inland.

Velanda was not impressed with her first view of an ikut winter camp—a cluster of dozens of dirty-looking brown and gray humps separated by muddy lanes. Unfortunately, Tep's estimate had been wrong—several days of clear skies and intense sunlight had thawed the entire camp to a depth of several inches. The Inutkak strewed bunch grass and other light material in the lanes to provide footing in the still-unfrozen mud, but Velanda distastefully observed that the ikuts' legs and feet were caked with muck. She saw that even Tep, an Inutkak born, trod lightly, attempting to keep his well-washed and curried fur from being soiled. It was lucky the Inutkak had only just arrived in North Camp. The Atulag had been gone for many months now, and the stinks of their long occupancy had dissipated. Of course the mantees who had come to the northern ice to mate had made no use of the abandoned ikut camp.

Their approach to the large central dome was heralded by a dozen scrambling younglings who ran ahead of them calling, "It's Tep! Tep and a funny black *hettopar*!"

"What's a *hettopar*?" she asked.

"A child—an adolescent, actually. They haven't seen any bors, and your smaller stature misleads them."

"Humph! As long as they don't try to play with me . . ." Some of the older children were as large as she was, and looked as if they had been wrestling in the ubiquitous mud. Of course she had not expected rudely bucolic ikuts to behave with the comfortable restraint and decorum of her family's retainers, but at least they could keep their cubs leashed, couldn't they?

"They would not play with you," Tep assured her. "They don't know your clan, so they would not know what was proper." He did not explain further. She got the impression that "clan," as Tep said it, referred to some internal division of the Inutkak, not to the band as a whole. There was no time for her to inquire further, though, as the lean children—so much more lanky than bors of similar ages—had announced their presence to the occupants of the largest dome.

Kelisat watched Tep and the pretty, black-furred woman from her obscurity among the roistering cubs. She was small for her age. A cub! she thought. He didn't even recognize me. He thought I was . . . a baby. Kelisat was no cub. She was only a few months younger than Tep. When they had been children together, everyone—including most of all Kelisat herself—had assumed that their relationship would continue, and that eventually the two of them would mate.

That had been a reasonable assumption. Two of Kelisat's grandparents had been Tehokag, and her father was an Atulag, so there were no blood barriers to the match. Their closest common relative was Shahm Hepakat's father. But then Tep had been chosen as a candidate for shahm himself, and suddenly Kelisat's goal to be the greatest Inutkak hunter and explorer since Apootlak himself seemed trivial and childish.

When Tep first went off to Metok, the true depth of the developing chasm between them had not been completely evident, but when he had returned to visit North Camp that first time . . . she had felt so *dirty*! Tep had smelled like summer flowers. His fur had been so white, even on his belly and lower legs. Later, she heard that city ikut bleached their fur to get rid of the "off" coloration all ikut shared, but at the time, looking at her own fur, she had felt stained and scruffy. Soon after seeing Tep—and after seeing how his eyes had just passed over her as if he really had not wanted to admit knowing her—she had gone hunting, and had remained away until he had gone back to the train.

"Barakh, Lis," her friend Topat had exclaimed when she had gotten him to help sledge her frozen prey back to camp. "Did you have to kill every ritvak this side of the continental divide? We should cache half this meat in the ice, for the next migration cycle."

Truly, Kelisat had proven herself a master huntress that time. But even that tainted victory went sour when she and Topat got back to camp. "This is very impressive," Hepakat had said to her, eyeing the laden sledge. "You have earned your spear this day . . . but this is more than we can eat all season. You have put yourself out of a job for the rest of the winter. I hope you like chewing hides."

Kelisat, being an ikut, did not shed tears, but she had turned away, her fur lying flat against her skin in spite of the bitter cold. Chewing hides? She was not a flat-toothed old woman! Even then, her humiliation was not complete: "And Lis? Some of these are quite young. Next time, leave those to graze and breed another year. We are Inutkak, not city ikut. The tough older meat is good for our teeth."

Now Tep was back—and with a pretty, exotic woman. Were those really gold rings dangling from her ears? Kelisat had never dreamed of such personal ornamentation. They would get snagged on branches, or pulled on by cubs, and would tear her ears painfully. She watched the two of them approach Hepakat's house.

The ikut who pushed aside the round, skin-covered door was huge! Velanda was startled by his great, yellowed teeth when he smiled. His fur had an overall yellowish cast, darkening to dirty red where it was shadowed. Once free of the opening he stood up, towering over Tep, who was the tallest man she had ever known. "Tep," the huge ikut growled. "Welcome. And you too, Srah . . . ?"

"This is Velanda Torsk," Tep said. "She is heir of the Black Peak bors."

"Then this is not a pleasure trip," concluded Hepakat, the shahm. "Welcome, Velanda Torsk. Let us go sit on a rock by the sea, and the two of you can tell me what brings you here."

As the sun lowered itself toward the southwestern horizon, they did so. Tep did most of the talking, except when Velanda interposed details an archaeologist understood better. She was glad to assume a secondary place—the huge old ikut intimidated her, though his manner was staid and restrained. His questions went right to the point; the ikuts' seemingly primitive living conditions were deceptive—Velanda was quite aware that the shahm was an educated man, and that he had put his long experience to good use too, integrating it with his book knowledge from Metok University, many years before. "There seems no harm in your brother's proposal," said Hepakat. "For now, we would merely agree to confer before taking unilateral action to save our respective peoples from mantee legal manipulations. Tell him I agree to that.

"Now, Tep," he said, "show me the sigil from the book." Tep unfolded the sheet of paper and smoothed it across his knee. Hepakat examined it at arm's length—he had not been a student long enough to become nearsighted from close work, and his subsequent years had been spent straining to resolve things on far distant horizons. "Ah," he murmured, "it is as I suspected. It is the mark of Apootlak the Bold."

"Apootlak!" Tep exclaimed. "Then it is a joke. Someone—the original borrower of the charter or one of the subsequent copiers—used it as a prank."

Hepakat peered curiously at the younger ikut. "Is that so? Why do you think it?"

"Well—Apootlak the Bold . . . mucking around in old records in Metok? What would the greatest adventurer in ikut history want with them?"

Hepakat snorted. "Was he a great adventurer?" he asked.

"Of course he was! He was . . ." Tep realized he was being baited. He paused, nodded, and allowed the shahm to explain in his own way.

"Once, Apootlak was a boy too," he said, "and perhaps was a student in Metok—or perhaps in Latobak, if it still existed in his era. Was there a university in his time? Who knows? Perhaps indeed he borrowed the charter. It is not unreasonable to speculate that his later feat—leading the Inutkak on their first migration, and thus saving them from the slow starvation of deficiency disease—began with a study of the Charter, to determine whether the migratory life was allowable under its terms."

"Of course!" Tep exclaimed. "He would have needed to know whether it was legal for us to pass through the mantee-settled islands, and how the successive occupation of the camps by three different bands affected land tenure, and . . ."

"And," Velanda interjected, no longer able to contain herself, "if the ikut migration was *not* legal under the charter, he had to remove the charter itself, so no one would be able to *prove* that the Inutkak were in violation of it!"

Hepakat nodded sagely, saying nothing. Tep did not speak either, because he was stunned by that implication.

"It can't be so!" Tep protested as he and Velanda walked back to the camp. The shahm stayed behind, to ponder all that had been said. "Apootlak was a hero! He would not have done that!"

"Now you are sounding like a schoolboy," Velanda chided him. "Just because he was a hero does not make him less human. He was a hero because he saved the Inutkak. If he had to bend the rules a bit to do so, he would have. Remember that people in ancient times were still people. It is their distance from us that gives them their idealistic gloss."

"You archaeologists!" Tep muttered. "You have no respect."

"But we do, Tep! Only we must try to understand ancient peoples, not worship them. Why, there is a little game I play, when I find myself waxing romantic about the glories of the old days . . ." She giggled.

"What game?" Tep demanded. "Tell me." She demurred, saying it was too silly to tell of. Tep insisted, and at last she complied. "When I find myself infatuated with some old hero or heroine—like Brant Odlum, who fought the slavers at the side of the Arbiter Rober IV, or Maira Traf, who founded the first trans-world bors council—I picture them . . . No! I can't say."

"Oh, come on! You can't stop now."

"Gas pains!" she blurted, then burst into embarrassed laughter. "I imagine them having eaten bad food, and . . . and farting, or I picture them grunting and thumping with their mates, or . . ." She could not continue.

"I get the picture," Tep said. He had childhood memories of hearing such grunting and thumping, in the close confines of his parents' tent on the ice, or in their hut in winter camp, accompanied by the howls of arctic winds outside. It would be impossible to maintain unrealistic, idealistic images of them, then. Sometimes when he had drunk too much beer, he had gas pains, and . . . "But if Apootlak stole the charter, what would he have done with it? If it contained some clause damaging to the Inutkak, he would have tossed it into the ocean, I suppose."

"That may be. It is gone forever, if that is the case. But what we have to figure out is just what that clause, if such it was, could have been." She sighed. "But now, I am tired. Have you given thought to where we will be sleeping tonight?"

Tep had not. When he had come home on other occasions, and before he had gone to Metok, he had always slept in his parents' hut, cuddled with his same-age sister and his three younger sibling-pairs. Crowding had not been a problem, as young ikut slept quite comfortably tangled in a mass of legs, arms, heads, and stubby tails. But now . . . Even if Velanda could have tolerated such sleeping arrangements, it was surely too late for it. If they arrived on his parents' doorstep, there would be hours and hours of getting acquainted with them and the younglings, and she would not get to sleep soon. Besides, as he remembered it, the first night back was always rough while everyone adjusted to the unfamiliar presence of another sleeper. How much worse it would be with two. Tep sighed. "I will have to ask the shahm," he said. "He will surely be coming back soon. You go on. I will find out."

Hepakat had not needed much time to think over what they had spoken of. Tep met him on the trail. "There is an empty hut. Potok and Merat left yesterday to hunt *riflik,* and will be gone for a week, at least. Velanda can use their hut." That decided, Tep rushed on ahead to find Velanda.

She peered inside the hut. "Here," Tep said. "I will light the lamp." The spark-wheel ignited the wick, and oily light illuminated the small chamber. The lamp itself was a bowl carved from gray stone, with a grooved "handle" for the wick to rest in.

"Where do I sleep?" Velanda asked, puzzled. "Is there another room?"

Tep had not realized how ignorant she would be of ikut customs. There was no bed, only a heap of animal skins on a broad shelf at the back of the hut. "There," he said, pointing. "We will sleep on the skins."

"We?" she blurted. Sleeping on a heap of smelly, fur-covered hides was barely tolerable, but sleeping with Tep—a man? "I can't do that!"

"Huh? What's wrong with the bed? It will be soft enough."

"Not that! I am not going to sleep with you, Tep Inutkak. You can find another place to sleep."

Belatedly, Tep remembered that she was a bors, not an ikut, and that bors had strange ideas—and that they became sexually mature at an unnatural age. "But . . . where will I go?" he asked plaintively.

"Tep, you can sleep on the floor, if you want to," she said, relenting slightly. "Or better still, I will do so, and you take the bed and half the furs."

Tep considered. He could, of course, find his parents' hut, and curl up among his siblings. It was a toss-up—a warm, soft bed among wiggling ikut younglings, or a cold, quiet one here. He admitted that life in Metok had softened him. Neither a shared bed nor a hard, cold one appealed to him. But he was here now, and it was late, and . . . "I will stay," he decided.

Velanda pulled the topmost furs from the heap and

spread them on the floor near the door hole. She arranged them, then crawled beneath them. "Good night, Tep," she said, her voice muffled.

Tep, who was not chilly, laid down atop the furs on the shelf, and considered his dilemma. Apootlak. The ancient hero himself had removed the Charter from all human ken. Tep, being an Inutkak and of the hero's own band, was perhaps in an ideal position to track down the missing document, he thought. The question was not whether Tep *could* do so, but whether he *should*—and whether "should" applied to his moral obligation to the Inutkak, to all the ikut folk of Glaice, or to all the people of his planet . . . including the mantees.

What had been Apootlak's reason for removing the Charter? Tep's decision hinged on that. If the hero had known what the present-day mantees claimed—that he and his folk remained on Glaice only at mantee sufferance, then Tep's loyalty to both his band and his ikut race would best be satisfied by his *not* finding the Charter. There was a reasonable chance that the mantees would not prevail in Metok High Court, that except for discipline of the Ketonak band, things might return to normal in a year or so.

If what the Charter might reveal affected the Inutkak band specifically, Tep's moral duty was less clear. What was the relative cost of his loyalty to his band, weighed against the future of all the ikut bands on Glaice?

Unfortunately he, Tep, did not know what Apootlak must have known, and could not make a decision comparable to the hero's until he had the Charter in hand—and there was a strong possibility that Apootlak had disposed of it permanently, perhaps at the bottom of some deep ocean trench.

As long as there were other options, other ways he might help his people in the courtroom battle, he could defer the search for the Charter, or abandon it entirely—and Tep had a good idea of what one of those other avenues might be. That decided, he at last drifted off into sleep.

* * *

"Tep? I am cold." Tep roused slightly. "There is a draft from the doorway that chills me when I try to sleep atop the furs, and when I put some over me, the chill from the ground seeps through, and it is very hard."

"Then bring the furs up here," he said. "We ikut keep each other warm. I am not a bors, you know. I will not mess with you. I do not even know how."

"I know. But I have never slept with anyone except Vols. If anyone found out . . ."

"I will not tell them, and you will not. Stop being silly, and come to bed."

Velanda did. And being exhausted and chilled, she did not stay awake long. But before she slept, she reflected that she did not mind at all being curled up with this big, warm ikut. And since he was safe . . . Benat was right. I can satisfy my yearnings to mate, unnaturally postponed by my studies in Metok, with the incomplete pheromones exuded by this overgrown cub. I will not become pregnant by him, or do more than sleep beside him, and I will be able to finish my degree before my urges overwhelm me and I am forced to mate, to breed another generation of rulers for Black Peak. Yet that felt quite mercenary. Tep was human, and had feelings. How could she use him so? No, she told herself sternly, it is just this once. When we return to Metok, it will be as if it never happened.

CHAPTER 7

Eskers and kames are positive landforms, raised features left behind by melting glacial ice. Moraines, on the other hand, are relics of ice movement, jumbled material scraped from a continent and deposited at the glacial front during summer melt. As glaciers recede in fits and starts, often lingering for decades or centuries, their recessions are marked by successive ranges of morainic hills.

There are negative features as well, most notably deep pits, often filled with water, called kettles. Those formed when huge ice remnants were left behind to melt slowly beneath an insulating blanket of soil. In the brief geological period between glacial recession and final melting, the buried ice becomes riddled with caverns called pingos.

Fando Bumpher, Ph.D.,
Glacial Geomorphology Lecture Series,
Metok University, Glaice, Xarafeille 132, 12030 R.L.

Rob closed the file he had been reading, and turned to his father, a question on his lips. John Minder, absorbed in his own reading, did not notice at once. Beyond the bubbly, hand-leaded windows and two stories below lay the cobblestone courtyard of the informal winter palace—and beyond the walls of stables and gardener's sheds lay all Newhome, Xarafeille Prime, a world peopled by all seven races of man. Newhome was the Arbiter's experimental laboratory, people said, where he observed on a small scale the interactions, troubles, and joys of all his people, on all the thousands of worlds.

Finally, Minder reached the end of his passage, and

sensed Rob's eyes on him. "It looks like the stakes on Glaice were higher than on some other trouble spots, Dad."

"I suspect you're right," his father replied. "What are you thinking of, in particular?"

"Well, the disputants were seriously considering war, if the courtroom decision went against them."

"There is that. But the motivations—and the specific battlefields—were strictly planetary, and Glaice's war-making industry was minimal. Too, there was no indication of an interstellar connection, and as long as that remained so, it was outside my mandate to interfere there."

"Did you want to?"

"Want to? I am Arbiter, not god. My wants are not relevant. Of course I would like to prevent violence everywhere, but I have to consider what I *can* do—and what the side effects might be. Have you considered those?"

Rob pondered, and took his time replying. "Involving yourself and the prestige of your office in a strictly planetary war that did not threaten to expand into interstellar space would risk revealing that you don't have a war fleet, or poletzai to back you up—and would create no general benefit among the worlds."

"Exactly so. And?"

"If there was another reason to involve yourself, say to have your consul do something . . . irregular . . . that *would* help everyone, by helping you do your job better . . ."

Minder smiled. Obviously, Rob had something quite specific in mind. "So are you going to tell me?"

"Well, I noticed that Glaice's number is 132, which means it was colonized fairly early, but it was not the first ikut world. When I tried to find the lowest-numbered one, I discovered that all of them had been abandoned—at least by ikut. As near as I can tell, Glaice is the earliest ikut-settled world that is still occupied by them—I know it's hard for them to find places that are right for them, and which remain so for more than a few centuries, because on most worlds, ice ages are temporary.

"Anyway, since Glaice is the oldest *existing* ikut settlement, wouldn't the ikut from earlier colonies have brought their historic records with them to Glaice?"

Minder's eyes brightened. "And you think that's why I hadn't found the ikuts' backup data module on the older worlds?" He knew where Rob was leading. For each one of the seven crystals his brother Shems had taken, the ones containing the codes to release his warships, and the ones with the location of his poletzia's homeworld—or homeworlds—there had been a backup copy. One copy had been given into the care of each race of man by John Minder I, to preserve as they saw fit. The present John Minder had gotten some of them back by one means or another, but he could not use them until all seven were in his hands. Rob suspected that one of them might have been on the planet Glaice—and that it was the reason for the tale their father had been telling the children.

"Let's find your sisters, then," John Minder said, "and we can get on with the tale. . . ."

"What will we do now?" Velanda asked Tep from the rear of the rattling car as they rode back toward the rail terminus.

"That depends on how much time you have," he replied. "Can you take a few weeks off from school to help me out? I want to visit some Inutkak burial grounds."

"Burials? But why?"

"With your help, I think I can find just what is needed to defeat those mantees—to prove your professor wrong."

"Of course I'll go with you, Tep. I wouldn't miss that opportunity for anything!"

"Ah!" said Tep. "That was easier than I thought."

"Well—I am an archaeologist, and that is what archaeologists do," she joked. "Those cemeteries are located on bors land—but by treaty, we bors do not disturb them. Unless I go there with you, I will never have a chance to see them. Professor Rakulit told me what a hard time *he* had, getting your shahm to agree to let him in.

"More seriously, though," she continued, "I too am quite curious about his conclusions. I wonder if the other evidence from the cemeteries supports them or conflicts with them. When we spoke with him, he seemed unsure of that himself."

"How can we determine that?" Tep asked.

"Archaeology is not just digging holes with shovels, Tep. Many of our tools are mathematical and quite sophisticated." As an example, she explained how one such mathematical tool, seriation, worked: with a moderately large sample of artifacts from stratified sites, ones occupied over long periods of time, the frequency of occurrence of certain stylistic traits—the changing patterns of incised decorations on ikuts' ivory harpoon heads, for instance, or the cross-sectional shapes of bors's tunnels—could be expressed as a graph.

She proceeded to demonstrate. She listed three kinds of decoration found on bors pottery: sinuous incised, geometric incised, and punched. "A fourth type is plain, or undecorated," she said. She then sketched two examples of seriation graphs. Horizontal lines represented the strata of two digs, with the frequency distribution of hypothetical traits looking like cross sections of lenses standing on edge. One she labeled "Site 1," and the other "Site 4." She folded the paper to cover Site 4; then she sketched a simple map. "Site One is stratified, occupied for many generations, and lies far west of the mountains," she said, placing a number "1" in a circle. "Site Two is on the west slope of the mountains, and is a single thin occupation layer, perhaps a temporary camp, with forty-five percent sinuous pots, forty percent undecorated, and twelve percent punched. What conclusion can you draw about Site Two?"

Tep studied her sketches. He pointed to the third stratum of Site 1. "Site Two was occupied at the same time as the 'c' horizon of Site One," he concluded. "The percentages are the same. The punched pottery at Site

Two must be a local variant or traded from somewhere else."

"Very good!" said Velanda, drawing a "3" in another circle, on the east side of the mountains. "Now at *this* dig, archaeologists find eighty-four percent punched ware, fourteen percent undecorated, and one percent each sinuous and geometric. What does that tell you?"

"I think Site Three belongs to a different tribe, one that traded with Site Two, and that it was also occupied at the same time as the 'c' horizon of Site One."

"Have you done this before?" Velanda asked. "You are quite good at it."

"The method is similar to the way geologists establish stratigraphic columns," he said. "But you, being a bors, know that. I saw it used in a paper on marine snails, where the variables were the sizes and shapes of the spines on their shells."

"Then I suppose I don't have to show you Site Four at all," she said, feeling somewhat deflated.

"Oh, no," he replied quickly. "This is fun. Show me."

Mollified slightly, she unfolded the paper. "Site Four," she said. The graph represented five strata labeled "a" to "e" in lower-case letters. The lower half of a "lens" labeled "punched" began wide at the top of stratum "a" at the top and tapered to nothing in layer "d." The upper half of another lens began in layer "b" and reached its thickest at the base of layer "e." It was labeled "undecorated."

"Now what can you infer from all four sites together?" Velanda asked.

Tep studied the latest graph. "The percentages of punched and undecorated pots from Site Three are the same as the 'b' horizon of the new site," he observed. "Thus those represent a single time period—the same one as Site One's 'c' horizon." He made a small, breathy sound. "This is fascinating. I also see that Site One was occupied from the beginning to the end of the tribe's existence—or at least during the entire time they made pottery. But Site Four was only settled in a middle period of that tribe's pottery-making span, and was again abandoned long before the end of it. The two small sites near the mountains were obviously outliers of the two tribes, and traded with each other, but the main groups at Sites One and Four may not even have known of each other's existence."

"Now do you see why I want to visit the cemeteries, Tep? If we can establish a similar relative chronology for your Inutkak sites, we can either prove or disprove Professor Rakulit's data."

"I agree," Tep said, and pulled a map from his pouch—a railroad timetable, actually, at a scale too small to be very useful. "About here," he said, pointing with his blunted fingernail, "there are three pingos, very old ones long since filled up. They are the very ones the seel professor . . ."

"Mantee, Tep! He is not a 'seel.' "

"Right. They are the ones he visited—and our own goal."

"Why?"

"Because when a culture changes through time, its material artifacts change also, don't they?"

"Usually, yes. Styles can change without major changes in religion, or new inventions, but usually technological change or mergers with other peoples—big things—show up in the 'tool kits' "

"Then let's formulate a hypothesis for disproof," said Tep. What he referred to was standard practice among scientists who adhered to good methodology; there was really no way to prove anything absolutely, to establish it beyond threat of eventual falsification, so Tep meant that he and Velanda should define not just what they *wanted* to find, but which simple tests could disprove, or falsify, their idea. They would then look carefully for such a thing. Just as a good hypothesis explains much and assumes as little as possible, so its potential disproof must be intrinsic to it—if no potential disproof can be defined, the hypothesis is invalid. Tep, only slanting things slightly, preferred to define a disproof of Rakulit's hypothesis, rather than his own. "Let's say that the Ikut One and Ikut Two cultures the seel . . . I mean, Professor Rakulit . . . proposes are really *one* culture. What would we expect to find?"

"Well," Velanda replied slowly, pondering, "we might see a considerable difference in the material remains—harpoon points, decorative styles, and such—between the oldest Ikut One burials and the youngest or latest Ikut Two ones, but we would find little difference between the artifacts from the youngest Ikut One and the oldest Ikut Two graves. Any variation from that pattern not explainable without recourse to the radiocarbon dates would falsify our hypothesis."

"Just so!" Tep exclaimed. "So if the difference between the latter two are greater than the differences within each of the . . . the professor's 'cultures,' then he is right, and our hypothesis is wrong, and . . . and we ikuts are soon to become 'displaced persons.' " He shook his head. "We will visit the Etonak pingo first. Rakulit called that one Early Ikut Two culture. Then we will look at the Pootorap cemetery, which he calls Late Ikut One. If there is less difference between their tool kits and styles than between the internal extremes of either Ikut One or Ikut Two, then we will have evidence to counter the seel's claims—though there are many other pingos, in both the northern and southern hemispheres. Ours will be a cursory study at best. We will save Todorat for last."

Velanda did not chide him for his slip about "seels" that time. She was beginning to realize that it was as much an artifact of ikut thinking as a reflection of any particular dislike of mantees. In his ikut mindset, "seel" did not mean the same thing that it meant to her—or to the mantees, who abhorred that usage. To Tep, it was merely a descriptor for *all* creatures who have fur, sun themselves on rocks, and hunt fish with their teeth and claws—and for their close kin, even in university classrooms and offices. Of course mantees saw huge differences between themselves and the less intelligent marine littoral mammals they shared their rocks with—but to ikut, both mantees and genuine seels were most often just sights seen from a distance, from a drifting ice floe.

"Your hypothesis is a good start," she said, "but alone, it is not conclusive. We will also have to visit the very oldest Ikut One sites, or we will not have a long enough baseline—a 'spectrum' of cultural change—to be truly meaningful, and to convince the court."

"We don't have time for that! The mantees are bringing their suit soon, and we must have the evidence to counter them."

"Well," Velanda replied thoughtfully, "maybe what we can get at Etonak and Pootorap will be enough to cast doubt on Rakulit's data, to buy us time."

When they reached Tebuk, they paid off their driver. There was no road in the direction they had to go, across the piedmont north of the town. "There is a livery stable near the railhead," Velanda commented. "I saw it from the train."

Tep, who had thought no further ahead than buying some food and beginning to walk northward, asked what a livery stable was. His experience of Glaice spanned parts of two hemispheres by sea, and the railway right of way between Metok and Tebuk, and not a bit more. He knew nothing of how inland dwellers lived or moved about on the vast continental plains.

"We must rent *moxen* to ride," said Velanda. "I am not going to walk several hundred miles to Etonak, and another seventy to Pootorap."

"*That* is a moxen?" Tep exclaimed, aghast. "I can not ride on that!"

"That is a *mox,* Tep. And if you will not ride it, you can trot along behind, but I will be riding." The stablekeeper, a fat old bors with dusty fur, chuckled aloud.

Tep stared. The beast's shaggy back was no higher than his waist, though it was as broad as it was tall. Its feet were huge two-toed pads covered with foul, mud-caked hair, and the legs that joined them to its sausage-like body were skinny little sticks. "Which way does it go?" he demanded. "Which end is its head on?"

"Look beneath its horns," Velanda said. "If you see little yellow eyes, then that is its leading end. The trailing end has no eyes under its horns, and the rearmost horns are often slightly longer."

Tep saw that it was so. "Then that appendage is a tail," he said.

The stableman guffawed. "That is its rear trunk," he said. "Its front one is currently curled under. Both are boneless, prehensile organs. It uses the front one for feeding, because with no neck, no real separation between head and body, it would otherwise starve. It uses the rear one in the opposite manner." Tep thought about that, then snorted in disgust. Yet the prospect of walking hundreds of miles out and back daunted him more than did the unsightly mox.

Velanda's credit had proved good in Tebuk's stores. Tep would have been surprised if it had not, after seeing the vast wealth on display in Black Peak. Had he been traveling alone, he would have had to pay in cash money. He and Fenag had both drained their cards for what cash he carried, and the train fare had almost cleaned him out. He dismissed his resentment of bors wealth as trivial and small-minded; after all, when he and Velanda had at last mounted up, they sat snug between great saddle packs containing tents and supplies. Still, he could not resist just one comparison. "It is much easier to travel on the ice," he commented as they rode northward out of Tebuk. "Ice moves more smoothly than this even in a storm. There are always nooks and caves in the ice to sleep in, and no need to put up silly cloth bags with sticks. And for food, there are always fish all around, and . . ."

"Tep! Shut up! Or at least change the subject."

Tep's mox, who the stableman said answered to the name "Volk," then said, "Yar! Shup!" Tep was too amazed to say another word.

"Does it really talk?" he asked Velanda later, as they made camp fifteen miles northeast of the railroad, on a high, desolate plateau.

"Moxen are not as intelligent as humans," Velanda replied, "but they have a language of their own, and are capable of learning human tongues, though not of speaking them well—as you heard."

"I know they're not as intelligent as me," Tep said facetiously, "because else I might have been carrying the mox on my back, instead of the other way around. I am curious how one treats such a creature. Does one eat mox steaks? Or are they really people—as some seels claim to be?"

"Tep!"

He grinned to show he had been teasing—after a fashion. "Seriously though, isn't it contradictory to use them for beasts of burden? I mean, does the stableman own them, or does he pay them a wage? If they feel unfairly put upon, can they appeal to the Arbiter's consul in Metok for a judgment against their bors masters?" Velanda did not know. She thought that the Arbiter only concerned himself with disputes between the *human* races—between bors, mantees, and ikuts on Glaice, and between fards, tarbeks, old-humans, and wends as well, though not on Glaice. She had not heard of any indigenous intelligent species of human caliber on any of the worlds of the Xarafeille Stream; perhaps, she speculated, there were such worlds, but they were left alone, and no charters were granted for human colonies on them.

The next day they made almost sixty miles, and another sixty the day after that. Tep had plenty of time to establish the limits of Volk's vocabulary, which seemed to consist of nouns, like guttural *h'ghrazz* for bunch grass—which by extension also meant, generically, "dinner." There was the affirmative "Yar," also, and there were several grumbles that indicated disagreement or dissent. Mainly, though, the creature expressed the latter by raising its nethermost trunk and emitting nasal-sounding yowls that reeked of the last stages of its digestive processes.

About noon on their fourth day afield, they made camp near the base of a low, domed hill. If their estimates were correct, the entrance to the ice caves of the Etonak cemetery lay within that jumble of rocks a few hundreds yards east of them. Cursory exploration confirmed that it was so. "Shall we wait until morning to go inside?" asked Tep, eyeing the clumps of fur and feathers, the strings of whale ivory and glass beads that festooned the narrow, dark cleft between two huge boulders. The Inutkak shahm wore similar tokens on ceremonial occasions. Had Hepakat himself placed them there as warnings to unwelcome intruders?

"Since there will be no sunlight inside the caves," Velanda said, "there is no reason to wait for daylight. But on the other hand, fulfs and vulpens hunt at night."

"Fulfs? I have never seen a fulf. Did we buy a gun?"

"They won't attack *us,* silly. I was just thinking that we should stay near camp at night. Our scent will protect the moxen from them."

"Exactly," Tep muttered, picturing a fulf. He could not imagine the whole creature, only great, gaping jaws lined with yellow teeth, its padded feet—four-clawed, but otherwise not unlike mox feet—and an unnaturally small, round body supported on four long, spindly legs. Vulpens, as he remembered them from storybook pictures, were much the same, but smaller and faster, with bushy red tails.

Their first night out they had dutifully set up two sleeping tents. "You slept with me in the Inutkak camp," Tep had protested. "Why must we have two tents now? No one can see us." He had not yet heard about fulfs or vulpens, but the thought of spending the night alone, in a flimsy tent in the middle of a vast, windswept plain, had not appealed to him at all.

Velanda had not relented right away, but some time before that morning, Tep had awakened to the sound of her soft breathing. The next night they made no pretense of erecting the second tent at all.

Tep did not wonder about his desire for companionship in bed. He considered it quite normal—it was the lack of such normalcy that had troubled him in his dormitory room in Metok, where he had slept with several pillows arranged as his siblings might have arranged themselves, were they there. He was uncomfortably warm, curled up among the pillows like that, but it was preferable to the terrible, bare aloneness he otherwise felt.

Velanda was more critical of herself. She, unlike

Tep, was of an age to mate; she was well beyond it, actually, and only by keeping emotional distance from bors males had she kept herself from an unplanned and potentially disastrous mating. Her willingness to cuddle with the huge, boyish ikut male, who was so like and so unlike her own kind, smacked of perversion, though there was no risk of him imprinting upon her as a bors male would have if they had mated, no chance of creating horrible misogamous children neither bors nor ikut, but reversions to the ancient, repulsive old-human type—hairless, skinny things with pink noses. She did not understand why the children of mixed marriages always turned out like that, but she had heard enough frightening tales.

Still, she knew that her desire to sleep with Tep was more than for comfort and companionship—that it was thinly veiled sublimation of a deeper urge, a chemical and hormonal command ill-suppressed beneath her civilized, human exterior.

By the third night or the fourth one, though, she hardly thought about her misgivings any more as they set up their single shelter.

Tep did not have misgivings. He did not think about the situation at all: he merely accepted that sleeping together—sleeping warm—was nicer than sleeping cold. Sometimes, when he awakened in the night to discover his heavy arm or thigh atop Velanda's smaller body, he withdrew it quietly. He was, even in sleep, aware that the bors female was more fragile than even his smallest sibling. Perhaps she made noises that disturbed his sleep—he did not remember them, but he was muzzy and dull in the mornings as if he had not slept well. Too bad she isn't ikut, he thought once or twice, remembering his siblings, Kelisat, and his other friends. Then he banished such disloyal thoughts with a disdainful snort.

"That is the mark of the Whale clan," Tep said, pointing with his flashlight at a carefully squared and incised tablet of slate. They had been walking—and crawling, and sliding—down the pingo's ice passages for a half hour, now. Velanda had begun to wonder if there were any graves at all, or just endless miles of honeycombed ice. "We must be close," Tep reassured her.

Two more turns in the passageway brought them into a chamber hollowed from the ice, an irregular room lined with niches the size of small single beds—and beds they were, heaped with layers of fur—upon which rested the mortal remains of . . . ikuts.

Velanda shuddered. Her professional experience with burials had been at inland bors sites, the ruins of abandoned warrens cut into the faces of rocky mountain peaks. What few individuals she had seen had been mere innocuous heaps of bones long stripped by hungry mahkrats and cave snails of such personal attributes as skin, flesh, and fur. At first glance, these ikut dead seemed about to awaken from their long sleep, ready to stretch and growl and to demand just what a bors interloper was doing in their bedroom.

Tep also seemed subdued as he read the names scratched into the slate or whale-ivory gorgets each corpse wore. "This is Kotanat," he murmured, "a famous fish-hunter of legend. See his spear? Kotonat was a sea hunter, not a net man. That must have been his best spear, which was called Bedorag. Kotonat is clearly an Inutkak. Many of us claim descent from him."

"Then we are not deep enough in the pingo, are we? Will the oldest . . . bodies . . . be farther in?"

"I think so," said Tep. "Supposedly the first tunnel is dug to the center of the ice mass, and subsequent chambers branch off it, until they would be too near the outside, and subject to warmth and humidity. See? This was the last chamber in this cemetery. It was filled just before the caverns were closed. See how Kotanat's nose has turned white with frost burn? That would not happen in the deep caverns where the temperature and humidity remain exactly constant."

Velanda, becoming slightly used to the presence of twenty-odd immobile ikuts, all dressed in their holiday finery of furs, imported paisley cloth, beads, and feathers, observed that they no longer seemed quite so alive. All their noses were frost burned, and their eyes were sunken with slow dehydration. Lips were drawn back to the brown roots of great ikut teeth in the rictus of death. She guessed that the dead Inutkak probably weighed only a third what they had in life—though she had no inclination to slip a hand under one and lift it to test her surmise. "Let's go, then," she said, not quite shuddering. "We do not have to photograph anything in this recent chamber, do we?" She glanced at her pendant watch. "It is already ten-thirty, and we can only continue downward until two, if we want to sleep in our tent tonight, not in a cold cave."

As they passed through chamber after chamber lined with "sleeping" ikut, Velanda made notes, while Tep took photographs of a representative sample of each chamber's denizens. She observed a tendency for the tunics or tool pouches of entombed ikut to be more elaborately decorated as they progressed deeper—a tendency that in other cultures sometimes reflected the relative busyness of a technological culture or the more relaxed pace of hunters or fishermen. Folk with holovisions and recorded entertainments did not as often spend as much time on personal adornment or the decoration of their tools. As they went deeper she noted greater proportions of handmade ivory and stone beads, and fewer bors-made trade beads of brightly colored glass.

Velanda made brief sketches of decorative motifs that could not be photographed without disturbing the dead—Tep had made her promise to touch nothing, to refrain from exertion and hard breathing that would create hoarfrost, and above all not to whistle or sing, which was considered to be an offensive reminder to the dead of all those happy things they were now denied. He did not really believe that, of course, but . . . there was no sense going against custom for no good reason. In one chamber, there had been a rash of unconventional decorations—sinuous water snakes swimming across geometrically incised waves—but in the next, and in the rest of them they had visited so far, there were more common depictions of food-fish species and the like, stiffly scratched on slate gorgets or more gracefully sewn of beads on tunic pockets and hems.

At one point, she observed that the orthography of written names had changed between one chamber and the next, but she attributed that to the death or retirement of one shahm and the accession of another, whose handwriting, and "hearing" of names usually unwritten, differed. "I wish they put *dates* on these gorgets," she said wistfully. " 'Born on the night of the least moon, in the year when the sun was eaten' is not very specific."

"It may be specific enough," Tep relied. "The 'least moon' is late summer in the southern hemisphere, and if 'eaten' refers to an eclipse, there may a record of it, or a way to calculate when it happened—once we get back to Metok." He sighed. "But I think all these graves are far too recent for us. Way back in one of the upper chambers, there was a 'sixth son of Parboorag,' and here . . ." He pointed at a large male. '. . . is Parboorag himself. If the 'sixth' refers to generations . . ."

"Then we are only a couple centuries in the past from the last burials, right here," Velanda concluded. "Tomorrow, let us not waste time taking detailed notes. We can just scramble as deep and as fast as we can, and get to the really old graves—those should be 'Incipient Ikut Two,' according to the professor's nomenclature. Then, having a preview of what is here, we can spend more time with the most significant burials on the way out."

Tep agreed and, as it was getting late, they trudged back through chambers now familiar to them. Going mostly uphill slowed them a bit, but that delay was offset by their knowledge of the way and by fluorescent markers they had left to guide them. The sun was still up, though low, when they reached the surface.

That night Tep's sleep was troubled. He seldom remembered his dreams, but the one that awakened him an hour before dawn was unforgettable. He stumbled out of the tent and settled atop a low boulder to ponder it, ignoring the moxen's grunting pleas for an early breakfast.

He had been atop a higher crag in his dream; he had stood tall and had stretched and grunted and howled over the low, domed roofs of the Inutkak winter camp. His siblings and other young ikuts had scurried into hiding at the ferocious noises he had made. He felt very strong, in that dream, and his claws were not blunted to preserve a university keyboard; they had made long, deep gouges in the frozen dirt when he bent down and lashed at it. It was a very strange dream.

When Velanda awakened, he said only, "I couldn't sleep. I think I am excited about what we will find in the lower caves. If the seel professor is right, I will see my earliest ancestors on Glaice. If he is wrong . . . but we will not establish that here alone. We will have to wait until we have seen Pootorap."

They did not finish at Etonak that day or the next. Near the center of the pingo ice the ikut graves seemed to change qualitatively. Some of the corpses were posed on their sides with their knees drawn up and their elbows bent and tucked close in, instead of lying supine with hands at their sides as was the custom among the later folk, including those of Tep's own generation. In the innermost—oldest—chambers there were fewer spears and harpoons with pivoting toggle heads left as grave offerings or sentimental decorations. Instead, many burials were accompanied by prosaic things—heaps of tangled cordage to which were attached crinkly, semitransparent wisps of something that resembled oiled paper. "Those are nets," Tep explained, "and fish-gut floats that have lost their air. I wonder why they buried so many fishermen here?"

"Perhaps because more people fished back then, than hunted." Velanda knew that Tep divided "fishing" and "hunting" along different lines than she would have. For her and her bors folk "fishing" was the acquisition of fish by any means, and "hunting" was chasing terrestrial, warm-blooded game. For Tep "fishing" was nets and floats, or hook and line, and "hunting" was spearing or harpooning things—even fish.

"Perhaps so," Tep agreed, "but I don't see why."

"Maybe Pootorap will help explain it—and other things too," she said.

The last few nights at Etonak, Tep's dreams became more intense. Upon awakening from them, he did not sit and ponder, but took brisk walks, sometimes for an hour or more. The content of the dreams had changed, also. The images were less clear, but the emotions underlying them were not: Tep felt strong; he felt invincible; he was big and strong and he wanted to prove it. "I am Tep!" he felt like bellowing. "I will fight anybody!"

The night before they were to leave Etonak, he decided he should tell Velanda about the dreams, but they had worked hard beneath the ice, making pencil rubbings of many early gorgets which seemed to be inscribed with different letters—ones they could not read. Then they had packed up everything but a few pots to make breakfast in, and their tent and bedding, so they could depart soon after first light.

That night, Tep's dream was absolutely, unequivocally clear. "I am Tep!" he growled—and Velanda responded.

"Indeed you are!" she murmured, in his dream.

"I am Tep! I am strong!" he growled.

"Yes," she whispered. "You are."

Tep felt hot—as hot as if he were in his room in Metok. He threw off the sleeping quilt. Velanda clung to him—she, he realized, in his dream, was the source of the unnatural heat. Yet he did not push her away—not then, and not for a long time.

Velanda was beneath him, her wrists above her head, held there by his hands. Her wriggling beneath him was inconsequential, a mere fluttering, yet tormenting. The heat was now fire, glowing coals centered low on his body, on his groin. He wanted to yowl with the pain of it, but he did not.

He thrust away from himself, as if to rid himself of

the tormenting embers and suddenly his pain ceased, and where heat had been was cool wetness—no, not cool. It was warm, yet without agony, only the tiniest throbbing ache.

He moved, and Velanda moved beneath him, making small, wordless mewling noises, wriggling now exactly with his own movements. What Tep felt next was indescribable. Even later, by the light of dawn, he could not quite recall the sensation that had overcome him.

When he awakened from that dream, he understood that he would no longer be able to share the tent with Velanda. He was no longer Tep, the big ikut child, a sexless being. He was Tep, a man, an adult male.

By wan predawn light, he examined his genitals. He understood then that while he dreamed, the concealing pouch that had held them all his life had ruptured, that no longer was his member involuntarily confined. It could now slide in and out of its furry sheath at his will—or, he realized, its own.

There was blood and mucus on his fur, but a close look assured him that his pouch had opened symmetrically, without undue tearing. The pain he felt would go away soon, he told himself. It had better, or he was not going to get far riding a mox that day.

Tep's feelings were quite mixed. He was proud to be an adult ("I am Tep! I am strong!" he remembered), yet he did not look forward to erecting two tents that night, or to many more nights, sleeping alone. He would, he decided, have to find a mate—there were a few young adult females in Metok, weren't there! He had not previously paid much attention to the sex or state of maturity of his fellow ikut students. Of course there were more choices at home with the Inutkak. There was Efrit, who was only a few years older than Tep himself . . . But had he not seen Efrit with that big male, Patork? Perhaps they were mated now. Then there was . . . He could not remember the names of any particular females of mateable age.

But why did that thought distress him? He was suddenly aware of *who* had been the subject of his dream! It had not been an ikut female from the Inutkak band or one he had met in Metok. It had been Velanda Torsk, a bors! He felt no pleasure in considering other mates because—because he did not *want* another mate. He wanted only one—Velanda, who was not of his own kind, who was possibly the *only* female whom he knew well, and she could not ever be his mate! Velanda was lovely and sophisticated. From the vividness of his dream, he was convinced that they would be . . . compatible in spite of the obvious differences. But when he tried to imagine announcing to tough Frant or the lady Bavant that he intended to mate with the heir to Black Peak . . . no, it was impossible. When he tried to imagine Velanda mucking through North Camp, or riding the ice, he failed even more dismally.

"I will tell her—warn her—as soon as she wakes up," he promised himself. "Perhaps she will not want to go on to Pootorap with me. It will probably be easier for both of us if I go on alone." His regret, when he imagined that lonely voyage with only surly Volk for company, was not because he would lose a valuable helper, a skilled archaeologist. No—not at all.

Tep did not tell Velanda right away, as he had intended. When he returned from his walk, she was preparing breakfast—a bowl of sweetened gruel for herself, and a tin of freshwater fish, and for him, gruel flavored with crumbles of iodine-rich seaweed, and an oilier ocean-fish chunk from a larger tin.

Afterward, they were busy folding and rolling tent and bedding, and loading their heavy saddle packs on the recalcitrant moxen—who, having had many idle days, were not anxious to return to work.

It was not until they had put several miles between themselves and Etonak that Tep broached the subject of his dream. . . .

CHAPTER 8

Amid all the DNA-based life-forms of the known universe, something like chromosomes have evolved, and one fact is incontrovertible (with one single, glaring, and notorious exception): mismatched chromosomes prohibit interbreeding and, in those rare cases where offspring result, they are invariably sports, freaks, or at best sterile. Except, of course, among mankind. Bors, with forty-nine chromosomes, breed with old-humans, who have forty-eight. The unmatched V-chromosomal "orphan" left over simply shrivels and disappears—and the offspring is always, without exception, genetically and morphologically old-human.

On the other hand, if a fard and a tarbek were to mate (however unlikely and repugnant such a union would be) the product would not be a smallish tarbek with lovely fard fur and graceful, expressive fard ears, or a largish fard adorned with bilous, gelatinous Tarbek wattles. It would be . . . an old-human.

Slith Wrasselty, Ph.D.,
Sex and Genes Across the Xarafeille Stream,
University Press, Thember, 12158 R.L.

"It was not a dream, Tep," said Velanda, not quite meeting his eyes.

Tep was at that moment glad that his mox chose to fart loudly, that his gasp was drowned by the mox's trumpet-bray. He was subsequently even gladder that this trail, presently crossing the divide between two creeks, narrowed to a path, so Velanda had to drop behind him, rendering further conversation impossible. It remained so for the rest of that day, and when they found a suitable flat campsite, they were still twenty miles short of Pootorap.

"I think I know how it happened," said Velanda, as they sipped hot tea after they had eaten. "A bors's bonding with his first mate is initiated by the *female's* pheromones. I am no biochemist, so I do not understand the details, but in layman's terms, the pheromone does two things: it stimulates the male's libido, and it 'keys' that stimulus to chemoreceptors for the female's very specific immune-system proteins, which are present in her body's various exudations.

"That it affected you, an ikut, is unusual, but not really surprising in retrospect," she went on. Tep was quite aware that she had chosen to distance herself from an emotion-laden topic by employing precise terminology and maintaining a scientist's superficial detachment. "Evolution is often conservative; often the same enzyme or other biochemical is used for many different functions—as both a digestive enzyme and a neurotransmitter in the same being, and as something else entirely in another species. The effect of my pheromone upon you—living as closely as we have these past days—was to accelerate the onset of your sexual maturation, and to take us both entirely by surprise."

"Then it's not my fault?" Tep squeaked or rather, he *attempted* to squeak. Already, responding to cascades of new biochemical cues, his boyish voice had deepened, and what came out was not a squeak, though not quite a rumble, either.

"Biochemically, it may be 'your fault,' in a way," she replied. "I have been fully mature for some time, and I have delayed mating to finish my studies in Metok. I suspect that your own pheromones, though formerly of a lower intensity than those of a mature bors male, may have clouded my judgment. Had you been less subtle, I would have been warned, and the issue of how many tents we used would not have arisen." That she *had* been warned, that she had consciously taken the risk, as a matter of her perceived convenience, did not arise at all.

She sighed a soft, delicate sound that made Tep's

guard hairs stand on end. "I think the damage was done that first night, in the Inutkak camp."

"You're not mad at me?" Tep inquired hesitantly, though he could no longer squeak, he still managed to endow his voice with a plaintive tone.

She shrugged—a graceful, delicate gesture that made Tep quiver all over. "Should I be? Did you have any more idea what might happen than I did?"

Tep, obviously, had not. "Then what are we going to do *now*?" he asked.

She smiled—a lovely expression that made Tep's skin tingle. "I am going to set up our tent," she said. "If you want to help me . . ."

Tep stumbled and almost fell into their small campfire in his eagerness to do so.

It was a very long night, and even though Tep and Velanda remained abed long after they would ordinarily have been up, breakfasted, and on their way, they roused only sleepily, and once awakened, did not emerge from the tent for quite some time. But Pootorap was only a few hours' journey, and there would be plenty of daylight for them to set up camp and prepare for the next day's explorations in the ancient pingo.

That day, on the road, neither one mentioned the events of the past two nights, and by nightfall there was no time for discussion, only for reenactment of what had transpired before, with what variation and innovations that struck either of them from one moment to the next.

The Pootorap cemetery's entrance was decorated similarly to the one at Etonak, but here the decorative fur and feather tokens nested in niches cut in well-dressed ashlar masonry. Columns carved to resemble bundles of poles or reeds held up an entablature of curved bas-relief forms that might have represented whale ribs. Tep thought that the very stones oozed a sense of extreme antiquity. Between the columns was a metal door.

"That is bors work," Velanda observed, fingering a brass boss mounted on the door's dark bronze face. "It is of the Middle Mount Barrow Period, I think."

"It may well be," Tep said eagerly. Then he grinned. "I wouldn't know the middle wheelbarrow from any other."

Velanda—after their last two nights' intimacies—was not inclined to be annoyed at his humor. "That period is well dated, and it give us one reliable date for this site."

Tep shook his head. She eyed him curiously, "Oh, I don't disagree," he said, "but just what event does it establish a date *for*? If the doors were commissioned by the cemetery's founders, it marks the age of the earliest burials here, but if it was ordered by the shahm who finally declared the cemetery full, the burials would have *greater* antiquity." He snorted. "What if a previous shahm merely bought the door used, from a junk vendor? That would do our cause no good at all."

"I don't think we have any way to find out which is the case," Velanda said. "We must explore the cemetery itself for useful information." She fiddled with the brass boss and the door opened. . . .

"Look at this!" Tep exclaimed, pointing at a well-decorated corpse. "This gorget is exactly the same as the ones in the deep levels at Etonak."

"Exactly?"

"Well—it is the same strange lettering as on the rubbings we made. I am sure of that."

"You're right about that, at least—I think it is ancient Universal, the original language. I am no linguist, though, and my own studies cover much later periods. Universal is believed to have become obsolete millennia ago."

"Then that is good news, Vel! If these so-called Ikut One folk and the later Ikut Two ones at Etonak both used Universal, it may mean they—and my ancestors—were here early on!"

Again, Velanda sighed. "But *how* early. It is the same problem as the door—perhaps the shahms merely copied old inscriptions from memory or from older artifacts. Let's go deeper. We still have an hour or so before we must turn back."

Tep had hoped that the inscribed gorgets would give some clue as to their dates of origin so that Rakulit's two "cultures" could be shown to be only one—but it was not to be; in the next chamber, only a few frozen ikut wore gorgets at all. Instead, they wore necklaces with ivory placards decorated entirely differently, with sinuous incised lines like seaweed, or they wore fat, faceted pendant gems. "Fire opal," Tep said.

"I'm not so sure," Velanda countered. "Fire opal is like a glass, with no crystalline planes. It is usually ground to shape, not faceted."

Tep wondered how she knew that. As if reading his thought, she smiled and said, "I *am* a bors, after all! I may be trained as an archaeologist, but geology is in my blood."

"Then what *are* those gems?"

"I don't *know,*" she admitted, frowning. "I *should* know—unless it is an artificial gem that does not occur naturally."

"Ah, well. it doesn't matter to us. The stones have no writing on them. Let's go on."

The next chamber held only one body.

"Huh? I wonder why they did this!" Tep shined his light on the corpse. Brilliant pink and vermilion shafts of broken light danced on the icy walls. "Look at the size of that jewel!" he exclaimed. "It's as big as my fist!

"It is at least that large," Velanda agreed. "But hurry! We have to go back soon, or the fulfs and vulpens . . ."

"Wait. Here is a slate tablet. It has some kind of writing on it. Let me make a quick rubbing of it." He unrolled a thin sheet of paper, and pressed it against the incised slate.

When he finished, Velanda informed him that even if they left right away, it would be dark before they got to the surface. Grudgingly, Tep followed her back the way they had come.

"What's that noise?" Velanda asked, just before they pushed open the bronze door.

"What noise . . . that is Volk!" Tep growled, pushing past her. "Something's out there!"

"Tep! No! If there are fulfs . . ." But Tep was already

gone. His thudding footsteps caused loose stones to rattle down to the base of the pingo's dome-shaped earth covering. Velanda peered timidly outside, now hearing Tep's bellows mingling with the mox's yowls, and with another sound, a low, penetrating gurgling. "Fulfs!" she breathed. She silently berated herself for not rushing to help Tep—but she could not move! She was as if rooted in place.

Tep saw his first fulf. It stood as tall as a mox—taller than Volk, now, because Volk was lying between the fulf's forelegs, twitching, making little mewling noises. Tep did not see all of the fulf, because its wide-open jaws spanned from its maximum height all the way to the ground—or so it seemed from Tep's perspective. Yet that threatening vista of shiny yellow fangs—hundreds of them—did not even slow him down. "You hurt Volk!" he shrilled, and leaped to the attack—right into the fulf's maw.

He kicked—and felt several fangs break from the beast's lower jaw. Its mouth snapped shut—but Tep's foot was already out of its way. He raised both fists and brought them down on the carnivore's long snout, and felt thin nasal bones break. "You hurt Volk!" he yelled again, and his still-dull fingernails dug into the fulf's nostrils. It yowled, and tried to shake him loose, but he reached down and grabbed a foreleg, which snapped like a rotten stick. Then he let go.

The fulf no longer seemed ferocious. It made noises much like those no longer issuing from Volk's trunks, and backed away from him, hobbling awkwardly, not daring to turn its back to him. Then it collapsed, and made no further sounds.

Tep ignored the fulf and knelt by the injured mox. Russet blood stained its throat—such as it was—and abdomen. One eye seemed shrunken and dull. Volk's forelegs both bent at odd angles. "Volk?" Tep said. "Volk?"

"Hh'kill por Volk!" the mox muttered weakly, flatulently, hardly raising its trunk.

Just then, Velanda appeared, glancing uneasily at the dying fulf—and at a half-dozen others that lurked a safe distance away. "I'm sorry, Tep," she said. "I should have come right away."

"Never mind that. What did Volk say just now?"

"He asked you to kill him. He is lamed. He wants to be dead before the fulfs begin to eat him."

"No! We will heal him!"

"Tep, we can't. Volk will never walk again. He knows that. We must kill him."

"I will kill *somebody*!" Tep rose to his feet. "I will kill a *fulf*!" He glared at the retreating pack, then abruptly scrambled toward them. The fulfs scattered. "Come back, you cowards!" Tep howled, but the fulfs kept their distance. One, though, made a whining noise and edged a foot or so closer to him than the others.

"Is this your mate?" Tep asked it, kicking the inert beast at his feet. "If I begin pulling its teeth, maybe *you* will come closer!" He wrenched the huge jaw open—about half the fulf's bulk seemed to be jaw, though its head was surprisingly light. "One tooth!" Tep brayed and held up a bloody yellow tusk. The living fulf muttered plaintively. "Two teeth!" Tep said, and jerked another loose. The female—if female it was—whined but came no closer.

"Bah!" howled Tep, realizing that his tactic was not working. "Cowardly, craven beasts!" He stood up, then jumped in the air. All of his mass was concentrated in his two feet as they landed flatly on the fulf's skull—which made a sound no louder than a seel cracking mussel shells as it flattened against the ground.

"Bah!" Tep said again. The other fulfs came no closer.

"Hh'kill Volk!" the mox muttered when he returned. A pained look crossed Tep's face. "Must I?" he asked Velanda who nodded solemnly, sadly. "How?"

"You did well with the fulf. Like that will do."

"Jump on Volk? I can't do that!"

"Tep," she said patiently, "dead is dead. Kill him now."

"Tshump onn Volk!" the mox said, very, very weakly. "Tshump ahh . . ." The word ended in a gurgle.

"Never mind," Velanda whispered. "Volk is dead."

"Good! I mean . . ."

"I know what you mean, Tep."

Supper that night was a gloomy occasion, though the food was better than usual—there was not much edible meat on a mox and less on a fulf, but Velanda butchered both animals efficiently, and wound thin strips of flesh around sticks, which she stuck in the ground over their fire.

The other fulfs did not depart immediately—until Tep began tossing joints from their pack-mate toward them. "Here! have a snack!" he snarled each time. The fulfs, evidently growing tired of being pelted with body parts and not being inclined to cannibalism, eventually withdrew beyond the limits of the fire's light.

"I hate to say this," Tep said as the fire diminished to embers, "but Volk was delicious."

"Yes," said Plunt, who was Velanda's mox, raising her anterior trunk from deep within the butchered carcass. "Volk yum-yum."

Velanda said nothing at all. She was busy picking her teeth with a sharp, slender clawlike fingernail. Tep thought her grimaces quite endearing, and he glanced longingly toward their tent. She smiled a bit wanly. "I am tired," she said, "and we have a long journey ahead of us tomorrow."

"Tomorrow?" Tep was stunned. "But we must explore the lower chamber tomorrow."

"We can't, Tep. We have only one mox. We must put all our gear and supplies on Plunt. We will have to walk, and it will take much longer than riding. If we are lucky, we will not run out of food until we are within a few days' walk from the railroad. Then we must wait for a train. We will eat . . ." She glanced meaningfully at Plunt. ". . . our emergency rations then, if we must."

The seriousness of their plight gradually sunk in. "Then we must come back later," Tep said, when it had done so. "And we have not yet visited Todorat, the really old cemetery."

Velanda agreed that they might do so. "But first, let's go back to the university, where we can spread our notes and photographs and rubbings out on laboratory tables and find someone who can translate ancient Universal." Tep agreed that was wise.

That night, their tent did not jiggle as it had on previous occasions, though when the two of them awakened in the morning, they were entwined limb with limb as they had been before.

The island could have been anywhere in equatorial Glaice. The roofed enclosures, though, were atypical, and those were what the satellites had shown. The activities that had gone on under them were atypical too, for mantees. An armament factory, the consul called it, though it was quite unlike a factory on a more sophisticated world. If he had not seen the dead ikuts a while back, he would not have recognized the bale of poknat ribs. The mantees had, from the ordered look of the place, set up an assembly line for their deadly "treats."

War, on Glaice, was of necessity different than it was anywhere else. Ikuts on their floes or in their camps were not very vulnerable, nor were mantees on their islands. He doubted he would see many outright battles, and no marching troops. He was sure neither side knew how to fight that way—but killing the young cut at the root of a people, and destroyed their future.

He was glad that all mantees had not fallen prey to this madness. Most of them—or so he hoped—were still willing to wait things out, to see what resulted from the hearings. After all, it was a mantee who had given him this location, had shown him where the satellite should look.

"Shall we wreck this stuff?" asked the captain of his small troop of bors police.

"I think not," said the consul. "They will know I have seen it." The mantees would just build elsewhere, and he did not dare allow himself to be perceived as running an ineffective police action against such things. Better the mantees believe him only an impartial observer. Without any real power, or any help from the Arbiter, he had to remain neutral, or lose any effective moral advantage he had, no matter how it hurt to do so.

CHAPTER 9

The first of the two problems faced by early generations of unaugmented men* was interracial warfare. Racially distinct colonies were the preferred norm. The founders were not bigots, but they recognized certain social truths: the customs of fards (to pick an example) who live in the fardish quarter halfway across town are seen as exotic to a bors, and pose no problems for him, but the customs of a fard family living next door, customs requiring the fards to be most active and neighborly at just those times when bors prefer to nap, are perceived less as exotic than as obtrusive and obnoxious. A certain distance makes the heart grow fonder.

John Minder IV,
Unpublished Manuscript,
Erne Museo, Newhome, 4321 R.L.

Neither Tep nor Velanda enjoyed the next two weeks. During the long hike to the railroad, their nights were mere brief episode of exhausted sleep and their days were endless trudging between a goal that seemed never to grow nearer.

When at last they reached the rails, they were not near any settlement. They erected makeshift flags along the tracks—the first ones two miles in each direction from their camp, and others at decreasing distances—in the hope that the engineer would spot them

*Note that the modern Universal I write in does not imply a sexual distinction with use of the "masculine" noun. Gender in language does not equate with sex in biology, and attempts to equate the two (and then to work around the confusions that result) merely trivialize the real and important dichotomies that faced (and still face) mankind.

and have time to slow, then stop, the train in their vicinity.

It was there, on this second night beside the tracks, that they eyed the great heap of gear that Plunt had carried uncomplainingly the whole way, and listened to Plunt's pleas for dinner. . . .

"Delicious!" Tep said, stretching his feet toward the fire. "I wonder why they don't serve mox at the Last Atopak?"

"As you surely noticed," Velanda replied with a wry grimace, "there is only one small meal's worth of decent meat on a whole mox—though I suppose a place like the Metropole Hotel might be a market for it—tiny little cutlets with a dash of fruit sauce, at a hundred creds a serving."

"Then we are lucky to enjoy a gourmet meal out here in the wilderness!"

"Tep, stop it. I know you feel just as bad about eating Plunt as I do. There is no need to pretend otherwise."

The train pulled through the next day. Happily, it was a northbound one and they did not have to ride all the way back to Tebuk before beginning the long journey home.

Tep felt somewhat hurt when Velanda obtained a pillow and slept leaning away from him as the train shuddered and rumbled toward Fulag. "It is not proper," she said when he offered his shoulder for her to rest her head. "And besides . . ." She did not complete her thought aloud. All the way to Metok, Velanda maintained her aloofness, which troubled Tep more deeply than he could have imagined—but she would not explain what had changed between them. Tep had to assume that it was merely the loss of their isolated freedom to behave as they wished, without fear of public disapproval. He began to ask himself if their relationship had a future—or only a past.

In Metok, all the news was of the court hearings that had begun a week earlier. Tep and Velanda bought newspapers at the station and brought themselves up to date on what had happened. "This is all preliminary stuff," Velanda concluded. "Only a summary of Professor Rakulit's evidence has been introduced. We still have time to arrange our own findings."

They did so. Velanda, a graduate student, was able to commandeer a workroom a floor below Professor Rakulit's office. The professor himself visited them frequently, and offered both helpful comments and more material aid—notably, a phone call to a retired emeritus, his own mentor, who had more than a passing acquaintance with ancient Universal.

"He has a guilty conscience, doesn't he?" Tep said once the professor left them. "He is helping us because he *knows* he is wrong."

"Professor Rakulit is a scientist. He wants to know the truth."

Tep was unconvinced. The professor had based his career on his carbon-14 dating sequences. He had published papers in scholarly journals. Would he willingly help shatter the chronology upon which his definitive history of Glaice was based?

"The linguist will be here soon," Tep said, walking slowly past the tables where their rubbings were laid out in order. He picked up several at random, and then rearranged the others.

"What are you doing, Tep?" Velanda.

"I am taking these rubbings. I am not going to let Rakulit's friend see them. When he finishes translating the rest of them, I will compare them with the ones he has *not* seen."

"What good will that do? *You* can't read Universal."

Tep held one of the documents in his hand next to another still on the table. "Some words appear on both of these," he said. "I will try to use *his* translations to 'translate' the ones he has *not* seen. If he is trying to fool us, then *my* translation will not make sense."

Velanda sighed. Judging the linguist's honesty by the degree of sense that Tep's "translations" would make . . . "Emeritus Barm is a *bors* linguist, Tep. He has no *motive* for deception." Still, she understood Tep. He felt helpless—dependent upon her, Rakulit, and the emeritus for help and information. They were all antiquarians, in a sense, while he was a biologist, and out of his element. His removal of the rubbings was no more than his attempt to maintain control of things. And, she thought, there are plenty of rubbings. There was no reason to think that the ones Tep had taken would contain especially significant information that would remain untranslated.

Her thoughts were interrupted by a loud, off-key whistling, from the corridor, then by pounding on the lab door. "Who or what is *that*?" Tep burst out. He opened the door.

"Is this where the scrolls are?" demanded the very short, white-muzzled bors who stood there, hand still poised as if to continue knocking—on Tep's nose.

"Scrolls?" Tep asked. "I have not seen any."

"Then where are they? That skinny seel—can't remember his name offhand—had some scrolls for me."

"I have no idea," Tep began.

"Wait, Tep! Sar—are you Professor Barm?"

"Exactly so, dear." He peered nearsightedly in her direction. "Have we met?"

"You are in the right place. The inscriptions Professor Rakulit wanted you to see are these—but they are rubbings of inscriptions, not scrolls."

The emeritus glared at Tep and said, "Why didn't you say so?" Wisely, Tep merely shrugged, at a loss for a polite reply. "Let me see them," the emeritus demanded, pushing past him.

Velanda led him to the tables. He held a rubbing close to his face. "Ah! Universal! I *thought* it might be that," he said. "Very interesting. Rubbings, you say?"

Velanda explained how and where they had come by them. "If you would care to sit here, there is a stylus and paper. . . ."

"He's quite a . . . a case, isn't he?" said Tep. The elderly bors had snapped at him twice—once for sniffling, and again for clacking his toenails on the stone floor tiles. Now Tep was waiting outside the room. "How is he doing?"

"He doesn't seem to have any problem with the text—but I had to spray the papers with a fixative because he insistently rubs them with his forefinger while he reads them. He smudged one badly before I noticed."

"I hope it wasn't an *important* one," Tep grumbled.

"I scanned copies beforehand, Tep."

"Oh. Good."

"Now we will see," said Tep, when he and Velanda were at last alone in the lab. "What has he written?" He leaned over the table where the professor's pages, the translations, rested next to the corresponding originals.

" 'Penotag, nephew of Rodrak, sixth son of Batorap . . . born in winter on the south ice.' Well, that's not very helpful, is it now?" he muttered. He glanced at another.

" 'Benag, fourth of the name, a warden of Latobak . . .' Hey! These are the *old* inscriptions from Pootorap! How did they get on this table?"

"Professor Barm was up and down so much . . . I tried to keep things straight, but . . ."

"It's no problem—just that it confused me." Tep rearranged rubbings and translations in their proper places. "Here is Benag from legendary Latobak, or so the translation claims, and over here is Rodrak, obviously an Etonak burial. . . ."

Then Tep stared. He was so very still that Velanda finally asked, "Is something wrong?"

"Wrong? Oh no—something is very *right*! This Penotag was '*born in winter on the south ice*'! See?"

"I see. Is that unusual? I thought most Inutkak were born in winter camp."

"On the *south ice,* it says! And this too is an inscription from Pootorap! How did a sedentary nonmigratory Ikut One man happen to be on the south ice?"

"An explorer, perhaps?"

"But he was *born* there! Even if his father was an explorer . . . his *mother* would not have been. Not while pregnant! No, the only answer is that the so-called Ikut One *were* migratory."

Tep, excited, now, went from one translation to another. None of the others were quite as interesting, though among the Pootorap ones there were several mentions of Latobak, which started him thinking.

"Ignoring the seel's C-fourteen dates, and using just the other evidence, what would you say about the history of all these folk?" he asked Velanda.

"Well, we know Latobak was, and *what* it was," she mused. "It is the legendary site of first landing on Glaice. It has not been excavated much, but instrument reconnaissance and a few test trenches indicate that it was a sizable town once, with a street grid and plazas."

"And if the Pootorap folk were from there—some of them, anyway, the early burials—then they were settlers or descendants of them *and* they are Ikut One. Right?"

Velanda nodded. "It implies that Latobak was the capital of the Ikut One, the sedentary ikut, but that Pootorap was a bors area, perhaps near the outermost limits of the then-settled area." She went to the chalkboard and began sketching a map of the peninsula, which jutted southeast into the sea. She marked the Inutkak camp on the southwest, and Pootorap farther north and east. Then she drew a dotted line enclosing Pootorap and stretching first north, then east along the mainland coast beyond the peninsula. "That is approximately the limit of sedentary ikut settlement," she said. "It approximates the shallow water breeding ground of the atopak fish, upon which it is believed they fed. And there"—another mark—"is Latobak, not on the peninsula at all."

She explained what she would deduce from what they knew—if, of course, she ignored the C-fourteen dates entirely. "The sedentary ikuts buried their folk near where they lived. If we indeed assume that some—like Penotag—migrated on the ice floes, then there is no clear gap between them and the later Ikut Two from Etonak. I would surmise that as more and more ikut began to migrate, as the atopak died out, they moved south to be nearer good places to embark on floes. Etonak would be an early one. Then later, as migration became the rule, not the exception, they moved farther south, around the tip of the peninsula at Tebuk, and finally ended up where the Inutkak now camp, where the floe ice is nearest the southbound current."

"In other words," Tep mused, "your surmise would be *exactly* what the sagas say happened."

Velanda moved to the tables where notes, photographs, and rubbings were arrayed. She put those that Professor Barm had misplaced in their proper spots. "All the evidence points to it," she said. "The 'fire opals'—man-made gems—were products of a high technology, probably made with offworld industrial machinery in Latobak, or else they were imported from offworld. When Latobak was abandoned, the gems were replaced with carved slate and ivory gorgets, easily made."

She pointed at small marks she had made on some of the Pootorap rubbings. "These were made of slate quarried from the Belorap Formation, on the south continent. So even their material argues for migrations by those original Ikut One people—and implies no gap between them and later folk who were clearly *your* ancestors, Tep."

She went on to cite further evidence. First, that the use of Universal as the language of choice for inscribing gorgets was not unique to the Pootorap ikuts, then that the custom of burying the dead in near-fetal position continued unabated from the earliest Pootorap graves through almost half the Etonak time span, when prone burials became the rule. Third, the Pootorap bodies were accompanied by nets and floats, not spears or harpoons, implying clearly a dependence on atopak fishing, and that too continued over to the earliest Etonak graves.

"We must write up our reasoning very clearly," she said, "in terms that will be easily understood by a layman—like a judge. 'The evidence that Professor Rakulit is wrong—that his *dates* are strangely skewed—is quite good.' "

"Write it up so I can understand it too," said Tep, jovial now. "Then we have everything we need!"

"Well—not quite. We still don't have an explanation for the radiocarbon dates."

"Who cares?" he replied ebulliently.

"How can a whole planet get lost, Dad?" asked Sarabet. "Didn't anyone check up on Glaice?"

"You must remember that the Xarafeille Stream was much less populated than now, dear. And the Arbiters then had fewer resources than I have today." Except, of course, the ones I really need—the fleet, and my troops, John Minder thought. "Back then, Arbiters did not control shipping as carefully as I must do. Often colony ships remained in orbit for generations, and then were used by a fresh, restless generation to go on, to start new colonies."

"So some of them took Glaice's ship, and the people on the planet couldn't maintain contact?" interjected Rob.

"There's no evidence of that!" Sarabet protested. "The people in that old city—Latobak?—would not have allowed the ship to be taken away if they still had need of its machinery and production facilities to make dietary supplements."

"Well, they lost *that* anyway, obviously," Rob snapped.

"We don't know what happened," their father said. "Perhaps they merely allowed their shuttlecraft to fall into disrepair, or to be destroyed in a volcanic accident—of which Glaice has many."

"Maybe they just didn't want anything to do with other worlds," Rob said grumpily. Later, when the story had been told in its entirety, he would remind his father and sisters that he had said that.

CHAPTER 10

Though separation initially by hundreds or thousands of miles made war a cumbersome and unlikely prospect, trade between desert and sea, between arctic ice and tropical forest, was not. The prime motivations of the races' corporate "designers" were exploitation of specific environments and the trade that enhanced—and latter-day folk saw the same advantages in their diversities.

Population growth and territorial expansion led, within generations, to borders no longer separated by vast wilderness, but where fards pressed cheek by jowl against tarbeks on one side, wends on another, and bors and mantees everywhere else. Wars over such borderlands (usable by more than one subspecies of man) were inevitable—as was the office of Arbiter, with its mandate to prevent such wars.

John Minder IV,
Unpublished Manuscript,
Erne Museo, Newhome, 4321 R.L.

Two days after returning to Metok, Tep and Velanda went to the Government House, where the Planetary Charter hearings were being held. The morning session had already started, so they busied themselves with the court's clerks, trying to arrange an appointment with the judge. Had it been a criminal prosecution—of the Ketonak band, for example, for their quasi cannibalism—that would not have been allowed, but the judge was acting in his capacity as the arbiter's consul now, and the clerks assured them he would want to hear their evidence in private, before they could be allowed to present it in open court.

"Tomorrow morning, first thing," said the chief clerk.

Having nothing further to occupy them, Tep and Velanda slipped into the public gallery of the courtroom, where a slender mantee woman held the floor. "We seek *prevention*, Consul Martinez," she was saying, "not vengeance. If the only way we can protect our innocent folk against being eaten by savages is to assert our proprietary rights as charter settlers . . ."

The judge interrupted her and pointed out that those proprietary rights had yet to be established.

"He's a funny one, isn't he?" Tep whispered. "The judge, I mean."

"He is ordinarily the Arbiter's consul. Haven't you seen old-humans before, Tep?"

"Not without those filter masks they wear." It was common knowledge that the bodily effusions of the old-human subspecies had strong, unpredictable, and—according to popular belief—erotic effects upon members of other races.

"He *does* look strange," Velanda admitted, studying the judge's face, which looked squashed, as if he had run into a door—except for the funny little pink nose that jutted from it. His little ears looked like clusters of pink worms, and the hair that framed them—black and shiny, wet-looking—contrasted strongly with the shiny baldness of his skull.

The rest of his body—at least what could be seen of it over the top of his bench—was clothed in a crimson jacket with black and gold trim, a uniform of sorts. He was, she noted, almost as skinny as a mantee, though his slight movements seemed stiff and angular, not graceful like a seel's . . . a mantee's.

Shortly thereafter, a large ikut took the floor. "This talk of 'proprietary rights' is not just premature," he said, "it is preposterous. Show us the Charter itself, I ask."

Tep saw the judge make an odd movement, like an ikut shaking water from its fur.

"What was that?" Tep whispered.

"A shudder?" Velanda was far from sure that it meant

the same thing to an ikut or a bors, let alone an enigmatic old-human. Whatever it signified, she was sure that the Arbiter's consul was not enamored of the ikut's bombastic oratorical style.

" . . . And let us for a moment postulate—no matter how ridiculous it seems—that indeed the seels arrived on Glaice, a few years before we ikut did, or the bors. Are we not *all* subject to the same Arbiter, to the Rule of Law that has guided us for twelve millennia on all the worlds of the Xarafeille Stream?"

"Sar Bottarak? Sar Bottarak!" The consul's voice was no higher than a mantee's, but it lacked mantee silkiness. It lacked all trace of the mellow resonance of bors speech or the baritone boom of even young, female ikuts. "Please, sir, restrain your rhetoric, your enthusiasm, and confine yourself to factual matters of relevance."

"I think he's the Megat band's shahm," Tep whispered. "Their sea route takes them near us, sometimes. I saw him once." The ikut speaker made little effort to restrain himself, and shortly later Tep said, "Let's get out of here. He's only making yellow snow on the judge's *tulap* floor." A tulap was a snow house, a temporary hunting shelter.

"You mean annoying him? I agree. You people could definitely use a better spokesman."

"We won't need one, once the consul sees our report," Tep said confidently. "Just watch. This crazy lawsuit will be old history in a week."

Velanda kept to her resolve to sleep alone—made easier than before because here in Metok they both had established quarters. Tep, with a good grace he did not feel, walked her home. When they arrived—she rented a small room at the rear of a private house, a room with its own entrance—she surprised him. "Please come in, Tep. I have something I must tell you."

What was it that could not have been said while they walked? With sudden dread, Tep knew exactly what she would say.

"You're leaving me," he blurted. "You're going home to Black Peak, aren't you?"

"Why, no, Tep," she said, somewhat taken aback by his behavior. "I may go home, but *that* is not what I need to tell you. It is . . ."

"Well? What is it?"

"It is that . . . I am pregnant."

At first, Tep had not understood the ramifications of these three words: "I am pregnant." He remembered his mother being pregnant. She got big and fat, and . . .

Oh, no! he thought. Pregnant. Babies! Velanda is going to have babies. For a moment, his realization went no further. It took him an interminable time (or so it seemed in retrospect) to get past "babies," to consider that they would not be Velanda's babies alone. Babies, he realized, have *fathers*. Him? No. He could not be a father! It was not that he thought someone else would be . . . was . . . it was just that he could not visualize himself that way. He was Tep, an individual, a student. He was not . . . yet . . . a *father.* Overwhelmed, he had almost staggered out of Velanda's room.

Wisely, Velanda had not tried to stop him from leaving, nor had she been deeply hurt. Actually, more than anything, she was confused. What had upset him so? It was not as if her pregnancy affected *him* in any material way. One thing Tep had forgotten was that fathers among bors are only a genetic source. Bors reproduction, she thought, *did* at times seem unfair. A male bonded for life with the first female he joined with—and yet *he* had no responsibility for her offspring, and no say in their lives. And females, once the urge came on them, could hardly stop themselves from getting pregnant. How had that come about? Her knowledge of human cultures did not go *that* far back.

She shrugged. Give him time to think and he won't be so upset. He is not a bors, after all. It wasn't as if *he* had imprinted on *her* . . . was it? Suddenly she was not so sure. He *did* seem dejected, now that they were sleeping apart, and a trifle sad even when they were together. He *did* seem . . . dependent . . . on her. *But he is an ikut*, she told herself. *Ikut do not imprint.*

It was not until far into the night that Tep realized one more ramification of Velanda's pregnancy. He sat up in his lonely bed, all thought of sleep forgotten. It went beyond pregnancy, even beyond fatherhood. Her children and his would be half-bors, half-ikut, and that meant they would be . . . He shuddered, remembering a small, sharp bump of a nose, of pink furless ears that lay flat against a head only spottily adorned with black, wet-looking hair.

"Oh, no!" said Tep. "Oh, no-o-o-o. . . ."

Old-human children! Tep knew nothing of the extra chromosome the variant races' designers had incorporated into their genomes, the V chromosome, so called because the centromere was placed almost at the ends of the two joined strands of DNA. Most of the V chromosome's codes merely activated existing genes common to all humans, even all mammals—as long as its predecessor's parents were of the same race. But when one parent was a fard or a bors, and the other a tarbek or a wend, or a mantee, certain specialized genes were activated—and the V chromosome destroyed itself.

Without an active V chromosome, a developing fetus did not grow fur like a bors, a wend, or a mantee, or vermilion wattles like a tarbek. Without the V chromosome, the fetus was not half-wend, half-bors, or half anything else; it was entirely old-human. It was as old-human as John Minder—and as Minder, or any old-human, knew, that was a less than ideal state.

Tep considered the possibilities. Would Velanda live at Black Peak with their old-human children? Surely not. Prejudices against old-humans ran deep. Even if so, *his* infants, however ugly, could not be allowed to suffer that cruel prejudice. But unlike more moderate worlds where old-humans could wander in itinerant bands, where they would not die if left outside city domes, or where each city had a shantytown for rehabilitated criminals, cretins, and old-humans, on Glaice there were no places for them except in Metok. But who would care for them there? Velanda? Would the lady Bevant allow her a stipend to stay there until the children were grown? Tep thought that unlikely. Surely, *he* could not maintain them there. The Inutkak band could not afford to keep him there longer than necessary to get his degree.

Old-human infants—or adults, for that matter—could not cope with the Inutkak's migratory life, either. Tep could not take them there. What could he do? Could he find a permanent job in the city? What was he qualified to do? He could not teach, not unless he earned a doctorate, and he did not have time for that.

It was a good thing that Tep had gotten a few hours' sleep earlier, because for the rest of the night he got none at all.

CHAPTER 11

Though both perpetrators of our hypothetical fard-and-tarbek union would possess proper V chromosomes, those chromosomes would not join one with the other as would their other forty-eight. Instead, those V chromosomes would merge in combat, and would destroy each other. By the time the offensive fertilized egg prepared to draw apart in its first mitosis, on its path toward becoming a blastula, there would be no trace of the V chromosome at all. The misogenous infant that eventually emerged, however repulsive it would seem to most of us, would not differ from any other old-human, and no phenotypic or genetic trace of its fard or tarbek origins would remain.

Slith Wrasselty, Ph.D.,
Sex and Genes Across the Xarafeille Stream,
University Press, Thember, 12158 R.L.

The next morning Tep could not get through Drumlin Way to get to Velanda's place. During the night, a barroom debate between ikut and mantee students had escalated into a fight, and the fight into what—for want of a better word—the Metok police were calling a riot. Now the street was blocked. Hologenerators clamped to the corners of buildings on opposite sides of the street created a wavery vertical plane of fluorescent puce and vermilion, a warning barrier. Tep stayed well clear of it; the holodisplay only indicated the approximate extent of the invisible shock screen.

"What happened?" he asked at the newsvendor's kiosk. "Was anyone killed?"

"They don't block the streets unless there's an

investigation, and they don't investigate name-calling or fistfights," said the newsman, a bors. "I saw the forensics van go in there."

"What's this town coming to?" Tep mused aloud.

"Don't ask me," the kiosk owner said, scowling. "I'm a *bors.*" The implication was clear: it was mantees and ikut causing the problem.

"I've been away," Tep said. "Have there been other . . . incidents?"

"Nothing this big, in Metok. Some rogue ikut band crashed their ice floe on a mantee island, went wild and killed a half-dozen seels. That was last week. Then there were several follow-up reports, but they contradicted each other—depending on whether the reporter was a seel or an ikut." He eyed Tep speculatively. "You look like an educated person. What do you think will happen? Is there going to be a war?"

Tep was taken aback. It was the first time he had heard *that* possibility spoken outright. War? He pictured troop movements, tanks, fortifications . . . how could there be any of those things on Glaice? "I don't see how that could happen," he said. "There's no weapons industry on Glaice, and everyone's so mobile—except you bors, of course. It would be hard to get enough people together in one place for a real battle."

"You may be right," the newsman agreed.

With a rattling wheeze, a battered utility truck pulled up next to the holobarrier and honked its shrill, electronic horn. Tep glanced in that direction. Several mantees got out of the vehicle. One looked familiar to him. "Kurrolf!" he called out. "Kurrolf! Over here! It's Tep!"

The mantee stared—coldly, Tep thought—and said something to his companions. Then he strode (if a lithe mantee could be said to stride) toward Tep. Tep had not been mistaken; it was Kurrolf—but a Kurrolf he did not know. His wedge-shaped mantee face was drawn into a stiff mask, and his large, soft eyes were half-lidded and unreadable. "What do you want, you fool?" he hissed angrily. "You should not have called out. Now I have much to explain to my friends. Are you stupid, Tep? Don't you know what's been happening?"

"I don't understand," Tep said, even thought he quite suddenly understood all too well.

"You are ikut, and I am mantee. Isn't that enough? And now, of all times!"

"What is wrong with now?" Tep asked.

"We are here to pick up the bodies from last night—the mantee ones—now that the police are done with them. And you call out to me as if nothing is wrong!" Kurrolf shook his head, expressing disgust with a short, vocalized exhale.

"*I* did not kill them!" Tep protested, beginning to become angry himself. "Why should that affect you and me? We are friends."

"You aren't a Ketonak, either!" Kurrolf snapped. "I am not of the Warm Stream band they ate, and neither were any of the ones who died last night—one of whom was my nursebrother, Terelt. Don't you remember Terelt, Tep?" Tep did. He remembered him as a small, brown bundle at Kurrolf's nursemother's breast. He remembered the tiny precious sounds of stridor, the infant's indrawn breaths as it nursed. He remembered wanting to make faces at the baby, to hold him and tickle him as he would have done with an ikut cub—but the nursemother had driven him away with snarls and bared fangs.

"I am so sorry about Terelt," Tep said, "but . . ."

"But nothing! Pretend we never played together. Above all, pretend we are lifelong enemies because . . . if we meet again . . . we will be." With that, Kurrolf, the fur all along his spine raised stiffly in spikes, his ears laid flat, turned and walked quickly back to the other mantees. Tep, having no reason to remain, departed before the police lowered the barrier to let the truck in.

Later, as he approached Velanda's by a circuitous route, he reconsidered what he had told the newsman, in light of his new experience. If there was war, it would be of a kind unique to Glaice and its peoples. There would be few pitched battles, but there would be many casualties, nevertheless. If ikut bands chose to alter their migration patterns so they would still be in their north camps after the autumnal equinox, mantee breeding and birthing patterns would be disrupted even if no directly fatal interracial encounters occurred. Fewer mantees would be born. Too, young ikut who missed their first trip across the equator would suffer from a lack of zinc and other nutrients they would ordinarily have gotten via the equatorial food chain. Weakened, they might die, if the winter were severe.

Tep's concentration wavered, or rather changed direction to something more familiar and comfortable. How long had he gone now, without once thinking of his own academic field? He allowed himself to think about food chains and nutrient cycles. On Glaice, zinc, manganese, and other important metabolic elements all came from one major source: the deep-sea vents caused by magmatic upwelling and the spreading oceanic tectonic plates. Most of the zinc—to follow the path of just one nutrient—eventually sank to the ocean floor, where it was metabolized by the quasi-living seafloor oozes into insoluble nodules, but small amounts were ingested by benthic plankton, deep-ocean microorganisms. Baleen whales dove deep to feed on such plankton, responding to occasional cravings when their internal supplies of vital nutrients became low.

Predators ate whales, and scavengers did also. Sometimes the predators were mantees or drifting ikuts. More often the mantees and ikuts consumed the scavengers or predators, mostly fish. Either way, the zinc from the deepwater geological processes found their way into the ikut children during their band's migration through the tropics.

Without migration, the ikut younglings would sicken or die. Tep believed that was the true significance of the Ikut I and Ikut II division—when first ikuts settled on Glaice they had not migrated. Either they initially had dietary supplements to provide zinc and other necessities, or else the lack had not become evident for several generations.

When it did, the hero Apootlak was the first to devise a way for his people to get what they needed—by abandoning the sedentary life and trusting themselves to the currents and winds on ever-melting chunks of ice—just as the Inutkak would do some time around the autumnal equinox, when Hepakat decided that conditions of ice, wind, and currents were just right. Perhaps, he thought, if Hepakat had already found a suitable floe for their journey, they might already be under way, their camp abandoned to the mantees who could soon arrive to practice their strange, unnatural breeding rites.

Tep shook his head, thinking about seels breeding—fifty males, or a hundred, all lined up waiting their turn to fertilize a few of their immense, fat throngmother's millions of eggs. It was a once-in-a-lifetime thing, he knew, or twice, maybe, if the male mated young the first time, and then lived a long time.

If there was to be war, he pondered, the ikut would have the greatest advantage in the south, where the mantees arrived to birth the young. He did not know the exact process or sequence of events, but he did know that when the throngmother gave birth, the other females, who were her sisters and older daughters, would take them and nurse them. Lactation was triggered by hormones or pheromones given them by the throngmother, or perhaps by the infants themselves.

If ikuts remained and raged along the coast chasing hopeful mantee nursemaids away, infants would be born on the cold rocks, one after another like clockwork, with no nursemothers' warm, fuzzy arms to pick them up, no breasts full of fat-rich milk to sustain them. Tep envisioned the gross throngmothers helpless amid their mewling, dying infants.

The image sickened him as much as did the other one—of sad ikut parents consigning one after another of their nutrient-starved infants to the pingo grave niches intended for adults who had died of accident or old age.

"Why?" he asked himself, agonized. "We have a system that *works* most of the time. We coexist—bors, ikuts, and mantees. Why should one incident—a tragic accident, really—set us all at each other's throats . . . or, worse, set us to killing each others' helpless infants?" He considered his disquieting meeting with Kurrolf; they had played together, mantee and ikut. Of course there had been conflicts—when were there not, when children played—and some of them were perhaps attributable to differences in their backgrounds. Whether those were ultimately genetically determined or cultural, they were no less intense; yet they had played well. They *had* been friends. Now they were, by Kurrolf's unilateral declaration, enemies. Lifelong enemies.

It was quite insane to Tep. It was pathological, and it had to be stopped. And now it would. He clutched his thick sheaf of documents close to his chest. The topmost one, itself some thirty pages long, was a copy of his and Velanda's report on the Etonak and Pootorap graves. Another copy lay in front of them, on the consul's desk.

The Arbiter's consul, Jacob Martinez, steepled his skinny, furless fingers and shrugged more eloquently than could a burly bors or massive ikut. "Ironically," he said, "the breakdown might not have happened if there had never been a Planetary Charter—or the belief that one existed. Left to custom and tradition alone, I suspect that you ikuts and the mantees would have reached a settlement. Only the existence of such charters in general, and the mantees' expectations of what one might contain, has lent relevance to their archaeological premise."

Tep nodded. "And now we can demonstrate the primary flaw, and put paid to all this," he concluded.

The consul raised a hand, palm outward. "It is not that easy," he said. "You and your colleague"—he nodded to Velanda—"have done admirable work. You have cast strong doubt upon the radiocarbon chronology—but unfortunately, it is not enough."

Velanda pressed on Tep's thigh, a largely symbolic restraint. "Hear him out, Tep," she said softly. Tep's suddenly bunched muscles relaxed slightly.

"Your study's results are clear," the consul continued, "but they are qualitatively different from Professor Rakulit's. His are simple numbers, easily understood. Yours depend upon shades of difference that ordinary folk might not readily perceive—and it is that *perception* we must change if order is to be restored."

"But *you* understand!" protested Tep. "You are the

judge. You have merely to rule in the matter, and it will be done with!"

"Tep, look at me," said the consul, sighing. Tep did so—and observed nothing different about the odd man. He was the same skinny, hairless creature he had been. The consul smiled, baring spatulate teeth that seemed to Tep to be uselessly small. "Exactly!" the consul said. "I am an old-human, a foreigner, and as ugly as a skinned blifet—right? No—no polite protestations. As long as I rule fairly, I am the Arbiter's consul, but if I go too far, if my ruling does not follow the common logic or if it results in clear disadvantage to one faction or another, then suddenly, I am . . . what I am—a meddling old-human.

"No," he continued, sighing again, "my decision must be clear to all, or I must not make it. I cannot undermine my authority by issuing commands that will not be obeyed."

"But the ships!" Tep protested. "The Arbiter's fleet, and his poletzai. They will enforce your decision."

The consul shook his head. "Force is the admission of failure," he said. "Surely you can see that. Consider that if I make no decision—if I stand aside and allow the dispute to fester, there will be war on Glaice. Yet, if I rule wrongly, and either mantees or ikut dispute my ruling and proceed to war in spite of it, there will be not only war, but war *in defiance of the Arbiter himself*—and the penalties that the poletzai would eventually impose on your planet would be far more severe than if I had issued no ruling at all."

That, Tep understood, had been a conclusive statement. The consul would not rule in the matter unless the issue was incontrovertibly clear—and Tep and Velanda's archaeological evidence, though well-founded, was not enough. If they had been able to discredit Rakulit's dates themselves, to show that they were intrinsically flawed, then the consul could have acted—but they had merely presented countering evidence too abstract for ordinary ikuts and angry mantees to consider.

"Sometimes a word—a few words—are worth a thousand pictures like these," said Jacob Martinez, taking in the photographs and rubbings on his desk with a sweeping wave of his hand. "The words, in this case, are written in the Planetary Charter of the planet Glaice, and without them . . ." He shrugged.

"The Arbiter himself has expressed interest in this situation. For reasons entirely his own, reasons I am not privy to, he suspects that a data module exists containing not only the original Glaice Planetary Charter, but other, earlier documents of importance to his historic research."

"A data module? Like the blue crystals in the basement of the Admin Building?"

"Just so—though being old, the module in question may be green, orange, or even black."

Tep pondered. The Charter again. But this news—that the Charter might exist not only as an oft-copied paper document, or as sheets of engraved metal in some permanent archive or ikut cache, but as a virtually indestructible crystal—opened doors he had not known were there. "Such crystals radiate, don't they? The university's basement storage areas always stink of ozone."

The consul confirmed it. "The energy stored in them dissipates slowly. Modern ones, that store more data than the old kinds, need to be recharged and rewritten every five hundred years or so. The older modules, especially the black, brown, and dark orange ones, give off less traceable energy, but they hold their information indefinitely. The Arbiter is said to possess readable modules from legendary Earth itself, never recharged."

"Readability is one important criterion," Velanda interrupted, "but detectability is no less important. Do the old modules give off enough energy to trace them with instruments? I need to know if the survey gear in the archaeology department labs will suffice."

"I will supply you with specifications for datacrystals of the approximate era," the consul responded. "It sounds as though you may have some idea where to begin looking."

"I may," she said, "but I will leave it to Tep to discuss that with his shahm—Hepakat of the Inutkak. I will not be involved in the search, because I have pressing business at home in Black Peak."

It was the first Tep had heard of Velanda's plans. Her sudden disclosure angered him, but there in the consul's office was not the time or place to discuss that, or to protest her decision.

"I have a general idea where the Charter may be," Tep told the consul, "but only my shahm will be able to help me pin it down." Tep sighed. "This is going to be a long, thankless search. I only wish it were possible to discuss Glaice's problems with the Arbiter himself. I am sure he could resolve things, even without recourse to poletzai, and the chances of the Charter being hidden at all, not lost forever, are quite slim."

"I cannot say," the consul replied. "That is, I cannot say whether the Arbiter could do as you wish, and equally, I cannot say whether indeed the Charter is findable. If you really want to speak with the Arbiter, I can schedule an appointment for you. You will have to arrange passage to Newhome, of course."

"But that is impossible," Tep protested. "Interstellar passage costs more than Metok's annual revenue. My band could not earn enough for a single ticket in a decade's trade."

The consul nodded his agreement. "Unfortunately, I suspect you are right." He did not offer to waive the fare—which was within his authority to do—nor did he explain the reasons why interstellar travel was so exhorbitantly expensive, while goods could be shipped between suns more cheaply than sending a package from Metok to Albiton, down the coast. Though not as obvious as white warships or soldiers, the cost of passenger travel was perhaps even more important, in terms of the control the Arbiter was able to exert.

John Minder XXIII alone knew the secret of the interstellar stardrive. The technology was only distributed to shipbuilders in "black boxes" that self-destructed when attempts were made to examine them. Thus was he able to dictate much of the nature of commerce and travel between the worlds of the Xarafeille Stream;

ships were built only within limited parameters—specifications that he alone dictated.

Cargo and merchants ships' crews traveled freely, and the cost of fuel and berthing were kept low, but passenger ships . . . There *were* no passenger ships, only specialized modules that fitted within the holds of ordinary working vessels—ornate suits of rooms carefully tailored to the requirements of the particular human subspecies that would occupy them. By keeping the costs of passenger travel artificially high, the Arbiter limited it to necessary trips. Of course there were still a few tourists—a few billion, actually, spread among all the worlds of the Stream—but they were an elite group and there were seldom more than a few score, a few hundred, persons on any one world who could afford to travel unnecessarily.

As hulls and passenger modules had to be specifically tuned to each other and to the resonance of the stardrive, it was virtually impossible to design and build a troopship module or a weapons platform that would not set up destructive echoes in the drive itself, rendering it useless. If that happened in a port, the resulting damage might turn a few acres to useless slag; if it happened in space, the damage might be less apparent—a brief flash recorded on distant-orbiting monitors, or simply a report of a ship that did not arrive at its destination on time, then never arrived at all.

Tep and Velanda rose to their feet, their meeting with Consul Martinez at an end. Tep turned to Velanda. "I'll meet you outside," he said to her. "I have a personal question . . . for Sar Martinez." Velanda raised an eyebrow, but departed without protest.

"She . . . my . . . my partner is . . . pregnant," Tep stammered uncomfortably when the two men were alone.

The consul nodded for Tep to sit down again, but Tep, quite uncomfortable, remained standing, shifting his weight from one foot to the other. He explained his difficulties. Surely, he hoped, the consul, an old-human, would be sympathetic to the plight of his poor babies—old human babies. Surely there was something he could do to help. Tep envisioned being offered a job—any kind of job—in the consul's employ, so he could raise them in Metok, if whatever Velanda planned or hoped for failed.

"There is really very little I can do," the consul replied, shaking his head sadly. "My actions are constrained, where the action would not promote the general welfare of the Xarafeille Stream."

"And this matter of Glaice does not?" Tep angrily spun about and strode toward the door. "Even finding the Charter has no *greater* importance, does it?"

"Wait!" the consul called out just as Tep emerged into the hallway beyond. "There is the other matter—the documents of purely historic merit. Were you to find *those*, the Arbiter would be personally obliged to you. I am sure he would find a way to express his gratitude."

Tep nodded, but said nothing, afraid he might say something he could not retract.

When his visitors departed, Consul Jacob Martinez allowed himself to smile. Obviously the young ikut was only a potential father. Potential, he thought, because bors females seldom carried their first pair of infants to term. Did Tep Inutkak know that? Or was Martinez wrong to assume that it was indeed her first pregnancy?

He poured himself a very small glass of Newhome whiskey—his workday was far from over—and sat down to ponder the situation on Glaice before composing a dispatch to John Minder XXIII.

The incident that had caused Tep to detour around Drumlin Way had not been an isolated one. Only a direct consular request to the news media had kept a lid on just how many such incidents there had been in the last few weeks. In Gladowak, a coastal town, three mantee females had cornered an ikut youth behind a slaughterhouse and had hung his skinned, gutted corpse on a meat hook within. On an ice floe just now approaching the equatorial islands from the north, a band of ikuts prepared special nets to catch any swimming mantees that came near. They had good cause to be concerned, because they had already killed and eaten a half-dozen members of the Rocky Reef throng who had become entangled in the long, deadly nets. They had not been starving or even especially low on supplies—it was merely an expression of how far the situation had degenerated, how high people's deadliest emotions were running. All across Glaice, such incidents were becoming common. Ironically, the various reactions to the mantee's legal measures had already caused fully three times as many deaths as had the initial Ketonak atrocity that had triggered them.

Martinez did not hold out much hope for Tep's and Velanda's success—but at the moment, he had no better options. He resolved to keep the hearings going, to stall as long as he could, to give them time.

Tep did not catch up with Velanda, but he would see her at her apartment, or later. Her about-face had angered him, as had her revealing her plans in the consul's presence, but now he thought he saw her motivation. He would have time to consider things, to become less angry, before he could confront her. Already, he was thinking, perhaps he was wrong to be upset. Perhaps she had a plan for the children.

None of that affected Tep's own plans. Whatever Velanda did, he had to return to North Camp, to speak with Hepakat and lay out a strategy for finding the Charter, the original, data-module Charter. If it was not at the bottom of a trench, there was only one logical place for Apootlak to have put it.

Perhaps whatever it contained would indeed hurt the Inutkak band, or even all the ikut on Glaice. That would be unfortunate, but either possibility was only a matter of degree; what was absolutely certain was that war, which otherwise seemed inevitable, would hurt everyone on the planet—bors, ikuts, and mantees. Tep knew where his true moral duty lay—and besides, if he *did* earn the Arbiter's personal gratitude . . .

CHAPTER 12

Given the evidence, it is clear that the distinctive behaviors of furred humankind are rooted in the more generalized and broad-spectrum ones of the old-human race. Whether that race is truly ancestral to the rest is more debatable. To extend the behavioral hypothesis to physiology, would we be forced to assume that bors hibernation, with its distinct hormonal chemistry, is no more than a latter-day evolution out of old-human sleep? On the other hand, if no genetic basis for behavior exists, what are we left with?

Slith Wrasselty, Ph.D.,
Sex and Genes Across the Xarafeille Stream,
University Press, Thember, 12158 R.L.

When Velanda found that Tep would be on the same train, she was at first angry, but by the time she boarded, she was able to smile, and to offer him the seat next to hers. The situation, however awkward for both of them, was hardly Tep's fault. She herself had to accept most of the responsibility for how things had turned out.

That, however, did not make the trip an easy one. Tep wanted to talk, to make plans for whatever eventualities ensued. She merely wanted to go home, to see her mother. As for the pregnancy, she would bear the infants or she would not, and the burden of deciding what to do with them was as much Bavant's and Vols's as it was her own. Only under very limited and specific circumstances would Tep Inutkak be involved or consulted—but she did not think he would understand that, or accept it even it he understood.

Velanda was able to steer what little discussion took place to Tep's own plans. Though her opinion and advice was useful to him, she had to pretend an interest, because she was no longer the same Velanda Torsk who had gone exploring with him. She was an entirely different person, one she herself hardly knew. She had gambled and had lost. She was pregnant, and whether or not the fetuses survived to term, her attitudes were no longer those of a student, an archaeologist, or a girl.

Perhaps there would be war. Would it affect Black Peak? If anything it would have a salutatory effect on the local economy. Neither ikuts nor mantees would be likely to storm the mountain city, but both would want weapons, which Black Peak's factories could supply in short order. Already wealthy, the town would become richer still, and her babies would be safe.

Her babies. Whether or not the first brood—Tep's—survived was not relevant. The constant in Velanda's personal equation was not those particular infants, but the fact of motherhood itself, a fact she could not ignore. If the half-breeds survived, they would only delay what must happen next: she must find a mate, a bors, and must breed the next generation of heirs to Black Peak. She was not particularly concerned who her mate would be; there were hundreds of likely males, and her mother would find one who was civil and who did not stink. Mating, breeding, she decided, was just an urge, a condition of being female and bors that would pass in time, leaving her again free to pursue other interests.

If Tep had been a bors—if he had bonded to her, imprinted on her, the first time they had coupled—she might have felt guilty about shuffling him out of her life. Had he been bors, that could have been a death sentence. Unable to mate with the only female he wanted or was capable of mating with, he would have gone mad and died unless he had access to expensive offworld drugs. But then, if he had been a bors, there would have been no problem, would there? Velanda had no one but herself to blame for using Tep, for trying to postpone the inevitable instead of bowing to her nature. How strange it was! She had been so enthused about saving his people, and perhaps the whole planet, from war. How trivial it seemed now, as long as it did not impinge on her and hers.

It did not take Tep long to become aware that Velanda would not discuss any of the personal matters that loomed so large before him. She would discuss what he planned to do, though without any of the enthusiasm the "old" Velanda would have demonstrated. Tep's idea was quite simple, in theory. Just as ikuts cached food in the glacial ice, caches carefully placed to arrive near the ice face where they would be found three or six years later, during another migration cycle, so Tep suspected that the hero Apootlak, all those thousands of years ago, might have cached the missing data module in the ice, perhaps far up the slopes in the mountains where it would have stayed hidden for many more than three or six years, but from which it would eventually emerge. Since data modules emitted identifiable radiation, he would, using appropriate detection equipment, search the ice for a recognizable signature.

Velanda was able to advise him on equipment he would need. Whatever he specified, the consul had promised he would get it either from the university or, if necessary, from offworld. "Happily for you," Velanda remarked after studying the listed specifications and emissions spectra for various ancient data modules, "the stuff you'll need is all portable. In fact, one deep-penetration scanner is all you should need. You won't have to drag a heavy sled across the ice. Brr! Will you be able to survive out there in winter? I almost froze, just going between the domes in Metok, saying goodbye to some friends."

Tep was touched by her hint of concern. She had not lost all human feelings. "I am ikut," he replied. "Cold is nothing to me." She nodded, evidently believing him. Actually, Tep was quite worried about that. Ikut were well adapted to cold conditions, better than bors or even seel-phase mantees; they could cope with dry cold that would stiffen mantees' oily fur and make it brittle; their fine mat of insulating down, unlike bors underfur, was hollow and a superior insulator. Still, ikuts did not ordinarily live on the high ice. Their adaptation was coastal, and even so, they did not often venture out of the warm winter-camp huts during heavy weather. Only hunters did that.

Hunters. Among ikuts, hunters were a special breed. In camp they were treated with great respect and allowed idoisyncrasies and irascibilities considered asocial in other ikuts. People moved from their comfortable spots near the warm oil lamps whenever a hunter wished to sit down. Did those small privileges make up for the suffering hunters endured as a matter of course, far from the comforts of camp? Surely, it was small recompense for what they gave the band, for without them, dependent on diminishing caches of food stored from warmer days, old ikuts and very young ones would surely die.

Tep Inutkak was well aware that he was no hunter. Worse, he was less than a fully-qualified camp-squatter, having spent too many years in comfortable, even-temperatured and windless Metok. Of all the Inutkak, with the possible exception of the younger cubs and the infirm old, Tep was sure he was least qualified to tramp around on the high mountain glaciers in the harshest conditions the planet Glaice had to offer. But of course, he did not tell Velanda that.

Topics of conversation allowable by his companion had long since been exhausted by the time the train decelerated into Black Peak station, and after an awkward, noncommittal farewell, Tep found himself quite content to be alone as the train gained speed for the run southward to Fulag.

On the slower train from Fulag to Tebuk, he peered often from his frost-rimmed window. At midday the sun rose quite high in the sky ahead. It was only days from the vernal exquinox, which on worlds less harsh, worlds with less of a lag between sidereal events and climatic ones, signified the coming of warm weather in the north. Among the Inutkak it meant other things. There would be a celebration of the season, but that was mostly bravado. Old, lean meat kept in the houses, swarming with nutrient-rich larvae, would be stirred and mixed with tender white shoots of bunch grass that had been force-grown from seed in flat trays. That reminded the band of the hardships they would have to endure before the shortening days of high summer came again. Oldsters and cubs would partake first, then nursing females, hunters, and at last the rest of the band would enjoy what was left. That order spoke well for the civilized nature of the Inutkak, of which they were justifiably proud. Some bands did not allow their old people to eat first, but the Inutkak valued the collective wisdom and experience of the old.

The Tehokag band, Tep knew, would at that time be preparing to depart from South Camp. All eyes would be watching for weather signs and changes in the ice underfoot. The Tehokag shahm, especially, would be studying winds and currents, alert for the perfect moment to push his chosen floe out into the westerly drift, to begin the long passage first eastward along the islands of the southern ring of fire, then northward until the jumbled island-threading currents of the south tropical "spine of the world" could be used to nudge the Tehokag floe ever northward and at last across the equator.

At that same time, the third band that shared camps and migration routes with the Inutkak, the Atulag, would be far to the west, having broken free of the equatorial winds and currents. The Atulag would be on the long, free run southward, readying themselves for their final, bumbling passage along the ring of fire to South Camp.

The Swift Current mantees, Kurrolf's throng—who occupied the island group that Inutkak, Atulag, and Tehokag passed through on their voyages north and south—would have left their warm islands for the long swim to the southern volcanic rocks, where their throngmother would give birth. Females destined to nurse the soon-to-arrive infants would swim freely, as scouts and guards for the rest of the throng. Well fed and strong, those adult males who had, in the season past, mated with and successfully impregnated the throngmother would take turns towing and supporting their massive mate, who in turn carried their genes and their hopes of immortality.

For Tep, far to the north, it was the bitter heart of winter already, and as he contemplated the arduous task ahead of himself, he wondered if he would be alive when summer came to the Inutkak.

Cold blasts off the high continent battered Tep's back as he stumbled from the hired car. "This is as far as I can go," the driver said. "Are you sure you can make it?"

"I am ikut, of the Inutkak band," Tep called out over the wind. "I am merely going home." The bors shrugged. *He* was not mad enough to stroll about in such weather. He had required Top to pay him twice the ordinary fare just to go out in his truck—and he had spent the entire evening before checking his vehicle carefully. If something malfunctioned from the intense cold, if his engine stopped, or his heater, he would not live long enough for rescuers from Tebuk to reach him.

Tep survived his hike. Shahm Hepakut ushered him into the dim warmth of his home. Seeing the lumps of ice on Tep's whiskers and the way his hands and knees trembled, he lit several more lamps for additional heat. He guided Tep from the low central area to his own high sleeping shelf, which was heaped with furs.

The ancient design of an ikut winter house had been discovered, lost, and rediscovered many times in the millennia before and since mankind had spread out from Earth. From the outer entrance, one crawled down a tunnel to well below the final floor level. At the lowest point, the cold trap, the temperature in the tunnel might be even lower than it was outside. Climbing upward to the main house floor, temperatures remained below the freezing point of water, but as long as people did not move about rapidly, disturbing the temperature-stratified air, the sleeping shelves remained warm enough for even a furless old-human to be comfortable.

When Tep had warmed himself and picked the ice

from his whiskers and from between his toes, he outlined the situation and his plans. The shahm, hesitantly, asked how hard it might be to train a hunter to use the instruments Tep had requested via the terminal in Fulag. "If he trims his claws and does not poke at and break the dial covers, an idiot could do it," Tep replied enthusiastically, not at all offended by the implication that someone other than he might be a better candidate to go up on the glaciers.

"Our hunters—even the least of them—are not idiots," Hepakat said sternly. "And for this task, I will select the very best of them."

"Of course," Tep said. "I did not mean . . ."

"I understand. I will call the chief of the hunters now, to listen and to advise us."

Tep stared. The hunt chief looked quite familiar to him. He was surprised to realize that she was female—not that half the hunters were not, as a rule, but he mostly remembered old Beluk, a male, who had been chief seven years before. He waited to be introduced. Why did the hunter frown at him like that?

"Tep," she said. "Don't you know me anymore?"

Her voice, even cracking with emotion, or perhaps with cold, was indeed one Tep knew. "Lis? Kelisat?"

Why, Kelisat asked herself, was he so surprised? Even when they had been children together, she had been a far better hunter than he. It stung. First, he had failed to recognize her at all, and then he cast silent aspersions on her prowess. Kelisat vowed right then that she would teach him to respect her—even if he no longer cared for her the way he once had. Shugging off her chagrin, she sat down on the far side of the shelf, with the shahm between her and Tep. She listened as the others explained the problems they faced, and the unanswered questions.

"I was thinking of something Apootlak said in the Fourth Tale, the Seventh Cantone," Tep said.

"Let me guess," Hepakat interrupted. " 'And when from the beginning five thousand cycles have passed, when the Inutkak have known many seasons in the north and in the south, when many crossings have been made, and generations born and died, then I will say to you, "Look at what I have hidden from you. Praise me or curse me as you will. I, Apootlak, whom you call Bold, have done this new, bold thing." ' That is the passage, isn't it?"

Tep nodded. "That is it."

Kelisat allowed herself no expression at all. She had not known the passage. She did not know the Seventh Cantone from the Seventeenth, and she only vaguely remembered, from lessons long past, the gist of the Four Tales. But I know how to hunt, she told herself, and that is why I am here with the wise shahm and Tep. They need me, or I would not have been summoned.

"If Apootlak was referring to the Charter, then five thousand cycles have not yet passed. I do not think we have been on Glaice for five thousand cycles. We are now in the thirteenth millennium of the Rule of Law, and the first Arbiter lived only twelve thousand years ago."

"What," Hepakat mused, "is 'the beginning' that Apootlak spoke of? That is what we must determine."

"Just so. If indeed Apootlak meant fifteen thousand years of the Rule of Law, then the Charter is not intended to emerge from the ice for two thousand seven hundred years. We must calculate how far the high ice has traveled so far, or where we might place a cache we wanted to remain in the ice for another twenty-seven hundred years."

"We must also determine where best to place a cache to emerge in three thousand five hundred years," Hepakat said. "Apootlak's 'beginning' could as well refer to the First Migration, which he led."

"How do you know when that was?" Tep asked. "The Tales give no dates."

"You told me, Tep. Did not Apootlak sign out the Charter in 871 R.L.? Then depending on how old he was, and knowing that the seventh cantone tells of his old age . . ."

"Of course!" Tep exclaimed. Then he frowned. "But

we now have two broad bands of ice to search, not one."

Kelisat's heart slowed perceptibly, a sign of distress. Hepakat's speculation had just doubled her labor and the suffering she would have to endure—and had halved her chances of success. Did either of them know just how *big* the high glaciers were, and how variable was the flow of ice within them? And they had both overlooked a third possibility that would worsen her chances yet again. "Heed the cycles of the sun," she chanted softly. "Heed the rise to heaven's height, the fall to Ocean's bed."

"What is that?" asked Tep. "I do not know that song."

Hepakat sighed. "Kelisat reminds us that we, shahm and candidate, are not so wise. That was from the Hunter's Guide, which teaches us to find our way in the trackless lands. We cannot assume that Apootlak meant 'three years' when he said 'cycle.' "

"But a cycle is three years!" Tep protested. "That is what 'cycle' means."

"Only to us, Tep. We are Inutkak, for whom a cycle is one pass, one complete migration round. But as Kelisat reminds us, there are sun cycles—years—also. Apootlak taught us to migrate, and he decreed the movements of the three bands, but in his time, had the word 'cycle' yet come to be as specific as it is today? What is to say he did not mean five thousand years, not fifteen thousand? And too, what if those early 'cycles' of migration were not three years long? Did Apootlak devise our finely balanced patterns without experimentation? The Tales do not specify them. With a little time, I myself could design and choreograph a different migration pattern, where perhaps bands indeed lingered an extra few seasons in the camps, and ate mantee. I could design a pattern with an extra loop in the tropic islands, perhaps. And it is known that those early Inutkak did not understand ice very well. The Second Tale mentions that they often finished migrations not on ice, but in skin boats."

"But if 'cycles' meant 'years,' then the Charter will

be buried in the rock and mud of the terminal moraine!" Tep looked defeated.

Hepakat shrugged. "Then that is one more place we must search for it. Can your instrument penetrate earth, or only ice?"

Tep sighed. "I will find out. It is an archaeological survey tool, and most archaeologists dig in earth, not ice, so I suspect it will work, but how well, how deeply, is problematical."

They spent the next several hours laying out a survey plan that Kelisat privately named a "fennet chase" after a game children played. They tied a thin fishing line to the tail of a fennet, then let the poor, frightened creature loose under the ice floe. They tried to guess which blowhole it might choose when it needed air, and tried to catch it when it surfaced. If no one succeeded at that, they had to follow the line, swimming under water like mantees, until they came to the end of it, and to the fennet. The winner was allowed to eat the fennet, but more often than not they all went home hungry, and the fennet was wasted, dying somewhere in the dark, cold waters at the end of its snagged tether. When the fish or the mantees had finished with the fennet, the ikut cubs could pull the now-freed line back up, and use it again, another time.

Kelisat wanted very much to succeed, to find the Charter for Tep. Perhaps then he would be grateful to her, and might even remember what good friends they had been. But the more they wrangled over the scope of the search areas, the less convinced she was that she would find anything at all—or that she and Tep would ever become more than two strangers, working miles and lives apart, though toward a common goal.

When all was accomplished that could be done, Tep offered to walk Kelisat to her hut, which was next to his parents'. Tonight, he would sleep among his younger siblings and would try not to think about two other babies who would never be tough enough to wrestle and claw their way into the middle of such a warm mass of furry bodies.

He expressed his gratitude to Kelisat for what she

was soon to endure, when she had made ready and when the consul's courier arrived with the archaeological survey instrument. He did not speak of their childhood years, or of how close they had once been. Was he thinking only of the sleek bors bitch with the dangly gold things in her ears? Kelisat bid him goodbye at the door of her house, and crawled inside. She had left a lamp burning, so it was not too chilly, but there were no other bodies there to warm the space further.

Her parents, with their last pair of youngsters, had been killed in the floe breakup off Pelander Island the year before—and Tep had not even asked about them. Tep was also unaware, as she was not, that he was not the only one to have attained physical maturity in the recent past. Had he come inside with her, their relationship might have rekindled quite rapidly, with an entirely new dimension added. She shook her head sadly. She had been afraid to ask him in, and by now he was surely rolling about with his parents' four cubs, unaware that she was here, so close, so far, and so alone.

"I'm a fulf!"a thin, high voice squeaked from somewhere beneath the heap of furs—of which some were white, and still attached to their owners.

"Aaragh! Stop that, Hent!" said a slightly older, less shrill voice: Tep's next-oldest sib, his sister Neriss. "Go to sleep."

"Yeah!" Tep agreed. "I killed the last fulf I ran into."

"Tell me! Tell me about it!" the high-pitched voice insisted, as Hent wriggled his way to the top of the heap, and up onto Tep's stomach. Tep opened one eye—and found himself staring into Hent's.

"Tomorrow," he said, rumpling the small one's ears, thinking how nice it was to be home. Until his last trip, he had never seen little Hent, but now it was as if he had never been away. "I'll tell you about fulfs and moxen tomorrow—if you quiet down *now*." Within minutes, Hent's breath smoothed in the easy rhythm of sleep.

CHAPTER 13

Be warned! The effect of endless night on wend physiology cannot be overstressed. We are diurnal creatures above all else, and even a week of polar winter can be devastating to us. Irritability and loss of appetite are only the early signs of daylight deficiency and can be quickly followed by episodes of violent, even homicidal rage.

Plan your visit to an ikut world with a careful eye to the seasons. The Parkoon Guide series provides calendars and seasonal tables for Harbinder (Xarafeille 971), Hembruch (X-3027), and of course the oldest ikut colony, Glaice, Xarafeille 132. Arrivists at Harbinder's Fetrak port might wait two months or more for adequate daylight to view the crags and glaciers local ikuts inhabit. Tourists who land at Glaice's southern hemisphere port in local winter face an uncomfortable and expensive shuttle trip north to Metok (and local summer, which is the only tolerable season).

The Wend's Guide to the Xarafeille Stream,
Volume XX, "In the Darkness of Winter,"
Amos Parkoon*, Bermat Press, Newhome, 11994 R.L.

"Did you make friends with Tep, Daddy?"

"I never met him, Parissa. He never came to Newhome, and I did not get to Glaice until many years later, and I did not see him then." John Minder did not admit that he had wanted to go there once he had verified what Rob had suspected, that a backup copy of one of the seven missing modules he required had found its way from one failed ikut colony to the next, and had

*Writing as Minirelifen Pentranipet, "the most far-traveled wend."

finally ended up on Glaice—where it had been lost. Had he visited Glaice then, he might have been tempted to bring hundreds of submersible vessels equipped with sophisticated scanning gear to plumb the depths of the oceanic trenches, and huge snow cats to scour the glaciers—and he would not have gotten even close to what he sought.

Too, massive intervention on his part would have telegraphed what he least wanted known: that there was an object so valuable to him that he did not dare leave the search for it to his subordinates, let alone to a humble ikut like Tep Inutkak.

John Minder XXIII knew well the cost of such intervention, without ships or poletzai to back it up. . . . Torag Benter was a bors, an interplanetary shipping magnate in the Falouse system—seven habitable planets orbiting the star numbered Xarafeille 2231. The Falouse worlds Brant, Falimer, Upkarch, Nerud, Mastipol, Phaleron, and Nord had been colonized by bors, wends, fards, and mantees, and the colonies were a mere few hundred years old when their plight first came to the Arbiter's attention. His offices on several planets, mostly those where Falouse colonists had originated, received complaints that letters and messages to their kin on Falimer, Upkarch, and the others were not getting through. Subsequently, Minder's consuls on the Falouse worlds lost track of the agents they sent to investigate. Then the consuls themselves stopped responding even to the Arbiter's most urgent queries.

Because he did not have warships to send, or troops, the Arbiter was forced to investigate covertly. To prevent the unknown malaise from spreading, he closed the Falouse system to interstellar traffic. The only ships that entered or left the system—or so he thought—were his own spy craft, which dropped new investigators onto the seven worlds. Few of them reported back, either. The few who did were all bors, and they had terrible, sickening tales to bear: the mantees on Brant, Upkarch, and Mastipol were gone. On Falimer, Upkarch, Nord, and Nerud, all the wends had disappeared too. On Phaleron, Falimer, Brant, Mastipol, and Upkarch, none of the fards who had settled in the desert areas could be found. Torag Benter, those agents pointed out, was a bors—and so was every living human in the Falouse system. It was genocide. There was no question about it.

John Minder had dithered helplessly. He had no forces he could bring to bear. Recovery efforts were under way on several worlds where backup copies of the seven missing data modules had been located. In every case, those efforts were indirect, because if anyone found out that the Arbiter could *not* call up ships and troops, then others, rulers less obsessed than Torag Benter, less fearless and defiant, perhaps, and less insane, might also decide to embark on courses of atrocity and genocide, for their own particular reasons. Only the Arbiter's reputation and his commitment to protect all the races of man stayed many hands.

Several major explosions had been reported by the Arbiter's spy ships. The radiation signatures indicated that their sources were tampered stardrives. That was not good, but at least they indicated that the Arbiter's monopoly had not—yet—been broken; a successful attempt to commandeer or create a stardrive would leave no such trace. Still, the very fact that Benter was experimenting with the few interstellar ships left in Falouse ports was ominous.

For the first time since the battles to free the slave worlds, an Arbiter had to destroy whole fleets of slower-than-light vessels with hastily modified peacetime starships. Rather than allow his vessels to be mounted with weapons, he merely ordered that their structures be reinforced, and their hulls armored. Once the technology again existed to mount weapons on starships, it might have been duplicated. The plans and specifications, the designers, engineers, and shipwrights who had built his original—and now useless—Arbitorial fleet were all dust these many thousands of years, and he doubted if, in today's closer-knit and sophisticated society, a similar construction effort could be mounted without dangerous "leaks." The vessels he commissioned were no more sophisticated than space-going rams but, able to move about at speed and at will, they made short work of Benter's vessels.

Only later, when the Arbiter's spies were free to come and go, when each of the seven individual planets was isolated, did reports begin to indicate that one starship remained unaccounted for. Only when planetary governments fell and new ones rose, ones not loyal to the bors dictator, was Minder sure that Torag Benter was no longer in the Falouse system, unless he lay in some unmarked grave. He was never found, and neither was the missing ship.

The Falouse system remained isolated, by Arbitorial decree. The populace was to be kept from contact for as many generations as it took to extinguish the last memories of what had occurred there. Only then, purged of genocidal guilt, would their descendants be allowed contact with the rest of the Xarafeille Stream. Yet was Torag Benter still out there somewhere, with the one starship he had successfully subverted to his will? Was he still experimenting with stardrives, and would he someday succeed? On the Arbiter's warships were detectors that could register the use of a stardrive anywhere within the Stream—but where were those ships, and the crews to man them? With them, hisactions could have been almost surgically clean and precise. Without them, his most delicate intervention was no more sophisticated than a heavy club . . . a battering ram.

But Minder could not tell Parissa much about things like that, though Rob had read the classified reports. For some time after he read them, Minder imagined he caught his son staring at him in an odd manner. Was his solution to the problem that much better than what the madman Benter had done in the first place?

"I would like to meet Tep Inutkak someday," Parissa said. "I would like to be a great hunter like Kelisat, too, and bring great heaps of ritvaks home for us to eat."

"Ritvak tastes like liver, Priss," said her brother. "You hate liver."

"I do not! I love liver, and I would like ritvak, too!"

"Mom?" Rob called out. "Can we have liver for dinner tonight?"

Parissa jumped up. "Daddy!" she cried. "Make Robby stop picking on me!"

Parissa had never been depressed; thus she would not have thought much of Tep Inutkak, right then, having little empathy for depressed people. Tep's melancholia stemmed from several sources, some obvious, some less so, and at least one of them was intrinsic to ikut nature—and to many other humans past and present, especially those with lifestyles similar to the ikuts'. Old-human psychologists and behaviorists on ancient Earth, whose scholarly musings now existed only in the Arbiter's archives and perhaps on lost Earth itself, would have recognized SAD, seasonal affective disorder. Long considered a disability, it was not until clinical studies had been cross-referenced with demographic data that it was recognized as an important genetic adaptation to life in the high latitudes of "wobbly" planets.

The symptoms—all of which Tep exhibited—were listlessness, a sense that any effort was too much and was surely doomed to failure anyway, cravings for starchy foods and sweet things—both usually in short supply in an ikut winter camp, foods that further promoted listlessness and sleepiness. A SAD ikut could sleep seventeen out of Glaice's nineteen-plus, just as a SAD old-human with northern European genes could have slept twenty out of Earth's twenty-four.

The advantages of such programmed behaviors were obvious, once one considered them from an evolutionary perspective. SAD people did not get cabin fever. They were too listless to be aggressive, so they did not erupt in the killing rages that sometimes overcame less-adapted people. Above all, they did not batter their mates or kill their cubs. They were too depressed to make the effort, no matter how intrusive and abrasive those other presences were.

Of course, as with all behaviors, SADness existed on a continuum, and was only useful when it fell somewhere near the middle; too little depression in winter camp resulted in infant deaths, and thus faulty non-

SAD genes were excised from the population; too much depression, on the other hand, usually led to a depressed person taking a long last walk in bad weather—and the result was similar: genes for extreme depression did not often survive in another generation.

Among the early old-humans of northern extraction (from whom it was suspected the basic ikut stock was derived) SAD incidence split sharply across sexual lines, which made a certain amount of adaptive sense; men, who could not nurse infants, tended to get out more, at least on mild days, and thus the pressure to adapt—to be depressed—fell more heavily upon women, who were more often left with the children, and who either nursed them or killed them.

Among ikut there was no clear sexual dichotomy—after all, half the hunters were women. It might be suspected that those women and men with the greatest susceptibility to being SAD gravitated early in life to hunting rather than hide-chewing or lamp-making. Kelisat, to be sure, had suffered greatly when she had been confined to camp. Tep's severe depression might be explained by his recent physiological changes and an imbalance between his male and female hormones. Before, estrogen and testosterone (to name only two) were in a certain neutral balance. After, they shifted to a strong testosterone preponderance. But depression often reflects—or creates—a shift to very low levels of testosterone, and of serotonin as well. Depressed people are not ordinarily aggressive or libidinous, states which are testosterone-dependent, and they are not very swift, or especially bright, either—which might reflect low levels of serotonin, a neurochemical. Their carbohydrate cravings may derive from low serotonin also, because carbohydrates are the building blocks for it.

Of course, biochemical considerations aside, Tep Inutkak really had things to be depressed about. First, he was the only Inutkak who had to take pills to maintain his health. All the others had stored up enough vitamins, trace minerals, and such in their subcutaneous fat and elsewhere to last until next migration. That made him feel not only different, but ineffective and less than fully Inutkak. "Tep Metok," he mumbled on occasion. "Tep Nobody."

That he was idling in camp while Kelisat braved the high country's winds and cold did nothing for his self-esteem either, nor did the taste of saliva-soaked hides. Ritvak hides were the worst, because they tasted like liver. Because Tep's well-adapted ikut body was getting enough vitamin A in his pills, it warned him against consuming liver that was rich in vitamin A by making livery flavors taste awful to him. Kelisat, he grumbled, did not have to chew ritvak hides.

Kelisat had her own discomforts. The worst of them, at the moment, was due to the snow. Inland, by the glacial face and the terminal moraine, snow did not compact in the same way it did on the coast, where it was often moister. When she tried to cut blocks of it with her slate snow knife the blocks crumbled and cracked. She could not build a snug snow house to sleep in. As the ground was quite frozen—by definition, "soil" on Glaice fit well with the geologist's definition of "rock" anywhere else—she could not dig a house pit, and anyway, there were no logs, saplings, or whale ribs for a house frame. The winds promptly knocked her little tent down; it was one of the two Tep and Velanda had taken with them, but *not* the one the bors bitch had slept in—at least she hoped not. It was cleaner, at any rate, than the other one. Yes, she had heard about their affair. Never mind how. Ikut camps were small places, and cubs listened everywhere, to everything. Maybe Tep had told Shahm Hepakat.

The only shelter she could create was a hole in the snow. Once inside, she pulled the snow back over herself, leaving only her nose sticking out. When it was windy, no one could possibly have spotted her nest. When it was calm, a passing observer—of which there were none—might have seen puffs of steamy breath coming from a projecting black nubbin the size of the imported walnuts that grew in Metok's sheltered parks.

She had surveyed about half of the requisite area of the moraine, the places Hepakat and Tep judged most likely for the Charter to be. So far, she had found nothing but rock, grit, and frozen silt held together with the most common mineral of all—frozen water. The tips of her claws were fuzzy and delaminated from scrambling over frozen boulders; ikut claws were designed to grip ice, not granite. Her nose was sore and raw from sticking up in the wind all night. The fur on her shoulders was rubbed thin by her pack straps, and she suspected she was developing a susceptibility to frostbite there, the way those patches burned when exposed to cold. Maybe, she hoped desperately, the snow would be better up on the glaciers themselves—it would be lovely to sleep inside again.

Tep seldom had the energy or the inclination to roughhouse with the cubs, yet his parents became annoyed when he merely sat on the sleeping shelf and growled when Turap or Patto, his young siblings, poked at him with rib bones or willow sticks. At Hepakat's urging, to get him out of the house, be became a schoolteacher, which was occupational training for anyone who aspired someday to be a shahm. Ikut schooling was less than formal; Tep sat on Hepakat's sleeping shelf in the big house, and his students arrayed themselves on the floor below. Tep could choose whatever topic interested him, and usually trusted that what was of interest to one Inutkak would be equally so to others, and perhaps of some use to them, someday. If his students lost interest entirely, they could leave—and be underfoot in their parents' houses—or they could, by a number of means including suggestion, request, and class disruption, get the subject changed.

Tep enjoyed talking about his adventures in the cemetery pingos, and he spiced his narratives with tales of the famous Inutkaks whose remains he had seen there. One particular day—one that would mark the end of his long winter depression and the beginning of an entirely new direction for his life—he explained how carbon-14 dating worked. Several younger cubs left before he got well into his subject, and he was left with the most mature intellectual core of the Inutkak youths.

"So the *old* Inutkak who didn't migrate ate lots of atopak because they needed zinc, right?" said Betak. Betak was a large, thoughtful cub Tep suspected might become male in a few years. He always made statements sound like belligerent questions. Tep merely nodded in response. "So the atopak got the zinc by eating sludge on the ocean bottom, right?" That was not precisely right; atopak ate crustaceans that ate bacteria that ate sludge. Nonetheless, Tep nodded again. If the other cubs got tired of Betak's pugnacious delivery, someone would tickle him, but so far, none had. "So carbon-fourteen gets made in the upper atmosphere, from nitrogen and cosmic rays, right? And then it breaks down into ordinary carbon, carbon-twelve, at a regular rate. Right?"

"Just so," Tep said aloud. He sighed. "Betak, do you have a point to make?"

"Yup."

"Well then . . ."

"So how long does it take for the carbon up there in the air to get all the way down to the sludge and ooze in the ocean?"

Tep pondered. "Why, it first has to find its way to the ground or the ocean surface, and to be taken up by plants or seaweed. Then animals . . . eat the seaweed . . . and are eaten by . . .

"Betak!" Tep yelled, leaping to his feet. "That's it! That's the answer! No—come back here!" But Betak was no longer there. The cubs, suddenly fearing that their teacher had gone berserk and was about to slaughter them, had all departed. Tep saw one last white-furred behind, a stubby tail, and a pink anus vanish into the tunnel. Cubs, despite their bulk, could move faster than the rats that infested Metok spaceport and the ships that called there.

Suddenly, even Hepakat's large home was too small for Tep's rapidly expanding thoughts. He followed the last cub out. The sunlight was bright, the sky clear, and the air frigid and still. His breath made huge puffs in front of his face. It was a fine day for a walk. "Food chains! Of course!" Tep exclaimed. "The deep vents release zinc and carbon dioxide, silica and lots of other things, and zinc, silica, and CO_2 precipitate as inorganic ooze. Bacteria metabolize oozes and excrete insoluble nodules of zinc and manganese and . . .

"Yes!" he cried out again. Speaking out loud helped slow and clarify his racing thoughts. Already, his brisk strides had taken him to the edge of North Camp. "Coelenterates and crustaceans and clams siphon bacteria-rich ooze, and the bottom-feeders eat *them*. The oceanic carbon—mostly $CaCO_3$, calcium carbonate, like limestone and shells—moves up the food chain; predator fish eat bottom-feeders, and *mantees* eat *them*! *Now*, in modern times, ikuts passing through eat a few predators and such, but not enough to affect their balance of carbon. Back then, ikuts only ate atopak, when they came to breed on the coast."

Suddenly everything was so clear! As he walked—he was almost to the Tebuk road, now—his mind was filled with a vast network of nutrients, among them carbon compounds, that pulsed and flowed from one animal or plant "node" to the next, becoming more concentrated or more dilute, traveling quickly or slowly. What it all boiled down to was this: carbon that came from oceanic sources was almost entirely C-12, both because C-14 was created in the atmosphere instead of coming from volcanic vents, and because by the time atmospheric carbon made its way to the isolated waters in the trenches, it had decayed into carbon-12.

Carbon dating worked because carbon-14 was radioactive, and because it decayed at a regular rate, with a half-life of 5,568 (plus or minus thirty) years, and because it was produced at a relatively regular rate in a nitrogen-rich atmosphere. The proportion of carbon-12 to carbon-14 in the atmosphere *and the bio*sphere remained constant and uniform. When an organism died, it stopped ingesting fresh carbon, but the carbon-14 in its tissues continued to decay at the same rate as before. By measuring the radioactivity of a sample a scientist could determine the ratio C-12:C-14, and could tell just how long ago that organism had died. It worked for mantees (bone), ikuts (frozen flesh), and burnt tree limbs (charcoal). It worked for any specimen that had carbon in it.

But a scientist testing an animal like the atopak that ingested only ocean-bottom carbon, which was almost pure carbon-12, would have to conclude that his specimen was very old, and had died thousands of years ago—even if he had killed it himself only hours before! People like the Ikut I folk—who got much of their carbon from the atopak they had eaten—would also be determined to be "old."

That was the Ikut I–Ikut II gap. When the Inutkak stopped eating "old" atopak and began meeting their dietary needs with a broad spectrum of land and ocean life-forms gleaned from a vast part of two hemispheres, their flesh, now richer in C-14, suddenly tested out as "young."

"Now," Tep exclaimed aloud, "I can get the proof I need to show Consul Martinez. I do not need the Charter anymore. Whatever Apootlak wanted hidden can remain so." Tep resolved that even if Kelisat found the Charter in the glacial ice—which had always been a slim chance at best, and grew slimmer even as he considered the ramifications of his, or Betak's, discovery—he would take the data module and hide it again. The Arbiter could pursue history in a different direction; that was of no account to Tep.

When he realized that the sun was quite low, and remarked upon how far he had walked, Tep turned around. His brisk pace—his stride and his thinking alike—did not flag, but it still took him until an hour after dark to get back to North Camp.

Even after dark, the Inutkak camp seemed less dismal than he had ever remembered it. Moonlight sparkled on fresh-drifted snow. The muted glows of occasional lamps set out to guide late-wandering ikuts home to their doorways cast a warmer light. It was, he mused, a perfect life for an ikut, on the one world that seemed right for his kind. Of course ikuts had adapted to Glaice, and that was the one true source of their contentment; the planet had not adapted to ikuts at all.

How had he ever thought North Camp, or anything else so purely, perfectly ikut, to be sordid or ugly? A city person might think so. A pampered bors lady from decadent Black Peak might. Had he been seeing his camp—and his people, his culture—solely through such unnatural eye filters? What else, he wondered, had he been seeing unclearly?

Suddenly, Velanda Torsk did not seem so pretty to him; she was far too small and puny to be pretty, and far too enigmatic. Kelisat, now, was ikut. Kelisat was big and strong, with lovely white fur that shaded almost to blond. She was a hunter, and she would be a fine mother to some lucky ikut's cubs.

Tep's thoughts darkened then, thinking of cubs, of his cubs, not yet birthed. What was Velanda doing about that? He realized that if he did not present the charter data module to the Arbiter's consul, he would not have the Arbiter's gratitude. How then would he be able to care for the babies? For all his exultation, that was one problem Tep had definitely not resolved.

CHAPTER 14

The second problem colonists faced when population expansion brought two or more races close was interbreeding. It was not as much a problem for those individuals who fell in love with someone different as for the races themselves: wholesale interbreeding would not have destroyed the *human* race, but it would surely have meant extinction for the distinctive variations.

The V chromosome was perhaps intentionally designed to aid in conversion of the variant races to the old-human "norm" once they were no longer needed. To prevent that from happening—as all products of misogamous unions were old-human—it was necessary only to inculcate in the other six race-based cultures a deep-seated revulsion for unfurred human skin.

John Minder IV,
Unpublished Manuscript,
Erne Museo, Newhome, 4321 R.L.

Hepakat hunched down, locking his knees as Tep sketched his objectives on the shahm's slate floor stones. "I have collected samples of flesh from every prey animal in North Camp's storage pits," he said. "When I return to Metok I will personally run radiocarbon tests on each one. Those—plus others I will obtain from the zoology department at the university, will be my 'controls.' Their C-twelve to C-fourteen ratios should be identical to atmospheric carbon." He sighed. "If I had known what I know now, I could have asked Kelisat to kill a *hootlap* for me while she is up there. The early

Inutkak—the so-called Ikut One folk—ate more hootlap than we do, here on the coast."

"I am sure Kelisat has enough to do," the shahm commented, in a reproving tone. "Already, she has been gone longer than any hunter in my memory."

"You are right, of course," Tep said, sighing again. "Perhaps I should go up there now and tell her to come home. Perhaps I could find a few hootlap and a crevasse dog or two also."

The shahm shook his head. "Kelisat will know when she must return. She is a hunter. You must pursue a different quarry: this new hope for our salvation. We may not need the Charter, but Kelisat's effort will not be wasted. She is our *getlag*, that is all." A getlag was a skin boat, but not a fish hunter's sleek craft. Its sole purpose was to provide temporary safety if an ikut floe turned over suddenly.

Tep felt that the Charter itself was a poor getlag. If his new plan worked, there was far less risk of harm to the Inutkak, because whatever was in the Charter, Apootlak had not thought much of it. Tep's way was better. Besides, he not only felt sorry for Kelisat, but he wanted to see her. Last night he had begun a dream of himself and Velanda in their tent on the way to Pootorap—was it always like that for adult males? Once they had experienced sex, was it never again out of mind for long? In that strange manner in which dreams transmute images, that one had ended in a snug snow hut with Kelisat. This morning, he had found himself looking for reasons to tramp up to the glacier where she was searching.

"As for hootlap and crevasse dogs, you can buy one of each at the market in Tebuk, when you get there. They will be reasonably fresh, and will be datable. The other samples you need should be available from the zoology department. They may be a few years old, but not thousands. They will suffice for what you wish to prove."

Tep reluctantly agreed that Hepakat was right—on that count, at least. "I will pack what I will need for the trip . . ." Tep had been about to say "for the trip home" when he realized that he now considered here, with his people to be home. "For the trip back to Metok," he concluded.

When the train stopped at Black Peak Station, Tep called Velanda's number. "Oh, Sar Tep," exclaimed Tabir, who picked up his call, "I will tell her it is you!"

Tep waited anxiously, keeping an eye on the train. Most of the other passengers who had gotten off to stretch their legs or to make calls had boarded again, and the line of newcomers not yet on board had shrunk to a half dozen by the time Tabir got back on line. "Sar Tep?" she began hesitantly. "Oh, Sar Tep! I am sorry! Lady Velanda does not wish to speak with you."

Tabir would say no more. She sounded as if her sinuses were plugged. Did bors cry? What had Velanda said to her? Unable to glean more than further apologies from Tabir, Tep disconnected and then had to run to get back on the train. The doors were already closed, and the noise of couplings coming under tension almost drowned out his insistent hammering on the glass. Finally, a bors sitting in the first banc saw him, and unlatched the door.

Once back in Metok, the chain of events, adventures, and ideas of the recent past compressed in Tep's mind into a whirlwind chaos of busyness from which a few images stood out, images like the heroic fish hunter reposing in his cold grave with his toggle-head harpoon, like the view of North Camp from the rise, all sparkling with moonlight and red-orange traces of lamplight, and like a particularly vivid image of Kelisat slinging her heavy pack as she made ready to depart, with a strange enigmatic smile on her face.

The zoology department specimens were as diverse as Hepakat had remembered them. Tep did not remove whole animals from the freezers unless they were quite small. From most, all he required were certain tissue samples, which he kept separated according to his own special considerations. First were those animals that were common fare for modern ikuts, mostly fish and seels (but not mantees, which they only called seels) that ikuts hunted while at sea. He had collected foods typical of camp life before he had left the Inutkak.

Next was a slightly different group representing those animals most common in middens associated with the abandoned coastal villages north and east of Pootorap, villages reasonably firmly associated with the old, sedentary ikuts. Only one creature whose bones had been common in those middens, so common they seemed to form the matrix in which all else was embedded—bones, broken pots, clumps of red rust that had once been steel—was not represented in Tep's growing collection. That was the atopak, of course, which had become extinct long before zoologists from Metok University had begun their collections—long before the university had come into existence at all.

The third group were specimens of species known to provide large portions of the diets of mantees. Those, in turn, he broke down into two subgroups: first, specimens matching the diet of modern mantees, all of whom lived on the coasts of their islands and migrated twice annually to the polar continental shelves. Those samples also corresponded with the diet of the first mantee shell middens, which Professor Rakulit had dated as early as 650 R.L. The second subgroup matched more closely the diet of mantees who had lived inland by the islands' streams and ponds, whose middens Rakulit had dated to around 990 R.L.

Tep was not sure what those mantee midden dates meant, but he had a feeling they would eventually fit in somewhere. He could not understand why mantees first settled the coasts, in 650 R.L., then moved inland 140 years later, then abandoned the inland areas until less than two thousand years ago.

With his samples in hand (or rather, in hundreds of tiny vials) Tep began the arduous process of testing them. Happily, the individual testing was not difficult; there was one large analytical computer, an automated laboratory which Professor Rakulit helped him set up. Tep did not even have to separate the carbon from the other constituents of his samples. The anlab did everything. Gratuitously—or so Tep thought at the time—it also logged a complete breakdown of those constituents by weight and percentage of the sample.

In spite of its simplicity, the testing of so many samples took many days. When Rakulit realized how extensive Tep's project was, he dug out a hopper that accepted ten specimen vials at once, so Tep did not have to feed them singly, and could catch an hour's nap between "feedings." Seeing how determined Tep was to get all the tests done immediately, he offered to help so Tep could go home and sleep for a while. Tep politely refused his aid—he did not trust the mantee, any mantee, too near his materials or notes.

The labor and the waiting proved worth the effort, though Tep did not realize immediately just how worthwhile they had been. The tests confirmed his suspicions. The land-animal carbon ratios corresponded closely with atmospheric carbon (and thus with the current date), as did the land plants. The dates for ikut marine fare spread out over a greater range of apparent dates, indicating that they were anywhere from contemporary to as much as two hundred years old. That was significant, because Tep knew that none of the samples he had chosen had been collected more than a decade ago. Still, as those contributed half or less of the total ikut diet throughout a given migration cycle, their skewed carbon ratio should not distort by more that fifty or a hundred years the dating of flesh from ikuts who consumed them—ikut like Tep's own folk, or the Ikut II people from Etonak whose remains Rakulit had dated.

Samples corresponding to animal and plant remains from old ikut coastal middens near Pootorap, the Ikut I middens, also tested as entirely current. Wherever the Pootorap folk had been getting carbon with a low amount of isotope 14, it had not been from the land-derived part of their diet. That, of course, implicated the single large part of their diet that Tep could not test: the atopak fish, because there was no atopak flesh to test, only bones. It was possible to test ancient bone, Rakulit said, as long as one dissolved away the mineral portions and tested only collagen (which was not soluble and thus liable to groundwater contamination). Tep pictured himself trying to explain that fine distinction to the Arbiter's consul. He then considered how little he trusted anything a mantee said, and he did not bother trying to find atopak bones to test, though the proprietor of the Last Atopak might have given him some.

The typical coastal mantee diet sources had dates that ranged over five hundred years. Not coincidentally, Tep was sure, those sources lowest on the food chain—mussels that thrived in deep water on the edges of the ooze-layered trenches themselves—tested oldest.

The diet of mantees from the short-lived inland sites (whose own bones indicated, according to Rakulit, that they had assumed the freshwater "otter phase" adaptation) consisted entirely of inland plants and animals, all of which gave carbon isotope ratios comparable to atmospheric ones. Tep wondered what "otter phase" meant. He understood "seel phase" well enough. Seel-phase mantees looked like . . . like seels. Did the others look like "otters"?

Tep, compressing the results of the data from hundreds of samples, sketched a simple chart:

Culture/source:	Rakulit's Dates:	Dietary skew:	Actual dates (?):
Ikut I	380-595RL	Land diet: +-5 years	?
		Atopak: ?	?
Ikut II	990RL to present	+5 to -200 years	1090(?)RL
Inland mantee	790-930RL	+-5 years	790-930RL
Coastal mantee 1	650-790RL	+5 to -300 years	950(?) to990(?)RL
Coastal mantee 2	930RL to present	+5 to -300 years	1230(?)RL to present

On the face of it, that did not look good. His tests, lacking any new dating based on the atopak's C-12: C-14 ratio, did not affect Rakulit's chronology as much as he had hoped. Actually, the Ikut II marine diet threatened to widen the gap, not narrow it.

His data on the inland mantees did not affect their placement in the sequence at all, but the results for the final group were significant. Conservatively allowing for a three-hundred-year skew in Rakulit's coastal mantee dates, they seemed to have appeared about the same time the inland mantees departed. That was progress. Instead of mantees arriving on Glaice around 650, moving inland for 140 years, then inexplicably moving back to the coasts, Tep's chronology indicated that the first mantee settlement of Glaice took place no earlier than 790 R.L., only two hundred years before the professor's date for the Ikut II—the Inutkak. The mantees had obviously settled the sheltered, forested island interiors, remained there less than two centuries, then moved to the coasts, where they had remained ever since. The move had taken place in the same general time period that the Inutkak began migrating. Was there a connection between those events? Tep was sure of it.

When he had cleaned up the lab, run all his vials through the washer, and printed out his test results, Tep went back to his dormitory room for the first time in what seemed months, at least. He slept in a bed, for a change. He should, he told himself later, have dreamed of pleasant things—like proving to Consul Martinez that Rakulit was all wrong, or like striding through North Camp, basking in the admiration of his people. Instead, he dreamed of pale, hairless babies.

The War Against the Children, Jacob Martinez entitled his private memoir—a document that would remain unread by anyone but John Minder, and perhaps some future Arbiter. Awake or asleep, the image of the mantee birthing ground haunted him. From his memory of those scattered heaps of brown fur and gnawed bone he could not help reconstructing, like a mental holoshow, the events as they had recurred.

Timing had been everything. The ikuts—a party of young males who had stayed behind when their band migrated—had watched the mantees arrive. They watched the ponderous throngmother, gravid with young, as she pulled herself onto the shore. They watched as the tiny infants came forth, and as the nursemothers, already swollen with milk, took them. They watched, and they waited.

When twenty nursemothers had been given young, the ikuts struck. A score of hooting, snarling ikuts armed with long spears and flint-edged bone swords swept down and surrounded the throngmother, scattering hopeful nursemothers and male guardians. She died quickly. A score of unborn mantees died with her, and the future of the throng died too.

Nursemothers with infants plunged into the water to flee. Males followed, to guard them. The tiny newborn things were not yet furred, and the water was cold. They died quickly. When long, fast ikut boats shot out from behind concealing rocks and ice and ran down the swimming nursemothers, those mantees died at spearpoint, trying to keep the infants up on their bellies and out of the water. Many males died trying to save them, but they only pulled over one ikut boat.

Many mantee males must have been left alive when the ikuts retreated, but what would become of them—a motherless throng? What would they live for? What but revenge? Even if the Charter was found, or if he accepted young Tep's proofs and declared against the mantees, those rogue males would still be out there somewhere, impossible to find, impossible to stop. The killing would go on. Only the massed support of the mantee throngs could stop them—and he might as well have wished for palm trees to grow on Glaice's icy shores.

CHAPTER 15

I could not have done it myself. At the time, I raged silently at John Minder XXIII, my young boss. I called him a monster, the reincarnation of some primeval demon. I think I hated him. I may even have wished his children might die as my ikut and mantee infants were dying, horribly.

It has been many years since I left Glaice, and there is no snow on the hills outside this village where I have retired. Still, I feel the coldness within—the cold of Glaice, and the greater coldness within the heart of the Arbiter of the Xarafeille Stream.

Jacob Martinez,
The War Against the Children,
Unpublished Manuscript

In the morning, Tep grasped his stack of printouts and stumbled into the refectory, where he drank several cups of black, offworld coffee and made brown rings on his papers. Coffee was unknown among the Inutkak—except for Shahm Hepakat, who had twice mentioned to Tep that it was the one "civilized" thing he really missed, some mornings. Coffee was not well known anywhere else on Glaice, either, though students drank it, and judging by the pots and cups in Consul Martinez's office, so did old-humans (or at least Arbiter's consuls).

As Tep had been away for some time and had not told anyone where he had gone, or what he intended to do, he would have thought his fellow-students would have clustered around him, with questions. It did not happen that way. Several bors students glanced curiously at him and his printouts, but they did not speak to him, and they took tables on the other side of the room. He had not expected the four mantees over in the corner to greet him, of course—not after the way Kurrolf had treated him. During his sojourn in the refectory, the only person who greeted him at all was Fenag, his "opposite number," the only other Inutkak in Metok. "Hey Tep! When did you get back? I thought you'd gone home for good." Fenag Inutkak glanced at the printouts. "Huh! I thought you'd already turned your thesis in. Why are you doing all this nutrient stuff?"

"This is something else, Fen."

"No it's not. Who are you trying to fool? Zinc, iron, phosphorus, manganese . . . What happened? Did you flunk? Are they making you do it all over?" Fenag shook his head, which was not ikut body talk at all. The odd motion, coupled with his inordinately thin body and long neck, looked effete to Tep, reminding him of the cartoon professor on a children's holoshow. Fenag, he then considered—not for the first time—was quite an actor. He did not do funny things by accident.

"You aren't going to get to be shahm that easily," Tep joked in return. "I didn't flunk." Fenag smiled. They both knew that neither of them really wanted to be shahm. They just wanted to stay in Metok as long as they could. Tep realized that was only half true now—Fenag wanted to stay, but he, Tep? He no longer knew what he wanted. "See for yourself," he said. "Look this stuff over, and tell me what you think I'm working on."

Fenag got himself a cup of hot water and a packet of fish-broth mix. Stirring thoughtfully, then sipping, he paged through the printouts. He really did skim it, Tep realized shortly, because he did not even mention the radiocarbon dates. Instead, he zeroed in on something Tep had seen, but had not paid any attention to. "You've grouped these samples by their metabolic zinc contribution, haven't you?" Fenag asked—or stated. He pointed at one particular column labeled "Zn comp," and ran his finger down each grouping. "No zinc," he said of the Ikut II land diet. "Zinc, no zinc, zinc, no zinc," he concluded, then asked, "What are these samples anyway? I recognize the first two—they are a breakdown of ikut camp food and floe food. That's undergrad stuff."

"I think you've just answered a really important question for me," Tep said, standing abruptly and gathering his papers.

"Where are you going?" Fenag demanded indignantly.

"Back to the lab, where I can sort this all out on the computer," Tep responded. "Are you coming?"

"Try to stop me," Fenag replied dryly.

"So that's the story," Tep said much later. "The atopak, we must assume, furnished the early ikut, our ancestors, with zinc. We must assume that the atopak, which resembles existing bottom-feeding fish, fed near the deep tenches, or in them, and came into the coastal shallows often enough for ikut to net them—and to wipe them out. There might have been some food they needed, every so often, or perhaps they laid their eggs in the shallows."

"If so, perhaps the early settlements' pollution killed the eggs," Fenag speculated.

"Exactly so," Tep said, not really hearing him. "While feeding in the depths, the atopak also consumed carbon that had little or none of the C-fourteen isotope. Ikuts, in turn, ingested that falsely 'old' carbon, and thus Rakulit's radiocarbon dates seemed to indicate that they were an early ikut colony that died out before we Inutkak arrived. Look here!" He pulled out his chronology chart, and wrote between the first two rows of the last column "680-895 RL" "See?" Tep said. "Even estimating a conservative three-hundred-year skew, as with the mantees' marine diet, we can now show that there is no more than a fifty-five-year gap between the Ikut One and Ikut Two, which is hardly enough to warrant calling them separate cultures, especially when all the other evidence—language, styles, seriation analysis—also shows continuity between them. Not only that, but it puts us ikuts, us *Inutkak* ikuts, here on Glaice a whole century before the greasy mantees arrived!"

"That's great—I suppose," Fenag said, not very enthusiastically.

"You *suppose*? What's wrong with it?"

"Well, now we Inutkak can take the mantees to court, and try to get them thrown off the planet, and . . ."

"Don't be a fool! We wouldn't do that—especially not over a measly century. What we can do is to put an end to the whole thing, and get back to our ordinary lives, migrating, trading with the mantees . . ."

"You think that's possible? Things have gone pretty far."

"Of course it is! We're all humans, and we've lived together for thousands of years. There has never been a war in recorded history, and there's hardly any archaeological evidence for one before that. Why can't we get over this stupidity?"

"You may be right," Fenag said, not very convincingly. "So what else do we need to prove our . . . your case?"

"It is ours. All of ours—ikut, mantee, and bors." He shrugged. "I'm not sure what I need. A live atopak to dissect and test would be nice."

Fenag snorted.

"Since that is not possible," Tep continued, "I will settle for a beer. I have not had one in months."

"I will buy some. We can drink it in my room, or yours."

"In our rooms? Bottled beer? I do not want to sit in our rooms, and I do not like bottled beer. I mean to go to the most appropriate place of all to get drunk and think about all we have discussed—to the Last Atopak Tavern. Besides, if I see any of those bors archaeologists there, I have some questions for them."

"Tep, that is not wise. Remember that much has changed since you left Metok. I, personally, would not dare go there. It is not a good place for ikuts."

"Not go there? Why?"

"It has always been mostly a bors place, but still, mantees drink there. Didn't you hear about the riot that started in that bar on Drumlin Way, a while back? That was ikuts and mantees."

"Did I hear about it? I was there! Well, I was there the next day, when the mantees came to collect their dead. I saw Kurrolf there. His nursebrother Terelt was one of the dead. Do you remember Terelt?"

"I remember Kurrolf, because you played with him when we were stuck on the island, that time."

Fenag watched Tep walk away, swaggering. "There," he muttered, "is what being a man is all about." He shook his head. He was quite content to be immature, especially if Tep's behavior was an example of what happened after one's pouch popped. Fenag would rather have stuck his head in a whale's mouth than visit the Last Atopak Tavern.

"I am Tep Inutkak!" Tep had declaimed. "I am a citizen of Glaice, a resident of Metok, and I am an adult. No mantees can tell me I must drink beer in a dormitory room. Are you coming, Fenag?" Fenag, understanding that he was not going to change Tep's mind, had declined.

The Last Atopak looked no different from the way it had the last time Tep had been there. There were no ikut customers, true, but there never had been many. He observed that the bors patrons who had looked up as he entered quickly looked away again, and stuck their noses in their beer mugs. He saw two mantees at a corner table, but both of them had left by the time he had seated himself at the end of the bar.

The two bors sitting nearest him tossed down their beer and then departed. Within minutes, Tep was alone at the bar, though the booths and tables were still well occupied. "You're a brave man," said the bartender, a bors whose name Tep did not remember. "You're the first ikut I've seen in here in a month."

"If it's really gotten that bad, why are you talking with me?" asked Tep.

"I am a bartender, and it's my job—but no one else in here will chance it. The mantees have taken to beating up ikut *sympathizers,* even." He shook his head in disgust. "Why did you come?"

"I wanted a beer!" Tep snapped. "And I wanted to find some archaeologist who could tell me if atopaks had zinc in them."

"Zinc? Atopaks were fish. I know that much, being around them all the time. And zinc is metal, isn't it? Fish don't eat metal."

"Bors don't eat iron, either, but that's what makes your blood red."

"I shouldn't know. I try not to think about blood. And speaking of that, maybe you'd better drink up and go, before those two mantees that left come back with the rest of their gang."

"Huh? What gang?" Suddenly, Tep had the sense to begin becoming frightened, and to feel just how alone and how isolated he was. He studied the room—as much of it as he could see in the mirror behind the bar. It looked no more threatening than before. It looked as it always had. Then he considered the street outside, and all the other streets he had to follow to get from here back to his dormitory. "Maybe I should just stay until a big group of bors leaves at once, and stick with them. Hey! That is Fand Bennep, over there. He used to live in my dorm. He is a paleontology student. Maybe he knows if atopaks have zinc."

"You just stay put! *I'll* go ask him. If you do, and those mantees come back and see him talking with you . . . He's been a good customer." The bartender—after wiping the already dry bar and making a busy clatter underneath it—carried a pitcher of beer to Fand Bennep's table and whispered something to him. Watching in the mirror, Tep saw Bennep shake his head vigorously as he replied.

"Ah, well," Tep muttered, "maybe someone else I know will come in.

"No luck, huh?" he said when the bartender returned.

"Depends on what's lucky for you, I suppose. He said to tell you *not* to come ask him yourself, and that he doesn't live in your dorm anymore, so he won't walk you home. He says he's got no idea if there's zinc in atopak fish, but why don't you find out for yourself?

He says there's a whole freezer full of them, ones some ikut's grandpa's grandpa hid in a glacier, once."

Tep's head spun. Atopaks? Whole, frozen, atopaks, not just fossils or old bones? "Where? Did he say where they are?"

"In a freezer. I told you that. In the . . . the . . . vibrating pay-lee-ogly lab, maybe?"

"Vibrating . . . you mean the vertebrate paleontology lab? Is that what he said?"

"I suppose so. Something like that."

Tep tossed a handful of money on the bar. "Here. A tip. And buy another pitcher for Fand and his friends, will you?" He got up, and headed immediately for the door. The bartender shook his head at all such foolishness.

Tep glanced around himself. When had Metok's streets been so deserted in late afternoon? What had happened to everyone? He had gone only a few blocks. He felt very vulnerable and alone, now that the initial sense of invulnerability his excitement had given him had worn off. His eyes darted between shadowed doorways and the mouths of alleys. The sun was already below even the lowest buildings, and was further muted by clouds scudding over the top of Metok Main Dome. Some distance away, he heard a high, breathy whistle. Somewhere behind him, he heard another. He did not know what the sounds meant, but he had heard them before—mantee hunting calls. Kurrolf had sounded like that, when they played hide-and-seek.

He quickened his pace and angled toward the center of the street, away from the shadows. The whistles seemed to come mostly from behind and to his left. The Last Atopak was in Southwest Quarter. Ahead a few blocks was Esker Radial, which led to the center of town, and intersecting it another few blocks to the right was Two Circle, one of three streets that ringed the dome's center at regular intervals. On impulse, Tep turned right at the next intersection, hoping to put distance between himself and his pursuers—because he was sure that the empty streets and the mantee hunting calls were no coincidence. Metok had indeed changed while he was away.

Northbound, his direction of travel now took him in dogleg fashion toward Two Circle, but he realized that the mantees had only to race along the hypotenuse of the triangle, Esker Radial. The other mantees must be even now rushing along Parmat Way, closing off his chance to backtrack. Could he reach the broad road, the open expanse of Two Circle ahead of them? There would be people there.

He heard whistles from his left—and now from ahead. He was cut off. Desperately frightened now, he headed east, running, then south a block, back toward the bar. They would not attack him inside it, would they? From there, he could call the authorities, and perhaps be escorted safely home. Then he remembered Drumlin Way, and where the riot had started in another bar. Would he be the triggering cause of another riot? Whistles came from three sides of him now. The Last Atopak was just around the block; he recognized the back of the larger building next to it. The bar had a back door; he remembered seeing people leave through it. One whistle sounded perilously close behind him, though he had not seen anyone at all—not yet.

There was the door. LAST ATOPAK, a faded sign read. DELIVERIES. Tep threw himself against it. It did not open. The hinges projected; the door would swing only out. He groped for the U-shaped handle, and pulled, but the door did not budge. From the inside, a push of hip or hand would unlatch it, but from the outside . . . Tep hammered with both fists, denting the sheet metal and the fibrous honeycomb core. Did no one hear him? He turned, figuring he would try to circle the tavern before the mantees were upon him. He stopped.

Silhouetted against the sunlight on a building back the way he had come were three human shapes—sleek, rounded mantee shapes. Seel-phase mantees were really not that much like seels at all, Tep reflected. They moved slowly forward on legs much like his own, not thrashing on stubby seel flippers. He saw no weapons, but the mantees moved tensely, like men holding spears or knives at the ready. Then he saw that their arms were spread out, their clawed fingers were curved like hooks, and the tips of them gleamed like metal. From Tep's left, motion flickered in his peripheral vision—and then from his right. He was trapped.

Abruptly, Tep felt something changing inside him. He felt different. Had he been fully male longer, he might have recognized it immediately. New chemical messengers rode in his blood, suppressing child/fear and replacing it with man/anger. It did not come from his brain, but from somewhere deep in his body. For a long moment, long enough for Tep to pull himself up and to bare his teeth in a hideous grimace, ikut and mantees were poised as if painted on the looming stone walls. There were twelve mantees now. Tep's fur-covered skin felt loose at his neck, tight at his groin, as his body readied itself. Beneath his skin, muscles heated and bunched. His claws—not as sharp as the mantees' steel accessories, but no longer trimmed for the keyboard—trembled at the tips of his stiffened, curled fingers.

A mantee darted forward, hissing. Tep lunged and roared, and the slick creature fell back. Others did not. They surged toward him. More mantees appeared and disappeared, at the edge of what he could see, visible only as movement, sensed only as sharp, stinging pain. They slashed at his exposed sides and buttocks. He pivoted, swinging one massive arm like a scythe and feeling one impact, then another, feeling flesh tear against his claws. He flexed his knees and dropped down to shield his vitals and his legs, still lashing out. Sound, in the narrow space, was dulled. Mantee hisses and screeches, deep ikut bellows, all sounded muffled and distant.

Tep felt bright pain in his arms as mantees darted forward, slashed, and retreated. A mantee, behind him, climbed up his broad back, claws digging for purchase. He howled. He shook a brown, furry mass from an ankle, and stood upright. Mantees darted beneath his flailing arms and tore at his belly, ravaging his loose skin. He could not shake the mantee from his back. Its claws were digging, seeking, at his neck, buried in fur and skin that rolled away under their pressure without tearing. His arms were heavy and slick with blood. Whose? His, and others'. Tep suddenly lunged backward. He heard the *whoof* of air as the mantee on his back thudded against the door of the Last Atopak. He thought he felt mantee ribs or arm bones break, but he was not sure. His own pain was intense, but it was very far away.

Briefly, all was still except for Tep's harsh rales and higher, quicker mantee panting. Then, again, the mantees swarmed over him. His arms and legs felt as though encased in thick, heavy clay, as if he were swimming in mud. Clawed, hissing shapes overwhelmed him, pulling him to his knees. Something sharp tore across the pads of one foot. He tried to turn, to slash and grasp, to no avail. His mouth gaped; then his teeth snapped shut on a slim, furry wrist. He shook his head. He felt bones grind, then break.

One of Tep's eyes no longer seemed to work properly, as if a floppy curtain first obscured it, then drew away, then fell back. New pain came more quickly than he could acknowledge it, sharp, icy pains that immediately dulled, only to be renewed elsewhere. His knees and thighs felt like cooked fat, and he could not regain his feet. Mantees darkened the spaces all around him, and he dropped to all fours. He rolled, and felt the weight on his back lighten as mantees leaped aside. He lashed out to keep them away from his eyes—from his good eye.

Abruptly, again, all motion stopped, and a dead silence ensued. Tep was only dully aware that he was lying down, half on his back, an arm protecting his face. The mantees had backed off. Tep rolled, and tried to rise. His hand slipped in thick blood on the pavement, and he fell back, his limbs too heavy. Blood from the flap of skin hanging across his eye ran into the other one.

Seeing dimly, hearing little over the rushing of blood, the thudding of his overstrained heart struggling to pump enough blood to make up for all he had lost, he was only dimly aware of the mantees, who seemed to be screeching at one another, arguing . . . "Mine!" he heard. "My right! The kill is mine." He knew that voice. Who?

Something glittered in the hand of an approaching mantee, something longer than a steel-sheathed claw. What was wrong with the mantee? Then Tep saw that it was walking backward, facing its fellows, keeping them at bay. "I know him! I claim the kill," said the mantee.

"Kurrolf!" Tep snarled—or tried to snarl, though it came out as a low grunt, like a snore.

"It is I, Tep," the mantee replied, a tenor snarl so low Tep hardly heard it at all. The soft sound did not carry far, and all the mantees except Kurrolf were several body-lengths away. They heard nothing at all. "I warned you before," the mantee said.

Again, Tep tried to rise. Again, he failed, not really understanding why. Had he been able to see himself as Kurrolf did, it would have been quite clear; his once-white fur was mostly red, soaked with his own blood that oozed from uncountable rents and slashes, tears that exposed masses of yellowish subcutaneous fat. Seeing himself, Tep would have known he was dying.

Kurrolf, satisfied now that his companions would not interfere, turned to Tep, a long knife in his hand. He crouched at Tep's side, and muttered in a very low voice. "Tep, hear me." Tep made no sign that he had heard. Even his good eye did not move. He was trying to ready himself for one last, desperate effort to get Kurrolf's throat between his hands, as soon as the mantee leaned nearer.

"Do not try it!" Kurrolf murmured—which was an odd voicing for a mantee. High, shrill mantee tones carried and echoed, but Kurrolf's words did not travel. It was as if he wanted only Tep to hear. "Tep, if you hear me, if you understand, do not move. I can kill you with one slash of the knife—but I will not. You must trust me."

Trust? Tep knew he was dull, stupid with pain and blood loss, and immobile. Trust Kurrolf! Trust a mantee? Had he ever really done that? He could not remember, not exactly. He had a vague impression of being slightly afraid of his childhood friend even then, afraid of mantee unpredictability, mantee differentness. Why did Kurrolf want him to trust? What difference did it make? And why was he bringing that knife so close to Tep's exposed throat? Tep did not trust him, but that did not matter. He prepared himself to die.

"Do not move, Tep. Do not thrash. The others would have killed you by now, but I do not want you to die." Kurrolf's words were low and fast, tumbling one over another, not quite a meaningless jabber to Tep. "I lied, Tep. I am not your lifelong enemy. I cannot be." Still, Tep felt the cold pressure of the knife against his throat. "Do not lunge!" Kurrolf growled as Tep again tried unsuccessfully to move. "I am going to cut your throat so the others will see the slash—but I do not want you to die. The others must see the cut, the blood, or they will not believe you are dead. Do not move, or I may slip and cut the arteries instead."

Tep's confused thoughts seemed to be racing, but in slow motion. Kurrolf was killing him, but was not. Kurrolf *could* kill him, but would not. Tep did not try to move. He was not sure if he had understood Kurrolf, and was cooperating with him, or if he had just given up—even when he felt the sharp, cold pain of the sharp knife slicing through his thick, fat-layered skin, even as he felt the rush of icy blood.

"Do not move until they are all gone, Tep. Be dead, and they will depart the more quickly." Kurrolf's voice faded, and Tep was only dimly aware of other voices, and of a warm splattering about his face and head. Who, he wondered, could bleed so much, and why were they bleeding on him? Then everything grew very cold, and very dark.

"Too bad he didn't bleed much," one mantee said as they slipped away. "He must already have been dead, eh, Kurrolf?"

CHAPTER 16

TO: ARBITER
FROM: MARTINEZ, X-132

JOHN—AND THIS IS OFF THE RECORD—THIS ISN'T RIGHT! THE YOUNG IKUT HAS ALREADY CONVINCED ME; I DON'T NEED THE GLAICE CHARTER TO SHOW PEOPLE THERE'S NO CAUSE FOR WAR, I CAN SAVE LIVES. ALL I NEED IS YOUR OK.

The sense of smell returned first: it was the odor of old blood, liverish, no longer sweet and tangy. There was also a thick, rich, acrid musk like urine and sex and spoiled fish.

Next came noises and voices. Voices that were noise, and made no sense. "He stinks!" one voice said.

"The mantees urinated on him," another said. "That did not hurt him at all. It was astringent, like an antiseptic, and it stimulated vasoconstriction, minimizing blood loss. If he had lost another pint, and if we had not gotten to him when we did . . ."

"Will he make it?" That voice was tenor, like Fenag's—or Velanda's. He wanted to ask her where the children were.

"I will know soon," said voice two—though Tep was not alert enough to count that high. "If he were a bors, I would say he was hibernating, but ikuts don't do that. I wish I had worked on more ikuts, but . . ." Voices faded. Tep's head seemed wrapped in thick black fur that smothered sound and light. "Velanda?" he croaked, but no one answered him.

* * *

The next time he awakened—or perhaps it was the time after that—everything hurt, everywhere. He was lying on sharp thorns, but when he tried to roll off them, claws dug into his flesh elsewhere, and the pain intensified. "I think he's awake," said the borrish voice, the one he no longer thought was Velanda. It was not a bors. It was Fenag.

The other one, though, was surely a bors. "Tep?" that one said. Of course he was Tep, wasn't he? Who else would he be? "If you can understand me, wiggle this finger." Tep felt someone wiggling his finger. They were doing it for him; why should he try? But he did. He wiggled it very hard.

"I think he's trying to," the voice said. "Yes! Good! Now listen, Tep. The drugs are wearing off, and soon you will feel a great deal of pain. Do not thrash, or you will reinjure yourself."

Do not thrash? Hurt himself? Tep envisioned something sharp and shiny, and a burning pain, a cold pain, at his throat. "Kurrolf!" he croaked.

"Yes," the voice responded. "It was Kurrolf who called to tell us where you were. Kurrolf saved your life." That was not what Tep had meant . . . but then, Tep was not sure what he had meant. A few moments later, someone again put the black pelt over his face.

The person who was not Fenag was, Tep saw for the first time, an old-human, not a bors. "Who're you?" he asked. "Y'not Consul Mar'nez."

"Good morning, Tep. I am glad you are awake. I am Shems Kruger, Consul Martinez's physician. I have been caring for you."

Tep did not care who he was, really. He was not sure why he had strained himself so to ask. Something was bothering Tep—something besides the dull pain everywhere, the sharp prickles and tormenting, itching bugbites. It was not a sensation; it was a memory, something important, something he had to do, and must not forget. "Las' Atop'k," Tep essayed.

"Yes, Tep. That is where you were. That is where we found you, behind the Last Atopak Tavern."

"No . . . I have to . . . to find the las' atopak. Where am I?"

"You are in Consul Martinez's spare bedroom. We moved you from the hospital last night, for security reasons, and to protect your friend Kurrolf. You rambled in delirium—so we know a little of what happened. If the other mantees knew you were still alive . . ."

"The las' atopak. Inna freezer, the bors tol' me. Vibrating pay-lee-ogolly."

Dr. Kruger shook his head. "He is not coherent yet," he told someone else, someone Tep could not see. "Perhaps later you can speak with him." The voices faded as if they were moving away. Tep tried to tell them about the atopak in the freezer, but they did not hear him. Then, for a long time, he drifted between strange images—swimming atopaks with eyes like great, glowing fire opals.

"A whole week has passed between your fight with the mantees and when you first became entirely coherent," said the old-human doctor as Tep slobbered soup down his chin. It was the first time he had actually tried to feed himself. Two spoonfuls, and his arm was already heavy and numb. He disagreed with the doctor's assessment of his coherence, because he remembered trying to tell him something about a fish, something he had been afraid he would forget. But he had not forgotten. "When can I get up?" Tep asked. "I have to find something. It's important."

"Tomorrow, we will remove the catheter, and will see if you're strong enough to get to the toilet."

"I have work to do! Important work! Where is Consul Martinez? He will tell you that."

"He *has* told me, Tep. You are looking for the Glaice Charter. But you cannot get up just yet. Even *your* work must wait, or you will suffer a relapse, or tear loose your healing wounds."

Tep finished his soup, only switching the spoon from one hand to the other twice. He had to exercise both arms, he told himself. Later, he asked to have the sheet removed so he could see some of those wounds. Afterward, he was not sure he should have looked. Many patches of his fur had been shaved off, revealing pink, bruise-mottled skin that was turning grayish-white where his fur had started to grow out. His arms, ribs, and thighs were almost entirely shaved, and were crosshatched with intersecting scabs, some V-shaped where mantee claws had torn the skin. Most of the stitches had already been removed, leaving little bug-tracks next to their respective scabs.

"Eyuck! I can't go out looking like this!" Tep exclaimed. The doctor agreed readily. If his orders, or Tep's common sense, would not keep him in bed, Kruger would settle for his pride keeping him there. "You look pretty ugly," he admitted. "In a week or so, when you have a bit more fur . . ."

Tep was not finished yet. "I need a smock to cover myself," he said. "I have to go to the vertebrate paleontology lab. There is a frozen atopak there—a whole fish, not just bones."

"You can order any kind of fish you would like, right here," Kruger said, being an offworlder and not knowing what an atopak was. "The consul's cook is a master chef."

Tep, thinking he had best not let anyone close to the consul know what he was planning, said no more. In fact, he hoped he had not said too much. After all, he needed the atopak to prove to the consul that Rakulit's radiocarbon dates were all wrong—and to show him *why* they were. Then he would not have to find the charter. The consul—actually the Arbiter—wanted the data module the charter was recorded on, but Tep had no intention of giving it to him. He sighed. "I guess everything will have to wait until I am better," he said, which relieved the doctor.

"How about *satap*?" Tep asked him.

"Satap?"

"It's fish. It is very good when it is steamed and wrapped in blue seaweed."

"I will ask the chef," the doctor promised.

* * *

By the end of the week Tep was up and walking from one end of Consul Martinez's suite to the other. He now sat for at least one meal with the consul, and found he enjoyed the old-human's company—the doctor was dry and greaseless, by comparison. Contrary to the myth, Tep had no evidence that old-humans smelled funny, or that their pheromones made other people do strange things. Perhaps ikuts were not affected.

"Some scientists believe that we old-humans are an ancestral type," Martinez said, skirting around the typical ikut belief that they originated on a world called "Ice," quite independently of the other kinds of humans. Of course Tep did not really believe that—else how could bors and ikut interbreed, and why would their offspring be old-humans? He did not want to think about that, right then.

"It is true that we old-humans produce pheromones that interfere with other races' mating urges," the consul continued, "but as you and I are both male, that is irrelevant to us." For that, Tep was grateful. He had gotten used to looking at the consul, but he could not imagine what an old-human female might look like, let alone imagine making love to one.

The night after that conversation, Tep had terrible dreams, and woke up snarling. His claws had torn holes in the sheet that he still wore because his fur was still short in places and made his skin feel oddly cool. When he was awake, he could successfully force his worry about Velanda and her condition out of his mind, inundating it with all his other pressing concerns, but asleep he had no control over what emerged from his subconscious mind. Talking about old-humans and thinking about mating had obviously triggered the dream, which had featured pink, naked children, like shaved ikut cubs, and mantees tearing at them with bloodied claws.

Tep did not get back to sleep. His mind raced uncontrollably from Kurrolf, whom he now knew had saved his life by pretending to kill him, to Velanda and babies, then to the consul and the Arbiter's gratitude—which might mean the babies' only chance for survival

—to his intention *not* to find the Charter, which might doom them. . . . "Tomorrow," Tep growled, "or rather, this very morning, I will get that fish, and I will be back on track again. If we can settle this mantee problem without the Charter, maybe I can get the Arbiter to promise not to reveal or enforce whatever Apootlak found in it, if I give him his historic stuff."

"We have only five of them!" the paleontology curator protested. "They are unique. And you want to *dissect* one? To *destroy* it?"

"You will still have four," Tep argued, reasonably, "and you will also have a complete report on the one I study—everything right down to the last tiny detail. You will have four fish about which you will know almost everything, instead of five frozen lumps about which you know nothing at all."

After much discussion the curator released one small atopak fish, less than a meter long, into Tep's care. Tep had to agree to perform much more extensive dissection, study, and tests, and to write a report that would surely qualify as a doctoral dissertation, if he could get his committee to agree to it. "It is not your only child," Tep remarked, seeing the expression on the bors scientist's face when he was about to depart with his prize.

"It is one of my five children," the curator replied without a bit of Tep's sarcasm.

Tep enlisted Fenag's help with the atopak. His initial urge was to plunge in as soon as it had thawed, to extract the contents of its stomach for analysis and radiocarbon dating, and to carve off a chunk of flesh to run through the anlab as well. He restrained himself, and between himself and Fenag produced a detailed study, with analyses of every tissue type, holos of the entire process, drawings, and microscope slides of everything else. Only when all that had been accomplished did he carry two dozen small sample vials to the anlab, and load the first ten into the hopper.

* * *

"So why aren't you happy, Tep?" asked Fenag later. "The fish tested really old—far older than any radiocarbon dates on either mantees or ikuts on Glaice—and some of its tissues had a lot of zinc in forms we ikuts can metabolize. Not only that, but she was full of eggs, so we know why atopaks came up in the coastal shallows—to spawn. Haven't you proved your point?"

Tep shook his head. "I didn't think everything through. How do we know how old that particular atopak is—or was, before we took him apart?"

"It came from an Ikut One cache, didn't it?"

"And isn't Ikut One just what we *don't* have good dates for?"

Fenag nodded. "I see what you mean. But the fish tested a thousand years older than any of the mantee professor's Ikut One dates, so you've shown why *those* dates are falsely old, anyway."

"I've inferred it," Tep corrected him. "I haven't *proven* anything. Now I have to do what I should have done in the first place; I have to get samples from Etonak and Pootorap . . . from Pootorap, at least. I may have to get dates on the mantee sites, too."

"You'll never get to them. I heard the mantees have been blowing up any ikut floes that come near their islands. I suppose you could sail there. . . ."

"Sail? In what? A skin boat? And have it go soft on me halfway there?"

"Well, the weather service has a metal one."

"Yeah—and only a planetary government could *afford* one! They don't sell tickets, you know."

"I suppose you're right. But why do you have to duplicate the mantee's work anyway? You yourself said there's nothing wrong with his samples or his lab techniques."

"I won't duplicate it. Hepakat only let him take little plugs of flesh from unobtrusive spots. I need more than that." He explained to Fenag what he intended to do.

"Will you be all right, by yourself? You aren't fully recovered, yet."

"I will take a few days to get ready. If you can help, I will be able to spend time resting—and I can rest more, on the train. I'll be okay." Fenag, eyeing Tep's patchwork fur and the still-evident scabs, was not so sure.

"I figured something out, Dad!" Robby blurted as he rushed into his father's study. "I figured out why those backup crystals were made!"

"Hmm," John Minder murmured. "I thought I already knew why—for just such a circumstance as I found myself in upon my accession."

"But Dad, who would ever have imagined that Uncle Shems would have taken them? No, there's another reason. Remember Occam's razor?"

"The principle of elegance? Yes. It states that the best hypothesis is the simplest one that can explain the most."

"Exactly. Simplicity. It didn't make sense to me that the First Folk would go to so much trouble—putting all the data about the poletzai worlds, and the code-keys to activate your fleet, into seven parts, any six of which were unusable without the seventh, if all that was needed was a backup for your crystals. It would have made more sense to have kept another set right here, in the Vault of Worlds, which is keyed to our family's genetic codes."

"I see what you mean. It does seem a bit . . . cumbersome."

"We've always assumed that the breakup into seven parts was to prevent any one of the races from getting control, if something happened to our family, right? But I kept thinking there had to be another reason for dividing things into seven mutually dependent parts—and then giving one part to the ruling body of each human race. It had to be *necessary*. Have you got it now?"

Minder smiled ruefully. Rob was turning the tables on him—it was usually he who asked such questions. "You haven't really told me anything yet," he protested.

"I have! Consider this: seven parts to a puzzle, a puzzle that the Arbiter has—supposedly—all the parts to already. What for? They could not be used unless all seven races cooperated to put them together. And if they did, what would happen?"

Minder's eyes narrowed. "Then your hypothetical consortium of the races . . ."

" . . . Would have control of your fleet and your poletzai! Checks and balances! If you—or some Arbiter, anyway—became unbalanced, or did horrible things, horrible enough to force all seven races to join together to overthrow you . . . they would have the means."

Minder nodded. "Presuming that *their* set of codes could override, or at least nullify, my own," he said. "It is Jefferson's one truly inalienable right."

"Jefferson? Who's he?"

"An ancient statesman and political thinker, one whom the original John Minder respected. He wrote a bill of rights for his new nation, which is virtually identical to the one incorporated in the Articles that define my own office. They are ideals, of course, and are not easily enforceable upon . . . diverse populations and governments such as those of the Xarafeille Stream, but . . ."

"But you said *one* right, Dad. What is that one?"

"It is the one the others are meant to preserve," Minder murmured. "The true reason for people's right to keep and bear arms, to assemble freely, to publish words unfavorable to governments—or to me—is to preserve the means by which they can exercise that one ultimate right, just as those seven crystals would do. Can you tell me what it is?"

Again, the tables were turned, and Rob pondered his father's question, framing a reply. "It is," he said at last, "the right to rebel against government that no longer serves the governed—and the seven crystals, brought together by a consensus of the races, would guarantee it."

CHAPTER 17

The history of the early millennia of human expansion is not well documented—in the public archives. Even the exact date of the settlement of Newhome itself is "lost." Yet the scraps and fragments that the Arbiter's archivists let slip point to an administrative system no less sophisticated than at present. One must wonder: Is there *motive* behind the apparently sloppy record keeping? Are there things our Arbiters do not want us to know?

Firko Slafex,
Letter to the *Salith Historic Society Journal*,
Salith, Xarafeille 957, 12020 R.L.

Tep uneasily eyed the luggage that stood by the laboratory door. He had sorted and culled it several times, rejecting everything not absolutely essential, and had packed his camping gear separately and had shipped it ahead to Tebuk, in care of the livery stable; weight and bulk would not be a problem later, once he had it strapped on the backs of several moxen. Still, the two large alloy cases at the door were both bulky and heavy.

One held sample vials in padded racks, and his few personal items. The other contained a minimal chem lab for certain tests he planned to make right there in the caves, a hydraulic jack, an infrared spot-heater and its tripod, and several other compact, but heavy, devices.

Tep was healing rapidly, but each time he hefted those two cases they seemed heavier, not lighter. Did he have the strength to carry them to the train station? He had to do that—and without tearing any of his wounds open—or else the doctor would not let him go until he recovered further. Thus far, he had been grateful for the physician's ignorance of unique ikut physiology, which had allowed him to convince the old-human he was more fit than he felt, but both the doctor and Fenag intended to see him off. If he displayed his weakness . . .

"Tep! Are you ready?" It was Fenag. Tep grasped one case in each hand, and lifted them. He suppressed a grimace and a moan as hot needles of pain jabbed into his arms and ribs. "Come on, Tep. The consul has sent his car to take us to the station."

Fenag, Tep noted, was wearing a leather utilitarian belt with several rectangular pouches. "What's that for?" he asked. "Have you found a part-time job as a mechanic?"

Fenag grinned toothily, unsnapped one pouch, and reached inside. "I have only one tool in here right now," he said, "but I will buy others in Tebuk."

"Tebuk? Why would you be going to Tebuk?"

"Stop being foolish, Tep, and put down those bags before you strain something. I am going with you. You are not strong enough to carry those bags to the car, or lift them onto a mox. Besides, I have never seen a mox, or the piedmont country, or a burial pingo, and I intend to see all three."

"I can't afford another ticket, or an extra mox for you to ride," Tep protested. "I have spent everything that was left in the Inutkak account with the university."

"That is what *this* tool is for," Fenag said, removing his hand from the pouch with a dramatic flourish. Between two fingers he held a small black, red, and gold debit card. "This is from Consul Martinez, who does not want us to go without whatever necessities we may need. Will you need a ritvak fillet with red mushroom sauce, served on a fine porcelain plate in the first-class dining car? How about a sleeping berth instead of a cramped seat? The consul has suggested . . . no, commanded . . . that we not stint ourselves."

Tep was nonplussed. He had not considered a traveling companion. He had contemplated with almost masochistic delight a long, very lonely voyage, a penance for his many failures—specifically his dalliance with Velanda, and his refusal to see what tragic consequences his self-indulgence would create: two small lives that could never *belong* anywhere, as Velanda belonged in Black Peak and as he did among the Inutkak. Then there was his foolish escapade at the Last Atopak, which could have resulted in his death and the loss of the vital knowledge he had not then bothered to write down. Tep had even considered his heavy baggage and the skimpy meals he anticipated as part of his self-punishment. It was not easy to turn himself around in a moment, just because Fenag was waving that card in front of his nose. "But . . ." he essayed. "But . . ."

" 'But' nothing! You cannot deny me such an adventure, Tep. You cannot deny me a chance to have *my* name in the thesis you will write—even if it is only a footnote, somewhere."

Tep had not considered a thesis. The Inutkak did not require future shahms to seek advanced degrees, only to acquire a broad, general education in those areas of use to them in their migratory lives. Fenag, who would not become shahm unless Tep failed disastrously, had obviously considered such things—probably as an alternative to returning to the band, when he had accepted his basic degree.

When Fenag elbowed him aside and lifted both heavy cases without apparent effort, Tep conceded that the young ikut's strength might indeed improve his mission's chances of success. "Very well," he said—unnecessarily, because he was following Fenag down the hallway instead of standing stubbornly in the laboratory doorway—"but have no illusions. It is winter out there, and this trip is not going to be fun." Fenag did not reply.

Tep realized there was another aspect to his penance—whatever cold and misery he might suffer was as nothing to what Kelisat was surely enduring. By now, having found nothing in the moraine, she must be up on the high glacier, where conditions were much worse than what he—and now Fenag—would have to endure. He irrationally resented that, as if Fenag's presence would dilute by half the payment he would exact from himself for his guilt. Guilt—because Kelisat was suffering for nothing. She would not find the Charter in the ice, because . . . it was not there. Guilt—because he, Tep, knew right where the Charter was, and he had no intention at all of recovering it.

Fenag attributed Tep's taciturnity to the lingering pain of his wounds, and he did not attempt to cajole him overmuch, though he insisted that Tep take his meals in the fine first-class dining car, and contradicted his orders to the waiter for plain, simple fare. "You must rebuild your strength," Fenag said in tones Tep's mother might have employed, "and groat pudding will not help you recover. Besides, our waiter will be offended if you do not order the crisped fish skins, which are a speciality of this train's chef."

Tep surrendered to Fenag's logic, but as he munched tasty crisped fish skins and dribbled nutritious oil onto his chin, he tried not to enjoy them too much.

Later, retiring to their capacious private stateroom, he told himself that the soft, roomy bed was a necessary comfort and that he would heal more quickly—and would thus be better able to pursue his goal—if he slept well and soundly now.

At some time in the night, before the train had reached the tunnel under the Hapnag Glacier, Tep's sleep was momentarily disturbed when Fenag crawled in with him. As the two ikut jostled and wriggled like cubs seeking a teat, Tep's injuries sent small jolts of discomfort to his brain, but he ignored them in favor of the pleasure he felt, not sleeping alone. After all, he thought muzzily, if Velanda had only been ikut . . . this is what I really wanted all along.

When the train pulled into Black Peak Station, Tep got to his feet. "Where do you think you're going?" Fenag queried him.

"I am going to the palace. Velanda will not speak with me if I merely call her, so I will present myself in person. Remain here—I have already spoken with the train's driver. We will not depart for over three hours, because station workers must purge the toilet tanks and replenish the dining car's supplies." The unintended apposition of two such incompatible activities, as if material was to be transported from the first place to the second, struck Fenag as funny, and before he stopped laughing and considering that, Tep was gone.

Tep had not walked around in Black Peak before, so he did not really know the way, but he knew two things: the aspect from his bedroom window in the palace had been southerly, and it was very high up. Too, he had gained an impression that the successive levels of occupied excavations that made up the bors town were widest at the bottom, and became smaller higher up, matching the slope of the mountain's face outside. The streets—the ways, they were called—were well marked, and there were water-lift elevators at almost every intersection. Tep was grateful for those, because his muscles soon became sore, and his skin felt oddly tight where hard scar tissue drew it up. Every movement seemed to elicit crackling noises, as if he had been fried, not cut and torn. He welcomed those sensations, though, because he knew that his activity was flexing his scars and would speed the breakdown of keloid tissues into ordinary skin and muscle. Still, his weakness went deeper than his visible wounds, and by the time he reached a level small enough to see from one end of its single street to the other, his legs were trembling uncontrollably.

He approached the only lift in sight, one much more ornate than any of the others had been. It was gold-shiny, not bronze-dull, and was manned by a uniformed bors operator. "Take me up, please," he requested, trying to make it sound like a polite command—and trying to keep his voice even, and not to pant.

"This car accesses only the municipal palace, Sar Ikut. Have you an invitation?"

"I am a dear friend of the lady Velanda," Tep replied.

"We often studied together at Metok University. I am unexpected. Because my train is delayed for restocking, I decided to say hello, but I have only a short time, so take me up at once."

"I must call ahead, Sar Ikut. What is your name?"

Against his wishes and better judgment, Tep told him. He did not think Velanda had any other ikut acquaintances of note, so he could not really use another name. The bors shuffled to the back of the elevator cab, and keyed an intercom—after pointedly removing his key from the lift's operation panel. After speaking in a low voice, he then turned to Tep. "Please wait here, Sar Tep. An escort will arrive shortly."

Tep waited. Hearing a commotion at the end of the short street, from whence he had come, he peered in that direction. There were six bors coming his way. He recognized one of them. "Vols!" he called out. "Vols—have you come to take me to Velanda? I must speak with her."

Vols was in the lead of the group. All but he were in uniform. "Ah—Tep. Why are you here? I thought Tabir explained that my sister does not wish to see you—or has something transpired?"

"Did she tell you what happened?" Tep blurted. "Don't you know?" Surely Velanda had not kept her secret from her family. How could Vols be so offhand about it?

"I know of nothing that concerns you, Tep," Vols replied, his expression seeming genuinely puzzled. "Is it to do with Uncle Frant's proposal for your shahm? Do you have an answer for him? You should have told the stationmaster, who would notify him. That does not concern Velanda."

"Velanda is pregnant!" Tep rumbled, hopefully too low for the other bors to hear. "We must discuss the babies."

Vols again looked puzzled—and he looked offended as well. "How do you know that? That is a family matter. How dare you speak of it!"

"A family matter? Did she tell you who the father is?

It is *me*, Vols! She carries my children. I must speak with her."

Vols's dark-furred face stiffened, and his ears lay flat against his skull. His large hazel eyes narrowed to thin slits. "You have gone too far, ikut!" he murmured angrily. "What matter who sires a pair of cubs? We are bors here. We are civilized folk, not shaggy ice-hoppers. Be gone now! Cease meddling in things you cannot understand."

Tep was taken aback by the other man's intensity. He had considered Vols a pleasant dinner companion and a humorous fellow. He now saw the bors in another light entirely—an arrogant fritterling, a cold stranger who stood between him and . . . and his cubs. "I understand what I understand!" he spat. "You cannot deny me my rights! Move aside. I must see her."

Vols backed up two steps, and the other five bors advanced. "There is no getting through to this . . . this foreigner," he snarled. "Remove him. Escort him to his train." The bors surrounded Tep, who drew himself up to his full height—an unaccustomed move that brought fresh new jabs and sparkles of pain in his back, ribs, and shoulders.

A bors grasped his wrist. "Come, Sar Tep," he said. "Do not make us use force." Tep shook his arm, which sent the smaller bors staggering away.

"Velanda!" Tep roared. "She has my babies!" He pushed toward the lift, intending to take the key from the operator. Again, bors surrounded him, grasping wrists and forearms. Again, he flung them away and pressed forward toward the cowering operator, who had the key in his hand.

Tep felt something cold and sharp prod his spine from behind, and suddenly agony spread from that touch! Tep's fur stood on end. It crackled with blue-sparked static, and his arms flung themselves out from his sides, unbidden. A yowl formed in his throat, but it came out as a breathless croak. He crumpled to the stone-tiled street.

Tep felt the hands that pulled and lifted him. He heard muttered complaints about his bulk and weight.

He heard Vols say, "Don't be too rough on him—he's a nice fellow, for an ikut, and he already looks the worse for wear."

"Rough," for those bors, was quite relative. Discovering that the five of them together could not lift and carry him, they settled for dragging him by his legs. Tep struggled to free himself, but his limbs failed to respond; they only tingled and prickled and shuddered as if he held his finger in an electrical socket. His head sparked and sparkled inside, too, and his eyes refused to focus, so he was not able to see where they took him. Evidently—or so he surmised later—someone found a cart or a wheeled pallet, and they rolled him on that. At least the wrenching agonies in knee, hands, and hip as he was dragged ceased, and were replaced with bumping, battering jolts to whatever parts of him he guessed were "down."

"Tep? Tep! Drink this!" Tep realized he was sitting up. At his left, next to his face, something flashed and flickered, a white, irregular light. His cheek, leaning against the light's source, felt cold. For that matter, everything felt cold, which was odd, because he determined that the flashing white light was a window, a train window, and most trains were kept much warmer than was comfortable for ikut. Tep was confused. There seemed to be a great gap in his memory. Had they reached Black Peak yet? He had to get off there. There was something he had to do. . . .

"Drink some soup, Tep! You're shivering. Those bors used a shock-prod on you, didn't they?"

Slowly, Tep's memory returned and his disorientation faded. "How did I get here?" he asked, sipping rich, fishy-tasting broth, holding the flimsy disposable cup in both hands.

"A bunch of bors carried you on board," Fenag said. "They said you'd be all right, but to tell you not to come back. They said for you to keep out of their family matters. What, exactly, did you *do*, Tep?"

Between sips, shakily, Tep told Fenag the details of his and Velanda's expedition—the personal elements he had left out, before. "So now they won't let me near her. She doesn't want to talk with me, they say."

"That's *inhuman*, Tep!" Fenag was indignant and appalled. "She's carrying your cubs! They have no *right*! You're the father—even if the cubs are going to be . . . ah . . . even if they're not . . ."

"Even if they're going to be furless as fish? As Consul Martinez?"

"Uh . . . yes. Like that. They're still your cubs, Tep."

"Just so," Tep agreed—though without much enthusiasm. "Inhuman," Fenag had said, and Tep had not disagreed with him. Tep was not an anthropologist, but he knew as much as the next educated man about the seven races of humanity. Inhuman? Not really. Mantee males made a big deal out of siring infants on their fat throngmothers, but once the infants were given to their breastmothers, their nursemothers, the males didn't pay much intention to them. And didn't fard mothers drive off their female cubs even before they were weaned?

Bors, Tep admitted, did not think much of fathers. Was Vols mad because Tep had sired half-breed cubs on his sister, or because he, Tep, had tried to usurp Vols's own position, his responsibility toward his sister's cubs?

"Inhuman," Fenag had said. But what was "human"? Bors, mantees, ikuts . . . He was ikut, so he loved cubs, his own cubs, even unborn ones. Vols was bors. Did he love those cubs too? Did Tep's entirely normal, but ikut, drive conflict with Vols's bors, but also entirely normal, one?

Fenag, whether he thought Tep was thinking deeply or was asleep, kept silent.

The races were so different, Tep mused. If the Arbiter, or his ancestors, had been so smart, why hadn't they planted bors colonies on one world, ikut on another, and mantees somewhere else, all by themselves? No—Tep knew why. There had not been time, or ships, for that. Wherever the races had originated, the original John Minder and his successors had been in a hurry. Hadn't all the colonists been in cold sleep or something, on the ships? How long could they have remained so without degrading or dying? When those ship captains found a good planet, they had plunked down colonists wherever they could—bors in the mountains, mantees by the water. . . The rest was up to them, to bors, mantees, ikuts, and the rest.

He considered Glaice. The three races didn't mix much. Places like Black Peak and Rabant were bors towns. No ikuts lived there, and no bors hung around North Camp. Tep envisioned the elaborate ikut and mantee migration patterns in a new light; there was more to it than just getting the right nutrients. The real genius of Apootlak's design was that it kept the ikut and mantees *apart* even while allowing them equal access to resources. Did the mantees get something special from what they ate during their mating and breeding seasons, something comparable to ikuts' need for zinc?

Tep pondered further. Mantees, bors, and ikuts needed each other. Ikuts traded nutrient-rich fish for bors tools, cables, and navigational instruments. Mantees and ikuts traded, or used to trade, whenever their paths crossed. For a moment Tep wondered what bors did to get zinc. Or didn't they need it, as ikuts did? Tep knew that zinc had something to do with ikut reproduction, specifically with the late maturation of males, and how everyone started out like females. But that was not relevant now. The main thing was that the varietal humans stayed apart, most of the time.

They met at the borders between territories, or where ice floe encountered equatorial island. Exchanges were often ritualized and formal, and each group was quite cautious of the other. Problems occurred when someone broke the rules, mostly—the rules that kept them apart. The Ketonak started the present conflict when they willfully disrupted their ordinary migration pattern.

Tep's problems stemmed from breaking the rules, too. When his parents had found out that he had been playing with Kurrolf, a mantee, they had not been happy about it. Neither had Kurrolf's nursemother. The adults had then done nothing, because the ikuts were almost ready to leave, and the problem would dissolve with distance. Yet it had not. Tep, an ikut, had expected an ikut-like reaction from Kurrolf, there on Drumlin Way, but he had encountered cold hostility and clannishness.

He had not expected what he had gotten outside the Last Atopak, either. He did not understand mantee hunting frenzy. The rules, the distance they promoted, would ordinarily have made that knowledge irrelevant. Then, when they caught him, he had expected to die—but Kurrolf had risked his own place among the mantees to save Tep, though in a strange and bloody way. Tep had interpreted that as the act of a friend, and as honorable. But was it friendly? Was honor even a consideration, or was it, for Kurrolf, something utterly mantee, and untranslatable?

His affair with Velanda had broken rules too—bors and ikut ones, ones all the races of man espoused. There, the immediate consequence was clearer than some—babies that would not fit anywhere except as orphans among the old-humans. What had ensued since then, including Tep's forcible ejection from Black Peak, had reflected differences less biological, but no less real. There seemed no good way to resolve such a situation . . . except to avoid it in the first place—which, Tep admitted, most people did, and sensibly so.

Obviously, places like Metok promoted such problems, places where different kinds of people worked side by side in classrooms, libraries, and labs, where the common factors of classes, grades, papers, and assignments overwhelmed the sense of difference mantees and ikut ordinarily felt, seeing each other across a stretch of open water or across the trampled dirt of a trading ground . . . or that Tep had felt in his palace bedroom, high in Black Peak.

The structure and the formality, the separate and exclusive territories and uses of the land that defined mantee, bors, and ikut, kept things clear in everyone's head, Tep decided. An ikut in Black Peak, a bors trader visiting North Camp or a mantee island, *knew* he was on foreign ground, and acted accordingly. He did not play with cubs, make sweet-talk with girls, or joke with people's grandfathers. He saw things clearly—the things that counted, and that he could count on, things like the self-interest of his trade partner, and the likelihood that he would honor a bargain once made, whether or not he was "honorable" in the way the trader defined it.

"Ah, Fenag," Tep sighed, emerging from his deep thoughtfulness. "I have been a fool, haven't I?"

Fenag, who had no desire to fiddle around with bors women—or any women, yet—or to renew acquaintances with childhood friends who were mantees, or to confront bors whom he had eaten dinner with (which of course he had not) agreed enthusiastically with Tep's self-assessment.

In Tebuk, they hired four moxen from the same trader as before. "Why are they so expensive?" Tep asked, dismayed. "The last time they were not."

"You did not buy the last two, yet they are not here, munching fodder, either. Their bones are scattered about, and I assume that what little flesh they possessed now makes up part of a bors and an ikut, or else of fulfs that live far out from here. Am I wrong? Only bring these four back intact and uneaten, and I will buy them back less the cost of their lease." Tep agreed that the liveryman was not unreasonable.

The voyage to Pootorap was uneventful, though arduous and not comfortable even at night. Tep was glad to see that the steady winter wind blew snow across their back trail immediately, obscuring it. No fulfs—if they ventured out at all in such nasty weather—would be able to trail them. Fenag, as unimpressed with stick-and-fabric tents as Tep had once been, tried unsuccessfully to cut blocks of snow into building materials. "Poor Kelisat," he remarked. "If the snow is no better wherever she is, I hope her little tent is better than ours is."

"It is exactly the same," Tep told him, then changed the subject. He did not want to think about Kelisat's suffering.

* * *

Kelisat herself would have preferred not to think about that, but it was impossible not to. The snow on the glacier was, if anything, drier and more friable than it had been on the moraine. When her raw nose and ice-fettered toes had become life-threatening, not just uncomfortable, she had laboriously chopped a shelter into an exposed bank of crystalline firn, snow that was well on its way to becoming glacial ice. She had remained there five days, recuperating.

Now she was back on the open ice again, checking the last possible places the Charter could be. If, due to some one-of-a-kind rockfall or weather shift, Apootlak's hypothetical cache had been pushed laterally within the flowing ice mass, and had hung up in a rocky pocket at one side of the glacier, it might never have moved downward at all. If it was not here somewhere just below the crags and cirques of the glacial head, then it was truly lost.

Kelisat promised herself another four days. In that time, the batteries that powered her search instrument would cease to function, and then she would begin the long hike downward, successful or not. Would Tep be there to welcome her into North Camp? Would he be happy to see her even if she did not have the Charter? What then? She supposed he would return to Metok and forget about her. She chided herself: "Such thoughts will not help you survive," she said aloud to herself, over the constant swish and hiss of snow driven by the incessant, cutting wind.

"You mean we have to thaw them out?" asked Fenag, dismayed. The younger ikut had been amazed, enthralled, and overwhelmed during this first trip downward into the depths of the Pootorap pingo. Here were his ancient and illustrious ancestors, laid out in all their primitive finery. Here were the spears they hunted with, the bone-beaded parkas they wore on the late ice, and the worshipful gifts of their families, their descendants. Fenag observed the stern expressions of bold fish hunters, and the grandmotherly grins of old women whose teeth were worn down to nubs. He squinted at inscribed gorgets and tablets whose ancient words he could not read, and he pretended to warm his hands over the lamp lit glow of their opalescent pink-and-vermilion jewels. "You didn't say we had to cut any of them open, Tep," he protested.

"I did too. I told you I needed two kinds of samples—what they ate in the summertime, and what they ate in the winter. I did say we would not have to duplicate Rakulit's samples, which he got by extracting little drill cores from their buttocks, but that was all."

"I thought you meant we would take food from jars of grave offerings, ones like I saw in those books Rakulit showed me. I do not want to cut open my ancestors."

"What you thought is of no account. If you will not help me, then find something else to do. Why don't you start by hiking back up and getting the saws, the hydraulic jack to break the bodies loose from their frozen beds, and the racks of sample vials?" Fenag was glad to do that.

Tep began his task by mounting a tripod over his first chosen "victim's" abdomen. He then suspended a tightly focused microwave dish from the tripod, and threaded its power leads to its power source. Then, while it hummed softly and began to thaw portions of the corpse, he reviewed his notes. Only those burials that could be clearly identified as to the time of year that they had died would be of use to him. Chief among them were burials with gorgets or tablets that said "died in high summer, his favorite season," or "crushed between floes in the spring breakup." Tep's knowledge of ancient Universal was not extensive, but between the translations Emeritus Barm had made and a copy of the emeritus's handwritten glossary, he managed to get the gist of most of the inscriptions. He was not sure he could trust unwritten evidence like a shriveled nosegay of touch-me-nots, but he had a degree of confidence in the bed of spruce boughs under one body, obviously laid there with tenderness, a soft deathbed. The length of the spruce "candles," the new year's growth, indicated it had been cut in the springtime.

Fenag's squeamishness—or his respect for the dead—annoyed Tep, who could not suggest enough other work to keep him busy. "Just stay out of my way if you won't help," he muttered. "When dusk falls, go up and guard the moxen against fulfs, until I return."

Tep's gory work took a full two weeks. He thawed abdomens, carefully unbuttoned, unlaced, or slit open what garments his chosen "victims" wore, then slit open the abdomens themselves and carefully removed samples of the corpses' last meals. He carefully cleaned and sterilized his inox steel tongs and his chrome-plated ice-cream scoop after each extraction. He then sewed up his incisions as neatly as he could, and smoothed the fur over them. In most cases, even where the corpses were unclothed, the wounds he had made were not obvious, though a few times he had to thaw out an arm and drape it over a botched cut.

Finally it was finished. Still slightly annoyed with Fenag, he watched while the youngster carried everything up the long grade to the surface. In the morning they would set out to the northwest, as he and Velanda had done, and would catch the train at midpoint between Tebuk and Fulag.

Tep had been careful not to form any emotional attachment with any of the four moxen. He had not even bothered to learn their names, and had stifled their attempts at conversation with him. Fenag, not knowing any differently, had imitated his way with them. Still, considering how Fenag had felt about carving open dead people who could not complain, he was dubious how his suggestion for dealing with the moxen would be entertained.

He need not have been concerned. Fenag, without the least squeamishness, held no qualms about disposing of their beasts of burden. "The liveryman will not give us any money back if we merely send them home by themselves," Fenag said. "We would be wasting the consul's money if we did not put them to good use, by eating them—that small part of them that is edible."

"Good!" Tep exclaimed. "Then as I have done all the butchering up to now, it is your turn. And do not snack while you do so—what little tasty flesh they possess is much better roasted. I will start a fire." He began digging for buried grasses and freeze-dried dwarf birch twigs.

After the most delicious meal either of them had enjoyed in a long time, both men settled back beside their small fire prior to retiring to the tent. The railroad's bermed roadway sheltered them from the west winds, and the sky above was clear and starry. Tep wondered where, in the great swath of hazy starlight, lay the star Prime, about which orbited Newhome, where the Arbiter lived. Despite the dim light of their camp lantern, Tep's eyes drooped, and he may have dozed. Half-asleep, he was aware that something was not quite right. The fire, when he had shut his eyes, had been little more than embers, but now the light of fresh flames flickered against his eyelids. He leaped up. "What is burning?" he cried.

Fenag, still seated, looked surprised. "Nothing is burning, Tep. You must have been dreaming." For some reason he held one hand closed in a fist. Tep looked first at Fenag, then at the camp lantern, and finally at the spot he himself had recently occupied, all of which were in a straight line, with Fenag in the middle. A suspicion, half-formed, because a certainty. "Fenag! What are you hiding in your hand?"

Fenag reluctantly opened his fist, which revealed . . . a fire opal. "You would not desecrate your ancestors' bodies? Yet you rob their graves of their treasures!"

"I did not!" Fenag said. "I took it from a grave niche that had no body in it, only this stone and one of those slates."

"Ah! And you think that is a lesser crime? Velanda surmised that those lone jewels, and the inscriptions that accompany them, are the only relics of folk who died, but whose bodies were lost and not recovered.

Shame, Fenag! I merely removed a few bits of food the dead could not digest anyway, but you have stolen the last remnant of someone, leaving nothing behind but words. Give me that!"

Shamefacedly, Fenag handed Tep the jewel, whose sparkling refractions in the lantern's light had first awakened him. He pushed it into a half-empty pouch on his belt, promising himself he would return it someday.

CHAPTER 18

TO: Martinez
FROM: Arbiter

Jake, I'm sorry. Ask me one more time, and I'll feel obliged to explain my decision—and I don't want to do that. I don't want it written down, anywhere. The Glaice Charter—the original data-module recording of it—is terribly important. How important? Consider that I have read your dispatches; I know the risks, and I have kept track of the casualties thus far. I know you are faced with a planet on the verge of genocidal war—yet that has not changed my mind. Push the ikut boy as hard as you have to. He is, I think, my last hope.

The train arrived during the night and, responding to the several reflectors Tep had placed along the tracks south of their camp, rumbled to a halt not twenty paces from their tent. Shortly, they were on their way to Metok again.

When they arrived, and had toted the sample vials and notes to the laboratory, Fenag displayed none of the squeamishness he had in the ice cave. Perhaps, Tep thought, his shame over the fire opal had improved his attitude. Their first task was to examine a portion of each sample for content.

Were those small bone fragments from *redopati*, rodents that ikuts usually fried in fish oil and ate whole? Careful comparison against the zoology lab's study skeletons was required to be sure. Microscopic analyses of pollens washed and filtered from each sample either confirmed or contradicted Tep's original estimates of the season of death, when pollen grains were matched against those in the lab's computer database of pollen types. Tep set seven samples aside as ambiguous—a burial dressed in winter hunting gear, for example, proved to have featherdown pollen in its stomach. Featherdown bloomed in midsummer, and ikuts ate only the fresh flowers, not the toxic leaves or stems.

No specimen vial was opened except within a sealed isolation chamber, where it was manipulated with robotic "hands"; no risk was taken that the second phase of the testing might be contaminated by anything in the lab. When all the samples' contents had been catalogued, Tep was ready to begin phase two—radiocarbon dating of selected foods.

That phase did not take as long as the first, even though over three hundred vials remained to be fed into the anlab, ten at a time. "That is a good job for you, Fenag," Tep said, stretching. "I will get some sleep so I am ready for the important work tomorrow and the day after." In spite of his words, Tep did not stay away long. Midway through the night he awakened, and returned to the lab to check up on Fenag's progress. Then, again, he slept for a few hours, but by first light he was back, and ran several batches while Fenag snored in an office chair nearby. By the following morning, the last analyses had been run.

The two ikuts spread printouts over the lab benches—neither of them had any desire to test the atmosphere of the refectory for congeniality, having been gone several weeks. Who knew how much further the hostilities had escalated? By midnight, Tep was droning his conclusions into a voice-writer's microphone, and by dawn he flourished his finished report in front of Fenag's sleepy face. "Read that," he said, slapping it down in front of his apprentice. "Then we will pay Consul Martinez a visit."

"But that's not fair!" Tep protested. "Look at those dates! Examine the evidence carefully." Fenag, sitting next to Tep on the far side of the consul's desk, merely observed.

Consul Martinez shrugged. "Let us go over everything

one more time," he suggested. "I will state how I believe things to be, and you may correct me if at any time I stray from the documented facts at hand." Tep agreed to that.

"First," Martinez said, "those ikuts who had atopak meat in their stomachs also had traces of summer pollens or fresh summer foodstuffs in them. That demonstrated that the atopak were in the shallows, where they could be caught, in the summer months. The presence of atopak roe in some stomachs, confirmed by DNA comparisons with both the atopak flesh from the burials and from the earlier specimen you dissected, tell us that the atopak migration to the shallows was for the purpose of spawning." He raised an eyebrow—an old-human expression Tep had learned to interpret as either skepticism or a desire to have his words confirmed. Tep nodded his assent. "Further," Martinez said, "your radiocarbon dates on unchewed gobbets of atopak meat indicate that the meat is up to a thousand years older than those ikuts who ate it—older, in fact, than the earliest evidence of man on Glaice." Again, when the eyebrow prompted him, Tep nodded.

"Second," Martinez continued, "those ikuts who died in winter—which you have confirmed by several indicators including the presence of fragmentary *ferinap* bones." Ferinap, being migratory birds that summered only in the high arctic, had mostly land meat in them, unlike ritvak and other species common to the coastal plains and lower plateaus. "Radiocarbon dates on those meats all indicate that the animals lived during a period from shortly after 800 R.L. to shortly before one thousand. Am I right so far?" Tep agreed that he was.

"Finally," he said, "the flesh of those latter individuals was dated by Professor Rakulit to the period 380 to 595 R.L. That summarizes the 'raw' evidence. From that evidence, you have concluded that the land-meat dates represent the actual age of the burials, since those creatures had no obvious source of 'old' radiocarbon, and you suppose that Rakulit's ikut-flesh dates represent a distorted 'average' between the actual dates and the much older ones that the atopak give. You have also tested chips of wood from spear shafts and bits of land-animal hide from the clothes of some burials, which confirm your 800 to 1000 R.L. estimates for the burials themselves. Have I missed anything?" Tep shook his head.

The consul then scribbled something on his desk pad, and projected it onto the screen on the wall to the left of Tep and Fenag:

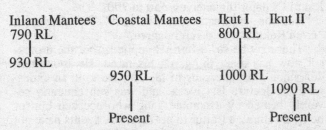

Inland Mantees	Coastal Mantees	Ikut I	Ikut II
790 RL		800 RL	
930 RL			
	950 RL	1000 RL	
			1090 RL
	Present		Present

"Does that approximate what you believe the actual historic sequence to have been?" the consul asked.

"Just so!" Tep said. "It is obvious that mantees and ikuts arrived on Glaice at the same time—around 800 R.L.—and that the present populations are lineal descendants of those settlers. No other conclusion is possible!"

Consul Martinez shook his head sadly. Tep was unable to interpret his exact expression, though if he had seen that fleeting look on an ikut face—drooping eyelids and a head turned slightly to one side, and eyes not meeting his own—he would have wondered what that ikut was ashamed of, or what he had to hide. "You and Professor Rakulit both accept the inland mantee dates, 790 R.L. to 930 R.L., as accurate," the consul stated, "and the later ikut dates as well, subject to possible skewing. Those begin, you believe, between 990 and 1190 R.L. and continue to the present. Further, you have astutely shown that the early ikut can be dated as early as 800 R.L." He made a looping motion with his stylus, and a rough circle appeared around the "Coastal Mantees" column on the wall. "There," he said, "is the problem."

"What problem?" Tep queried indignantly, sitting forward in his chair, his fur standing out on his neck. "The inference is clear! A marine diet caused Rakulit's dates to be falsely old. My estimate of 950 R.L. is *conservative*! They may actually be later—as late as 1200."

"Yet it is, as you say, Tep, only an *estimate* based on an *inference*. The only 'hard' evidence is still Professor Rakulit's dates themselves, 650 to 790."

"But the implication is obvious!" Tep protested. "Even Rakulit would surely agree."

"That may be so," Martinez replied, "but the professor now has other things on his mind. He spoke out, denouncing the accuracy of his own work, in an undergraduate lecture last week, and was subsequently severely beaten by a mantee gang who accused him of being a sellout, a traitor to his race. My agents have not apprehended any gang members; there are so many gangs, now." He sighed. "I do not think Professor Rakulit will be of much help to you."

"That is no matter," Tep said. "*You* know the truth! Tell the Arbiter what we have found. Surely, he will send poletzai to quell these mantee gangs. Then Rakulit can speak out without fear, and this insanity will be ended."

"Tep, Tep," said the consul, holding his hands out palms up as if to quell the ikut's internal tempest, "I have been in frequent communication with the Arbiter. You must understand that he cannot send poletzai to every world having local difficulties. Could his warships, from orbit around Glaice, stop mantees from swimming under ikut flows and detonating explosives? Could missiles and lasers aimed from orbit stop ikut bands from raging across mantee islands without killing ikut and mantees alike? Can Glaice afford to maintain offworld policemen on every corner in every town to prevent the resurgence of the gangs, once the poletzai depart? No, this is an internal matter, Tep, and it must be settled here on Glaice, not on Newhome."

"But what can I do?" Tep asked desperately. "What evidence must I obtain that will convince you to act?"

"I think you know that, Tep."

"The Charter," Tep growled. "That's what you want, isn't it?"

"You must admit it would resolve everything, and in a way everyone could understand."

Tep had no reply to that. The Charter. Somehow, despite his efforts, the consul always came back to it. Tep lifted himself heavily from his chair. "I will not waste time pleading with you," he said. "I must report what I have discovered to my shahm, and find out what he wants me to do next." He bade goodbye to Consul Martinez and departed. Fenag followed him out.

"He is lying, isn't he?" Fenag asked when they were out in the street. "Our evidence is good enough!"

"What makes you think he's lying? Why would he?"

"Because he just doesn't care about evidence. He doesn't care about anything but that damned Charter!"

Tep nodded silently. "On the face of it, I would say you are right. But *why*?"

Consul Martinez spoke, though no one else was in his office anymore. "Memo to John Minder, confidentiality level one," he said.

"Ready for message," said the AI that handled such tasks. Its voice seemed to emanate from a point just left of the consul's head, whichever way he turned it. Martinez was used to it, but he did not use the AI when others were present, because it seemed to disconcert them. Even his secretary had not gotten used to the disembodied voice.

"Against my express wishes and my better judgment, I am again pressing forward with your plan," he said. "I have once again obfuscated with the ikut, Tep Inutkak, and have—hopefully—discouraged him from the archaeological course I formerly supported him on, and have set him back on the trail of the elusive Charter.

"John, I cannot stress emphatically enough that this is a risky scheme. With Tep's evidence, and the mantee Rakulit's cooperation, I could defuse the tensions here. The index stands at a present high of zero-point-seven-eight and will surely go higher, and without decisive intervention, genocidal war is almost inevitable." He sighed. Why did Minder want that particular data module so badly? What else was on it? It had to be something really old, something from long before the ikut had brought the module to Glaice. "If I knew what it was," he muttered, "maybe I'd feel better about screwing over the poor dumb ikut."

"Query last sentence," his AI said. "Apparent non sequitur."

"Delete the last sentence, please," Martinez said. "Continue from what I said about the tension index." The AI repeated that sentence. "Conclude and sign off," the consul dictated. "Send it priority prime. End memo."

As the seasons slowly changed across the face of Glaice's ice and oceans, so they changed elsewhere. Newhome, larger and less dense than Glaice, with less ocean and more habitable land, changed according to its own unique constraints. John Minder and his family had recently moved to the Winter Palace—one of several winter palaces, actually.

This one, high on a rocky spine that wound north and south across Newhome's equator, had balconies that looked out over thick forests broken here and there by roads and rivers, spotted with villages, marred in two places by the gray spread of towns.

Newhome, said the folk of the Xarafeille Stream, was a microcosm of the human-settled fragment of the galaxy. There dwelt folk of all seven races, and in the interactions between them the Arbiter studied the larger conflicts that arose between men out among the far-flung stars. Yet, Rob Minder reflected, there was no place on a glacier or an ice floe, or even on a "tropical" isle that remained free of snow only seven months out of a long Newhome year. There was, he was sure, no true microcosm of Glaice on the Arbiter's laboratory world.

"That was dirty, Dad," Rob Minder said. "That poor guy Tep was doing everything right."

"I don't disagree with you, son," Minder responded.

"And Consul Martinez was right too. With Tep's evidence, he could have staved off war on Glaice almost indefinitely. Of course, relations between the ikut and mantees would never have returned to what they were before the Ketonak atrocity, but . . ."

"How could you risk all those lives, even for the code module for your fleet?"

Minder gestured at the display that hung in the shadows of the broad stone dome over their heads. It was a holograph, without mass, but it sometimes seemed to Rob to be a bright, jeweled weight over his father's head and his own, a weight that might someday crush them. The projection depicted—though not all at one time—the whole of the Xarafeille Stream.

Responding to Rob's question, Minder asked, "How many people are up there?" That question was more exact than it seemed, because from any vantage point on the balcony rimming the dome, an observer saw the Xarafeille Stream exactly as he might if the dome had not been there, as if he were looking at the night sky itself, but enhanced, every star a colored gem, indicating population density, instead of a pale speck in a swath that, from outside, could have been only a moonlit cloud. "I must consider *that* context."

"I know that," Rob replied, "but it's hard to maintain perspective when what I see, what we talk about, is individuals like Tep. I can't bring myself to look at people like him as . . . tools."

"You should not have to do that, son," Minder said. "But an ideal universe would not need an Arbiter, either—or at least, not a helpless one like me."

CHAPTER 19

We Arbiters, old-humans all, have thus purposefully maintained the sense of repugnance that the furred races feel toward us. What bors or fard in his right mind would seriously consider conceiving and parenting repulsive, furless offspring? Of course that has led to social problems for old-humans, who are so universally shunned, but we old-humans created the problem in the first place, didn't we?

Individual races of man have provided their own solutions as well. Tarbeks, because of the solitary nature of their reproduction*, have no taboos against misogamy, which is so improbable as to be unthinkable. Fards, lacking the tarbek "advantage," have inculcated the ideal of racial "improvement" into their basal culture, and actively practice eugenics on a broad scale. The possibility of a foreigner infiltrating a mantee throng during their mating frenzy is hard to imagine, and bors also have a certain edge, brought on by minor biochemical disparities. . . .

John Minder IV,
Unpublished Manuscript,
Erne Museo, Newhome, 4321 R.L.

"Are you sure you don't want to come with me?" Tep asked Fenag. "How long has it been since you were home?" He gestured at the waiting train.

"Last cycle," Fenag replied, "but I think I'll stay here. That way, if you need anything done, you can hike into Tebuk and use the terminal to call me."

Tarbek males deposit semen in warm pools that females of their kind frequent, and consider physical contact between the sexes to be quite disgusting—Ed.

"Well then . . . be careful. This town isn't safe anymore. Maybe you should dye your fur black or something."

"I can take care of myself," Fenag insisted. "*You* be careful, and don't get off the train at all, in Black Peak."

Before the train had drawn completely to a halt in Black Peak Station, Tep was on his feet, waiting at the door. He was ikut, and male, and people like him did not give up, where cubs were at stake, unless they were more thoroughly broken than Tep had been. Still, he was no fool. He would not put himself needlessly in jeopardy; he would again try calling Velanda. He would tell whoever answered that his name was Berran Fendo, that he was an archaeology student, and that he had a message for her from Professor Rakulit. He suspected that Velanda herself did not even know he had tried to get in touch. Once he was on the line with her . . .

"Oh!" exclaimed Tabir, answering the call. "Lady Velanda is not taking calls. What did you say your name was?" Tep repeated it. "I do not think that is so," Tabir stated. "I think I know who you are, though I will not say it aloud. Sar Vols has instructed me to rebuff you immediately if you called." Tep, not being expert in disguising his voice, decided that this last effort had failed—until Tabir continued. . . .

"The Lady Velanda, however, gave me different instructions," she said. "I am to tell you to wait at the station, where she will meet you. She will arrive as soon as she can." Tabir disconnected.

Tep had almost a quarter-hour to adjust his thinking to this new turn of events—though when Velanda arrived, in the company of a rather stumpy bors male, he was no less confused than before. He had not recognized her at once, even though he had expected her to have a bulging abdomen, from a distance, she looked merely short and rather middle-aged.

"Oh, Tep!" she blurted. "I am so sorry! I did not intend for you to be hurt, the last time. I should have come myself."

"The cubs?" Tep said, far too abruptly. "How are the cubs?"

Velanda looked confused. Then her eyes dropped to her slightly protruding belly. "You mean my cubs?" she asked. "Why . . . I am sure they are doing well." She shook her head as if to deny something. "Tep, there is something you must be told. There has been a terrible misunderstanding. Please, hear me out."

"I will," Tep rumbled, "but you must understand that I am ikut, not bors! We must work things out. We must compromise, not merely do things the bors way."

"That is what you must understand. There is no need for compromise, Tep."

"You are wrong! You cannot just dismiss me. We must make arrangements concerning the cubs."

"Tep, they are *not* your cubs! You are not the father of my cubs. They are entirely bors cubs! I am sorry. I wanted to break it to you easily, but you are so precipitous . . ."

Tep could not reply immediately. Not the father? But how could that be? "Ah!" he said. "That is a low trick. I suppose there is some fine bors distinction between 'father' and 'sire'? Do not quibble, Velanda."

"There is no such distinction. Tep, I *was* pregnant, as I told you—as I should never have told you—but those cubs died unborn. I am now pregnant by my mate, Aluf Hadlo, who is standing right over there." Velanda stood panting, as if her effort to blurt everything out before Tep could override her with further misunderstanding had taken all her breath away.

Tep had also gasped, but with shock and disbelief. "You are lying! My cubs are not dead." He glanced toward the husky bors who kept position several yards away, but who eyed him carefully. Bors gave fatherhood short shrift, but that did not make bors men less concerned or possessive of their mates, especially since by the act of mating, they bonded with that one female for the rest of their reproductive years.

"Tep, we bors often lose a first-conceived pair of cubs. It is expectable. And they were not ordinary cubs. They were . . . incompatible. I lost them the very day I arrived here. Oh, Tep, I am so sorry. I thought you would know all that!"

Tep did not believe her, she could see. "I was a fool, Tep. I did not really understand how you ikut men feel about children. If you had been a bors . . . it would not have mattered so much. If you had been a bors, you would have bonded to me, and would not care about cubs, except your sister's. But you are ikut, and you did not imprint on me—which is why I felt safe mating with you in the first place, and . . ." She put her face in both hands. Beneath them, Tep saw, she was weeping. Her bors mate shifted from one foot to the other, unsure whether to intervene. "I was so *confused,* Tep," Velanda cried. "I should have told you. I should not have made Tabir send you away, but I . . . I did not know *how* to tell you."

"So you had Vols and five thugs beat me up and shock me, instead?" Tep felt numb. Velanda was not acting. He was now convinced that she was telling the truth. His cubs were dead. Worse, they had never really been alive, no more so than a wart, less so than a bug, which could at least crawl away from its egg casing. Tep knew that. He knew that he had been worrying and suffering not over two fetuses with little arms and legs, little almost-people halfway between conception and birth, but over clusters of undifferentiated embryonic cells that had long since been sloughed off, rejected as incompatible with their host. Tep was numb. He knew that he would grieve later, not for the lost cells, but for what he had believed, that had never really been. But now . . .

"I did not send Vols to beat you up," Velanda stated. "Tembo used the shock rod, because he is only a boy, and he was afraid of you—you are a big ikut, Tep. I am sorry he did it, but I do not blame him; he is no larger than me."

Tep sighed. "And Vols," he said, "only reacted to me as a threat against *his* cubs—his sister's cubs, for whom he is responsible."

Velanda looked up in surprise at Tep's calm and

rational face. "You understand that? Oh, Tep! Now I am sorrier than ever that I did not trust you to understand."

"I am not so sure," Tep responded. "*Now* I understand, but only because I have been thinking about how different we humans are—bors, ikuts, and mantees. I do not know what I might have done, had you told me earlier."

Velanda wiped tears from her eyes, making the fur under them flat and shiny. "What are you going to do now?" she asked him.

Tep had told her nothing of his recent adventures and efforts, and he did not think that was what she meant. "I am going to the Inutkak," he said. "There is a girl . . . if she is back from hunting . . ."

"Oh! I am happy for you, Tep. Perhaps you will have cubs together—and if you and she visit here, they can play with mine."

Tep had not thought *that* far ahead. He had intended to tell her about Kelisat's search for the Charter, and his dilemma over what to do if she found it. Still, when he considered the new idea she had planted in his head, it did not seem preposterous at all. Kelisat? Cubs? Kelisat! He had not considered *mating* with Kelisat! As his thinking along those lines caught up with Velanda's, he considered the implications of what she had said, and was surprised by the odd heat he felt deep inside himself. Yet his thoughts quickly returned to her comment about cubs playing together, and the difficulties that messing around outside the subspecies boundary had caused him—first with Kurrolf, then with Velanda himself. "As for our cubs playing together," he said, "might that not confuse them about what they are, bors and ikut? I think that is what happened to us, in Metok and after. We were not sure, for a while, what we were—and we did not understand what we were *not*."

"I see," Velanda said in an icy tone that had not been apparent before. "You may be right—every time I think I *do* know what to expect from you, you surprise me again." She glanced toward her stolid mate. "I must go now, Tep. Aluf's forbearance must be near its end." She lifted her eyebrows, a wistful face. "We may not see each other again, at least for many years."

"I suppose not," Tep replied, feeling only relief, somewhere deep inside, underneath the dull agony of his perceived loss of the cubs. "It would be for the best."

Velanda nodded, unable to speak. She turned away, and hurried to her mate. Tep watched them depart, and then reboarded the train. He knew he would not quickly recover from this day's revelations, but he was eager to begin that process. He was free, he realized. It hurt, but he was free to be just what he was—ikut, and a man.

Shahm Hepakat eyed Tep by the light of a single oil lamp, aware, even before Tep recounted his litany of failures, of the changes in the young man who was a candidate for his own responsibilities. Hepakat himself had not been forged in as hot a fire as Tep; he was, he reflected, the product of a quieter time, and had been less inclined to fan flames others had kindled. Perhaps, he told himself, he would retire early when all this present turmoil was done with, and would see what Tep would do, as shahm. The boy obviously felt responsibilities as heavy as a shahm's, or heavier, and was holding up under them. Now he intended to add another parcel to Tep's load.

"Until the Ketonak disrupted the balance," he said, "the Inutkak—and I personally—enjoyed good relations with the Swift Current throng, and with Heloset, their throngmother. Yet my recent messages to her have had no replies . . . until this." He handed a slightly crumpled sheet of paper to Tep. "This came by courier, though my own messages went via satellite link to the government weather station on Farilan Island."

> Once I was throngmother to a single throng, Hepakat of the Inutkak. Then I oversaw many trades between my folk and yours, and welcomed your younglings to play with my own. Those days

are gone, perhaps forever. Life is not as nice as when we were young.

Your messages, seen by my opponents before I myself see them, bring suspicion upon me, and I dare not reply openly. Even a hint that this letter exists would mean my overthrow from the Council of Throngs, where I am a voice for reason still—a voice, some would say, of traitorous concession.

I cannot give your young man permission even to tread the "sacred soil" of our islands, let alone to dig and poke among the "relics of our ancestors." Should he choose to come here, I would have no choice but to preserve my position by ordering him slain.

Heloset, Throngmother,
Second Speaker, Council of Throngs

"So that's that," Tep said in disgust. "The last chance to prove that the hostility between us is needless . . . destroyed by that very hostility. What is she afraid of?"

"Don't judge her too harshly, Tep. Read between the lines. Heloset rides a current that cannot be diverted, and that at risk not only of her position, but her life. Mantees are more excitable than we ikut, and are often violent among themselves—witness Professor Rakulit's beating, for no greater offense than doubting his own data. Heloset merely wishes to survive—and to be on hand for that one moment when her reasonable vision might be heard, and might turn the tide of unreason."

The shahm shrugged. "Still, you are right. Our last hope rests upon Kelisat, now." Tep did not think there was much hope there, at all, but he kept his suspicion to himself. If by chance he was wrong, and Kelisat returned with the Charter, there would be new and painful decisions for him to make. If he was right, his choices would be no less painful.

A cub, Putanap, half-ran, half-rolled into Hepakat's house. "Kelisat!" he squealed. "Kelisat is back."

"I will meet her," said Tep, arising. "I will bring her here to report."

"She will be cold and exhausted, Tep," the shahm said. "Whatever she has—or has not—found, it can wait awhile." He smiled. "But go—your face will be a more pleasing sight to her than my old one."

Tep followed Putanap outside. "Where is she?" he asked, squinting, even though the sky was overcast.

"Perhaps she went home, Tep," the cub replied.

Sometimes, even after spending weeks here with the band, cubs' informality still surprised him. In Metok, a youngster would say "Sar Tep," as would most adults who were not close acquaintances. Here, he was just "Tep," most of the time. It was not disrespect; among the Inutkak a name *was* a title, and was imbued with a sense of what the name's holder had accomplished. If the great heroes of the past were to return today, cubs would not say "Sar Aripat," or "Sar Apootlak"—but the very breathlessness with which they spoke those names would be title and honorific enough.

When someone addressed a person in some specific capacity, he might say "*Shahm* Hepakat," or "*Hunter* Kelisat" . . . or, thought Tep, even "*Chief* Kelisat." But "Tep" had no such ring to it, and "Scholar Tep," as the cubs addressed him when he was teaching them, was not much better. How lucky Kelisat was, he thought enviously, to have stayed and worked her way up within the band. Everyone knew she was the best hunter; they saw her bring in her kills, and they partook of them. It would be nice to belong, like that, he thought. The promise of someday being shahm did not stretch very far, when few people knew anything he had done, and would not have been impressed, anyway. It was hard to be content with textureless "Tep."

There were fresh scufflings in the feathery drifts that had accumulated in front of Kelisat's house. Tep lifted the skin flap over the tunnel, and stuck his head in. "Kelisat? Lis?" No one answered him. He crawled into the entry tunnel, down through the cold trap, and up again. "Kelisat?" he said.

"Tep! You *are* here." Kelisat sighed from the sleeping shelf. A lamp was lit, but the small room was very cold. Not knowing when she would return, no one had warmed it for her beforehand. "I almost wish you had not been here," she said.

"Why is that?" he asked. She did not respond, but could not conceal her shivering. "You are cold!" he exclaimed. "Let's go see Shahm Hepakat. His house is quite warm."

"No! I have not been beneath a roof, a real roof, since I left here! I am not going outside again!"

"Then I will light more lamps. You will have a warm sleeping shelf in no time at all." He bustled about, finding four lamps. She watched him untwist their fiber wicks so they would hold more oil and would burn brightly. Ikut lamps were unsophisticated, no more than shallow stone or pottery bowls of oil with an extended, grooved lip on one side, where the wick lay.

Tep found an oilskin, filled the lamps, and set them about. The house filled with warm, smoky light. In his rummaging, he had found a stiff hide box half-full of old sweetbark, but no real food. "Are you hungry? I can get food from my parents. What would you like?"

"Fish! A big bowl of oily fish, and something—anything!—that is *hot*! Oh, Tep—I have never been so cold, for so long!"

"I will bring soup, too," Tep said, on his way back outside.

When Tep returned, Kelisat was asleep. He at first considered letting her rest—but the soup would get cold. He climbed up on the sleeping shelf, with a bowl in one hand—after hanging the larger soup pot from a peg and setting a lamp under it.

"Here, Lis. Be careful, it is more than warm." Her hands trembled so violently that he had to help her hold the bowl, his hands over hers. She spread her fingers wide to soak up the soup's heat through the bowl.

Kelisat savored that moment; soon, Tep would ask her how she had fared, and she would have to tell of her failure.

"I am so sorry, Kelisat," Tep murmured. "We . . . I . . . have made you suffer so."

He was sorry? How strange! It had been Hepakat's order, not his. He was not shahm, not yet. Not for a long time . . . but he would be. And until then . . . he would go back to Metok, to his black-furred bors female. . . . Oh, what was the use! There was no point in stalling further. "I did not find the Charter, Tep," she blurted.

"I know," Tep murmured, not taking his hands from hers. "That cannot be helped. The fault is mine, for allowing Hepakat to send you, on such a forlorn hope. Will you forgive me?" He lifted her hands and the soup bowl to her lips. "Drink more. You are still trembling." She drank, welcoming the opportunity not to reply. Forgive *him*? Nothing was happening as she had thought it would.

When the bowl was empty, Tep refilled it, and then brought her a plate of other things to eat—fat crustaceans, their shells already cracked, chunks of fish, and red meat, just thawed. She ate greedily. "Finally I am warm!" she said, settling contentedly onto the furs.

"Tomorrow," he said, "we will talk with Shahm Hepakat, and will decide what to do next. But for now . . ." Kelisat was suddenly disappointed. She had almost . . . almost . . . thought he was going to move closer to her, but instead, he was fumbling in his pouch. "For now . . . I have something for you."

It looked as though he held a glowing ember between his fingers. "Here," he said, pulling on her wrist, and placing the object on her palm. She tensed—but it did not burn. It was a crystal, a bright bauble that caught the light of the lamps and released it clarified and warm.

"It is lovely, Tep," she said, trying to force herself to sound enthusiastic—though the prettiest, strangest bauble was no substitute for . . . for what she had wanted from him. "What is it?"

She half-listed as Tep explained about opalescent crystals, inscribed slate gorgets, and the wonders he had seen in the caves of Etonak and Pootorap. "But you are exhausted," he said at last, misinterpreting her mood. "Here. You must sleep." He pattered her furs. "I will send a cub to wake you in the morning." He regained his feet awkwardly, half-slipping from sleeping shelf to floor.

How much nicer it would have been, she thought, once he had gone, if he had said, "I will wake you in the morning," and had then settled next to her. She held the fiery bauble up so it caught the lamplight and painted flickering fire-patterns on the roof over her head. It was not warm, though. Its false flame was cold, a poor substitute for real warmth, the kind of warmth she was afraid she would never feel.

CHAPTER 20

> The pingo burial caves are, unfortunately from the tourist's point of view, closed to the public. There are, however, several reputable shops in Metok and other sizable towns, where genuine (though unconsecrated) burial tokens can be purchased. Your Parkoon & Parkoon tour agent or guide will be glad to furnish a list of recommended sources.
>
> The tokens, lovely creations of naturally colored bird feathers, amber, whale ivory, and fish scales, are designed as mnemonics, and each feather or bead represents an ancestor or a notable event in a particular family line, enabling native wise men to recite the entire history of one who has died, without recourse to notes, computers, or other recordings.
>
> Parkoon & Parkoon Tourist Agency brochure

When Kelisat awoke—on her own, with no rowdy cub shaking her—she felt no warmer than she had when she went to sleep, though now her body was rested, and she was not—physically—cold. The stars were still out, and dawn was no more than a low haze along the horizon. Automatically, without conscious thought, she noted the height of Ferak, the Hunter's Star, above the conical silhouette of Shepag's Breast, the northernmost volcano of the ring of fire. Being a hunter, intimately familiar with the progression of stars and seasons she knew that the summer solstice was not far off.

In three short months, the snows would melt from North Camp, and the south-facing hills would become green. Shahm Hepakat would spend long days on the offshore ice, searching for the perfect floe, the perfect vehicle for the Inutkak's coming journey southward.

Even now, she thought, the Atulag band was surely settling in at South Camp—if they had survived their crossing of the equator, and had not run afoul of the shoals, or been attacked by mantees returning from their birthing rites, or been swept off course, to struggle desperately along the south coasts, clinging to a melting, cracking ice vessel.

The Tehokag band might, if all was well with them, be drifting already in sight of the mantee isles, their shahm peering outward from the highest crag or pinnacle of their ice, seeking the best channel, the perfect combination of wind and current that would propel his band westward and north through the equilateral current-races, and again outward, onto the broad, free northern sea.

Even now, the Warm Stream mantees would be struggling more directly north, some males towing the throngmother's fat bulk in her hammock of netting and fish bladders, others swimming farther out, encircling the throng. New nursemothers would be cresting the waves, swimming on their backs with their newborn charges clinging to fur and nipples. Half those infants would die before the throng reached their warm harbors, their forested caves.

For all of them, Atulag and Tehokag, mantees and Inutkak, it was a terrible, hard life. Only madness could account for them making it harder than it already was. Only madness—yet that was what faced all of them. Madness, the end of the perfect, precise dance of bands, throngs, winds, currents, and seasons, the end, perhaps, of mantees and ikut alike. Without the Charter, without *some* settlement for the hateful, growing dispute, would some future Glaice be left only to the black-furred, decadent bors huddling in their mountain caves, leaving all the rest of the world to the empty winds, to the mindless beasts and fishes?

"Without the Charter," Hepakat said, "we have no hope. . . ."

"I still think Heloset should . . ."

"Tep! Hold! What we discussed yesterday must never

be spoken of!" Hepakat was emphatic: Kelisat had not been apprised of the throngmother's message.

"But we don't *have* the Charter!" Tep exclaimed. Kelisat cringed inwardly. She had not found it—but had she missed it somehow? Had cold, fumbling hands and bleary, wind-reddened eyes conspired so that she had set the scanner wrong at one critical moment, or missed the subtle flicker of a dial that had registered an anomalous emanation far beneath the ice?

Her fingers even now ached with remembered cold. She stuck one of them in her pouch, where she carried a small bone vial of analgesic ointment, tallow infused with an extract from the spines of a tropical fish. Her hand bumped something hard and rounded.

"We don't have the Charter, and we can't get at the only other evidence that would render it unnecessary," Tep said.

"Then we must come up with other ideas of where to search for it," the shahm replied. "We have not searched the southern hemisphere glaciers, the one nearest South Camp." Kelisat again cringed. But no—though South Camp was a long way from Amberdin, the southern shuttleport, a message could be gotten through to the arriving Atulag. They would send their own hunters, if the southern glaciers need be searched. The consul had arranged for her to have the scanner—surely he could equally well order it sent to the Atulag. *She* would not have to go back on the ice. And anyway . . . "No one can search the south glaciers now," she said, tossing something back and forth between her hands, working to restore their nimbleness. "It is summer there, and the lower glaciers will be slick with meltwater and impossible to traverse."

"Then where else?" asked the shahm. "And stop tossing that data module, anyway! Your fiddling makes me twitch!"

Tep stared. Now Kelisat's fist was closed, but he had caught the warm firelike glimmer of what she held, what she had been tossing hand to hand. "Lis? Is that what I think it is?"

She opened her hand. The Pootorap fire-gem nestled

there, glowing softly by lamplight. Tep turned to Hepakat. "You called *that* a data module?" he said.

"It is a small one—no more than a few hundred gigabytes of data. Where did it come from, Kelisat? There are no computers here in North Camp—and unless I am mistaken, that one is far too old even for the students' computers in Metok. Most modern ones are green or blue."

"A data module," Tep breathed. "It is an *old* data module indeed. It is perhaps eleven thousand years old!

"Now I understand!" he said, standing up. "The inscribed gorgets! Now I understand what we found at Pootorap!"

"Then tell *me,*" demanded the shahm. "I too would like to know what has excited you so."

Tep explained where the crystal had come from, and how Kelisat had come by it. "It is a personal record!" he said, quite sure of himself now. "The early colonists who founded Latobak, the first city, must have kept their medical histories, their diplomas, résumés—who knows what all?—on them! When they died, they were buried with them."

"That is likely," Hepakat said, "but the gorgets?"

"When Latobak was abandoned—or perhaps even before that, when contact with other worlds was lost and when the Latobak machinery and computers began to fail—such data modules could no longer be read! The gorgets replaced them—pieces of slate, with only a few statements on them, and a name. It took thousands of years for the custom to die—we do not use such things today, having built a strong body of oral tradition to replace them, but think how important that sense of identity must have been for them!"

"So now you understand about gorgets," Kelisat remarked, not very impressed. "What good does that do us?"

"The fire opals are not baubles, they are data modules!" Tep said, as if that explained everything. He grinned. "I think I will give you the chance to find the Charter, Lis. Would you like that?"

"The Charter? The Charter is . . ." She had begun to say "lost." "The Charter is . . . one of those things?"

"A *big* one!" Tep said. "Like these, even to the color. The consul said 'vermilion,' which to my mind evoked katvak shells, not fire, but *that* is what he meant." He pointed at the crystal Kelisat held. "I am sure of it. And I am sure just where it is."

Tep paced, unable to contain his excitement. "We must go to Pootorap at once!"

The next several days were a blur of activity for Tep and Kelisat. Tep's camping gear was now all in Metok, so they had to make do with Kelisat's, and with what they could gather from other hunters.

The hike to Tebuk, towing a sled loaded with Inutkak gear that was much heavier and bulkier than Tep's, took twice as long as unhindered walking would have.

"Ah! You! How was your meal, ikut?" asked the bors.

"Meal?" Tep wondered what he was talking about. "I have not eaten all day."

"My moxen!" the statesman said. "You did not bring them back."

"Oh. You are right. Now I need more moxen."

"Do you want all of them?"

"How many is that? I think four will be enough to carry our gear."

"Oh. I meant, did you want *entire* moxen or only steaks and chops? I see now you will need them alive, for a while, before you decide to consume them."

"This time I will be returning with them," Tep said.

"So you say—but I will still charge you what I did last time, and the same terms and conditions will apply."

"Fine," said Tep, in a hurry to be on his way. Then he smiled toothily. "This time," he said, "make sure you give me *plump* ones. . . ."

"I am tempted," said Tep, when he and Kelisat were mounted, and on their way northeastward out of Tebuk, "to make camp one last night when we return—just outside Tebuk. There we can celebrate with a fine meal."

"I do not want to eat my mox," said Kelisat. She thought for a moment. "Do they have names?" she asked.

Tep laughed. "I have named them! This one, under me, is Steak. Yours is Fillet, and the others are . . ."

"Tep!"

The winds on the piedmont were not as strong those Kelisat had endured in the high country. The heavy Inutkak tent, borne by moxen, was strong enough to stand against it. Being ikuts, they had given no consideration to bringing two of them. Kelisat and Tep would of course sleep together. Whether they, adults both, slept like cubs, or whether they had sex as newly matured ikuts might be expected to, or whether they made love as adults, in full understanding of a relationship that was developing between them, only time would tell.

Tep now understood that what had happened with Velanda had been mostly a trick played on both of them by their subtly different pheromones, their vastly different expectations. With Kelisat he expected nothing. If what he felt for her was no more than companionable affection, they would cuddle as cubs. If his feelings and interests went beyond that, and if she reciprocated them, then playful sex might result—but no babies could be conceived. Among ikuts, the act followed the emotion, and the results reflected it. Neither of them had to weigh consequences when they decided, on purely practical grounds, to take only one tent.

There was no lovemaking. Kelisat, having slept mostly alone since the deaths of her parents, was quite content to cuddle, to be warm without an excess of furs, burning lamps, or a severe metabolic tax, as when she had slept in the snow.

Tep seemed distracted and troubled, though he would not discuss what was bothering him, and she could make no sense of it. He was sure he knew right where the Charter was. The Charter—and the end of their problems. Whatever it contained, the consul would be able to resolve the mantees' dispute, and surely the festering angers that had been created in the aftermath of the Ketonak band's ill-advised migration would fade in a generation or two. So why was he . . . depressed?

Despite such questions, the journey was not an unpleasant one. While it was daylight, they rode. The days were at their longest now, and they made good time, only stopping when their moxen expressed fatigue. On a more hospitable world such lands, between the forty-fifth and forty-eighth parallel, would have a temperate climate. On Glaice that was not so, but still, they were not so far north that there was daylight throughout all the night hours.

Kelisat eyed the heavy bronze door, the niches with their tokens woven of fur and bright songbird feathers. "Wait, Tep!" she said, just as he put his hand on the tarnished brass fitting that released the hidden latch.

Tep observed curiously as she unwrapped bark twine and soft leather from a small bundle. She fluffed soft fur with her fingers, and smoothed the barbels of red and blue feathers. Tiny bone beads clicked against each other. "*Telamor fenad ab,*" she intoned slowly, hoping that her pronunciation of the words the shahm had taught her was not too distorted. "*Sentas rey nobor, en transim fal.*" She brushed the dust and crumbled remains of some long-decayed offering from a carved niche next to the portal, and reverently placed her new token in it. "*For narat ley, sento ken telam,*" she concluded. "We can go in now," she said to Tep.

"What was that all about?" he asked as the ornate bronze door swung open upon the blackness within. Kelisat shook her head. Had Tep's visit here, with that insensitive bors female, corrupted him completely? Within this ice cave were the remains of her most ancient ancestors. She had begged the shahm to teach her the ritual, and she had made the token with her own hands, while Hepakat explained the importance of each feather in the spiral whorl, red within green.

They had none of the modern equipment that Tep had used the last time he had been here—for which Kelisat, had she considered it, would have been glad. The flickering light of her oil-soaked wick lit the stone-slabbed vestibule with the same mysterious and subtle light by which shahm after shahm had seen it, down through the long generations, for eleven thousand years and more.

Even Tep seemed to be affected by the light, by her reverence. At least he did not bark out more loud questions. His voice, when he said "This way," was a mere whisper.

Beyond the stone slabs that held back the glacial earth of the entryway was ice. It was not the clear stuff that formed on quiet water, or the green, jadelike ice that formed in the bays of the continental coast—ice for which ikuts had names. It was not the firn or névé of which glacial geologists spoke, using words older even than the most ancient remembered tongues. This ice, Kelisat saw, was a different stuff, unnamed and unique, formed first as snow in some high cirque, then recrystallized, compressed, and jumbled in its long voyage as part of some ancient glacier, long before Glaice's sun was even a numbered dot on some ancient star map. First it had been snow, then loose, columnar hexogonal crystals, then firm ice consolidated by the pressures of glacial movement. Then, when that glacier receded, perhaps a hundred thousand or a million years ago, it had been left, an outlier buried in the silts and gravels of meltwater streams, like an immense diamond crystal embedded in blue clay.

The walls were coated with ice like glass—formed when the body heat, the torches, lamps, and breath of men passed by. The path Kelisat trod was dark with gravel and silt melted from the clarified ice of the walls, and was smoothed by the tread of more hundreds of generations of Inutkak shahms than anyone but a shahm, reciting the lineages of the band, could count.

In silent awe, Kelisat passed through the first burial chambers, pausing to say "*Felan a manor sen,*" at every niche where lay one who had gone before.

This she repeated in the second, the third . . . and the eleventh chambers, but then Tep whispered impatiently that there were still twenty chambers to pass through before they reached their destination. In the twelfth chamber, Kelisat said *"Felanton a maneven sen"* instead, which was a plural form. "May our deeds honor you," it meant. She said it only once.

For Kelisat, there was no longer a "destination." There was only *now,* and somewhere far below, a *beginning,* not an end.

It was not the *last* chamber. There were still older ones, where rested the remains of the oldest Inutkak ikut. Or were they really "Inutkak" yet? Those most ancient ikuts were men of the coast-hugging early days, men who had likely visited Latobak when lights still shined in its windows and traffic coursed its streets. The old ones had lived in a time and place when personal histories had been recorded on data-modules, not inscribed on slate or kept alive only in the minds of shahms, in the epics and the begats of the tales.

This chamber Tep thought, marked the true beginning of the Inutkak, first of the far-travelers. There were still fire-colored jewels adorning these graves, and those of a few generations after them, but there were slate gorgets also, marking the time when the data modules could no longer be read, when the machines to read them no longer functioned. Jewels they seemed, and jewels they became, bright and pretty, but revealing nothing of what was inscribed within their glowing depths.

Tep was now glad for Kelisat's reverence. Before, he had suppressed his own instincts, imitating Velanda, the blasé and sophisticated researcher. Now Kelisat's mood and attitude had affected his own . . . no, her uncritical acceptance of the old, Inutkak ways had freed him to be wholly Inutkak himself, to walk the icy corridors of this shrine in the spirit it deserved of him.

"What you have suffered to find," he said in formal

tones, "is within." He stood aside to allow the hunter the first glimpse of her long-sought prey.

Kelisat stopped to enter the room cut from the ancient ice. There was only one body within it. It rested not within a niche, but on a huge slab of clear, translucent ice. The weight of the massive ikut who lay there had caused the body to sink into the ice, until it was half-concealed.

On the floor beside the bier was a crumpled fishnet, its floats long since collapsed and shriveled, but atop the net was a device made of wood and bone, with two clear, sparking lenses: a sextant not unlike Shahm Hepakat's, the tool of a navigator, a band leader, one who rode the ice. There were spears, too, bundled and laid beside the big man's body. Some were two- and three-pronged gigs, fish spears with barbed tines of once-flexible bone; two were toggle-headed harpoons that would separate head from shaft when plunged into the flesh of whale or seal. Three more were short, light hunting lances like those Kelisat herself might have carried, seeking ritvak in the foothills above North Camp. Two were headed with carefully flaked obsidian, and one with a blade that seemed to be ground from inox steel. The shafts were bound together with stone-weighted spear throwers that extended the length of the hunter's arm and multiplied the speed of her throw.

This man, Kelisat knew, had been a hunter among hunters; each spear, she knew, had been blooded, had brought down prey . . . food for the people, the Inutkak.

Tep had seen this man's grave before. He had seen it on his first visit to Pootorap, but had not had time to look closely, before rushing out again, to drive off the fulfs that had killed Volk, his first mox. He had made a rubbing of the slate tablet that rested by the man's head, and later had removed that rubbing from among the ones spread on the lab tables for Emeritus Barm to translate, and it had remained folded in a lab drawer, untranslated and unread.

He followed Kelisat into the chamber. He was sure that he would not have to read the old Universal inscription to know what it would say.

The flickering light from Kelisat's lamp was magnified by the jewel that rested on the chest of the ancient hunter and shahm.

"There is what we came for, Tep," he heard her whisper. "*That* is the Charter, isn't it?" She did not rush forward to grasp what she had sought and suffered for. She seemed hesitant—even afraid.

Tep stepped past her. "That is the Charter," he confirmed, but reached instead for the slate tablet. "This," he said, "is what *I* came for." He read the first line silently, struggling with the odd syntax and unfamiliar words. When he next spoke, it was as if he was reading the words in the contemporary Inuktak tongue, not translating at all.

"Once we were strangers here," he intoned, in words long memorized, words familiar to every Inutkak youth. "And we clung fearfully to the shore. Once we looked to the city and to the stars for succor and sustenance, and did not seek it at sea. We were not, then, what we are: a new people, wedded not to the land, but to the winds, not to the rocks, but to the currents.

"We are the world-folk who span the seas between our fingers. We are the world-folk, who belong, no longer visitors, no longer afraid, nor hungry. We are the world-folk, who have chosen here to remain."

Tep's eyes blurred, though ikuts did not shed tears. "*Terod nepata Inuktak,*" he repeated, in the old tongue. *Inutkak,* which meant "people of the world," or "people of *this* world and no other."

"There are more words, aren't there, Tep? You did not read them all?" Kelisat stood beside them. He felt her hand resting on his shoulder.

He realized that his finger still rested on a line halfway down the slate. He had stopped there because what followed was not phrases from the tales he had memorized, but something unique to this place, to the slate tablet. He read those lines to himself, several times, before he attempted to say them aloud, in words Kelisat could understand.

"This flesh we called Apootlak," Tep said, at last, "but Apootlak is not here. He is one with the currents of ocean and our blood. He is one with the wind and our breath. He is Inutkak, the first hunter of this world, the first of us, and he is among us. He is not here."

Tep turned to Kelisat. "There is the Charter, Hunter," he said. "Take it."

"Tep, I can't! I don't dare. That is . . . that is Apootlak!"

"Take it," Tep said again. "*That* is not Apootlak. *That* is just old dried meat. Apootlak . . . is *here*." He squeezed her arm. "You are Inutkak, Kelisat, and *you* are chief hunter of the world-folk now. It is yours to take. Do you want a new spear—or a very old one?" He touched a fine obsidian point. "Take this one, because it is your spear, hunter, by right of the blood that flows in your veins and the profession you follow."

Kelisat straightened. Tep felt it beneath his hand. Then she stepped from beneath it, and forward, and lifted the fire-lit crystal from the hands that had held it for eleven thousand years.

CHAPTER 21

And Tegat sailed alone, unmated still,
His honor bright, his hands still wet with blood;
Though woman cherished not his blighted seed,
His sons are every man; his shame lives on.

Inutkak First Tale,
Sixtieth Quatrain of the Eighteenth Cantone

The Charter was wrapped in soft skins, buried in Kelisat's pack, where it lay padded with sleeping furs and her foul-weather parka. In the morning they would begin the trek back to Tebuk. Now they had made a lean-to out of one of the tents, and had heaped sleeping furs beneath it on soft spongy spruce boughs that kept them dry and off the snow. There was no wind, no cloud cover, and yet the air did not have the bite of winter. Was the worst of the season behind them?

Tep had gathered wood for a fire, and flames now reflected off Kelisat's fur and his own.

"Is that really what 'Inutkak' means, Tep? The 'world-folk'?"

" 'Inut' does not mean 'world' in general. I don't think there is such a word in the old ikut tongue, and when we want to say 'world' or 'planet,' we use the Standard word, 'world,' or we say 'Glaice,' which is a bors word, I think. It means 'ice.' Inut is a *name,* not an ordinary noun. There was never another 'Inut,' only *this* world, this place."

"Then we are *Inutkak* because our ancestors were the ones who learned to live here, to survive by migrating, when the starships stopped coming and the old technology was lost."

"That is what the words on that slate seem to say," Tep agreed, "but . . . somehow I keep feeling I'm missing something. '. . . Who have *chosen* here to remain' is what it said. Did they really have a choice? Does that mean that some ikut did *not* choose to remain on Glaice, on *Inut*? Does it mean some of them *left*?"

"Does that matter? If they left, they did not become Inutkak, did they? I wonder if the Charter will say anything about that 'choice'?"

"I am more concerned that it will say something else—that we may only migrate through the equatorial zones at the sufferance of the mantees who live there, or something even worse."

He shook his head angrily. "If *only* I could go to Paldernot Island! I *know* I would not have to give the Charter to Consul Martinez, then!"

"What is on Paldernot? I have been there twice. It is not a very nice place—all those trees, so thick I could hardly breathe. At least that's what it felt like. Even the mantees don't live in those forests. We wanted *serifalt* furs, but they had none to trade and there was only one male in the entire throng who was willing to guide us, so we could hunt the serifalt ourselves. There were only tiny little paths, as wide as my two feet together! I was lost in ten minutes!"

"Paldernot isn't a very big island, though," Tep mused. "Do you know of a place called Sea-Bite?"

"There is a shallow cove by that name, on the south shore. The mantees say it was bigger, once, until an eruption of Mount Paldernot cut it in two with a lava flow."

"*That* is where I wanted to go," Tep said. "I have a map—a copy of one of Professor Rakulit's maps, actually. The old cove is now a freshwater lake. One of his 'old' mantee sites is at the north end of the lake."

Kelisat wondered what was so important about that particular digging. Tep explained that there were actually two archaeological sites there, one on top of the other. "Archaeologists refer to the 'law of superposition,' " Tep said. "That means that what is underneath something else has to be older than what is on top of it."

"Why is that?" Kelisat asked. She patted the furs she

sat on, then lifted the edges of the layers. "I happen to know that my ritvak hide, this one, is older than I am, because it was a mating gift from my father to my mother. I also know that this *narmot* fur, which is under it, is only three years old, because I made the kill, and prepared the pelt myself."

"That may be so," Tep said, "but tonight, which fur did you spread on the spruce boughs *first*? This one?" He fingered the topmost fur.

"Don't be silly, Tep. First I laid the narmot fur on the boughs, and then . . . Oh! I see what you mean. This 'law of superposition' does not truly apply to the age of the furs, but to the order in which they were laid down."

"Exactly so. You could not have laid the ritvak fur down first, and then slid the soft narmot one under it, any more than the mantees could have slid the charred ruins of a village, which was composed of wooden and stone houses, underneath a midden—a refuse heap, which is mostly mussel shells and other trash. The village had to be there first, and to have been burned, before the mantees began dumping the shells of mussels they had eaten on top of it."

"That is so. But what does it matter?"

Tep explained briefly how radiocarbon dating worked, and his conclusions about the falsity of Rakulit's dates. "Since the village was mostly wood, from trees that grew on land in the very forests you detest so, they will produce true and accurate dates. Rakulit's dates, on the other hand, were derived from the mussel shell in the upper layer."

Kelisat nodded briskly. "So if you collected charcoal from a burnt roof beam, and dated it, you believe it would be younger than the shells on top of it—which cannot be!"

"Just so. Only one of the dates can be a true one—and I have already shown that marine materials cannot be relied on." He shook his head. "But the throngmother, Heloset, has said she will kill me if I set foot on any of the mantee islands."

"There is that," Kelisat replied. She patted Tep's arm sympathetically. Then Tep felt her fingers stiffen.

"What is it?" he asked, turning to look at her.

"We will discuss middens and burnt villages later," she said, quite firmly. "Now there is something else I wish to do." The glow in her eyes was more than fire, warmer even than the tongues of flame outside their shelter. Her fur was softer than the smoke that drifted up and away. Her eyes, her fur, her softness consumed Tep as no flame could do. As for Kelisat, when at last they joined as one, and when they later, much later, separated, she knew that the embers within her would not fade. "Never again," she whispered, when Tep was asleep, "will I be cold."

Their lovemaking, Tep thought later, lying awake, listening to the soft sounds of Kelisat's breathing, had been an entirely new experience. What he had felt with Velanda was boisterous cub-play, and the scratching of an adolescent itch. This had been different. They had made love not just with their bodies, but with their eyes. He felt a shuddering, wonderful twinge remembering Kelisat's eyes, and how he thought he could have swum in them. He admitted that he was not wise enough to know if their tender intensity had crossed that ill-understood line between experimentation and adult love—love that might result in . . . in babies—but he suspected it had.

Dawn glazed the easternmost sky with iridescent haze, obscuring the lowest stars just arisen. He and Kelisat had, he decided, slept long enough. "Wake up, Lis," he murmured, nudging her. "I have a question."

"It is still night!" she protested sleepily.

"No—look there. Dawn."

"The sun won't be up for an hour. Good night, Tep!" She rolled away from him. He did not again try to awaken her.

When she at last awakened on her own—still before the sun was up, but seeming hours for Tep, she immediately said, "Now, what is this important question?"

Tep wanted to know if she might have gotten pregnant. "I think it is possible," she said, softly. "My mother died before she could teach me about such things. If you suspect it—if you felt as I did . . ."

"I am sure of that!" Tep blurted. "It was . . . it was . . . I do not know how to say it."

"Then we must hurry," Kelisat said. "We have much to do before I get fat, and cannot travel."

"Fat? Travel? But we have moxen to ride, and doesn't it take three seasons for babies?"

Kelisat promised to clarify what she had meant. "It is something I thought of, and it may entail another voyage. But first, I want *you* to answer some questions."

Tep agreed immediately—and was even more confused by the nature of her questions—which concerned Paldernot Island.

"Besides this 'superposition' of burnt villages and mussel-shell heaps," she asked, "why is the Sea-Bite site so important to you? Could there not be other similar sites, perhaps on islands the mantees do not currently occupy or watch closely?"

"There may be," Tep admitted, "but I do not want to take time to return to Metok, to search through old records from before Rakulit's time. And besides, this site is special."

When Kelisat asked why, Tep quoted a passage from the First Tale:

> "Fat Sorelf's hold was forest trees and mud,
> And Tegat's weapons fire and earth-spewn glass;
> 'No peace is free, no passage safe for us
> Except the deed is done, the battle won.' "

"I remember that," Kelisat said. "Tegat fought the mantees—Sorelf was throngmother—and when they saw that their villages could not be safe from us, they agreed to allow the Inutkak to pass through their islands on the swift current for which they named themselves." She pondered her own words, and then her eyes widened. "Is *that* the village that was burnt? How can you tell?"

"We Inutkak did not burn others. The Cantones are clear that Tegat's act was unique. 'Tegat, no-sons,' he was called, because no woman would mate with him, to pass on his murderous blood to children. That is in all the tales. And Rakulit says he knows of no other villages that were burned—at least no Swift Current ones."

"That is interesting, Tep, but I do not understand why it is important."

"Because with a date on that village, we will also have an unimpeachable date on an event in our oral tradition—one several generations after Apootlak. Then Consul Martinez will have no excuse not to declare the mantee lawsuit invalid, and we will not have to give him the Charter."

"Not give it to him? But I . . . we . . . worked so hard to get it! And you said there were files on it that the Arbiter himself wanted."

"Old historical stuff! Who cares about that? If I could read the Charter first, maybe. If it said nothing that would hurt us ikuts, then I would hand it over."

"I think that is wrong, Tep. The Charter belongs to everyone on Glaice—on Inut. It is not yours to dispose of as you wish."

"Apootlak did! *He* kept it for eleven thousand years!"

"You are not Apootlak, Tep! And I very much doubt that the Arbiter asked *him* for it! I do not like this at all. I do not want to be pregnant, either. Not by a . . . a . . ." She could not continue. She arose, and began rolling her sleeping furs.

"Kelisat, I am sorry! I want to do what is right! I will ask Shahm Hepakat what to do."

Kelisat seemed satisfied with that. Still, they did not make love that night or the next. She seemed as eager as Tep to get back to North Camp and throw the burden of decision on Hepakat's shoulders. Tep then realized that mating—with an independent ikut female like Kelisat, at least—was not going to be a simple thing, that his life was no longer entirely his own, and that the two of them were not always going to agree. Kelisat was, he realized, a moral being. He, he decided, was not. "Perhaps that is why people mate," he speculated. "Somebody in a family has to be honest."

CHAPTER 22

Ikut boats, though often elegantly designed and built, suffer from a notable flaw: their waterproof hide membranes become waterlogged, and thus render them unsuitable for long voyages. This, and the deterrent cost of maintaining a major fleet of all-wood ships, may wholly account for the ikut use of cumbersome, unstable, constantly melting ice floes as a primary means of transportation.

Tok Metorap,
Ikut Studies,
University Press, Metok, Xarafeille 132,
12090 R.L.

In Tebuk, they resold the moxen to the stable master, who expressed amazement that the beasts still lived. "Volk!" he exclaimed, patting one male's rear end. "Plunt!" he crooned, stroking the broad back of a female.

"That is not Volk!" Tep said. "Volk is dead."

"No-o-o-! Volk *not*!" said the male mox, bucking and then dashing back into the darkened stable.

"Now you've frightened him!" said the bors.

"But that was not Volk!"

"It was! It is a common name. Moxen are not very smart. There are only a dozen names among all of them. Now do not frighten Plunt!"

"I will not. I have my money. Our business is done." Tep backed out the door.

The sky was clear, and most of the snow had melted from the road west toward North Camp. Unlike the last time, several drivers vied for the chance to take them there by car. Tep negotiated what he considered a reasonable fare.

When the thawing countryside slid by outside the window, Tep turned to Kelisat. "What was it you said about travel?" he asked. "You never finished telling me."

"I am no longer sure I want to," she replied. "Let us see what Shahm Hapakat says about the Charter, first." She refused to say more.

"Kelisat is right," Hepakat said. He and Tep were alone in the shahm's house; Kelisat had gone home to light lamps and warm hers—and had not given the slightest hint whether Tep should join her there or plan on sleeping with his parents and siblings. "We must send the Charter to Metok. I will take it to Tebuk—but not right away. I will be too busy for the next few months. I must prepare the Inutkak for our departure from North Camp. Perhaps by the time you return from your own journey . . ."

"*My* journey? What journey? Kelisat too spoke of such—but she will tell me nothing! Her lips are as tight as a clapclam!"

"Tell her I have agreed to her proposal—and then she may loosen them a bit."

At first, even after Tep had relayed Hepakat's message, her lips remained sealed, though the way she arranged her sleeping furs seemed to suggest that she did not plan to sleep alone on them. Tep had brought food—selecting from his mother's stores several delicacies he hoped Kelisat would like. "Those are for the celebration!" his mother protested. "Now there will be none left for when we cross the equator!" Her words would afford Tep a good chuckle later, after Kelisat told him what she had in mind.

Before that was to happen, however, Kelisat had decided to punish Tep a bit more for his dishonest intentions. She nibbled at the rich old meat he had bought, picking small, fatty larvae from it and ingesting them without even a smile, as if she were an old, old person who had lost all sense of taste. She crunched Tep's mother's spicy ground nuts—pickled, they had been brought all the way from the South Continent valley where they grew—without so much as a murmur of pleasure, though Tep watched her closely for the slightest sign that her mood was improving.

Finally, though, after every edible bit was consumed, as she sat picking her lovely teeth with a splinter of yellowed whale ivory, she relented. "How long," she asked him, "will it take to gather what tools and things you will need to excavate the Sea-Bite site, once we get there?"

Tep stammered. He fired a dozen questions at her. She waited until he was entirely finished with them before she explained what she had in mind. "I can get us to Paldernot Island," she said. "It is a long trip, especially in a skin boat, but it is not an impossible one. If we are lucky with winds and currents, we can finish digging up what we will need, and can meet the Inutkak in South Camp at the summer solstice."

She explained her plan. Instead of bumbling eastward along the north coast for weeks, in order to catch a good southwesterly current, as the Inutkak on their ice floes must do, they would catch the first southwesterly current out of North Camp, and ride it halfway to the equator. Then, using sail, they would tack sharply south, at right angles to the equatorial current, and would, she hoped, be able to land on Paldernot Island after only a short monthlong journey.

"We will have to make it in less than six weeks," she stated, "because for all the grease we put on the hull, the skins will still absorb water. In a month, they will already be getting soft and floppy. In five weeks, our boat will begin to fall apart."

Tep, who had studied the winds and currents deliberately, as a prospective shahm, was less worried about the dangers of the voyage than what they would encounter when they got to Paldernot. "I do not think the mantees live near Sea-Bite Lake," Kelisat said. "If we lower our sail as we approach the island, and if we avoid villages on the coast, we should be relatively safe once we are inland.

"And if not," she concluded, "it will not matter. I do not intend to allow the mantees to commit atrocities upon my body unless my spirit is free of it!" Her emphasis, and her meaningful glance at Tep, indicated that she knew what the mantees had done to him, in Metok. Tep was too ashamed of that even to ask her how she had found out about it.

She explained that Hepakat would delay delivery of the Charter datablock to Consul Martinez. "If you and I can make our way to the weather station on Farilan Island without being caught by mantees, we should be safe until we can arrange to be picked up. The bors who run the station will have no reason to turn us over to the mantees, and they might even help get us to the Inutkak floe in their metal boat." Then she smiled, and patted the sleeping furs. "Come here. We will make further plans tomorrow."

"I am too excited to sleep!" Tep blurted.

"Sleep? Whoever mentioned sleep?" asked his mate.

The first task that faced Kelisat was to build their boat. The small craft the Inutkak used for fishing and hunting at sea, she said disdainfully, were not adequate for such a voyage as they planned. Tep wondered how she knew so much.

"I did not spend years learning hunter lore—and becoming the Inutkak's youngest-ever chief hunter—for nothing," she said. "We will be sailing, not paddling, so we need a deep keel. We will be drifting westward anyway, and a shallow boat would make so much leeway, sailing close to the wind, that we might overshoot Paldernot by a thousand miles."

Tep looked at his lover with a strange light in his eyes, his expression half amazed admiration that he had caught such a brilliant mate, and half chagrin, because she was surely much smarter—well, just as smart—as he was, in her very different way.

Their boat had to be larger than a hunting craft, Kelisat explained, indicating the sheer-strakes laid out on a patch of clean-swept ground, because they would need a tall mast to get their sail up above the wave crests. The low air in the troughs was too often weak and variable. The mast, she said, would be as tall as the boat's keel was long.

"Waves don't get *that* high . . . do they?" he asked, suddenly anxious, gazing at the long keel pattern. "I never saw waves that high when I was on a floe."

"On a floe, you don't see them," she explained, enjoying his discomfiture, "because a floe is big enough to ride over the crests, not between them. A boat goes up, and over, and down the waves. It is a delightful sensation!" Tep could not tell, from her bright-eyed grinning face, if she was enjoying the memories of such "delightful" rides, or getting most of her pleasure from his horrified expression.

Finally—actually only a few weeks passed, but to Tep, burdened with anxieties, it seemed longer—the boat was finished. Kelisat had gotten much help from the other hunters, who knew the skills and who were eager to have a part in realizing the grand design of the large craft. It was almost forty feet long, very narrow and deep, and their baggage and stores did not take up a quarter of the available space beneath its deck. Beneath the cabin sole were several tons of rock ballast. Overhead was a tent of raw skins stretched over wooden purlins. They had been allowed to harden before they were varnished and heavily greased.

The rig—had Tep known enough about boats to describe it—was as simple as Kelisat, with the help of her hunters, could make it. A tall triangular mainsail, fully raised, reached all the way to the masthead, and the foresail was just as tall, but not as wide at the foot. Kelisat explained that the large spar at the bottom of the mainsail was a boom. "That is the sound it makes when it swings over," she said, "and hits the empty head of someone who forgets to duck!"

The smaller spar at the bottom of the foresail—the jib—was too low to the deck to hit anyone, but that one was called the "club." "It makes no sense!" Tep said disparagingly. "The big one should be called the club, not the little one."

"I will be glad to pick it up and hit you with it, if it will make you feel better about its name," Kelisat said.

"The club is intended to make it easier for a single sailor to work the sail, and I will be sailing single-handedly."

"What about me?" Tep said. "I'm going too."

"I know. What does *that* have to do with anything?" Sometimes, Tep mused, there were disadvantages to having a very smart mate—especially a witty one.

They pushed off at dawn, and once away from shore, headed southeast along the coast. "Are you *sure* we won't tip over?" Tep asked, anxiously eyeing the water that boiled past on the boat's left side, only inches below the deck. At that moment, his first lesson in seamanship began.

"I can see that I must teach you how to talk," Kelisat said, smiling. "Imagine what trouble if we were in a terrible, gusting storm, and I said, 'Tep! Run forward and cut loose the thingy-dingy.' We might *capsize* before you found the *jib sheet.*"

Tep, stung by her humor, shrugged. "I would just start cutting things until I found the right one. Perhaps I would start with the *main halyard,* and then the *outhaul,* which are at the *mast.* Then, if I heard nothing from you, I would begin sawing away at that thick, tarred 'thingy-dingy,' the *forestay.*"

"Tep! You have been studying! Who has been helping you?"

"The shahm's dictionary. The big thick one has a diagram of a sailboat, with the ropes and spars named. But you are right; I need a few lessons. I need to know what is dangerous, and what isn't—and I assume that sailing with one edge of the boat in the water is not . . . is it?"

She laughed, entirely good-naturedly. "Then let us begin. We are on a point of sail called a *beam reach.* That means the wind is coming almost directly from one side, which causes the boat to *heel* to the other side. If the wind were a bit more *astern* of us, we would be on a *broad reach,* where we would heel a bit less, and go a bit faster. I'll show you." She pulled the tiller toward her, and the mast immediately straightened up.

"It doesn't feel any faster," Tep said, "but we are now headed toward the shore. Is that Tebuk over there?

The smoke?"

"That is Tebuk. If we had a knot-meter you would see we are actually going a bit faster than before. More of the wind's energy is pushing us forward, and less is expended on making us heel. Now I will show you what 'pointing' is—but you will have to help, by sheeting us in."

"I'll be glad to as soon as you tell me what that means. I know what 'sheets' are—those ropes that pull the sails tight, but . . ."

Kelisat instructed him. Shortly thereafter, the water was splashing past Tep within reach of his white-knuckled fingers, right over the edge . . . no, the *rail.* Now the boat's bow was pointing south, and Tebuk's smoke columns were well aft, off the port side. "Shall we go faster?" Kelisat asked, grinning, her whiskers glistening with spray.

Tep almost said "No!" before thinking about it. Then he, too, grinned. "Yes!" he said enthusiastically, realizing that if the wind was unchanged, and much of its effort was being expressed in forcing the boat to lean so perilously, they were not *really* going fast at all. "A beam reach, I think. Not a broad reach, because we do not want to run into Tebuk."

"We cannot run into Tebuk, Tep," said Kelisat, "because a *run* is the *other* point of sail—when the wind is directly behind us. If we were *running,* we would go aground somewhere between North Camp and Tebuk." That time, despite her grin, she had the grace to lower her eyes slightly, as if ashamed to be enjoying herself so at Tep's expense.

By nightfall, the lights of Tebuk were only slightly astern, and Tep began to consider just how long a month at sea was really going to be.

Two days later, Tep noticed that their compass bearing had changed slightly. "Why don't we just sail south, close-hauled," he asked, "and then follow the Swift Current right to Paldernot Island?" He indicated the course on the map—no, the *chart.*

"If wind were all we had to contend with, we could

do that," Kelisat said. "Of course, pointing is not as fast, and we would have to swim the last few hundred miles. . . ." She pointed at small blue arrows on the chart. "We are following the current, just as we would on an ice floe, only with the wind's help we are going faster than the current is. If we sailed directly south, the current would neither help nor hinder us, and we would actually take longer."

The voyage wore on. Tep learned what the several chunks of soft swamp-cedar Kelisat had insisted upon bringing along were for. "Whittling is kind of fun," he said, as he cut chips from the small model of their boat that he was making. "I wonder if this will sail, when it's finished."

Kelisat looked up from the sweater she was knitting. Several skeins of variously dyed ritvak yarn were also among the "extras" she had stowed aboard. "It will float, if that's what you mean. As for sailing . . ."

Tep grinned. He now allowed her all the little jokes she cared to make at his expense. Besides whittling and knitting, there were few distractions besides talking, and he had come to understand his lovely mate—in some limited way, at least. He know, though, not from anything she had said outright, that she had been infatuated with him long before he was aware of her in a romantic way, and that it had been very painful for her to be ignored by him—and agonizing, when he had brought Velanda to North Camp. He also knew that right now, she was the expert, and in charge. When they reached Paldernot Island and started digging, it would be entirely his show. Maybe by the time they arrived there, she would have gotten the last of her gentle but vindictive bitterness out of her system.

A week later, they hauled the sheets in a bit, and the compass now read due south. Tep's tiny boat model was finished, as were the sleeves of Kelisat's sweater. The water stretched in every direction, and gave Tep's eyes no relief, nothing to focus on except the shifting glimmer of sunlight.

"Where are those big waves you told me about?" he asked.

"When we pass the tropic, and our current swings south and moves with the northern edge of the equatorial current, we'll have waves," Kelisat promised. "From then until we put ashore, we'll have nothing but waves."

Tep was sorry he had asked. Now, he would have something new to think about—and worry about.

Several days later, Kelisat announced that they had reached the halfway point. The current beneath them was already flowing more west than south, and indeed the boat lifted and fell rhythmically on great swells too large and slow to give a sense of real motion, but which made the horizon rise and fall in a slow, dizzying manner.

"It's time for a swim and a climb," Kelisat told a puzzled Tep. "We have to grease the hull."

"We did that already—in North Camp. Besides, the boat's in the water now. We can't grease it."

"We have to do it again. Grease doesn't last. Waves beat on it, fish nibble on it, bacteria turn it into slippery goop that runs off. And we will get the boat *out* of the water—one part at a time." Tep was dubious about that. What could they do, take it apart? When Kelisat explained, he was even more dubious. "You want me to climb up *there*?" he asked, gazing with ill-concealed horror at the masthead. "And then you want me to *tip the boat over*?"

Kelisat stretched hides over the cockpit and hatches, securing them by laying rope around the coamings and the hatches, and pounding the skin tarpaulins and the ropes into precut grooves. Tep had never even noticed those grooves before.

Climbing the mast was not as hard as Tep imagined it to be, either—not once he saw the scornful look on Kelisat's face. With the encouragement of Kelisat, holding a sharp fid—an ivory tool for splicing cordage—he half-climbed and half-hoisted himself to the masthead, where he clung, swaying through wide arcs. At last the motion damped itself out, and the mast stayed vertical—as long as Tep did not move, and did not even breathe heavily. "Thread the peak halyard through that pulley on the end of the spreader," Kelisat ordered. Tep did so.

Kelisat filled a large skin bucket with ballast, then tied its bail to the peak halyard, and began to pull, hoisting it up. "Hold the rope toward the port side!" she called to Tep. With one hand to push on the mast, and one to pull the rope away from it, and only his feet on the spreader and a loop of rope holding him up, Tep did so. As Kelisat raised the eccentric weight, the mast began to lean. When it was all the way up, it leaned so far that when Tep looked straight down, he saw only water.

"Tep! You're going to have to rock it. Make it tip."

"How do I do that?" he asked, in a weak, tremulous voice.

"Loosen your safety rope, and stick your feet out to the end of the spreader. Maybe that will be enough." It was. With a motion that seemed slow and graceful from where Kelisat was—in the water next to the boat—but that seemed to accelerate at a terrifying pace to Tep, as he rushed toward the water.

Tep was quite content to remain clinging to the mast while Kelisat splashed and clambered about spreading gobs of thick grease on the exposed hull. He was equally willing to stand on the keel with her, and to lean backward until the mast rose clear of the water, slowly at first, then quite rapidly, until it reached a position about twenty degrees from plumb, passed it, then swung back.

"I will go below and shift ballast to the other side," Kelisat said. "Why don't you get ready to go up again." Tep did not even allow himself a waterlogged groan.

They could not have put off recoating the hull long, because over the next days the water became quite rough, and the waves seemed to pile one atop another in unpredictable pyramidal peaks that indeed seemed as high as the masthead—though the mast was seldom vertical enough to tell.

"This is where the two currents meet," Kelisat said. "It will get a little rougher, and then we're going to sheet in the sails and head as near to south as we can. If we're lucky, we'll go fast enough to reach Paldernot before the equatorial current sweeps us halfway around the world from it."

Not for the first time, Tep gave serious consideration to telling Hepakat to find someone else to succeed him as shahm. He was not at all sure that he could endure the tension of voyages much like this every eighteen months—and without the ability to control the floe, a much larger craft without rudder or sails.

The last week and a half of the trip went very fast, because they were too busy to snatch more than a few hours of sleep at a time. The waves lifted and plunged them endlessly, and Tep was amazed that the chaotic water even permitted a steady enough wind to fill their sails, let alone to keep them heeled well over, pointing within fifty degrees of the wind direction the whole time. Someone had to cling to the tiller all the time, because each wave was unlike the one before, and it was difficult to keep the ever-more-waterlogged craft on a proper heading. It was exhausting work, and neither of them could keep it up for a full four-hour watch.

At last, land loomed dark on the ever-moving horizon. "We're in luck!" Kelisat exclaimed. "That's Seneratap. The current bears around its east side and heads south a way, so we'll get a rest and a free ride before the really hard stuff!" The *really* hard stuff? Tep wanted to cry. Kelisat saw his mournful expression.

"I was joking, Tep! It won't be any harder than this last stretch was. We'll be on a broad reach, and we'll only have to fight the current a bit when it swings west again, past Seneratap. We'll be at Paldernot in a few days."

That thought comforted Tep—for a few minutes, until he considered the entirely different but no less dangerous situation they were sailing *into.*

CHAPTER 23

Archaeology is not a science. It has been called so because it employs scientific processes gleaned from physics, chemistry, zoology, oceanography, and countless others, but those do not make it science. It employs the scientific method at times, the relentless creation and culling of hypotheses and theories, and through them can sometimes predict what is still unknown, undug.

Archaeology has been called an art, when inspiration has led to discovery, and has been considered drudging labor when nothing is found. One description alone is not in dispute. Above all, good archaeology is a discipline; only rigorous consistency of method permits synthesis of information from one site to the next, one excavator to his successor, by which new insights can be gained.

Penderithamin Elteranibet,
Archaeology,
Scholastic Press,
Newhome, 11994 R.L.

Paldernot Island again divided the westward-flowing current, and with much effort, the sailors got their increasingly cumbersome craft into the southward flow, which swept them along the southeast littoral. There were, according to Kelisat, only a few of the rocky habitats mantees preferred along that stretch of coast.

Paldernot Island looked small on Tep's chart, but the physical reality of it was not. It was slightly over two hundred miles long from southwest to northeast, and about half that in width. The great, gray, truncated cone of Mount Paldernot dominated it, rising from a spreading base of heavily forested ancient lava flows.

Kelisat and Tep lowered their sails as the current swept them around the island, and then unstepped the mast as well—no easy task, while afloat. They had periodically thrown ballast rock overboard as their craft's skin took up water, and had pumped most of the foul-smelling bilge overboard. Now, in full sight of any mantees who might be basking on the offshore shoals, they allowed it to accumulate, and moved their remaining stores and equipment on deck. They treaded carefully, because even half full of water, with only two feet of freeboard, the craft was unstable, and if it were swamped by an unpredictable wave, or by their own motion, it would surely sink immediately.

Low in the water, there was little for any alert mantees to see, and as the current kept them twelve to fifteen miles offshore, they did not feel immediate fear of discovery. Mantee eyes were not as good as ikut ones.

As they rounded the southernmost joint of the island—the low eastward headland that defined Sea-Bite Cove—Kelisat unshipped the boom and lashed it astern, trailing in the water. She then instructed Tep in the art of sculling—moving the pole back and forth in the water to propel the craft just slightly faster than the current.

"We need steerage way," she said. "We must catch the shoreward edge of the current, which will sweep us into the cove."

The final stage of the ocean voyage was, as far as Tep was concerned, best forgotten. It was wet, hard work, in muggy heat that he was not accustomed to, and his anxiety was hardly lessened by the fact that, from headland to headland, Sea-Bite Cove was almost fifty miles wide, and no mantee ashore could see them. "Mantees fish offshore, not in the cove," Kelisat said, "and even the mussels on the cove bottom lack something their diet requires—though they harvest them for trade with us. As the Tehokag have already passed north of here, the mantees would have no reason to be in the cove in this season."

The waning current—and Tep's effort with the boom-turned-oar—took them past a low marshy shore. It was, he realized, looking at his map of the island, the delta formed by drainage from the inland lake that once formed part of the cove itself. They were now drifting northeastward, and when a low, gray wall of lava met the delta reeds ahead, Kelisat pointed. "That looks like a good place to go ashore. We may be able to hide the boat among the rocks."

When the boat was turned over, allowing the water-logged skins to bake in the equatorial sun, and when they had made a sledge of poles and planks from the cabin sole for the tools and supplies they would need, they set out for the site they had marked on his map.

Tep did not choose to remember much of that part of their voyage, either. They skirted the landward edge of the delta, keeping for the most part on the dry, shelving lava that formed its border. Sharp stones cut his feet, and occasional slogging where arms of marshy delta made inroads into the rocky shelf kept his soles soft and tender. Insects as large as Tep's thumb clattered, wriggled, scrambled from beneath his feet, and flew about his head. "Twenty-five miles of this," he muttered, despairing that it would ever end. "Twenty-five miles," he muttered that night, trying to sleep under circumstances no different from the heat of day, except that the awful, white glare of the equatorial sun did not blind him—the darkness, the mist obscuring all but the brightest stars, did so instead.

He dreamed he was in Metok, running down empty streets. From the tall, black buildings, darker even than the Paldernot forest's trees, echoed a distant shrilling: mantee hunting cries.

Near the end of their second day afoot, Tep looked up from his compass, and pointed. "Down there," he said. "It should be there." A half-hour later, they found a patch of disturbed soil that had not yet been obliterated by new growth. Tep traced its rectangular outline with his eyes. "That's Rakulit's test pit," he said. He referred to his notes, then cut several stakes from saplings, and drove them in at the corners of a square area next to Raulit's excavation.

"He must have left a datum stake or marker somewhere nearby," Tep muttered.

"What's that for?" Kelisat asked.

"A permanent mark that will give us an absolute elevation to work with, so we can map what we find according to the exact depth and compare it to Rakulit's stuff."

"Why don't we just start digging until we hit burnt stuff, take some, and then get out of here?" she asked, glancing around. "We're awfully exposed."

"I thought you said no mantees would be around here," Tep commented.

"Well, yes, but . . ." She shrugged. "I suppose you're . . . I suppose I'm right. Well? Let's get the shovels . . ."

When she returned with them. Tep stood over the backfilled pit, not the untouched area he had staked out. "It will save time," he mused, "if we dig out Rakulit's pit again first."

"I think I misheard you," Kelisat said. "I thought you said it will *save* time . . . to dig *two* pits instead of one? To do *over* what Rakulit already did?"

"You'll see. Anyway, his backfill will be softer than the undisturbed soil."

They dug. Indeed, redigging the end of Rakulit's pit nearest the one Tep had marked out took only a few hours, and long before dusk, their shovels clanked against hard lava. Tep used a flat trowel to scrape smooth the side wall of the pit, and studied what he saw there in profile, a section through all the strata laid down. Superposition, Kelisat reflected. Successive "blankets," differently colored, one laid atop another.

"There!" Tep said, pointing. "The white layers are the late-period mantee shell midden. Those dark flecks lower down are the village the Inutkak burned."

Kelisat felt a sense of complete anticlimax. "That's it? That's what we came all this way to see? Marks in the dirt? Bits of shell and charcoal?" She could not articulate just what it was that she had expected to see. She had known that it would not be two intact mantee villages, one on top of the other, of course. She knew what time and weather did to man-made things. But this? She could not interpret such subtle signs.

"Now we can dig the area I have marked," Tep said. "Hopefully, there will be enough artifacts there to establish continuity with the ones Rakulit removed." But instead of digging immediately, Tep untied the cord from a roll of wire screening and began fashioning a frame for it from another sapling—a frame with two sides that extended beyond the others like handles. When he was done, he laid it a few feet outside the marked area. "Let's toss a few shovelfuls of sod in here, and see what turns up," he said. Kelisat stuck her shovel in the ground and put her foot on it.

"No! Not like that!" Tep cried out. "Here, I'll show you." He cut around the marked edge of the undug pit with the flat shovel blade, then lifted a precise, thin slab of rooty sod, and tossed it on the screen. "We'll go down by exactly two inches each time, and draw in the locations of any artifacts we find on these charts, one chart for each level. Take those handles," he commanded, nodding toward the saplings projecting from the screened frame.

Kelisat then learned how to sift dirt—something she felt would never serve her again, if she were so lucky as to survive this journey. When they shook the sifter, the dirt fell through. She learned how to pick out roots and rootlets, and how to examine the pebbles that remained for tiny flecks of bone, chipped stone, and mussel shells.

By dusk, she had gotten quite good at it—but what was the point of it? "We have established that a layer of 'sterile' soil has accumulated over the most recent mantee occupation layer," Tep said.

"We didn't find anything," Kelisat protested.

"That's what I mean by 'sterile,' " Tep said. "The accumulation of several inches of topsoil proves that the mantee midden below is undisturbed. If we *had* found any artifacts, any signs of human occupation, it would just have confused the issue. Tomorrow, we will remove the first layer of the shell midden. We may find things of interest there."

"Do we have to sift every shoveful of that, too?" Kelisat asked mournfully. Digging out this little pit, not as long in either dimension as she was tall, promised to take a long, long time. "Only every fourth one, I think," Tep said. "We must keep our eyes open for artifacts, though." Kelisat wanted to ask him how he had learned so much about archaeology, but she was afraid he might say that the bors woman had taught him, and she did not want to hear that. Actually, the technique Tep was using was common to many fields, and his own experience had been gotten while studying the changes in the ecology of a sandy bog below a retreating glacier. The "artifacts" there had been fish bones and samples of soil containing ancient pollen grains, but the principle was the same.

Even digging out the entire pit in layers only two inches thick, the next day's effort went quickly, because they did not stop quite as often to sift the soil, and because there were few roots, and almost everything fell through the pencil-fine holes in the mesh. What was left was mostly white fragments of mussel shell, the remains of mantee meals. When they found bits of flint—reddish stuff that did not originate on the entirely volcanic Paldernot Island—Tep examined them with a hand lens. "This red flint is quarried in the Mootratok Hills, on South Continent," he said. "The source was discovered when Temotlik was shahm and we Inutkak began trading it to the Swift Current mantees. That was only seventeen generations ago, so if we take some of these shells, and date them using the C-fourteen method, and the dates come out very old . . ."

"Then it proves that the dates are false," Kelisat concluded dully. She was tired of digging and sifting, and they were still a long way from the bottom of Rakulit's neighboring pit. She was so tired, at the end of the day, that she could not remember whether or not she left several small bags of artifacts lying out when the two of them retired for the night. She was sure she had packed everything, but she couldn't actually remember doing so. Thus when, in the morning, Tep grumbled and complained about the bits of now-useless flint, fish bone, and mussel shells scattered about by some curious night creature, she was unable to reply. She dug in silence most of the next day, until Tep apologized for his harsh words.

Three days later, the last of the shell-rich overburden lay heaped around the pit. Three days. Kelisat had set traps made of cord and sticks, and the mouselike rodents that made so much noise thrashing in fallen leaves at night didn't seem to catch on. They kept being caught in the traps. She and Tep ate them raw, sometimes still alive. When Tep suggested skinning and gutting them, Kelisat shook her head. "Most of the fat's next to the skin, or adhering to the organs," she told him. "We are ikuts. We need fat, or we'll get sick. Fur's not bad, as long as you don't choke when you cough it up."

Tep had quite a collection now: a heap of tiny fur balls intermixed with equally tiny white bones. He counted them. Nine. Three meals a day. He yearned for a nice, cold fish, for a big chunk of ritvak flesh—for anything but warm, bony little crunches.

"Now we must be quite careful," Tep said, eyeing the state of their work. "Rakulit noted many large chunks of charcoal in this layer, which is the burnt village. We need to find a piece that not only shows some sign of having been worked by human hands, but that is from a fairly young tree." He explained—though at that point Kelisat was far too tired, dirty, and bored to care—that the heartwood of old trees would, when dated, indicate when the particular growth had occurred, not when the tree was cut up into timber, which could have been three hundred years later.

Rakulit's pit, from sod to bedrock, was about seven feet deep and Tep's was at present just over five. The charcoal flecks and chunks, to judge by the evidence in the wall of Rakulit's pit, would be all in the middle eight to ten inches of what remained to be excavated in Tep's. "This top layer," he explained, "is sedimentation that occurred after the burned village was abandoned, but before the midden was begun. We will take it off and sift it first." Kelisat groaned. "We have to sift it all," Tep explained, "because if my hypothesis is correct, there will be no human artifacts in it." He explained that he further expected the bottommost soil to be similar—washed-down sediment from before the village had been built, with the human artifacts—and charcoal confined between the sterile layers.

"I suppose we'd better get started," Kelisat said, picking up her shovel.

What they found was just what Tep had predicted. Happily, too, though the fire had been intense enough to oxidize and redden the soil, it had not destroyed everything. Kelisat found small lumps of slagged metal that clinked against heat-shattered pebbles in the sifter. "Mantees today use little metal," Tep reflected. "That there are so many of these lumps indicates that the ones who built this village were unlike modern mantees—perhaps more dependent on technology."

"How do you know they were mantees at all?" Kelisat asked. Tep pointed to Rakulit's chart of his pit, and to the sketch of a partial skeleton. "He found mantee bones—charred ones—right near the edge of his pit. That is why I decided to put our pit where I did—because I expect to find the rest of the mantee in our own pit. His leg and foot bones, anyway. They should be right about . . . there." He pointed.

"Here are some bones, I think," Kelisat said, shortly later, as she picked something brown and glossy from the sifter. "They do not look like roots, and they are too light for pebbles. Not being a Ketonak—or otherwise having butchered mantees—I cannot say for sure, but they look like ankle bones to me."

Tep, remembering where the last shovelful had come from, scraped and brushed soil from that area. "You are right. There are still bone fragments in place here." He picked at a fist-sized chunk of charcoal still in place. "This is probably as good a charcoal sample as we're going to get," he concluded. "I can still see the growth rings of the wood, and they form a complete circle. This was a smallish pole—probably a roof pole that fell on our mantee when his house burned."

As they carefully uncovered the bones, first loosening the compacted matrix of ash and soil with sharpened twigs, then sweeping it aside with brushes made of tough, fine ritvak whiskers, more bones emerged: the rest of a foot, including five horny, clawlike fingernails that had not—quite—rotted away. Then, angling into the corner of the pit, the found a thick tibia and thinner fibula.

"I will dig back in there and get them out," Kelisat said.

"Wait," Tep cautioned her. "If the bones project more than an inch or two into the undug soil of the pit wall, we will have to leave them in place and carefully backfill around them."

"Why is that?"

"We must not tunnel sideways out of the pit we have defined. Someday someone else—someone like Rakulit, who is more skilled than we are—will come back here to dig again, and would not thank us for messing up *his* dig."

"You really think anyone will bother?"

"If we succeed—if we get this stuff back, and avert a war—I am sure of it. This is an important historic site that represents a key event for mantees and ikuts alike. The battle fought here was the last one, and it precipitated a treaty that has lasted many thousands of years." And, he thought, a treaty that will surely be terminally broken if we do not succeed.

The leg bones did not project beyond the pit's vertical wall. In fact, the knee joint was right in the corner. The mantee, Tep decided, studying Rakulit's drawing, had died with his legs bent, so that one was in Tep's pit and the other was in soil yet undug by either man.

"Here is his kneecap," Kelisat said, "and another odd bone."

"Probably the femoral ephysis," Tep said, hardly glancing her way.

"No, it is not," Kelisat replied, brushing soil from the

thumb-sized morsel. "It has a hole in the pointed end, just like a . . ."

Tep was immediately on his hands and knees beside her, having crossed the intervening distance in one rapid motion. "A harpoon toggle!" he crowed, blowing sandy grains from it. "An *Ikut One* toggle! That hole is where the rope was tied."

"I know how a harpoon works, Tep," said his companion, slightly miffed. "I have not spent the past two migrations in a dormitory."

"I'm sorry. I am excited. Mother always said I babble when . . . This is wonderful! It proves I am right. Look. There is a groove in the patella, the kneecap, where the harpoon head lodged in the mantee's joint. I'll bet there is a corresponding one in the femur that Rakulit removed."

When the excitement of the find died down, when the bones and the artifact were drawn and photographed in place, they returned to the digging, but no other material artifacts were to be found in that level. Once the bones, harpoon toggle, and charcoal had been removed and stowed in plastic-lined bags and little glass vials, they cleared the remains of the soil down to the dark layer of original sod, the sterile stuff upon which the village had been built. Tep was not content. There was not—quite—enough concrete evidence. If the radiocarbon dates on the charcoal from the lower occupation level, just excavated, were what he expected, they would provide proof, but it was thin, nebulous proof—a date, a number, without anything to fasten the imagination to. If those metal blobs had not been melted—if they had indeed been artifacts of some high technology . . .

Kelisat interrupted his gloomy musing. "What are those spots?" she asked, pointing to several dark, round patches in the smooth-scraped dirt.

"Those are post molds," Tep said offhandedly. "They are marks left when the unburned, buried parts of the house poles rotted away. There must have been a wall there. The mantee was probably trying to break out when the burning roof fell in on him." Dutifully, Tep drew the markings on his latest chart.

There were no other artifacts in that soil, when they excavated it, but still Tep insisted they sift most of it, just to be sure, even sweeping the last shovelfuls of drying dust from the smooth, hummocky lava floor. "Well, that's it," he said, dusting off his hands. He made as if to climb back out of the pit.

"Why are there holes in the lava?" asked Kelisat.

"Those? Bubbles, I suppose, from when the lava was molten."

"But they go in a straight line—the same line the post molds went in. And wouldn't bubbles be different sizes? These look as if they had been drilled."

Tep got down on his knees and poked at one of the holes. There was indeed a whole line of them, running diagonally across the pit. "You're right! They are too regular to be natural." Eagerly, he swept what soil remained from the part of Rakulit's pit they had reexcavated. There, the holes made a right-angle turn and vanished into the pit wall. "Lis, climb up and get the drawing of that last layer—and Rakulit's drawings too. And the measuring tape." Tep studied the drawings and the holes, then measured the distance between them. "They are laid out on exact centers of one and nine-tenths of a foot," he remarked.

"Isn't that an odd increment?" asked Kelisat. "Why not two feet exactly?"

"It is two feet, using the old bors foot."

"Does that mean bors made them, not mantees?" asked Kelisat.

"It was once a standard measurement, but we ikut have bigger feet, I suppose, and we adopted our own standard, in the forgotten past. It is another hint of the age of the village." He squinted at the drawings. "They match exactly with the post molds from the layer above," he concluded. "I think that because the original soil was too thin to support house posts, the builder drilled holes in the rock to anchor them. And drilling precision holes in hard lava is not typical mantee technology."

Kelisat had gone back to poking in one of the holes. "I think they used bolts, or steel pegs. This orange stuff is surely rust."

Tep was elated. Mantees—at least mantees of historic periods—did not use steel, except for a few fishhooks purchased from the bors. That a mantee house had been made using a machine drill and steel for something as prosaic as pins to hold house posts suggested an economy and a style of life that was radically different from anything previously known. "That clinches it," he said. "Those were colonial period mantees for sure. Now I will be able to face Consul Martinez without a doubt in my head."

"Well, that's it," Tep said, tossing the last shovelful of dirt back into the refilled pits. He had, with difficulty, convinced the weary and dirty Kelisat of the necessity of backfilling. "If we don't, the soil will erode, and the pit walls will wash down into the holes, destroying part of the site. If Rakulit had not backfilled his pit, even the mantee bones we found might have been jumbled, and our carbon sample rendered useless, for being disturbed, even contaminated."

They tamped the humped earth. Everything but the shovels and other tools more practically abandoned than dragged back to the cove was packed on their clumsy sledge. They were ready to leave. Tep was not optimistic about the progress they would make, now burdened with filled sample bags and vials that weighed three or four times what they had, empty. Kelisat commented that she hoped their boat had dried out sufficiently for them to make the voyage at least to Farilan Island and the weather station.

She need not have concerned herself with that. The high, breathy whistling began almost immediately. This time, it was no dream. Tep was wide awake, and they were among not the stone buildings of Metok, but the deep shadows of the forbidding trees of Paldernot

Island. The mantee hunting calls alone were the same as before. Sometimes they came from ahead—as if they were on the trail leading to the boat. Sometimes they came from the north, inland, from the dark forest. He also heard them from behind. The ikuts were surrounded. Worse, thought Tep, he was now sure they had been there all along. He had not just dreamed those horrible tones that night, had he? And the rustling leaves, at night? How much of that had been rodents? Tep remembered scattered bags of artifacts, and how he had blamed Lis for leaving them out. Mantees. It had been mantees, snooping, sneaking in at night, going through everything.

He felt sick with despair. This—all the work, the misery—was for them too! It was not just for the ikuts, the Inutkak, but the mantees did not know it. Kurrolf had not known. Visions of war, of white, furry cubs stained with bright crimson blood, of brown little mantee infants dead . . . War, devastation, and all unnecessary. If only they would listen. But those were hunting cries, and he was the prey; you didn't talk with prey.

CHAPTER 24

The value of archaeology is not above dispute. What is the worth of knowledge gained if the gaining destroys the source? The archaeologist must assume that the artifacts he unearths and the drawings of telling patterns in the soil he digs will be as safe in some museum as they were undiscovered, snug within their mantle of earth. But cultures and civilizations rise and fall. Who has not speculated that the treasures they see in museum cases may someday be reburied in the plaster dust and rubble of that very museum, or in the rotting hull of some ship lost at sea before they are ever displayed? Who has not wondered if some future archaeologist might not excavate museum or shipwreck, and conclude no more from the useless, displaced relics they find than that fools and archaeologists are themselves quite ancient?

Fenag Inutkak,
Personal diary, undated

They came on as silently as the thick mists that lingered until midday. Mantees. Shadows at first, gray, then taking on color. The first one emerged in front of them, on the path, arms akimbo, confident. "Ikut thief!" it hissed. Eyes glowed greenish in the dim light coming from behind Tep, shafted sunlight through a break in the oppressive, encompassing trees. The mantee eyed the loaded sledge with vast distaste.

"It's not theft," Tep said softly. "This is for you, too—for everyone."

"For me? Hah! How nice. Then I will take it—and will throw it in that water." He gestured in the direction of the landlocked lake. He sidled closer, toward Tep and the sledge. He heard a low, threatening rumble—Kelisat. *No,* Tep thought, *not yet.* There was still a chance to settle things peacefully. "Where is your throngmother? I can explain this to her. . . ." Even if the mantees would not let them go, even if they were killed, the artifacts could still speak. The notes remained. Rakulit could interpret them, could run the C-14 dates. Consul Martinez could still act on that. He, Tep, did not matter. Even Kelisat did not, on the scale of deaths that would happen, otherwise.

"My throngmother! Hah!" The mantee spat. "I'll give her your skin to lie on." His long, webbed digits arched, tipped by sharp, clawlike nails.

Behind Tep, and alongside the trail, brush rattled. More mantees. He did not look around. The one he was talking with was their leader. Tep was not sure how he knew that. More mantees crowded ahead. He heard more, behind. Kelisat's low threat-noise intensified, wordless but unmistakable. Mantee snarls intermingled with ikut, shriller, no less fearsome.

"Back, Tep!" Kelisat snarled. Tep did not dare take his eyes from the mantees in front. He backed up until the sledge ropes at his shoulders drooped, until he felt the sledge's bundles at the backs of his knees. "When they come, get up on the sledge," Kelisat whispered. "Back to back. We can hold them a while, give them something to think about. Maybe their throngmother is near. Maybe . . ." She did not finish.

"If we can keep stalling them . . . If we fight, then there's no going back. If we kill any of them, then even the throngmother won't listen."

The mantees pressed closer. Tep thought he could see ten—and how many more were behind him? The triggering event, when it happened, was a small thing. A slight mantee, probably a female, pushed through her companions, snarling, eyes shiny and unnaturally wide. She reached not toward Kelisat, but past her—toward the sledge. Her outstretched claws caught, and something tore. Kelisat snarled, and slapped her hand away—and suddenly, there was no more talking. With a single movement, the mantees surged forward.

"Quick! Up!" Kelisat yelled grabbing the loose skin on the scruff of Tep's neck. He—somehow—got up atop the sledge. Mantees snarled, edged closer, now a mass of brown fur, individuals were indistinct except for eyes darting and flashing, and white and yellow teeth and claws.

The ikut could outreach the smaller mantees. Back-to-back with Kelisat, on all fours, one massive arm outswept, Tep's aspect kept them momentarily at bay. Animals, he thought, irrelevantly. We're not human, not anymore. No better than fulfs and moxen. That was, had he thought of it, an advantage, right then. Humans plunged right in. Disciplined humans—which the mantees were not—marched into combat, knowing they would be hurt, would die. Animals did not. Animals threatened; they avoided hurt. They sought advantage, a weak spot, a carelessly left opening, because wounds cost too much. These mantees had no steel-tipped claws, only their natural ones, sharp, but for grasping and tearing, not slashing.

But there were so many of them. The lull ended. A small female darted in low, lashing out at Tep's big braced arm. He knocked her aside with his free one, but others pushed near, interfering with each other. Tep felt icy, stinging pain in his left leg—teeth. He shook off a mantee, who fell among its companions, yowling angrily, spitting white ikut fur. Another went for his right leg. Then teeth found the wrist he supported himself with. Tep stood up, battering a mantee head with his free hand, sending the little brown man flying.

He kicked at a snarling, dun shape that dragged at his ankle, but could not shake if loose. Mantees were small, a third the mass of an ikut male, but they were wiry, fast, and tenacious. Tep realized his and Kelisat's mistake: high ground—the sledge—would have been advantageous fighting ikut, but was not now. Upright, he couldn't keep them off his ankle and calves, couldn't reach them with his arms. Kelisat, realizing that too, jumped down just as he did. They remained back-to-back, moving away from the sledge.

Now he could fight. Massive ikut arms swept dark,

snarling bundles aside, away from his legs. The short fur on his hands and wrists was streaked with blood—his blood?—but he felt nothing.

Mantees dropped low in front of him in a smooth heap, four or five of them. What for? He remembered; a childhood memory flashed by: mantees playing. Mud slides down to the water; mantees heaped up like that, then one running up from behind, flinging itself . . . When it happened, he was ready. A mantee sprinted up over its hunching companions, and flung itself at his face, hands out in front, squalling. He knocked it aside, feeling claws rake his cheek.

Another launched itself, and another. One clung, blinding him with brown, slick fur in his face. He dug in with both hands, trying to get a grip in an oily pelt stretched tightly over writhing, hard muscle so different from loose ikut skin, which was fat-layered and easy to hold. Redness washed into one eye—blood from a slash—Tep's blood.

He got a forearm under a mantee belly and thrust it away. Another dark shape flew at him. He straight-armed it, and it fell, mewling, into a vast, moving mass of others.

For a moment, there was a lull, a silence without motion. Tep heard some forest creature—a bird?—chattering overhead. He heard Kelisat's heavy panting, but didn't dare take his eyes off the mantees. Several were down, he saw. One's face was bloody—a pink tongue darted out, swiping a crooked nose.

One mantee chattered loudly, a meaningless sound to Tep, who recognized the leader's voice, rallying them. Tep's knees shook, loose as fresh-cut blubber warmed in his mouth. His arms felt heavy, weighed down by the blood that soaked his fur. One eye was clear, the other shut. Blood congealed behind his eyelid.

One more rush, he knew, and he would go down—like in Metok, outside the Last Atopak. That thought—the memory of rank steaming mantee urine-smell—restored him. He roared, a wordless, inarticulate noise from deep in his throat. Mantees hesitated; for a moment he thought it was because of his roar.

It was not. There was another sound, a high-pitched, ululating cry, coming from somewhere toward the water. Mantees backed off. There was now a body-length of churned humus between Tep and the nearest of them. Into that space stepped the mantee leader. "You got your wish," he said, none too clearly. His lip was swollen and cracked, and blood on his chin had already begun to crust, Tep saw with some satisfaction. He did not remember hitting that mantee—but he hoped he, not Kelisat, had gotten that particular blow in. But what was that about getting his wish? "Heloset comes," the mantee said. "Now we will see what happens."

He had something dark and glittering in his hand—obsidian; a volcanic-glass blade. The mantee slashed the cords that held the results of Tep's and Kelisat's labor to the sledge. Tep jerked forward, snarling.

"What treasure is this?" asked another mantee—a young male, full in his prime of strength and grace, uninjured. He held a small drawstring sack. He sniffed at it, questioningly, it seemed, then poked a finger inside. "Dirt?" he asked, rhetorically. He tossed the bag on the ground. Some of the dirt—a carefully gathered sample, its provenance marked on one of Tep's charts, intended for analysis of pollen grains, and thus of climatic conditions—spilled out on the ground.

"This looks like ashes," said the mantee, addressing his companions as well as the two ikuts. "Are these things the treasures of our ancestors? Bits of knucklebone, pebbles, ashes and dirt?"

"Leave them alone," Tep growled. "They are more a treasure than you know."

"Then you confess to stealing from us," the first mantee snapped. "For stealing worthless dirt, perhaps, I might let you go with the wounds you have received, but if these are really treasures—you must be punished more severely." He picked up Tep's notebook, and flipped idly through page after page of drawings—the entire structure of the pit they had dug, layer by two-inch layer, showing the exact location of every artifact, every soil sample taken. Tep trembled uncontrollably, wanting to do something but aware that the ululating cry, announcing Heloset, the throngmother, was sounding nearer, now. "I do not understand this," the mantee said. "Is it mere useless scribbling—or is it a code? Have you hidden maps of our defenses in here?"

"It is what you see," Tep said. "It is also proof that we need no war, no 'defenses.' "

"This? Drawings of a hole in the ground?"

"You know that? How . . ."

The mantee drew himself up stiffly. "This is my island, you bumbling fool! Do I feel it when the wind twitches my whiskers? We watched you come ashore. We watched you drag your bundles, and we watched you dig. At night when you slept, we examined your hole in the ground, and everything you took from it."

"Then you know we were doing you no harm!"

"I know nothing of the sort! I know you are ikut trespassers, and spies! That is all I need to know." He threw the notebook on the ground. It broke open with the impact, and pages scattered about, though there was no breeze to carry them away.

"No!" Tep howled, as the mantee ground several pages into the dirt with his foot.

"No!" another voice echoed. It was a deep, resonant, booming voice—for a mantee. Their captor stiffened, then turned toward the source of the command. The other mantees also turned—as did Tep, and Kelisat.

The mantee who pushed through the bushes was like no other present. It—she, actually, for there was no question in Tep's mind just who the enormous mantee was—was as tall as an ikut, though hunched and dragged down by roll upon roll of flesh. Six lissome females clustered close about her, holding her upright. Several more scurried about her on all fours, removing stones and the debris of the forest floor from her path and guiding the placement of her overburdened feet.

"Heloset!" Tep's mantee captor snarled. "You should not have come here! You should be in the water where it is safe! These murderous ikuts. . . ."

Heloset, the Swift Current, throngmother and Second Speaker of the Council of Throngs—snorted derisively. She pointedly examined Tep, whose white fur was spattered with his own blood, and which hung in tatters in places, leaving red, gaping flesh wounds. She then looked Kelisat over just as carefully, as pointedly, before turning her gaze upon the other mantees.

"I do not see two 'murderous' ikut! I see two ikut shredded by mantee claws. Was there a fight here, Fanerolf?" she asked the mantee leader. "Who, then, did these 'murderous' ikut fight? You? Come here, Fanerolf, and show me *your* wounds. Did the ikut bruise your lip?"

"I was not badly injured, Heloset," he spat. "We took them by surprise, and . . ."

"And received hardly a mark from those great ikut claws? None of you? Only bruises?" She shifted her attention to another male. "Saref—show me *your* wounds. Why is your arm hanging like that?"

"The ikut female hit me, Heloset. My arm is broken, I think."

"She *hit* you? And when you were thus disabled, did she rend your belly? Did she tear your bowels from you, with those sharp ikut claws?" Obviously, Kelisat had not. "Shall I ask the *ikut* why you are still alive? Perhaps *they* can explain why none of you—not one—has more than bruises, scratches, or a broken arm." She turned to Tep. "Well? What does the murderous ikut have to say?"

"We did not want to fight, Throngmother Heloset," Tep murmured.

"Speak up!" Heloset commanded. "You did not want to fight? You merely wanted to run free with your loot?" With a wave of her hand, she indicated the crumpled, half-torn pages on the ground. A female scurried to pick up several of them, and handed them to the throngmother. Heloset made a great show of examining them.

"You were probably wise. *These* don't seem worth fighting over."

"Oh, but they are, Throngmother!" That was not Tep, but Kelisat. "I mean . . . what's in those papers—and those little sacks—can *stop* the fighting between our peoples."

The throngmother replied to Kelisat in the same barking, sarcastic tone she had applied to her male progeny. Despite his desperate circumstances, Tep did not listen closely to her words because he now understood what she was doing—and he was quite busy planning just how he would help her do it.

". . . It is not a peace treaty, throngmother," Kelisat was saying when Tep's attention returned. "But with these notes and papers, we can show that there is no *need* for us to fight. That is why we risked *our* lives coming here—to try to save other lives. Ikut and mantee lives."

"Show me!" Heloset said. "Show me how this . . . this *stuff* can end a war."

"No! The ikut is lying!" That was Fanerolf, who had led the attack. "You must not talk with him!"

Heloset did not look at her son. Her eyes, instead, swept across her assembled throng—or that part of it that was present. "The Council of Throngs think I am too easy on the ikuts," she said. "They have not called me traitor—not yet. *You* are my children. The Warm Stream mantees and the others are distant cousins, at best. I need not heed them—but *you,* my babies, I will listen to you. Do you want war with the ikuts?"

Heloset's manner was not far from oratorical . . . but the response was, perhaps, less than what she wanted, or expected. There was muttering, and a few shouted noes, but only a few. Tep thought he understood what she was trying to do: mantee throngs were not democracies, they were . . . families. Most Swift Current throng members, except for the oldest, were *literally* Heloset's womb-children. A few, the oldest, were her siblings. She birthed between twenty and fifty infants every year, and the nursemothers who raised them were, also, her daughters. So . . . a family matter.

But the Council of Throngs—which included the Warm Stream throngmother, whose infants and older children had been eaten by the Ketonak ikuts—were not family. Without the support of her own band, Heloset did not dare defy the Council or make separate peace with ikut—any ikut; *with* the backing of her throng, she might pull that off, and that was what she was angling for. A mother, Tep thought, could command her children by ones or twos, but if they *all* rebelled at once . . .

But the throng's response had been less than overwhelming. What would Heloset do now? With much effort, she struggled toward Tep, her flesh bobbing beneath her stretched, sagging skin. Her eyes were tiny black beads almost buried in the flesh of her short-muzzled face. She took Tep's arm—his bloodied arm.

"I want to tell you about *this* ikut," Heloset said, addressing the throng. "Forget about other ikut, for now. *This* ikut—Tep Inutkak, who may someday be shahm of his band. In Metok, when my son Kurrolf and his friends attacked him with steel claws on their fingers. This ikut did not kill a single one of them. He could have—Kurrolf told me that. He could have killed mantees, but he didn't.

"Today, here . . . he didn't kill any mantees either." She motioned to Fanerolf. "Come up here, fat-face," she said. "Yes! You! Fanerolf." Reluctantly, he complied. She grabbed his wrist in an unbreakable grip, almost lifting him from the ground. "Stop wiggling, child!" she said. Then she reached for Tep's hand. Fanerolf was growling, a tenor monotone, but he did not struggle any more. It was undignified, and he had no hope of getting free. Tep himself was amazed at the strength of the throngmother's grip on his wrist. "Look at this!" Heloset held Tep's and Fanerolf's hands up. "Look at those ikut claws! Look at Fanerolf's."

She let Farerolf down. "Look how big the ikut is, how strong. He is stronger than me. And he is all bloody. He was clawed. He was gouged and slashed. Maybe he's dying, all the blood he's dribbled on the ground!" Tep, whose forearms, legs, and face hurt, but who was far from dead, maintained an expressionless face.

"Where are Fanerolf's cuts? Didn't you say you fought him, or were you only playing with him? Where are your slashes and gouges?" She thrust him aside.

"I will tell you about *this* ikut!" Heloset bellowed. "He could have killed you—dozens of you. He could have sat on your little brown heads and smothered you! That ikut *girl* could have pulled your arms off. But they didn't! *These* ikut didn't want to hurt mantees. That's what they said, and the evidence is clear! Look at Fanerolf, who could have bit his lip while eating fish." Several mantee chuckles could be heard—chuckles quickly stifled as the angry Fanerolf's eyes raked the small crowd.

"So, if we decide—if all the throngs decide—to war against ikut, against the Ketonak, the Atulag, the Tehokag, even the Inutkak, then what will we do about these two ikut who don't want to kill mantees—and who took terrible wounds to prove it? Shall we kill them too? Shall we start the war right now, by killing them?"

There was a quiet murmur, no clear negatives from the throng, but no hostile calls, either. Then somewhere at the back, nearest the lake, there was a disturbance. Several new mantees pushed forward, still dripping water from a long swim. "I'm late!" said Kurrolf. "I came as soon as I heard!"

"Ah! Kurrolf," the throngmother greeted him. "Perhaps you can help us decide. What would we do with this ikuts who won't kill mantees?"

"Do? What do you mean? He is Tep Inutkak! I played with him when we were cubs. I suppose we should give him something to eat—and a bath!" Kurrolf sniffed disdainfully. That time, the chuckling sounds were louder.

"A bath!" someone called—a high voice, female. "Give him a bath—and his friend too!" Several slender mantee females rushed forward. Tep heard Kelisat stifle the beginning of a growl. It ended with a funny out-of-breath squeak as the mantees tugged her toward the water.

Tep felt Kurrolf's hands grasping him. "I thought you were dead," the mantee said in a soft, joking tone.

"But for you . . ." Tep said, as he waded into the tepid—for an ikut—lake.

CHAPTER 25

Mantee generational metamorphosis is one of the great puzzles yet unsolved. From most ancient times, it has been axiomatic that environmental factors do not rewrite genes. Stretching the parents does not create taller children. Yet the environment in which mantee parents live determines the morphological expression of their offsprings' genes—or it seems to.

Throngmothers claim no conscious role in the determination—whether their cubs will be seel-phase, and adapted to oceanic living, otter-phase, and more suited to temperate pools and creeks, or dugong-phase, most content in the warm lagoons and weed-choked channels of vast deltas and swamps. Yet someone, something, determines such things.

Slith Wrasselty, Ph.D.,
Sex and Genes Across the Xarafeille Stream,
University Press, Thember, 12158 R.L.

Later, Tep did not remember much of the trip home. The mantees loaded everything in the boat, and towed them to Farilan Island, where a radio message to Metok, to Consul Martinez, was all it took to get them home aboard the weather station's powerboat.

If the consul declared that the evidence Tep and Kelisat had found was sufficient, said Throngmother Heloset, then her position on the Council of Throngs would be secured. With that—and the backing of her own band, her children—she was quite sure she could swing the other throngmothers from their warlike position. "Kurrolf and I will travel with you as far as your band's camp, and await the Consul's decision," she had decided.

Tep was ill, most of the way. "Seasickness," Kelisat said, laughing at him. Tep was not sure. Maybe it was all those warm-water mussels he had eaten. It felt as though they were still alive, in there. Or perhaps it was the fumes from the powerboat. One kind of fume bubbled up behind the vessel, and it smelled like a small volcano had erupted in the vicinity. Another stink, sharper, with a nasty, oily tang, seeped up from below-decks, where Tep refused to go, even when his fur was beaded with cold spray. "Seasick?" he said as the boat's unnatural straight-line forward motion raised it crookedly atop one wave's crest and sent it spewing drunkenly into the following trough. "Ikut don't get seasick." Heloset, who had, with Kurrolf, decided to accompany the ikut to North Camp, burped loudly, and leaned over the lee rail. "Neither do mantees," she said afterward. "I know now why nobody but bors use these awful boats."

Ashore at last in North Camp, Tep and Kelisat had plenty of help unloading the samples—now packed in waterproof fiber boxes with official-looking government labels. "Aren't you going to Metok with them?" asked Hepakat, the shahm.

"What for?" Tep asked. "Professor Rakulit can run the C-fourteen dates, and Consul Martinez can do the rest."

"But you won't know what he finds out until you get to South Camp, nine months from now!"

"I already know what he'll find. I don't have to be there." He explained. "Once I was sure that the site we dug was the one the old Inutkak had raided, and once I saw those holes drilled in the rock . . . Seel-phase mantees do not build elaborate shelters. Niches among the coastal rocks suffice." Kurrolf and Heloset nodded their agreement. "Whoever built the village that Tegat sacked," he concluded, "they lived in permanent houses. They were not seel-phase." Just as the ikut had been forced to adapt to make radical changes in their lifestyles, when contact with the other worlds of the Xarafeille Stream had been lost, so had the mantees.

Contrary to what everyone had believed, the *earliest* mantees were otter-phase, not seel-phase. Coming from a warmer world, a world perhaps more like Stepwater, Xarafeille 578, or more like the temperate zones of Old Earth itself, the mantees had naturally settled in the most hospitable places for them—the streams and forests of the equatorial islands. That, Tep said, had been about 800 R.L.

When the ships stopped coming—and with them, the supply of food supplements containing zinc, and other things—the mantees, too, had to migrate to get what they needed. Glaice's odd geology was behind it. Tep said he would have to talk with some bors geologists to get the details right, but it had to do with the different natures of the island rocks created by upwelling from the equatorial mid-ocean ridges, the eroded batholithic soils of the polar continents, and the fresh, volcanic rocks of the rings of fire.

However different mantees and ikut were, both were still human, with virtually identical Earth-based metabolisms. Both needed things that could not be gotten in one place alone. Bors? He did not know about that. He supposed they got what they needed during their endless tunneling. There had to be traces of almost everything in the rocks, if someone knew what to look for and how to make it into metabolizable pills—but bors had shared neither that knowledge nor their pills with ikut or mantees, whom they traditionally considered savages.

About 900 R.L., or somewhat later, a few generations after the first ikut migrations, the mantees moved from woods and streams to the rocky shores to be nearer the ocean foods their deprived systems demanded, and they began migrating too—north to breed, and south to give birth. The long swims kept them tough, and within a generation, all of them had become seel-phase, adapted more to water than land. Of course, the winnowing effect of migrating was a secondary benefit. The main one was the broadening of their diet.

"You know," Tep mused, addressing Heloset, "I wonder if Apootlak didn't work things out with the Swift

Current throngmother of his time, way back then. The whole thing, the timing of our migrations and yours, is too precise to be accidental."

Kelisat, who had come to know Tep better and better recently, recognized the avid, curious gleam in his eye. Tep was on to something. "Don't you mantees have an oral tradition too? I'll bet if we wrote it down, alongside ours . . ." Kelisat was now convinced: Tep would not be going back to Metok for quite some time. But would he follow the current south with the Inutkak? He might—unless she acted quickly—decide to stay with the mantees, on Paldernot Island, with a recorder and a notebook. . . .

"Come on, Tep," she said impatiently, rising. "I have something to show you." Behind his back, she winked at Kurrolf and his throngmother. Shahm Hepakat, she was sure, already knew what she had in mind.

"What is it?" Tep asked. "Where are we going?"

"Inside," she said, indicating the doorway of her house. "Go on!" she pushed on his rump, hurrying him down through the cold-trap tunnel.

Tep looked around. One stone lamp was lit, its wick giving off fat, smoky light. Ahead, he saw nothing out of the ordinary, nothing to justify Kelisat's hurrying away from what had promised to be an absolutely fascinating discussion. . . . Kelisat did not explain. She climbed up on the sleeping shelf, and patted the thick furs—his furs and hers, together.

For a long time thereafter, Tep was far too busy to ask questions or to wonder just what it was she had planned to show him. Several months would pass before he noticed that his mate was getting a bit heavier as a result of what happened that night.

But Tep did not stay with the mantees. Kurrolf could write down the mantee "begats," he told Kelisat, and he would read them later, perhaps the next time they were in North Camp. For quite a while he was far too busy bringing Kelisat special things to eat. Shortly after the band's arrival in South Camp, little Etop was born, squealing and vituperating even as she was pushed from her mother's warm womb, never, Tep was sure, to be silenced again, even in sleep. Her brother Apootlak came forth moments later, blinked, and seemed to gaze about himself, his expression at once immensely curious, yet serene.

"He will live up to his name," Tep stated proudly. "I can tell already."

"Perhaps we should have named him Tep," said his mate, without discernible expression. Tep tried to figure out if she was joking. Obviously, she was not entirely serious, because two Teps in one small winter house would be far too confusing.

Within months—because ikut cubs experienced rapid growth in their first year, in preparation for the hardships of their first migration—Etop and Apootlak learned to predict their father's movements, and to station themselves exactly underfoot, with always-entertaining results, and to pull their sleeping father's ears, or to push bits of *hatok* feather up his nose, which was great fun also. Almost incidentally—or so Tep believed, though Kelisat did not—the cubs kept Tep far too busy to think much about mantee oral traditions, carbon-14, or planetary charters. Someday, of course, when all the furor had settled down and his cubs were grown, he would get back to those things, but for now, there was only the vast, cold sea, the ice, the warmth of a winter hut, and the sounds of his family settling in for the long night.

EPILOGUE

A pheromone trigger has been proposed by the eminent Dr. Felerithem, of this university, to account for the mantee change—but upon whom would it act? Would an otter-phase throngmother, shivering in arctic cold, forced to ingest only salty seawater, unknowingly release a pheromone that caused the nursemothers who adopted her infants to produce a different milk chemistry? Or would a seel-phase nursemother, panting and suffering in some brackish tropic lagoon, herself involuntarily produce milk with growth-hormones that cause her nurseling to develop as a dugong-phase mantee?

Perhaps Professor Felerithem, who is easily of an age to retire, might well consider the benefits of emeritus status, and dedicate his waning years to traveling to worlds where, unlike dry Phyre, mantees of all phases could be observed, and such adaptive changes recorded.

Slith Wrasselty, Ph.D.,
Letter to the *Inter-University Journal of Evolutionary Physiology,* Vol XXX,
Newhome, Xarafeille Prime

John Minder leaned back on his uncomfortable seat, which was a small, wooden barrel with wrought-iron hoops. Over the centuries, all of the staves had severally been replaced as they rotted and crumbled away, and the hoops exhibited varying degrees of pitting and corrosion, as if they too had been repaired or remade. Still, the essence of the ancient artifact was unchanged: it was still a powder keg, and he still sat upon it.

"There's still one thing I don't understand, Dad," Rob said pensively. "I've read this Glaice Charter, and

I can't find anything at all that would have been damaging to the Inutkak on the other ikuts. Why *did* Apootlak take it?"

Minder smiled. "Any takers?" he asked, glancing first at one and then the other of his daughters. "What *do* we know about it?"

"The Charter was signed in the same year the colony ship set down near Latobak," Sarabet said. "That was 790 R.L. We know that there was only one ship, and it carried bors, mantees, and ikuts—so there was no danger of one group claiming precedence. That couldn't have been what Apootlak feared."

"I know!" stated Parissa, smiling smugly.

"Oh, come on, Priss!" said her brother.

"I do! Daddy *told* me already!"

"Dad! That's not fair," Sarabet reproved him. Then, to Parissa: "Well then, tell *us* what it was."

" 'Pootlak had relocation claws, that's why," stated the youngest Minder child.

"What?"

"Daddy? *You* tell them."

"The relocation clause," Minder said. "From the beginning, Arbiters pushed the races of man to spread out, to colonize new worlds, diverse worlds, so that they would never again be trapped or enslaved for the benefit of a few. Of course, some worlds were better than others. Bors are quite flexible. Their adaptations, like the ability to hibernate, allow them to survive the rigors of cold winters without food, but they don't *need* cold to survive. Much the same can be said for mantees, who adapt within two generations to arctic ocean rocks, the 'seel' phase, to temperate forests, otter-phase, and to vast warm swamps, like their namesakes, which were called *dugongs* or *manatees*."

Minder shrugged, then continued. "Ikuts were more narrowly 'designed.' They *need* the ice and the cold to kill off parasites that other races are immune to. They need long, dark winters to set their reproductive clocks, and summers when the sun never sets. Many worlds, even warm ones, can support small ikut populations in the high arctic regions, but such colonies by their nature remain marginally small. Only on Glaice was there such a vast coast, such broad oceans, to give the ikut race its full scope, and Apootlak knew that."

"Of course," Sarabet exclaimed. "But they had to take diet supplements to live there!" She frowned, realizing that she didn't have all the pieces of the puzzle.

"That's right," her father said. "Glaice was almost perfect—but not quite. Remember that there were few commercial ships voyaging to places as remote as Glaice, and the problem of offworld supplies must have been a source of chronic anxiety to Glaice's folk, especially to the mantees and ikuts. When enough years went by without ships calling—when supplies ran low, and the original machinery the colonists brought with them wore out—don't you think that *some* ikuts would want to move on to find a *completely* perfect world for their children?"

"And there *weren't* any!" Parissa interjected. "No place is as nice as Glaice!" She said that about every place in her father's stories.

Minder smiled. "For an ikut, maybe," Rob muttered, looking out over the balcony edge at distant green and misty hills bathed in warm, humid sunshine.

"But some people are never satisfied with what they *have,*" Minder said, "especially if the only way to keep it involves much hard work, like migrating on ice floes that melt as they go.

"Remember," he said, "that the data module containing the Charter contained many other things as well—not least, from my point of view, part of the codes I must have to operate my fleet of warships, and a vital fragment of the coordinates to locate the planet where my warlike poletzai live. But for the ikuts and mantees, what mattered most was the relocation clause that guaranteed them the right to a ship, or ships, to take them on in search of a more suitable world if they failed to adapt to Glaice, or to adapt the world to themselves. They had the right—but Apootlak made it impossible for them to exercise it."

"The codes!" Rob cried out. "Not *your* codes, Dad,

but the ones they needed to call for ships to take them away!"

"Exactly. Apootlak knew that ikuts would find no better home than Glaice. He knew—as, I am sure, did at least one unnamed mantee throngmother—that migration, difficult as it was, was the key to their survival. So he hid the data module that held the communication codes. No more ships came, and in time, the ikuts truly made Glaice their home, and made themselves one with it."

"Cut that cable," the shahm cried out as the great ice floe ground ponderously over the rocky shallows and out into the wide northern sea. "I, Apootlak the Bold, have brought us safely past the treacherous shores."

From not far away, a soft feminine voice called to the hero and his sister.

"Poot! Etop! It's time for school. Do you have your lunch sacks?"

"Aw, Mom," said the bold adventurer, pushing his great ice floe away, with a casual backhanded gesture. "We were having fun!"

Kelisat emerged from the tent they lived in while on the ice, and poured the contents of a stone jar into the puddle—the great, wide ocean of just-pretend. Small, glittering minnows flickered back and forth in the clear, shallow water. "When school is over, perhaps the mighty hunter Etop will wish to teach Apootlak how to catch a whale. . . ."